From Now On

CONTENTS

FROM NOW ON

C.W. FARNSWORTH

CHAPTER ONE

EVE

My world upends mid-sip of merlot.

"I'm not sure we're forever."

I swallow. Sputter. *Stare* at Ben Fletcher, my boyfriend of almost four years. My *ex*-boyfriend, I guess, as of approximately ten seconds ago.

Because those five words—now on an endless loop in my head—aren't ones you recover from. They're words that haunt you late at night when you can't sleep. They're *final*.

I wish I could say this is the first time I've had my heart broken. It's not. But it's the first time it's happened when I haven't seen it coming. Experience counts for something, though. My hand doesn't tremble as I set the wineglass down on the flawless white tablecloth.

Ben chose to utter that life-altering sentence in Somerville's nicest restaurant, La Bella Napoli. Unless I want my legacy in this town to be stained linen and a public outburst, I have to keep it together.

I'm too *shocked* to react, I think. My lips are numb. My tongue is numb. I understand exactly what the true crime podcasts

I listen to mean when they say *the blood drained from her face*. I can feel it taking place, a chill appearing as warmth sinks.

Ben drags a palm down his forehead and over his nose. He swears under his breath before dropping his hand. His Adam's apple bobs once, like a nervous tic. "I—I didn't mean to say it like that," he tells me.

Didn't mean to say it like that. Not *Didn't mean to say it*.

I'd just told him "it won't be forever" while we were discussing our living situation in the fall. *Arguing* about our living situation in the fall would be more accurate, actually.

For two years, The Plan has been for us to move to New York City together after graduation. I'd waitress or bartend or work retail until I became a famous artist and every gallery was clamoring to sell my work. Ben would attend NYU's graduate film program and become an Oscar-winning director. We'd live in a shoebox that probably wouldn't have air-conditioning and probably *would* have mice, eating ramen for most meals. But we'd be together, and we'd both be chasing our dreams.

That *was* The Plan.

It's astonishing, how a single sentence can obliterate years of planning. Erase countless hours of conversations. It feels like I was halfway up a staircase, and the rest of the steps ahead just… vanished.

Ben exhales so heavily the taper candles on the table flicker.

"My uncle offered me a job."

"At the *seafood store?*"

Ben frowns. "It's a profitable business, Eve."

It's a lobster shack. Calling it a *store* was generous. They don't accept credit cards; it's cash only. There's no public restroom, and the bathroom that does exist is not exactly a privilege to pee in.

"But…you want to be a director," I remind Ben, like he's

possibly forgotten about the dream he's had for as long as I've known him. "You got into NYU and you're—"

"I turned NYU down."

I gape at him, jaw open and eyes wide. "You— What?"

This is feeling a lot less like cold feet or second thoughts and a lot more like deliberate decisions made without me.

Another beleaguered sigh comes from Ben's side of the table, but the candles stay lit. "I already have student loans, Eve. Taking out a bunch more just to indulge the fantasy I become a famous director one day?" He shakes his head. "It was fun to think about. To talk about. To hope for. But we're graduating soon, and it's time to face reality. Rowan said—"

"You discussed this with *Rowan*?" I hiss.

Ben blows out a deep breath *again*. He's always been a sigher. And I used to find the deliberate exhales reassuring. A grounding rhythm whenever I was unsure. Ben's a constant, someone who shows up and sees things through.

Except, his reliability dried up. So, right now, Ben sighing is the most irritating sound I've ever heard.

"She's my best friend, Eve."

I know Rowan is his best friend. That's a fact I've been uncomfortably aware of our entire relationship. Because Rowan is a cheerful blonde who grew up in the same small coastal town in Maine.

Ben's always been insistent he doesn't see Rowan as more than a friend, that nothing romantic has ever happened between them. And I believe him, but I've never understood *why*. Because, honestly? They make perfect sense together.

"You discussed changing The Plan—*our* plan—with Rowan before talking to *me*?" I'm incredulous, hurt, and pissed, all of which are evident in my tone.

The tops of Ben's ears turn bright red. "I just needed an outside perspective. You're…too close to things."

"Too close to things," I repeat.

Too close to things? Of course I'm too close to things. I'm his fucking girlfriend!

Or, I *was* his fucking girlfriend.

"Should I bring over some dessert menus?" The smiling waitress who served us dinner appears to clear our empty plates. "The cannoli are always popular. And our tiramisu is incredible."

Ben looks to me. Ordering dessert is a decision he wants my opinion on. Just not what he chooses to do with the rest of his life.

The pasta I ate has turned into a leaden lump in my stomach. My appetite is nonexistent. But I nod because I'm desperately trying to act normal, and that's what I'd ordinarily do—dessert is the best part of the meal.

"Great. I'll be right back." The waitress disappears.

"I know I handled it terribly," Ben says as soon as she's gone. "Honestly, I brought it up to Rowan because I knew you'd talk me back into it, and—"

"Talk you back into it?" I scoff. "This was not *my* plan, Ben. It was *our* plan. What we *both* wanted."

His eyes close briefly. "I know."

Moving to New York together was my *suggestion*, though. I pushed Ben to apply to NYU over other film programs. I planned the color scheme of our shoebox apartment. I gave him three guidebooks to the city for Christmas.

I reach for my wineglass, chugging the remaining inch of merlot in one go. I don't even *like* red wine, but the chalky aftertaste barely registers.

I feel…lost. Not sure what to do or say next.

"I'm *so* sorry, Eve," Ben continues. "I never wanted to hurt you. I—I'm just trying to be honest with you."

At the table next to us, a laughing couple clinks their glasses together. A celebratory soundtrack painfully ironic for this moment.

I'm not sure we're forever.

I *was* sure we were forever. Or, I stopped considering us temporary. I thought I was done dating, that I'd met my future husband at eighteen.

"So, you're moving back to Maine," I state.

"I—yeah. I am."

He's playing it safe. He's returning to his loving, supportive, *whole* family. To the tiny town that smells like salt air and seaweed, where everyone knows each other's grandparents. To marry Rowan and have little blond babies with her.

I can picture it perfectly. Suddenly, Ben's future is so much clearer than I ever saw our planned life together unfolding.

There's nothing wrong with familiarity. But I'm realizing how much of our relationship was future-focused. How it felt like we were working toward a goal together, never living in the moment. In the hour we've been at La Bella Napoli, I can't recall anything we've discussed that was unrelated to New York. I'm sure we *have* touched on other topics; I just can't remember a single one.

I don't want to do long distance. Ben knows I don't want to do long distance. That was a central component of The Plan—us ending up in the same place.

He changed The Plan, and he did so without consulting me. The sense of security I've always experienced around Ben is gone, shriveled up into nothing but an empty hole of loss in the hollow center of my chest.

I pluck my napkin out of my lap and toss it on the tablecloth. My skin feels tight and itchy, like it's shrinking around me. Or maybe that's the room itself. Either way, I can't keep sitting still.

"I need to use the restroom," I announce, louder than necessary.

I've lost my volume control tonight. Among other things.

Ben nods. Swallows. "Okay."

He looks miserable, but I don't gain any satisfaction from it.

I get why he changed his mind. Ben's responsible and steady. He's not a risk taker. For months, he's gotten this wrinkle between his eyes when the topic of New York has come up. I knew he was stressed about money and worried about finding an apartment, but I thought he was excited about film school and a new chapter in a new place. It never occurred to me that he would change his mind. That Ben was even *capable* of blindsiding me like this.

I underestimated the allure of safety. Overestimated how much he loved me.

I stumble as I stand, nearly knocking my wineglass off the table. Shattering glass would be a more appropriate sound to accompany this moment.

Because that's what Ben and I are—irrevocably broken. This awful moment, those five words, will always sit between us. I'll never be able to go back to the *before*. We're ruined.

I'm not mad.

I'm shocked, recalibrating to a new reality.

I'm sad.

La Bella Napoli is fancy. As fancy as Somerville gets, at least. The restaurant's restrooms are single-person ones with plush cloth towels and soap scented like lavender and a vase of eucalyptus next to the sink. I'm most appreciative of the fact I won't have to worry about anyone coming in while I sob in a stall, but the soothing scents are nice too.

Standing in front of the mirror, studying the bouncy curls it took me an hour to style and arrange, no tears come. I study my somber expression, my face so pale that the few freckles on my nose stand out in stark contrast. I sniffle a couple of times, but that's it.

For the best, honestly. This evening is humiliating enough without spending the rest of the night with red, swollen eyes. My body still feels numb, and I silently pray this apathy will last long enough for me to get home, grab the emergency stash of vodka out of the freezer, and cry on my best friend's shoulder. Harlow will know what to say to make this shitty night better. She'll also suggest we egg Ben's car or tissue-paper his house.

The sooner I leave this bathroom, the sooner I'll be home. I wash my hands with a thick lather of lavender soap and hot water, then step back into the hallway.

My eyes fall to the floor as I resent each step forward. I don't want to return to that table. Sit back in that chair. Look at—

I collide with a hard body. A hard body that does not belong to Ben.

I know that instantly. It doesn't smell like Ben. It's taller than Ben. And it's not Ben's voice that says, "Eve?"

A rapid flurry of flutters appears in my stomach, the jolt of giddiness fracturing former numbness. The same silly sensation that appears every damn time I see Hunter Morgan.

Tonight is only the second time I haven't felt guilty about the strange reaction.

Hunter raises his left eyebrow, the one split by what I assume is a hockey injury, and that's when I realize that I haven't moved. That I'm standing and staring at him. Inhaling his masculine scent and absorbing the heat of his body.

I jerk away like I was just electrocuted, heat flooding my face. Everywhere that was pressed against him tingles.

So, basically my entire body consists of crackling nerves.

"Hi. Hunter. Hi."

One corner of his mouth kicks up as I babble out a flustered greeting. That's as amused as I've ever seen him—slightly smiling. "Hey, Eve."

I wonder if girls invade Hunter's personal space a lot, because he seems completely unfazed by how I just collided with him. My guess is yes, and not accidentally.

"Sorry about that." I gesture between us. "I wasn't looking where I was going."

He knows you're a klutz, Eve. No need to draw more attention to it.

Hunter doesn't acknowledge my apology. He asks, "Are you okay?" and peers at my face more closely than I'd like, considering I was just almost crying.

"Fine," I chirp. "Great."

Then I remember that his best friend is dating my best friend. Harlow tells Conor everything, and hockey players gossip a lot, based on how many rumors Conor shares with Harlow. Sooner or later, Hunter will hear why I was distracted enough to overlook a six-foot-something hockey player in my path on the short walk from the restrooms to the restaurant.

I decide on sooner.

"Actually, it's been a crappy night. My boyfriend and I just broke up."

It sounds real—and sad—spoken aloud.

"Oh."

Hunter looks startled. Unsure what to say beyond that single syllable.

We don't know each other, not really. He's the hot, popular hockey player. I'm the awkward dork whose hands are always stained with paint. There was one night, freshman year, when it didn't seem like we were so different. But since that conversation I doubt Hunter even remembers, our brief interactions have all been because our best friends fell in love with each other.

He clears his throat. "I'm really sorry, Eve."

I think—hope—that's pure sympathy in his voice. Not pity.

"Thanks." I force a small smile. "Good to, um, see you. And congrats on the championship. I only got to one game, but I could tell you guys were…" My voice trails. I don't know much about hockey. I don't know much about sports, period. Maybe if I did, my monthly conversations with my dad would last longer than two minutes. "Winners," I conclude lamely. "So anyway, good to see you! Bye!"

Did I already say that? I think I already said that.

Hunter Morgan makes me nervous. Reduces me to a fumbling mess, more like. It might be the piercing blue eyes. The dark blond hair that always appears stylishly mussed. Maybe the muscular, athletic frame.

Or, how, when he looks at me, I feel like I'm standing at the edge of a cliff.

Whatever the cause, being around him has the unsettling effect of my mind going blank and my mouth spitting out repetitive gibberish.

It sounds like Hunter says "Bye, Eve," as I hurry back into the dining area, but I'm moving too fast to tell for sure.

A dessert menu is waiting at my place when I return to my seat.

"I'm not hungry," I tell Ben, sinking into the chair.

"I figured," he replies. "I already asked for the check."

I nod, arranging my napkin back in my lap simply for something to do. Then, I stare into space. I can't think of one thing to say to him. My brain is vacant, and not in a pleasant, relaxed way. Just…empty. Same as the void in my chest.

Ben's silent too, playing with an extra fork.

I sip some water while surreptitiously watching Hunter return to a booth where Holly Johnson is waiting. I had a freshman seminar with her. She's smart, nice, and pretty. Exactly what I picture Hunter's type being.

Holly leans forward as soon as he sits down, a seductive smile spreading across her face.

I bet she's never accidentally tackled a hot guy. And if she did, she'd have something clever to say.

I look away, busying myself with pulling on my winter coat while Ben pays the check. Head for the door as soon as he receives the receipt, pulling in deep lungfuls of cold air once I'm outside.

Icy wind nips at my calves as I stride toward Ben's parked sedan, the sheer tights I'm wearing no barrier from the chill. I stop and lean against the hood as I wait for Ben to catch up, staring toward the south end of Main Street. During daylight, you can see the Sound. Right now, it's a black abyss past the streetlights.

Snow is falling, fluffy flakes drifting down from the dark sky and dissipating on the salted sidewalk. It's March. It still feels—looks—like winter. But soon it will be spring. Soon I'll be leaving this place. And moving to New York on my own feels very different from moving to New York with Ben.

The chirp of the car unlocking makes me jump.

I straighten, watching Ben approach with his shoulders slouched. Everything about his appearance is familiar. The glint of the chain attached to the dog tag that belonged to a childhood friend who enlisted after high school, then tragically died in a motorcycle accident last winter. The dark jeans he's wearing that I helped him pick out at a store down the street. The green beanie his little sister knit him.

I hate every second of this.

He shoves his hands into denim pockets. "Didn't know it was supposed to s—"

"We're done, Ben."

A few feet away, he stops, a pained look spreading on his face. "Eve…"

That's all he says—my name. Nothing else.

Because Ben knows.

He knows I don't want to live in a small town in Maine. He knows I don't want to do long distance. He knew this was where his decision would leave us.

Our relationship already shattered. You can't glue broken glass back together.

No matter what Ben says—now, next week, next month—it will always be drowned out by the sound of *I'm not sure we're forever.*

"Goodbye, Ben." I turn and continue down the sidewalk.

"Where are you going?" he calls after me.

"Walking home," I reply, my steps adding more distance between us.

I can't get in his car and let him drive me home like every other one of our dates have ended. Everything's changed, and I won't pretend it hasn't.

"Eve! Eve, come on. Just let me drive you—" The rest of Ben's words get lost in a gust of wind.

I tuck my chin into the collar of my coat.

Ben calls my name again, but that's the only sound he makes. There aren't any footsteps. He doesn't chase after me, and I can't remember if he ever did or if we always stood in the same place.

Three blocks later, my legs are completely numb.

So I call my best friend, and she answers on the first ring.

CHAPTER TWO

HUNTER

"Do you want to share the spaghetti?" Holly Johnson asks me.

"I'm going to stick with pizza," I respond, same as I have the last five times she's suggested we share an entree. I'm rapidly running out of ways to say *I already decided, get whatever you want* in more polite terms.

Either Holly's extremely indecisive or she has some *Lady and the Tramp* fantasy of us sucking noodles during this date.

Twin lines appear between Holly's eyes as she leans forward. The neckline of her top gapes, showcasing a clear view of her cleavage. She's also done *that* several times since we sat down. Intentionally, I think.

My knee bounces beneath the table. I wince when my shin bangs against the metal leg, swallowing the swear that wants to slip out.

Her frown deepens. "Is everything okay, Hunter?"

"Great," I answer quickly. "I'm really glad we're doing this."

I must be a better actor than I thought, because Holly's concern clears.

"Me too," she says sincerely, reaching out and resting her hand on top of mine. Her fingers drag along the back of my hand in lazy circles. "And you'll be even *more* glad later."

The suggestive lilt to her words and enticing touch would work on most guys. It *should* work on me. Instead, it has me running through exit strategies and fighting the urge to knock her hand away. It's ticklish—like a spider's crawling across my knuckles.

Holly winks before settling back in her chair and scanning the menu for the thousandth time.

I keep the smile fixed on my face in case she glances up suddenly. And tug hard at the tight collar of my dress shirt, trying to let some heat out. The back of my neck feels like it's being blasted by a furnace. Winter hasn't left Somerville—I think the high today was thirty—so the radiators in here are cranking.

Plus, I sweat when I'm uncomfortable, and I'm rather uneasy right now.

Holly's undeniably gorgeous. I've thought so since the first day of our shared International Affairs class. Before then, I'd seen her at parties and around campus. We'd never really talked, not until she took the seat next to mine back in January, flashed a megawatt smile, and immediately intrigued me. We usually make small talk before and after class, and once the season ended, I decided to ask her out. Mostly because I couldn't think of any good reason *not* to ask her out, which I'm learning now wasn't exactly solid reasoning.

I've accomplished everything I set out to in college. I'm graduating summa cum laude, I was accepted into every graduate school I applied to, and Holt's hockey team won a national championship. I also met my two best friends—Conor Hart and Aidan Phillips.

By any metric—academically, athletically, socially—my four years at Holt University have been a smashing success.

But sometimes I feel like I overlooked something important. And I hear that niggling voice, the one that often accompanies the drop of dread when a necessity gets forgotten. The sensation hits randomly, and it hits hardest when I look at Eve Driscoll.

As soon as I think Eve's name, my gaze veers in her direction. Looking that way is an urge I've been battling since I ran into her outside the restrooms. Eve's fiddling with the white napkin on her lap, seemingly lost in thought, while the guy sitting across from her scans the bill.

Her hair is curly tonight, bouncy and cheerful and untamed. But her expression is blank, her shoulders stiff and the line of her jaw jutted straight.

My eyes wander to the guy across the table from her. Ben Fletcher. I know his name. Know he's a film major. He's from the Northeast—Maine or New Hampshire, I think.

Holt's a small school, and I have a good memory.

Also, it's hard to forget details about the guy who got your dream girl.

Ben looks even more miserable than Eve does. I wonder who ended it—him or her. None of my business, but the first question I wanted to ask Eve.

The odds are high they'll get back together. They've been a couple for years. But right now, Eve Driscoll is single.

She's also leaving. Standing and walking out the door without a single glance back at her ex. He stands, dejectedly shoving his wallet into the back pocket of his jeans. His posture isn't proud, like Eve's. It's slumped. Defeated, like he's given up on something.

Some foreign feeling—hope, maybe—sparks a little brighter in my chest.

"The sweet corn and basil ravioli sounds really good. What about sharing that?" Holly suggests.

I tear my attention away from the other side of the restaurant just in time to meet her gaze as she glances up. Smothering a sigh, I acquiesce. "Yeah, sure. Ravioli sounds good."

Maybe if I agree to share, we can finally move on to a topic besides the menu.

Holly grabs the napkin from her lap and tosses it on the table. "I'll be right back. Order if the waitress comes by, okay? I'm starving."

"Okay." I relax a little at the temporary reprieve.

Maybe my memory will improve while she's gone.

I blow out a long breath and slump back against the booth when she disappears down the hallway, yanking at the collar of my shirt again in a feeble attempt to cool off. Is dating supposed to be this hard? This *sweaty*?

My gut says no. My parents haven't run out of words to say to each other in the twenty-five years they've been together.

I asked Holly out because I wanted to get to know her better. But she's treating this like a prelude to a hookup. And it's not that I'm uninterested in having sex with Holly—she's gorgeous and I haven't slept with anyone since the start of the season—it's that I had higher hopes for tonight *beyond* tonight.

Conor talked to his girlfriend, Harlow, for two hours last night. *Two hours*. I doubt the mindless chatter Holly and I have exchanged even totals thirty minutes, and I'm already out of ideas.

Maybe *I* just suck at dating. My high school girlfriend, Jemma, would agree with that assessment. And I don't have the same excuses now that I did then.

I glance at the empty table where Eve was seated earlier. A

waitress is arranging clean plates and silverware on the white tablecloth.

My boyfriend and I just broke up.

Her voice reverberates through my hollow chest, and that flicker of hope appears again.

Just as quickly, I extinguish it.

Hope has burned me too many times before.

When I get home, there's just enough of a dusting of snow on the front path for my boots to leave an impression. I walk slowly, listening to the low crunch as flakes collapse under each step.

I love snow. I love winter, which I associate with hockey. I love hockey, and ending the season hoisting a trophy didn't entirely erase the ache of realizing I'll never play competitively again.

Aidan is sprawled out on the couch in sweatpants, scrolling on his phone, when I enter the living room. A Kings game is muted on the flatscreen. Phillips is a California boy, born and raised in Los Angeles. The exposure to endless sunshine could explain his cheerful personality. He rarely takes anything as seriously as Conor and I typically do.

"Hey. How was your night?" he asks, glancing up.

"It was fine," I reply, pulling off my jacket. The sleeves are damp with melted snow. I should have left my coat in the entryway with my wet boots, but there was no room. That's where all of our hockey equipment is currently being stored.

I hang it off the knob of the television console instead.

Aidan whistles when he notices my outfit. "Damn. What's with the fancy clothes?"

"I was out on a date."

He makes a choking sound. "A *date*?"

Phillips doesn't need to sound *so* shocked. Tonight's outing was partially his fault. Part of an unfortunate attempt to find the happiness my best friends discovered effortlessly.

I'm still confused how my two best friends—Conor the commitmentphobe and Aidan the jokester-slash-sex fiend—ended up in serious relationships while I, who got sick of casual sex a long time ago, am struggling to make it through a single date. I'd be a *great* boyfriend.

Unless you ask Jemma.

But I was seventeen. Young. Dumb. Overwhelmed. I apologized to her when we were both home for Thanksgiving freshman year, and she smugly informed me she was dating a football player at Lincoln University. And then, less smugly, said she hoped I was doing better.

Aidan's still staring at me, his phone and the hockey game totally forgotten. I purposefully didn't tell him or Conor about my date beforehand, and now I'm thinking I should have kept my mouth shut altogether.

"Yeah, it's when you take a girl out to dinner and talk to her," I explain.

Aidan rolls his eyes, then sits up. "I know what a date is, dick. I just didn't know *you* were dating."

"Yeah, well…" I loosen my tie before taking a seat in the armchair. It's a relief to sit and sprawl without worrying about the expression on my face or any potential injuries. I'm going to have a bruise on my shin. "It didn't go that great."

Understatement.

The rest of dinner was fine. Slightly stilted, the conversation more of a leaky faucet than a steady flow, and unpalatable, because it turns out corn ravioli tastes terrible, but nothing catastrophic. *That* happened when I dropped Holly off. She invited me in, which wasn't unexpected. What *was* unexpected was her response to me saying I wasn't feeling well and should get home. *That sounds like an excuse,* she told me. *If you're not interested, just be honest.*

And since I *am* honest, I told her I wasn't interested. Plus a whole bunch of other stuff about how I enjoyed talking to her and how special she is, but those three words—*I'm not interested*—were the only ones she heard.

Holly proceeded to stomp inside her sorority house, but not before she slammed the door of my SUV so hard I'm surprised it isn't dented.

So, yeah. *Didn't go that great* is an understatement.

"Sorry," Aidan says.

I nod, then sigh. "Thanks."

"So how long have you been, uh, dating this girl?"

If I were in a better mood, I'd grin at his uncertain tone. Aidan is usually the guy you ask for a spare condom at a crazy frat party, not the one who prompts heartfelt conversations about feelings. He's changed since meeting Rylan, and I'm happy for him. Also feeling a little left behind. I'm spending spring break with Aidan and Conor *and* their girlfriends, and if anyone has ever said fifth-wheeling is fun—they were lying.

I grunt, then toss my tie on the coffee table piled with text-books. "Tonight was the second date. I don't think we'll make it to a third."

I'm actually *certain* there won't be a third date. But *don't think* sounds a little less pathetic.

I'm not even sure whether I should consider getting coffee with her after class last week—when I asked her out to dinner—a date. But if it was one, it went a hell of a lot better than tonight did.

"Bummer. Isn't that supposed to be the best one?" Aidan grins.

Like he ever waited for a third date. Or a first one.

"This isn't about sex."

"Then what is it about?"

I slouch down in the armchair, staring at the television. A car ad is playing on the screen. "You and Hart have both settled down. I thought it might be nice to meet someone. I was never crazy about the party scene, so I thought I'd try dating."

"I have not settled down," Aidan insists. "I'm twenty-two—still a wild stallion."

I snort.

Aidan doesn't take much seriously, but it's obvious he's helmet over skates for Rylan. He still gets shit—and gained legendary status—about the scene they made at the championship game. Rylan is Coach Keller's daughter. Aidan snuck into her hotel room before the game, and then kissed her in front of the entire team after it. You don't do *that* and then keep your options open.

"Please *never* say that again. And call yourself whatever you want. It's a Friday night, and you're on the couch, sober, waiting for Rylan to text you. You've changed, and it's a good thing. So has Hart. If he and Harlow don't get married, I'll be shocked."

Conor in a relationship was less of a surprise than Aidan. He's had an intense personality as long as I've known him, it was just always focused on hockey. And, based on how he used to act around Harlow Hayes—entirely ignoring her—I wouldn't have bet any money she'd be the one to shift Hart's priorities. But now, he's as serious about Harlow as he is about going pro. *Very* fucking serious, in other words.

I miss playing hockey, but a break from Hart's drill sergeant routine has been nice. We still skate together on the weekends, but it's not the same grueling pace of practices and weight sessions and film sessions and traveling to away games.

"Did you mention marriage on the second date, Morgan?" Aidan teases. "Because that might have been where you went wrong."

I flip him off. "You hear about your retake yet?"

That's how Aidan met his girlfriend. He failed Stats last semester, and she got assigned as his tutor. Maybe straight As are why I'm single.

"No." Aidan glances at his phone. His expression is suddenly sober, and I immediately feel badly for reminding him about the impending decision. He needs to pass the retake in order to graduate.

"I had this weird moment earlier," I blurt.

Partly to distract him, and partly because…I have this strange urge to talk about it.

"What do you mean?" Aidan asks. "What kind of weird moment?"

"I was talking to this girl, and it was just…I dunno. Weird."

If I tell him I feel an inexplicable buzz of electricity around Eve—a girl I talked to *once* and who has been dating someone else most of the time since—I'm ninety percent certain Phillips will burst out laughing. A couple of months ago, I would've said a hundred, but he hasn't changed that much. *I'd* laugh, if our roles were reversed. Internally, at the very least.

"Dude, you're going to have to come up with another adjective. Weird *how*? She was staring at your dick the whole time? She was bleeding? She was on a date with you, and you mentioned marriage?"

"No, I…" I don't know how to describe my short conversation with Eve earlier. Around her, it's just…different. I noticed it the first time we spoke. Since then, I've waited for it to dissipate. To see her and feel nothing. That still hasn't happened. I shake my head, second-guessing sharing. She and Ben might already be back together. "Never mind."

The front door opens and slams closed.

Conor's eyebrows rise when he strolls into the living room, bringing a gust of cold air with him. "Wow. You're *both* home."

"Phillips is waiting for girls' night to end," I say.

"Morgan had a shitty date," Aidan shares at the same time.

"Oh-kay." Conor sinks down onto the couch next to Aidan. "I got none of that."

"Hunter just got back from a bad date that involved a weird moment," Aidan tells him.

Panic seizes my chest as Phillips cheerfully relays that information. What if Hart mentions my weird moment to Harlow? What if she says something about it to Eve? She'll assume it was about my date, not her, I *think*. But what if she doesn't?

Nearly four years of friendship, and I've never mentioned the girl I met the first week of freshman year to either of my best friends. It was stupid to break that streak now, especially since Hart is dating her best friend.

But I'm always careful and constrained and guarded, and I wish it hadn't worked so well because it makes it a hell of a lot harder to change.

"Phillips is waiting for his girlfriend to invite him over," I inform Conor.

"How'd you know that?" Aidan asks, frowning.

"Because you told me Rylan had a girls' night on Friday two days ago."

"Oh." Aidan shrugs before he glances at Conor. "What are you doing home?"

"He got kicked out."

A realization I meant to say in my head, yet accidentally got spoken aloud. Another slip.

Conor and Aidan are both staring at me. I shrug a shoulder, attempting to act casual. "Right?"

Harlow would have wanted to comfort her best friend. As soon as she heard about the breakup, I'm sure she kicked Hart out for girl talk.

"Yeah," Hart grumbles.

"Shit," Aidan says. "What'd you do?"

"Nothing. Eve had some emergency and Harlow went to pick her up."

"What kind of emergency?" Aidan asks the question before I can.

Did something else happen? My brain is trained to always leap to the worst-case scenario.

"Something about her boyfriend, I think. I dunno. I only heard Harlow's end of the conversation."

I relax some. It doesn't sound like anything else happened, and Harlow is with her now.

"Huh," Aidan says. "Well, since we're all home, sitting around like losers instead of champions, why don't we—"

His phone buzzes, and Phillips snatches it before I can blink.

Conor snickers.

I smile, holding in another sigh. No matter what he says, Aidan is smitten.

"See you guys." Aidan leaps off the couch, then hustles toward the entryway. He has no jacket on. I hope he stops for shoes, or else he's going to have an unpleasant surprise when he steps outside.

"You're a fucking tamed stallion, Phillips!" I call after him.

Conor's still laughing when the door slams shut.

CHAPTER THREE

EVE

Forty-one months.

Ben and I started dating in October of our freshman year. It's March of our senior year now. I'm not counting March in the total tally, even though we're more than halfway through the month, because I *can*. And because forty-one sounds slightly better than forty-two.

"Forty-one months," I announce, flinging my phone away without bothering to close out of the calendar app. "That's how much fucking time I wasted."

"You didn't waste anything," Harlow says. She's curled up on the couch next to me, feet tucked under her. My best friend hasn't left my side since she picked me up on the street thirty minutes ago. "Don't let the ending ruin the rest."

That sounds like philosophical bullshit to me. Harlow is trying to be supportive, and I appreciate the sentiment, but how can the ending *not* ruin the rest? I don't know how I'll be able to look back on the past forty-one months with any sentimentality.

I exhale, tilting my head back and staring at the plaster ceiling. There's a semi-concerning yellow stain I've never noticed before. Hopefully the roof doesn't cave in before we move out in May.

Ben isn't impulsive. This was a decision he thought through. Has he known for weeks? Months? All the planning, all the conversations. Was there a part of him that *always* knew he wouldn't be able to follow through, while I was looking ahead, oblivious and excited?

I don't want to know the answer.

It's what he decided. The *when* doesn't really matter.

Bitterness curdles in my belly, so I reach for my half-full cup as a remedy. I added some seltzer to the vodka, but the drink's strong enough to use as antiseptic. The sip burns at first, then settles and spreads into pleasant, warm numbness.

"Want to watch a movie?" Harlow asks. "Take your mind off it?"

"No." I blow out a breath. "Thanks."

"What about donuts? I can make a quick run to Holey Moley."

"Not hungry," I reply.

Harlow already sacrificed her night with Conor for me. I'm not going to send her out on a fried dough mission solo, and I'm in no shape to be seen in public.

Holt is a small campus, and I used to love that about this school. The sense of community was comforting. Now, it feels constrictive.

Now, I have people to avoid.

"We could go spread instant mashed potatoes in his front yard," she suggests. "The snow's supposed to switch to rain soon, so he'll have a late-night surprise snack. Oh! Or we could cover his car in plastic wrap. I saw that on a TV show and I've always wanted to try it."

I groan a laugh. I knew she'd suggest pranks at some point. Harlow's fiercer—braver—than I am. I'm the type of person who likes to pretend unpleasant moments never happened. Or, in this case, get drunk on the couch. "Dozens of Holt students live in his apartment building, Harlow. And the car thing sounds…like a lot of work."

I don't care enough. I can't say it aloud, even to my best friend.

When Conor broke up with Harlow—on her birthday, which I haven't totally forgiven him for—Harlow was hurt. She was also furious. *I* should be feeling that way, I think. Not this detached processing, like I'm watching someone else write my life and am waiting to see their decision on what I do next. I skipped right past denial and anger and bargaining and depression and already reached the final stage of grief. Acceptance. There are vestiges of all sorts of emotions swirling inside of me—sadness, surprise, sentimentality—but I've already accepted their cause. It never occurred to me to disagree, when Ben said *I'm not sure we're forever*. To argue or to attempt to change his mind. Partly because of pride. Partly out of apathy.

"I'll keep brainstorming." Harlow reaches for her glass and gags on a sip.

I measured both drinks.

I smile, but it collapses quickly.

Harlow reaches out and squeezes my knee. "It'll be okay, E. Even if it doesn't feel that way right now."

"It does feel that way," I admit. "I'm not worried. Just kind of…numb."

"That could be the vodka," she tells me. "Did you add *any* seltzer to these drinks?"

"A splash." I sink lower on the sofa. "I didn't see it coming. Not because there weren't signs—because I didn't *want* to see it coming. Because I thought if I kept forging ahead…he'd keep following me."

Hindsight is a bright light, casting what I should've done in contrast to what I did. The funny thing is, I don't think it would have prevented my breakup with Ben. I think we would have broken up a lot sooner.

"You don't need him," Harlow says softly.

"I know." I take another generous gulp from my drink.

But I wanted him. Wanted the security of constant companionship and support.

I know having a few people in your life who care about you is better than having more who don't. More is nice, though. I like being able to say "I talk to him regularly" when the topic of my father comes up. I liked being able to say "my boyfriend is moving with me" when someone mentioned how far or expensive New York City is.

Want and need are different. I don't *need* more, I remind myself.

Harlow's phone—half tucked under her thigh—lights up, a new notification adding to the many messages littering the screen. I can make out the heart next to Conor's name from here.

I try to remember the last time Ben texted me nonstop about something. About *anything*.

I come up blank.

He did text me twenty minutes ago, asking if I made it home safely. I replied *Yes*, because I'm not petty enough to make him worry about my safety. Even if he'd always dismiss my fears of being kidnapped by saying it was statistically unlikely.

Ben didn't respond to my reply.

I swallow more fizzy vodka, avoiding Harlow's concerned gaze.

The first half of spring semester felt frenzied, like graduation was imminent. Now, time has come to a standstill, and the remaining seven weeks of college appear an eternity ahead. Seven weeks of avoiding Ben. Seven weeks of screening potential roommates to ensure I don't end up sharing space with a serial killer. Seven weeks of submitting job applications alone.

Spring break starts next Saturday. Or Friday, if you're one of the lucky few with no classes on that day. I didn't want to spend any of my precious savings on a trip, so I planned to stay on campus. With Ben. We were going to take a day trip to Seattle… and discuss New York.

Even if Ben's in Somerville for break, I won't have to see him. I can stay, slouched, on this very sofa for the entire week.

"Answer him," I tell Harlow, nodding toward her phone. "Way more productive than staring at me with that wrinkle between your eyes."

The wrinkle deepens. "Do you want to go to Gaffney's? Throw some darts? Hit some pool balls?"

I consider it, then shake my head. "No. Thanks. Honestly, I just want to stay on this couch the rest of the weekend. I'll get through next week, and then I can camp out here all break."

I'll stock up on cookie dough and browse the library's fiction section and order a new face mask and—

"Absolutely not." Harlow looks horrified.

"No, it's a good thing," I assure her. "Like a rest, recharge, and revitalize kind of retreat—"

"You are not spending spring break—our *final* spring break—on the couch. That is *not* on the bucket list." Harlow points toward the kitchen. I don't turn my head, but I know where her finger is aimed. Right at the creased piece of paper attached to the bulletin board hanging next to the stove. The senior year bucket list was my attempt to prioritize all the things I told myself I'd do in college but didn't. It was a short list to begin with, and all I've crossed off was *attend a sporting event.*

"There's nothing about spring break on the bucket list," I say, reaching for my drink again. It's become an emotional support glass at this point.

"Not *yet.*" Harlow hops off the couch, returning a few seconds later with the worn paper. Something red—pasta sauce, I hope—is splatted at the bottom.

Harlow picks up one of her thick marine biology textbooks off the coffee table and flops down on the couch with a pen poised in hand.

She scribbles something, then holds the paper out to me.

I have a bad feeling about this.

Yes, I wrote the list to be more adventurous. But Harlow is much more adventurous than I am. I barely remember what made the original list, but it was nothing that wild. *All-nighter* was on there, I think? *Attend more parties*?

Hesitantly, I take the paper from her. The title I wrote—*Senior Year Bucket List* has been crossed out. It's now called *Eve's Fuck-It List.*

And *spring break road trip* has been added to the bottom.

I sigh. "Harlow, I can't afford—"

"It's free," she tells me. "The whole trip has been planned and paid for."

"*Your* trip?"

Harlow told me last month she was driving to a small town in northern California with Conor over spring break. She invited me at the time, but I told her I had plans with Ben.

"*Our* trip." She grins. "Come on, it will be a blast."

"I appreciate the offer, H. I really do. But there's no way I'm freeloading and third-wheeling for a week—"

"Fifth-wheeling, technically. Aidan's coming too and he has a girlfriend now."

"Even worse. I'm happy here—what are you doing?"

"Texting Conor to check with him. But I'm sure he'll say it's cool."

"Harlow, *no*!" I grab for her arm, but it's just out of reach.

"Conor thinks it's a great idea," she tells me a second later.

I silently add *slow responder* to my growing list of grievances against Ben. By the time he replied about something, it was usually null. I'd already eaten lunch or left for Gaffney's or gone to the studio.

As with his sighing, it started out charming. I liked that Ben wasn't constantly on his phone like most of our peers. He always apologized for taking so long to get back to me, and I always said it was fine. I also started texting him less frequently.

"So, you're in?" Harlow asks enthusiastically.

I scramble for some excuse.

"You said you're leaving Thursday afternoon. I have my Poetics of Narrative class on Friday morning, and I can't miss it." I mean, *I could*, would actually love to, but I shouldn't. And it's the best excuse I can come up with while drunk and on immediate notice. "So..." I shrug, and then let my voice trail, leading Harlow to the inevitable conclusion.

"That's fine," she says, shocking me. "Better, actually. Now Hunter doesn't have to drive nine hours alone. He has a Friday morning class too, so he's coming separately."

"*What*?" There's pure panic in my voice, but Harlow is too busy texting to notice. And I'm too stunned to stop her.

Hunter...as in Hunter Morgan. I cannot ride *nine hours* with *Hunter Morgan*. I barely made it through our five-minute interaction earlier. I barreled into him, smelled him, and then babbled nonsense. Me, him, and a small enclosed space? I'll probably self-combust. I'll *definitely* say or do something embarrassing.

"Conor checked with Hunter. He said you're welcome to ride with him." Harlow delivers the verdict cheerfully.

Fuck, fuck, *fuck*.

My brain's stopped working. I can't come up with a single believable excuse for why I can't ride with Hunter. I could fake an illness closer to Friday, but then there's a risk Harlow would insist on staying with me. I already ruined her night. I don't want to ruin her spring break too.

I could tell her the truth, but it sounds ridiculous even in my own head.

See, the first night of freshman year, I met this guy. And I've barely spoken to him since, but he's stuck in my head, so I can't be stuck in a car with him.

I never mentioned meeting Hunter to Harlow, and I'm fairly certain he has no memory of it. If he does, he's never said anything. I tested Harlow last fall, the first time Hunter said hi to me, acting like *I* had no clue who he was, and she definitely didn't respond with *Oh, yeah. He said he met you freshman year.*

I never expected him to remember me—it was a long time ago. But it makes me more self-conscious about how well *I* remember *him*.

I take a deep breath. "Harlow, I really don't—"

"Do it for me, Eve." She gives me a pleading look. "I know I've been distracted by Conor lately. This will be a chance for us to hang out a ton. Aidan's girlfriend, Rylan, is awesome. You'll like her. It'll be a fun, chill getaway. The perfect distraction. I promise."

"You do realize the flaws in your *quality time* pitch are that we already live together and that Conor will be on the trip too, right?"

Harlow rolls her eyes. "Only for two more months. And Hunter is going. I swear it's not a couples thing. The house Aidan rented is *right* on the water." She nudges my ribs with her elbow. "*Way* better scenery to paint than our living room."

"It's not just the couples thing. I'm going to feel like an outsider. I don't know Conor's friends."

"You've met them. Aidan's super friendly. And Hunter's more reserved, but he's cool. Driving with him will be fine."

I *know* Hunter's cool. He's part of the crowd that's beautiful and popular and athletic. It's one of the reasons why being around him makes me feel like I've swallowed a sparkler. He's so firmly outside my comfort zone being around him makes my world feel bigger. Makes me feel reckless, like maybe I should try to capture something out of reach.

And it's also why driving with him will *not* be fine. It will be the most thrilling nine hours of my twenty-two years on this planet.

Fuck it.

I swallow another long gulp of vodka and tell my best friend, "Okay. I'm in."

HUNTER

"**S**orry I'm late!"

Aidan's apology beats his arrival by half a second. He flies past me and carves a clean circle in front of the bench, sending a spray of ice shavings into the boards.

Phillips is never one to make a subtle entrance. His shout echoes across the empty ice and cavernous ceiling. The open bleachers and (former) silence don't bother me. This is how I prefer an ice rink, actually. The cool, still air feels hallowed, filled with the same peaceful majesty disciples experience in a church.

I glance at the giant clock located above the scoreboard. 9:09.

Phillips is rarely punctual. But it's almost guaranteed he runs late if he's coming from Rylan's. Hart and I have been here for fifteen minutes, waiting for him, because Conor has the opposite problem and aims to always be early.

Holt usually melts the ice after hockey season ends. Predating Hart's arrival on campus, that was before playoffs even started. This year, at Conor's request, the school agreed to keep the rink frozen until mid-April. They probably would have agreed to keep this building open until graduation, if he'd asked.

Division III teams in Middle of Nowhere, Washington, don't win national championships. Forget unlikely. Plenty of people said it was impossible. I'll be shocked if this arena doesn't get named after Conor whenever they get around to updating the facility. He brought a ton of positive press to a college that'd never been known for anything extraordinary. I'm praying it was enough of a splash that I'll be able to buy a jersey with my best friend's name on the back this fall, but there are no guarantees in professional sports. It's not the standard nine-to-five. There are injuries and salary caps and all sorts of other factors to consider.

Conor sends the puck he was handling into the open net. It's a beautiful shot, one I'd admire if I wasn't accustomed to Hart shooting bullets like that regularly. "You don't sound sorry," he comments.

Aidan grins. "Yeah. I'm not. Seemed polite to say it, though."

"Since when do you care about being polite?" I ask.

Phillips yanks his hand out to flip me off before adjusting his chin strap. "Good morning to you too. Sorry you two had sucky nights, but mine happened to be *fantastic*."

"Hart!"

We all glance toward the bench. A reflex that's been drilled into us for the past four years. Holt's head hockey coach, Anthony Keller, is standing with his arms crossed, a familiar, inscrutable expression stamped on his face. Coach Keller is infamous for his stoicism.

Coach's gaze travels to me as Conor skates toward the bench. I give him a respectful nod, which he returns. Then Coach glances at Aidan. Phillips immediately straightens, the cocky smirk on his face dissipating instantly.

I skate toward the opposite end of the ice before anyone catches my grin.

Now that the season is over and I don't have to worry about

Aidan's decisions affecting the rest of the team, I mostly just find Phillips's mild terror around Coach amusing.

"Thanks for the moral support, man," Aidan says sarcastically, catching up with me mid-lap.

"What?" I ask innocently.

"I'm going over there for dinner tonight."

"Whoa. Meeting the parents. Big deal."

"You've gotten more sarcastic lately, Morgan."

"Too much time around you, I guess."

Aidan laughs reluctantly. "I…I want her folks to like me."

"Why wouldn't they like—oh. I guess there *was* the whole *getting caught in their daughter's hotel room the night before the championship* thing. And the *making out with their daughter in front of the entire team* thing."

Phillips groans.

"Plus the four years of practices where you either showed up hungover or fucked around during—"

"Wow, you're crabby. How long of a dry spell has it been? One month? Two?"

My mouth stays firmly shut.

"*Longer* than two?" Aidan sounds aghast.

I sigh. "It'll go fine with Rylan's parents, Phillips. They'll see how much you like her. Coach cares more about how you treat his daughter than how subpar a hockey player you were."

Aidan scoffs, then clears his throat. "Thanks, Morgan."

That's the thing about Phillips. Everyone on this campus knows who Aidan Phillips is. He's the life of the party—the first to crack a joke or tap the keg. It's not a facade.

But there's a lot to Aidan beneath the boisterous exterior. He reminds me of my brother, in a lot of ways. But unlike Sean, who displays selfishness most of the time now, Aidan is all sincerity and loyalty at his core.

We skate a few more laps in silence. I feel the tension dissipating from my body a little more with each circle on the ice.

I love playing hockey. But what I really love? Skating. There's something addictive about the smooth strokes on a flawless surface. The scrape of metal against ice is audible when there's no raucous crowd or whistles. All the stressful shit in my head—mostly about my post-graduation plans—settles, like it got left behind at the blue line.

It'll catch up to me, I know. At some point, I'll have to decide what I'm doing and commit to what's next.

But for now, I can skate with a clear head.

A blur of black blazes by on my left.

Conor's chat with Coach is over. And, fuck, is Hart fast. He's training as much—maybe more—than he was while we were in season.

Even after playing with him for four years, I'm still in awe of his talent. It's rare, witnessing someone excel at what they were clearly meant to do. I've watched a lot of hockey, and I've never seen anyone look more at home on the ice than Conor Hart.

I've never been jealous of it. I knew I was good enough to play in college—good enough for Division III, at least. But I never thought playing in college would involve getting to observe someone chase a dream the way I've gotten to see Conor pursue his.

If he doesn't make it all the way, it'll break my heart too.

"What'd Coach want?" Aidan asks.

"Just some drill suggestions," Conor replies.

There's a new tension to his expression that wasn't there when we first arrived at the rink.

Our team had two goals this season: win a championship and get Hart to the pros. We *earned* that trophy. Every guy busted his ass to get us there. So did Coach Keller. Because we weren't after a trophy. We did it for Conor. And when I look back on my college hockey career, I won't remember the early morning practices or the bruises on my ribs. I'll remember how special it felt to be part of a team that rallied because of such a selfless outcome.

As stressed as I am about my own future, at least I know what the options are. Hart is waiting to find out what his will be, and uncertainty is unsettling.

"What are you wanting to run?" I ask Conor.

He comes here by himself during the week, but weekend mornings have become the designated time for me, him, and Aidan to skate together. We mostly just fuck around, playing pickup. Once, we talked Aidan into playing goalie while I defended Conor.

Phillips put on the pads and everything, waddling across the ice like a baby penguin. Hart and I practically pissed ourselves laughing, and Aidan swore he'd never play goalie again.

Willis, our actual goalie, has practiced with Conor a few times since the season ended. But most of the guys on the team are still riding the high of the championship, knowing it'll be the only one they win. Few share Conor's competitive mindset.

It's what makes him such an incredible athlete, excluding his natural talent. He's driven in a way that elevates everyone around him but that only some can sustain.

"Thought I'd start with some shooting," Hart answers.

"I am *not* playing goalie," Phillips announces.

I laugh, and then skate off to grab the bucket of pucks. They spill onto the ice, a few rolling into the boards.

The next hour passes quickly. It always does, when I'm on the ice.

We head into the locker room to change. It's strange to be in here without the ruckus of the whole team. Slamming my metal locker shut sounds louder than a gunshot.

The final time I clear out my gear will be weird too. Wherever I end up living this fall, I doubt I'll be skating regularly. Definitely not with my best friends.

I'm exiting the showers when Conor brings up spring break.

The break snuck up on me, maybe because the weather has felt like we're stuck in the dead of winter. It's warmer today, over freezing at least. Last night's snow was melting into icy rivers when Conor and I left the house this morning.

"—Eve's coming with us, by the way."

My shoulders stiffen as I reach my locker and start getting dressed.

My sweatshirt muffles Aidan's indifferent response. "That's cool. She driving with us, or Morgan?"

"Morgan. Eve has a Friday class too." I yank the hood off so Conor's reply is clearer.

"Okay. You guys in for breakfast burritos?"

That's *it*. That's their whole fucking conversation about Eve coming with us before Hart replies that he's starving.

I can't decide if Harlow's best friend joining our trip is a positive development or will be a worse week than I was anticipating. When we made plans for spring break—in hopes it would be right after we'd won a national championship—neither Aidan nor Conor had girlfriends. I said I was fine with Rylan and Harlow joining us, and I am.

Graduation is rapidly approaching, and once it arrives, everything will change.

Conor's praying for a shot at the pros. Aidan, I have no clue where he'll end up. My guess is he'll try to stay in Washington since Rylan has another year left at Holt. And me? I got accepted into every graduate program I applied to, and I haven't told a single person.

I knew having Harlow and Rylan join our trip would change

the group dynamic. And I'm not sure if adding Eve to the equation will make the week any less uncomfortable for me. She's single—still, apparently—but she also just broke up with her long-term boyfriend. If she's looking for anything, it'll be a rebound.

"Morgan? Breakfast burritos?"

I tug a pair of Holt Hockey sweatpants on and shut my locker carefully. "Yeah, I'm in."

"Cool. Let's go."

It's drizzling when we head outside, washing away the last of the snow.

Aidan scowls up at the gray sky. "I checked the weather for Calaveras earlier. It's not supposed to be much warmer there than it's been here." He makes a face, then brightens. "But I double-checked the rental comes with wetsuits. And—there's a hot tub."

I clap a hand to my chest. "*Really*? No way!"

I couldn't tell you anything about the place Aidan rented *except* that it has a hot tub, with how frequently he's mentioned the feature. At least he's stopped suggesting we install one in our tiny yard.

"Have you noticed Morgan has been extra sarcastic lately?" Aidan asks Conor. "I think it's a side effect of celibacy."

I roll my eyes. "Know a lot of sassy priests, do you?"

Hart laughs. "What is it with you and hot tubs, Phillips?"

He shrugs. "What's not to like about them? It's where I met the love of my life."

Conor snorts. "You were naked *and* drunk."

"I don't want to see *anything*, Phillips," I remind Aidan.

That was a stipulation before I agreed to the girls coming. I'm glad they're both happy—Conor in particular is way more relaxed when Harlow is around—but that doesn't mean I want to spend the week being reminded how single I am. Or see anything R-rated. It's bad enough our house has thin walls and Aidan abandoned his *no girls over* rule when he got with Rylan. Earplugs are one thing, but I refuse to walk around wearing a blindfold.

"I can control myself, Morgan," Aidan retorts.

"News to me," I reply.

I found him and Rylan making out in the upstairs bathroom three days ago. Fully clothed—thank fuck—but lots of wandering hands. The door was half open, so I walked in without realizing *what* I was walking in to.

Aidan rolls his eyes. "How come you're not lecturing Hart?"

"Because I've yet to find him hitting second base in the bathroom."

I don't think that's because of consideration of me, though. Hart's just possessive of Harlow. He wouldn't hook up with her anywhere there's a risk of someone seeing.

Conor groans. "The bathroom? Really, Phillips?"

Aidan shrugs. "Why not?"

"Because it's a communal space. Because I can't use the bathroom if you're—"

"Relax, Morgan," Aidan interrupts. "We'll keep it in the bedroom at the rental. I don't want to make Eve uncomfortable."

"So thoughtful of you to do that for *her*," I say, rolling my eyes.

I'm acting normal—I think. But there's a clench in my chest, hearing Aidan toss Eve's name out so casually. I'm not used to it. I'm used to her name being a thought in my head, not a word spoken aloud.

We reach Conor's SUV. It's the only car in the entire lot. Aside from Coach and the facilities staff, Conor is the only one with a key to the rink. And not many people are lining up to exercise first thing on a Saturday, so the rest of the athletic center is empty as well.

As soon as we're in the car, Aidan starts blasting a new band he found and has been listening to at full volume most mornings. He's a terrible singer—totally off-key—but his enthusiasm makes it sound better, somehow.

"Come on, Morgan," he shouts, catching my gaze in the rearview. "I know you know the words."

I do. Not by choice.

Aidan and I rock-paper-scissored for the front seat. I lost, so my legs are crammed against a bunch of extra hockey equipment. I assume Conor is planning to clear his car out before driving to California. If not, Aidan and Rylan are in for a *long* trip. Actually, they're in for a long trip regardless.

Aidan is the only one with money to spend on expensive plane tickets, which is why we chose a spring break destination we could drive to. Calaveras is nine hours from Somerville. A doable day drive, considering I've gone all the way home to Wyoming—seventeen hours—in a straight shot before. I was fine with driving alone rather than cramming in Conor's crowded back seat. Now that Eve is joining me, I'm more unsure about the arrangement. I'm not dreading it. I'm…nervous about it, I guess.

Nine hours is a long time to be trapped in the car with someone you barely know. Phillips would fill that time with endless chatter about who the hell knows what, but I've never had that talent of spouting random shit to fill silence. I'm not shy, more deliberate. I don't say stuff just to talk, I say what needs to be said.

That could translate to an awkward road trip.

"Morgan! Come on."

Hart is grinning as Phillips bugs me again.

"Why doesn't Conor have to sing?" I whine.

"I'm driving, man," he yells. "Requires full concentration."

I can barely hear him over the music. There's a chance Aidan is going to blow out Hart's speakers. We're waking up every single squirrel on campus.

Reluctantly, I start singing.

CHAPTER FIVE

EVE

Pop music blares through my headphones as I dab my paintbrush against the canvas. My breathing is even, my heart rate steady.

The last class in this building ended a couple of hours ago. I'm alone, inhaling the distinctive scents of an art studio—wood and ash and Turpenoid and linseed oil and clay and chalk.

Long before anyone suggested I had any talent, art was my happy place. Studying it. Interpreting it. *Creating* it.

It's my outlet for everything I bury inside, either by necessity or by choice. When there's a pencil or paintbrush in my hand, it feels safe to let it out.

Art is subjective. Up to interpretation. It's a secret code to my most private thoughts.

Like the painting I'm working on now. It was an assignment for my Advanced Painting class. At first glance, it's a happy portrait of a little girl and her father. No stranger would immediately know that it was inspired by last year's Christmas card from my father. The card is sitting in one of the drawers of my desk— the spot where I shoved it after I opened it.

I flipped the perspective, so all you can see of my dad's face is his profile. Mostly a wide, proud smile crinkling his cheek. And I replaced his four-year-old son with a younger version of myself, even including the tulip-patterned dress I wore to preschool until the pink cotton was threadbare.

Rather than the large backyard of the cul-de-sac my dad resides in now, I changed the background to the apartment I lived in until I was twelve and my mom met her current boyfriend, John. A building my dad never visited.

The little girl is beaming. The exact expression I would have worn had he ever shown up.

I dunk my brush to switch colors.

Swish. Swish. Swish.

I don't realize how furiously I'm swirling my paintbrush until a few droplets of dirty water splash onto my denim-clad thigh. I drop the paintbrush's wooden handle, snatch the stained rag off the table, and head for the shiny industrial sink in the corner.

A quick glance out the window reveals it's still raining. A dreary day that matches my current melancholy perfectly.

I soak a rag, and then dab at the droplets on my jeans. The sleeve of my striped sweater snags on the buckle of the belt I found at my favorite vintage shop in Phoenix, yanking some threads loose. I swear under my breath as I survey the damage. It's not the first time I've ruined clothes in this room—one of the main reasons most of my clothing is secondhand, aside from my financial situation—but it's especially annoying today. Small grievances seem much bigger when you're already upset.

Rhythmic tapping draws my attention to the doorway. Thea Lewis—head of Holt's art department and my favorite professor-slash-advisor—appears in the doorway wearing her signature stilettos and carrying an armful of blank canvases.

"Thought you might be in here," Thea says, sending a cheery smile my way as she taps her way across the linoleum.

"You thought right," I reply, wringing out the wet rag and heading back toward my station.

I, like all senior art majors, have a private studio space to store canvases and work on projects uninterrupted. But barely anyone showed up for this afternoon's class, and those that did disappeared as soon as it ended. Since my private studio space is approximately the size of a closet and I had this room to myself anyway, I just stayed in here.

"Oh, Eve. I *love* this one." Thea has stopped in front of the painting I'm working on.

"Thanks."

I've been working nonstop for three hours. I squint at the canvas from a distance, agreeing it's some of my best work. I usually prefer to work with oils, but watercolor was the right choice for this piece.

Too bad it's not possible to actually repaint the past.

Too bad I kinda want to light it on fire.

"Does it have a name yet?" Thea asks.

"Um…Homesick."

Daddy Issues would be more fitting.

Thea nods. "It's stunning. The colors are perfect. Sweet and nostalgic."

She stares at my painting for a few more seconds before walking over to a nearby table to stack the canvases she's carrying.

Once she's deposited them, she turns back toward the doorway. "I'm headed home. Have a wonderful break."

"You too," I tell her.

Thea studies me, traces of concern appearing on her pretty face. She's one of my younger professors and has always treated me more like a little sister than a student. "Eve, dear, please tell me you have some fun planned for next week."

"I do," I assure her, opting not to mention it wasn't entirely voluntary. "I'm going to Calaveras."

I'm expecting a blank look—my expression when Harlow shared the name of the California town that's our spring break destination—but Thea lights up instead. "How wonderful! Calaveras is beautiful. Make sure you bring some materials with you."

"I always do," I reply.

And I wouldn't forget them for this trip. Not only do I have a nine-hour drive with Hunter to act busy during, I'm not totally sold on Harlow's assurance that I'll fit in with their group. Having the option to go off and paint or sketch seems smart.

"Great. Good night, Eve."

"Night, Thea," I call after her.

She's the only professor or teacher I've called by their first name, and it felt strange until sophomore year. Now, it's second nature.

Twenty minutes later, my growling stomach convinces me to call it quits. Lunch with my friend Mary feels like eons ago. We grabbed sandwiches in the student center before Mary left for the airport. She, like most of campus, has already departed for spring break. Harlow left this morning.

I clean up my station, store my canvas, and grab my backpack.

Automatic lights flicker on as I walk down the main hallway, hiding a wide yawn with the back of my hand. The doors ahead are blurry, thanks to my tired eyes and the water streaking the exterior of the glass. I can't tell if it's still raining out, and decide it doesn't matter. I'm going straight home to shower and change into pajamas either way.

It *is* raining out, I discover when I step outside.

It's raining steadily enough that my scalp is thoroughly soaked in seconds, water drenching the strands and clumping them in wet ropes.

I tug the sleeves of my sweater down over my knuckles and wrap my arms around my waist as I stride toward the parking lot. I wore rain boots today, at least, although that was a lazy decision, not a practical choice. I deliberately step in the center of a puddle, just to watch water splash red rubber.

"Eve!"

I startle, glancing in the direction of the voice.

Ben is standing next to one of the black metal benches that line the campus's brick walkways. His hands are shoved into the back pockets of his jeans. Unlike me, he's wearing a raincoat. The hood is up, covering most of his forehead and shadowing his expression.

For a few seconds, staring at him, I pretend.

I pretend tonight is identical to every other time Ben has waited for me outside the art building. I pretend my life looks exactly the same as it did last week. I pretend everything is simple and nothing has changed.

Then, I blink, and reality returns.

I haven't seen or talked to Ben since the night we broke up. His text asking if I got home okay, followed by my affirmative answer, was our last communication. Since I gave up on texting him unless necessary over a year ago, it hasn't even felt that strange not to see his name on the screen.

A long exhale leaves my lungs before my steps angle toward the right. Toward him. I release my hold on my ribs and swipe my face with the back of one hand. The green buds dotting the broad branches of the oak tree above aren't acting as much of an umbrella.

"Hey," I greet.

A sharp stab of pain in my left hand alerts me to the way my nails are digging into my palm.

I relax my grip before I can break skin.

"Hey," he repeats.

I hug my middle again. The sun is sinking in the sky, chilling the dampness in the air. "What are you doing here, Ben?"

"I wanted to see you. Talk to you."

I glance at the bench covered with tiny puddles. "How long have you been standing out here?"

Ben shifts his weight back and forth between his feet. "About an hour. You usually leave by six."

I don't ask why he didn't come inside the art building. He never did. I used to think it was out of some respect toward letting it be *my* space. Another clue I missed indicating that Ben was never going to follow me anywhere.

"Yeah, well, I was trying to finish some stuff before break."

He nods. Pulls a hand out of his pocket and scratches his jaw. "Eve…I'm sorry. I'm so fucking sorry about Friday night. I was nervous about how to bring it up, and it came out all wrong, and I know you're pissed at me. You *should* be pissed at me. I acted like an asshole who—"

"It's fine, Ben," I interrupt, wanting to get through this conversation as quickly as possible.

I'm tired and cold and wet and drained. An emotional sieve.

"*Fine*? What's fine?"

"Friday night. I wish you'd brought up your decision about New York somewhere else, but there was no right way to tell me."

Ben stares at me for several seconds, confusion and uncertainty warring on his face. "So, we're…good?"

"We're good," I confirm.

He exhales. "Okay. Thank God. I told David that I'd stop by

the theater to preview some shorts for the documentary. But I can swing by your place later. Is nine okay?"

I blink at him, dislodging some raindrops from my eyelashes. They slip down my cheeks like tears. "What are you talking about? Why would you come over later?"

"To talk." Ben's response has an unspoken *duh* at the end, like I'm the one making no sense right now. "We have a *lot* to talk about. There's really no good train option from Port Haven down to Manhattan, but I was considering getting a car anyway—"

"Ben. We *broke up*, remember? We don't have a lot to talk about. We have nothing to talk about. I meant *we're fine*, as in, *we're done*. I already told you that."

"I was hoping you'd reconsider," he says quietly.

"I haven't. I won't."

He sighs heavily, then knocks his hood off his head. His light brown hair is saturated to a darker shade in seconds. "I didn't mean it, Eve."

"Oh? So you're *not* moving to Maine?"

"No. I mean, yes, I am moving home. But that other shit I said? About not seeing forever and not wanting to go to film school? I thought that would just make the decision easier, convincing myself I was making the right choice. I just—I need some time. I need to go back and see what that's like and then decide what my next move is. Port Haven isn't *that* far from New York. I'm not asking you to change your plans. I'll be able to visit on most weekends and—"

"I get why you're moving home, Ben. But…you had to pick, and you did. You can't have it both ways."

He runs a hand through his hair. "Why does it have to be one or the other? We're adults. I don't see why we can't figure out a plan that—"

"Because I don't want to! You knew I didn't want to, you knew we *had* a plan, and you changed it without consulting me."

"I said I was sorry, Eve."

"That doesn't change that you did it!"

"So, that's *it*? Three years together, and you're just *done*?"

I *really* resent how he's attempting to make it sound like *I'm* the one who lacked faith in us. "You're the one who changed."

"People change, Eve! You've changed. I can't even remember the last time we had a conversation that didn't include New York. You were obsessed with it. It felt like you wanted a built-in roommate in New York, not *me*."

Irritation flares hot in my chest. It seems like my soaked skin should be steaming. "Fuck you, Ben. I'm allowed to plan ahead and be excited about my future. And I was talking to you about it because it was *our* plan. Because I thought you were excited about it too."

"I was. But...my dad's getting older. My uncle's handling a lot on his own, and I just—"

Bob Dylan's "Like a Rolling Stone" interrupts. Ben's favorite song. He pulls his phone out and silences the call. "I'm late to David's. Can we...can we grab lunch after your last class tomorrow? *Please*?"

"I can't. I'm leaving right after class for spring break."

It's the first time I've felt relieved to have plans to use as an excuse, rather than wish I had an excuse to back out of my plans.

Ben looks stunned. "You're...you're leaving—what? Where are you going?"

"California. With Harlow."

I don't mention who else will be there. On the few occasions Ben was around Harlow's boyfriend, he didn't say much. If I had to guess, I'd say he was intimidated by Conor. Even if you don't follow sports, it's impossible to attend Holt and not know who

Conor Hart is. He's Holt's biggest celebrity, and Aidan and Hunter are talked about a lot as well.

Ben doesn't seem to know how to respond. The possibility that I'd leave for spring break doesn't appear to have occurred to him, and I feel a rush of gratitude toward Harlow for insisting I join her plans. Lying—or admitting that I have nothing going on —would feel extra pathetic right now.

I take advantage of his temporary muteness. "Have a good break, okay?"

I stride away before he says anything, eager to escape the drizzle.

Ben doesn't call my name.

He doesn't chase me. This time, there's no pang as I try to recall if he ever did.

All I feel is relief. And the realization that it feels exactly like an ending.

CHAPTER SIX

HUNTER

I t's strange walking around a silent house that's normally noisy. I can hear the creak of each step as I descend the stairs. The duffel bag slung over my right shoulder bangs against the wall, the rasp of nylon against plaster audible between creaks. If we'd ever gotten around to hanging up anything on the walls, it'd all be askew.

I dump my duffel by the front door when I reach the entryway, and then head into the kitchen.

The fridge is basically cleared out. I pour a bowl of cereal, sniff the milk, and decide to toss the carton. Brewing a whole pot of coffee for a single cup seems wasteful, so I munch on my plain cereal and down a glass of water to wash the dryness away.

Phillips clipped his Stats exam to the fridge door—the retake he just found out he passed, not the original he failed. I stare at it as I sip, trying to rouse some more excitement about the upcoming trip. Aidan is graduating with us. That's cause for cele-bration—and a reminder we'll each be headed our own ways soon. Even if the approaching drive is awkward and I have to watch multiple make-out sessions, this trip will be worth it.

I add my dishes to the dishwasher and take the trash out. I'm not planning on coming back here after my morning class, so I double-check that all the doors and windows are locked before carrying my duffel to the car.

The sun is covered by clouds, but the air feels a little warmer than it's been. Teased by the barest hint of spring. I roll the window down as I drive to campus, hanging my elbow out an inch and drumming my fingers against the wheel as I wait for another car to continue through the intersection.

Arriving on campus is as strange as walking around the house was. Holt's a ghost college today. Spring break doesn't officially start until tomorrow, but there aren't many students with Friday classes. Even fewer who are bothering to attend them the day before break begins.

I'm a responsible rule follower. *Dependable*, my teachers and coaches have always called me. I hand in the extra credit. I'm always on time for practice. Part of it is intrinsic to my personality. The rest, I blame Sean for. Even before addiction twisted my brother into someone who's barely recognizable, he was the impulsive, devil-may-care Morgan brother. That didn't leave many rules for me to break.

As much as I admired Sean, I saw the aftermath of him missing curfew or skipping practice or failing tests. When you witness how burdens you refuse to carry fall onto everyone around you, it's hard to justify imitating that destruction.

I score one of the coveted parking spots right by the student center, grabbing my backpack off the passenger seat and then heading toward the door that leads directly into the campus coffee shop.

There's a line at the register, but it's not very long. I should have plenty of time to grab a coffee and make it to the political science building on time.

"Morgan! Should have known you'd still be on campus." Robby Sampson, one of my hockey teammates, punches my bicep as he appears beside me.

The two girls who are in line directly ahead of me—they look young, so I'm guessing they're freshmen—turn to look at us.

Robby winks at them.

One blushes and one giggles before they turn back toward the counter.

"What are *you* still doing on campus?" I ask Robby.

Phillips barely eked him out for the title of *irresponsible rule breaker* on the team. If Coach had two daughters, it might have been a tie.

"My flight got cancelled," Robby replies. "Tornado warning back home."

"Shit," I say. He's from Tennessee.

Sampson shrugs. "No biggie. I changed my flight to Kentucky instead. I have a good buddy who goes to Lancaster. His spring break was last week, so I'll bunk with him for a few days before heading home." He punches my shoulder again, in the exact same spot, and I hide a grimace. That hurts a lot less when I'm wearing pads. "What about you? I ran into Phillips in here yesterday morning, and he said he was about to head out."

"Yeah, he did. Hart and Phillips left yesterday. I'm driving separately."

"Long drive to make alone," Robby comments.

I shrug, not correcting the assumption and telling him Harlow's best friend is coming with me. Even though I've had almost a week to get used to the idea, I still feel…strange about the approaching trip with Eve. Uncertain. A nervous sort of excited. Maybe I'd feel less weird if I'd talked to Eve directly about it. But Harlow and Conor arranged all the details—telling me where to pick Eve up and Eve when to expect me—so I truly have no clue what to expect when I show up at her and Harlow's place later.

"Hey, Robby. Hi, Hunter."

We've reached the front of the line, where a blonde is standing behind the cash register. *Brooke*, I recall, even before I glance at the name tag on her shirt. She and Aidan had a fling earlier this year. Before he met Rylan, Aidan had a lot of flings and no relationships.

"Morning." I aim a polite smile Brooke's way before scanning the contents of the pastry case. Dry cereal wasn't much of a breakfast.

Robby orders while I deliberate between buying a muffin or a bagel.

"Wanna skate later?" he asks me once we've paid and moved down the counter to wait for our drinks. "Rink's still open, right?"

"Can't," I answer around a mouthful of muffin. "I have class. That's why I'm still on campus."

"Oh. I thought you just didn't want to ride in the Lovemobile."

I snort at his apt description of Hart's car, then swallow another bite. "That factored," I admit.

"Have to say, I figured you'd get a girlfriend *way* before Hart or Phillips."

"Yeah, well…" I take another bite of my second breakfast.

"Don't look bummed about it, man. Monogamy is totally overrated."

I keep chewing, hoping Robby will move on to another topic unrelated to my single status. Thankfully, he does.

"Did you see the email about the dinner?"

I shake my head. I was busy packing all morning. "What dinner?"

"The school's throwing it to celebrate the championship.

Coach Keller sent an email to the team this morning. Sounds like it'll be lame—no open bar or anything—but—"

"Two black coffees," the barista calls out.

I catch a glimpse of the clock as I grab my cup. "Shit. I've gotta run, Sampson. Have a good break, 'kay?"

"Yeah, you too, Morgan," he calls after me cheerfully.

I make it across campus in record time, thanks to the wide-open walkways. I only pass five people in total before reaching the three steps that lead into the brick building housing Holt's political science department.

The door is swinging shut when I reach it. I yank it back open, planning to hustle down the hallway, and then slow when I spot who's entered just ahead of me.

Shit.

"Hi, Hunter," Holly greets as I screech to a stop to avoid barreling into her.

"Hey, Holly," I say carefully.

She wasn't in class on Wednesday, so this is the first time we've interacted since she left my car under…tense circumstances.

I was *nice* about not wanting to come in, to be clear. But maybe I misread some signals, or didn't know the right ones to look for. And rejection—even polite rejection—sucks.

"Figured you'd be gone for break," she comments as I fall into step beside her.

I clear my throat. "Yeah…leaving right after this. You?"

"Same. I'm flying to Cancun with some of my sorority sisters. I'd skip today, but I already missed Wednesday to go shopping in Seattle, so…"

It's occurring to me we didn't discuss our spring break plans during our date last weekend. I'm not sure how it didn't come up during one of the awkward pauses, but it didn't.

"That'll be fun," I say.

"Yeah," Holly agrees. "Are you headed home?"

Another awkward pause follows the question, like Holly just realized she has no idea where I'm from. That she never asked.

"No. California. Aidan rented a place."

"Oh. Cool."

We've reached the doorway of the lecture hall. Most seats are full. Professor Hayden only allows one unexcused absence a semester—which explains why Holly is here. He also uses and allows limited technology during his classes. There aren't any slides to look up online. If you miss a lecture, you have to get notes—handwritten notes—from a classmate. Laptops are only allowed for students with learning differences. That enforces the attendance policy pretty well.

Professor Hayden is standing at the front of the room, his hands clasped in front of him. "Miss Johnson. Mr. Morgan. How lovely of you to join us. Please take your seats."

It's 11:09—class starts at 11:10—but we both shuffle to our joint row quickly.

Once I've sat down and opened my notebook, I tap a pen against the spiral ring anxiously.

I'm not nervous for class. I'm nervous for *after* class.

Holly leans closer. I can tell instantly, because she wears a perfume that smells like some sweet fruit. Strawberries, maybe? I drove from her sorority house back home with the windows down —despite the snow—simply to clear the smell out.

Cherries, I decide. Holly smells like cherries. The maraschino kind that come in a glass jar of red syrup, so they're extra sweet.

"Can I borrow your notes from last class?" she whispers to me.

"Yeah. Sure. I'll give you my notebook after class."

I won't need it over break. And if it smooths things over with

Holly, she can copy whatever she wants. I hate confrontation and unnecessary drama. And dating, I think. Right before I graduate wasn't the ideal time to start up a relationship, anyway. I don't know what Holly's plans are after graduation. I didn't ask—on purpose—because I was worried it was a question she might reciprocate.

Class passes quickly. Despite my classmates' complaining about Hayden's lack of materials—the only way you can study for one of his exams is by reviewing your notes—I don't think any of them would deny that we learn better because of it. The girl sitting directly in front of me during one of my classes yesterday was playing Solitaire on her laptop the entire time.

But here, everyone's hanging on to Hayden's every word, worried the sentence they miss will be on the next test. I write nonstop, my wrist cramped by the time class ends.

Professor Hayden wishes everyone a good break, and then calls out a gruff "Hunter, stay back a minute?"

"Of course, Professor." I zip up my backpack, hand Holly my notebook, and walk toward the desk at the front of the room. My grip on the strap tightens as I approach the podium he lectures from.

I know what this is about.

Predictably, Professor Hayden doesn't bother with any small talk. "You haven't responded to any of my emails," he states as soon as I reach him.

"I know. I'm sorry."

"You must have heard back by now."

I nod. "Yeah. I have."

He sighs, but his expression is sympathetic. "I'm your academic advisor, Hunter. I can't *advise* you on anything, academic or otherwise, if you keep me out of the loop."

I nod again. "I know."

Truthfully, I shoved all future decisions out of my head and focused on hockey. That worked—until the season ended. And skating with Conor and Aidan on weekends isn't a commitment I can justify as an excuse.

It's silent in the lecture hall. Everyone else hustled out of here, eager to start their break.

"I got in everywhere," I admit.

Professor Hayden's bushy eyebrows rise. He looks surprised. Impressed. And Hayden isn't easy to surprise *or* impress. "Everywhere?"

I applied to some pretty competitive schools, mostly at his urging. They all waived the application fee, so that wasn't a factor, and honestly? I didn't think I would get in. I thought the decision would be made for me.

"Yep," I confirm.

"Hunter. That's incredible."

"Thanks. I'm just— It took me by surprise. And everything with hockey…"

"Your season is over, correct?"

I hide a smile. "Correct."

He's really asking.

Professor Hayden might be the one person on campus who has no idea that we won a national championship. He's not oblivious, just selective with what he focuses on. He's like Hart with hockey, except he's dedicated his life to being a political science professor. No wife, no kids. He does sabbaticals around the world every few years, researching ancient Roman and Greek civilizations and assessing the origins of democracy and empires.

"You have until the fifteenth to decide, but we should really discuss your options sooner."

"I know. I'll make an appointment after break. I promise."

Hayden nods. "Very well. Do you have exciting plans?"

"For break?" I fidget with the strap of my backpack. "Uh, not really. I'm visiting California with some friends. What about you?"

He gives me a small smile. "I'm visiting my brother. He lives in Vancouver."

"Okay, well…" I'm as uninspired by small talk as he is. "Have a good break."

"You too."

I nod, then turn to leave.

"And, Hunter?"

I glance back.

Hayden smiles. The widest one I've ever seen from him. "Congratulations."

I smile back. "Thanks."

CHAPTER SEVEN

EVE

I peek out the curtains for the tenth time in two minutes. Drop the blue fabric like it burned me when I see the street is still empty. Glance at the clock, and then resume my anxious pacing.

Hunter isn't supposed to be here for another five minutes. Anxiety is stretching each second to feel like hours. I'm wired from the three cups of coffee I had this morning to combat the mere four hours of sleep I managed, the stress of worrying about running into Ben on campus, and the nerves about this drive with Hunter.

I haven't spoken to him since the awkward encounter outside La Bella Napoli's bathrooms. Harlow arranged everything related to me joining her spring break plans—I'm guessing because she thought I'd try to back out otherwise.

A valid concern.

I turn into the kitchen at the end of my next lap, pouring a glass of water to keep my hands busy. I've drained half the contents before it occurs to me that gulping water right before a nine-hour road trip isn't the wisest choice.

I dump the rest of the water into a succulent, then hustle down the hallway toward the bathroom.

Halfway there, I hear a knock on the front door.

Fuck. He's early.

I spin back around, toward the front door, then complete the turn and jog into my room. I glance into the mirror above my dresser to assess my appearance—not great, but not awful either—apply some lip balm, and then sprint back to the entryway.

I'm already breathing heavily, my heart rate a wild staccato in my ears, when I open the door.

The sight of Hunter makes my vitals even more irregular.

He's his usual gorgeous self, wearing a navy waffle-knit shirt that shows off the broadness of his shoulders and the impressive bulge of his biceps. The darker shade makes his eyes pop. And when he smiles… Shit. Even the lingering chill in the spring air isn't affecting me. And I'm *always* cold, like a lizard. The climate is the one thing I miss about living in Arizona.

"Hey, Eve."

"Hi, Hunter." I sound like I just ran a marathon. Hopefully he'll think I was training with Harlow earlier or something. Except…he knows Harlow left yesterday, so probably not. "Thank you for doing this. You know, uh, driving me. It's really nice of you."

"No problem at all," he replies easily. "I'm glad you're coming with us. Should be a fun week, but I wasn't totally thrilled about the fifth-wheeling part. It can be…a lot."

I nod. "Trust me, I know."

Hunter gifts me with a full grin, and I almost have a heart attack. "Yeah, right. I'm sure you do." He glances at the suitcase standing next to a pair of Harlow's sneakers. "This your bag?"

"Yeah. I just need to grab my backpack from my room, and then I'm ready to go."

"No rush. I'll stick this in the car. Come out whenever you're all set. Unless you need help carrying anything else?"

"No, I'm good. Thanks."

He nods, then bends over to grab the handle of my suitcase. The fabric of his pants stretches tight across his ass, and my mouth immediately goes dry. An entire flock of butterflies takes flight in my stomach.

I don't know what's wrong with me.

I mean, I *do*. I've never been suave around guys—let alone devastatingly attractive ones.

Also, I just got out of a long-term relationship that wasn't exactly *sizzling*.

It's been years since I kissed a guy other than Ben, let alone done anything else.

I'm wanting a distraction from the breakup.

And…it's *Hunter Morgan*.

I know—even though I'm going to lie to myself for the next nine hours out of sheer self-preservation—that's the main reason I'm a human inferno right now.

"Be right there," I say, then hustle down the hallway.

A few seconds later, I hear the front door shut.

After grabbing my backpack, I pee, pull on my jacket, take five deep breaths, and then head outside. I double-check the front door is locked before heading for the green SUV parked along the curb.

"Have a nice break, Eve!" Mr. Goodman calls from his front yard. Our neighbor is outdoors mulching his front flowerbeds.

"Thank you," I respond, waving before opening the passenger-side door.

The interior of Hunter's car is very clean. I imagine the messy, sweaty jock stereotype exists for some reason, but Hunter appears to be the exception.

Underneath the lingering aroma of pleather, all my nose can detect is a subtle masculine scent. I inhale deeply a few times, trying to catch a stronger whiff. No luck, which is disappointing, although I also appreciate that he's not one of those guys who smells like he bathed in cologne, since it's not really warm enough to have the window open.

"All set?" he asks, shifting the car into drive.

I nod, buckling in. "All set."

I glance in the rearview mirror as he pulls away from the curb. My home at Holt is out of sight in seconds, along with my plan for spending break solo.

This is a new chapter, I tell myself. College isn't over yet.

———

I turn my head, but the ache in my awkwardly bent neck doesn't improve at all. I reach back to rub the sore muscle, and bang my elbow on the car door. Every nerve ending in my right arm protests.

It doesn't feel like we're moving. I open my eyes, expecting to see cars on the road ahead, same as before I started dozing.

But there's dirt and grass and guardrail, and past it—the Pacific.

I sit up straight, a burst of adrenaline bolting through my system. Glance at Hunter, who's turning off the car and picking up his phone. I guess the lack of movement is what woke me up.

"Uh, what—what's going on?" Remarkably, my voice sounds fairly normal. Like I wake up on the side of the highway regularly.

Hunter doesn't reply right away. He's scrolling on his phone screen, this sexy crease of concentration between his eyes.

Absurdly, I'm wondering what it would take to get another

grin from him. We didn't talk much before I fell asleep, and, ridiculously, I'm more focused on what I should say than why we're motionless.

Hunter lowers his phone, reaches toward the dashboard, and turns the flashers on. "Your phone went off a few times. I'll be right back."

He opens his door and climbs out without offering any more of an explanation.

Maybe he has to pee? That would explain the unplanned stop and sudden urgency.

I yawn, then grab my phone from the cupholder and scroll through the notifications. A missed call from my mom, even though I talked to her last night. A few messages from Harlow, asking for progress updates on the drive. And two texts from Ben.

BEN: *Since you won't be around, I'm going home for break. Call me if you want to talk.*

Ten minutes later, he added:

BEN: *Please call me, Eve. Anytime.*

I blow out a long breath, zip up my coat, and then climb out of the SUV. I'll stay close to the car to give Hunter some privacy, but I might as well stretch my legs a little while we're stopped.

Hunter didn't stray far. He's crouched by the rear tire, frowning at it. I walk closer, keeping my gaze fixed on the Holt Hockey bumper sticker stuck to the fender, instead of ogling his ass again, as I ask, "Is something wrong?"

"Yeah. It's flat."

"Shit," I say.

We're a few hours into a nine-hour drive. The navigational system already had our ETA projected as 11:45. A delay isn't ideal, to say the least.

He glances up, the right corner of his mouth kicking up a half inch. Not another grin, but it still makes me feel unsteady. "Yeah. Shit."

I shove my chilly fingers into the pockets of my coat, wiggling them in an attempt to encourage circulation. "Should I call a tow truck?"

"Nah, I can change it myself. There's a spare." Hunter's already shoving up his sleeves and rounding the trunk, the thud of his Timberlands loud against the asphalt.

I move back a couple of steps so he can lift the tailgate. I like to think of myself as capable and competent, but I have nothing to contribute to this situation unless he wants a sketch to remember it by.

I've never gotten a flat tire, let alone changed one myself. So I stand awkwardly as Hunter sticks something behind the other rear tire. He shifts our bags to the side and pulls the floor of his trunk up, lifting a heavy-looking tire out of the hidden compartment like it weighs nothing, followed by a diamond-shaped jack.

He pulls a wrench out of the jack and crouches back down beside the tire.

His efficiency is impressive. Hunter strikes me as one of those people who always knows what to do in any given situation, but witnessing it firsthand is different.

I take a seat on the hard ground, pulling my legs into my chest, wrapping my arms around them, and resting my chin atop my knees.

Hunter glances at me, his hands still busy working at whatever's holding the tire in place. "You don't need to stay out here, Eve. Get back in the car."

"I don't mind," I say, even though my butt is already numb. Sitting on cold asphalt is as uncomfortable as it sounds.

The sun never emerged in Somerville today. It doesn't seem to have shined much in Middle of Nowhere, Oregon, either, because the ground feels the same temperature as a block of ice.

"It's warmer in the car," he tells me. "Safer too."

Warmer, definitely.

Safer is debatable. This two-lane highway is quieter than the road that runs through the sleepy neighborhood Harlow and I live in. Not a single car has passed by since we stopped.

Plus, I've never sat on the side of a road with a handsome stranger before, or helped him change a tire. Not that Hunter is a complete stranger or that I'm "helping" him per se, but it feels good to do something that could be considered uncharacteristic. Maybe I'll even add it to my fuck-it list, just so I can cross something else off.

"I'm good," I respond. "What's the worst that could happen?"

"While sitting on the side of the highway? You really want me to answer that?"

"At least I wouldn't die alone."

Hunter huffs a laugh. I can't tell if it's a sound of genuine amusement or a pitying *This chick is crazy* kind of chuckle. "I guess."

"Sorry. That was dark. I'm usually a little…cheerier. It's just been a rough week."

I trace one of the wildflowers I painted on the pants of my overalls—a yellow lily—avoiding looking his way after that admission.

"Yeah, I know." Hunter's voice is soft. A gentle tone you might use to soothe a scared animal.

He feels badly for me, obviously.

Which is *exactly* what you want from your crush. *Not.*

Admitting I have a crush on Hunter feels freeing. And a little uncomfortable, since he's *right here*. But also healthy, a sign I'm moving forward, and a definite improvement from guilt. I never would have cheated on Ben, but the fact that Hunter made me feel giddy while I was in a supposedly happy relationship isn't something I'm super proud of. Maybe if the same giddiness had happened around several guys, it would have mattered less.

But it didn't—doesn't—around several guys. Just Hunter.

"Have you changed a tire before?" I ask as a distraction from my thoughts.

"Not by myself," he answers. "My dad got a flat once when we were on a fishing trip. I helped him change it. I remember the basics, and I double-checked an article after we stopped."

That explains what he was doing on his phone.

"Don't worry," he adds. "It'll be fine."

"I'm not worried."

Hunter glances over as he cranks the jack, hearing the sincerity in my voice.

Getting stranded in the middle of Oregon? Not ideal. But I'm not worried. Hunter makes me nervous, but he also makes me feel safe. There's a reason that my unsure freshman self struck up a conversation with him, which was wildly out of character. My mom drilled *don't talk to strangers* into me a little too strongly. Or maybe that's just the excuse I've used to stay in my comfort zone.

"You had class this morning?" he asks.

"Yeah. You?"

"Yep. My professor only allows us one unexcused absence a semester, so…"

"What class was it?"

"Comparative Politics and International Relations," Hunter replies.

"So, you're a political science major?"

"Uh-huh."

"That's cool."

And unexpected. Most of the sports guys major in business.

I have this vague sense of who Hunter Morgan is. Bits and pieces I've collected over the past several years like some secret project.

He's like one of my favorite paintings. For years, I've treated glimpses of Hunter as a chance to survey, to observe more of the details you miss at first glance. But there are some answers you can't obtain by observing, no matter how hard or long you look. And I've never had the opportunity to ask questions before.

"Are you going to law school?" I wonder.

"No. Grad school."

"For poli sci?"

"Yeah."

Another surprise.

"Where are you going to grad school?"

"Not sure yet. I applied to ten different schools wanting to have options, and now—now I have to pick one. I used hockey as an excuse to put it off, but now that the season's over..." He shrugs.

"Well, how many schools did you get into?"

"Ten."

"Ten," I repeat. "As in, every school you applied to? You got into every school you applied to?"

"Yep." There's no bravado in his voice.

If *I* was a genius, I'd brag about it.

"Wow. I—wow. Congrats, Hunter."

He smiles a little. "Thanks."

"So unfair that you're smart too."

Another full, heart-stopping grin appears. "*Too*, huh?"

"I mean, you're athletic. And most athletes aren't academics. I mean, not *most*. I don't really know many athletes, and I didn't think you were dumb. Or that anyone is, that's a really mean thing to say, I just…" I exhale. "Congrats on being smart *and* athletic. I'm going to shut up now."

I should have sat in the car when he suggested it. I'm going to have to pretend to sleep for the rest of the drive so I can't say anything else embarrassing.

When I gather enough courage to sneak a peek at him, Hunter is grinning at the wheel he's working on. The old one is off already. He's attaching the spare. "What about you?" he asks.

"What about me?"

"What's your post-grad plan?"

"Oh. Uh…" I run my tongue along the backs of my teeth, stalling.

I used to enjoy talking about my plan. Back when it wasn't only my plan. Ben backing out didn't just devastate me because he was my boyfriend. It made me question everything.

I saw a dream. He saw a risky bet.

Am I just fooling myself, thinking I'll be able to make it in New York? I'm not afraid of hard work, but I *am* intimidated by failure. I've saved as much as I can from summer jobs, but that still adds up to a sad total. A sad total that would stretch a lot further in Chandler. I think my mom has reluctantly accepted my move to New York, but she still makes a point to mention I could paint in Arizona almost every time we talk.

Be practical was my mom's mantra. Because she had limited choices. She chose a career that allowed her to stay home with me and not have to pay for childcare. She stayed in the same town she grew up in because it was familiar.

But I'm not sixteen and pregnant. I can be selfish.

And my dad? My dad hasn't even bothered to ask the question Hunter just did.

Hunter's still waiting for an answer. Not in a way that makes me think he's impatient or just trying to be polite, more that he's asking because he actually wants to know the answer.

"I'm moving to New York," I tell him. "Hopefully to be a full-time artist, but probably to wait tables or bartend. Whatever pays the rent."

For some reason, I hold my breath, waiting for his reply.

"Good for you."

"Yeah." I exhale. "Working in the service industry. *Really* exciting stuff."

"That's not why you're moving to New York, Eve."

A thrill runs through me when he says my name. Just like earlier, I'm not cold anymore. Even the asphalt under my butt feels softer.

"No, it's not," I agree. "But pursuing art isn't exactly…realistic. I'm probably setting myself up for failure."

It's the first time I've admitted that aloud. Because two of the people who know me best—my mom and Ben—have expressed concerns.

And you can't share doubts with someone who's casting aspersions. I've had to be unfailingly optimistic and upbeat and *certain*, and it's a relief to be the worried downer for a change. To admit I'm scared it will be a mistake.

"That's better than never trying at all," Hunter says.

"You think?"

"Yeah. I do. But it doesn't matter what I think. It's about what you think."

I think he's right. That, as worried as I am about not succeeding, I'll regret not trying a lot more.

I also think my crush on him is bigger than it was yesterday.

CHAPTER EIGHT

HUNTER

"You can turn on a light," I say. "It won't bother me."

The scratch of Eve's pencil abruptly stops. "Oh. It's, um, fine. I'm just doodling."

I've been trying to tell what she was "doodling" for the past two hours, ever since she pulled a sketchpad out of her backpack. She seemed more relaxed as soon as it was in her hands, sitting cross-legged and balancing the bound paper on one knee. I basically went cross-eyed trying to look over there while simultaneously keeping my gaze on the road.

Now, it's pitch-black out and we're in standstill traffic. We were moving—crawling—for a while, but the tires haven't rolled an inch in ten minutes. The GPS is estimating our arrival time as 12:30 a.m., and I'm guessing the next update will be even later.

Ahead of us is an endless stretch of red brake lights. I glance in the rearview mirror, and immediately regret it. Pretty sure the truck behind me has its brights on.

White dots dance across my vision as I squint at the GPS. Arrival is estimated at 12:43 now.

A half hour later, we've barely moved, another hour has been added to our ETA, and I have to piss so badly it's physically painful. The fast-food place we stopped at for dinner oversalted the fries, so I downed an entire root beer plus most of the water bottle I brought.

I blow out a long breath. "We should stop."

"For the night?" Eve sounds surprised by the suggestion, but I don't see a better option.

"Yeah. This isn't looking like it'll clear up anytime soon." I nod toward the red lights ahead. "We get off the road, get some sleep, and leave early in the morning. We should make it to the rental by noon."

Eve closes her sketchbook and sits up straight. "Okay. Uh, yeah. Okay."

I flick on my blinker.

It takes us fifteen minutes to make it to the next exit—which thankfully has a hotel and a motel on the sign—and we aren't the only ones getting off. Several other cars take the same ramp. Three of them pull off at the first hotel, so I keep driving to the motel farther down the street. The *Vacancy* sign is flickering, but the parking lot is pretty full. There are two leather-clad men straddling motorcycles in the spot next to us.

I park in the closest open spot to the office and hand Eve the car keys so she can lock the SUV if she wants. "I'll be right back."

When I enter the small office, a middle-aged couple is talking to the man at the front desk. I duck into the tiny bathroom. By the time I reemerge into the small lobby, the couple has disappeared.

"Good evening, sir," the man greets. His name tag reads *Alfred*. For the late hour, he seems awfully chipper.

"Hey. Could I get two rooms, please?"

Alfred shakes his head. "I've only got one room left."

"With two beds?"

Another headshake. "Just the one room with the one queen bed."

Of course. With the way this trip is going, I wouldn't have been shocked if he'd said he had *no* rooms available. Having to turn around and inch my way back onto the highway holds no appeal whatsoever.

"Okay. I'll take the room, please." I pull out my wallet. "Fifty-nine, right?"

"Sixty-nine. Plus tax."

If Aidan were here, he'd make a joke.

I glance at the laminated price sheet, which lists a queen room as fifty-nine dollars a night.

Alfred reaches out and grabs the sign, stashing it under his desk. "Prices are subject to change based on availability."

No wonder he looks so cheerful. Business is booming tonight thanks to the gridlock on the highway.

I hand him my credit card and then sign the slip.

Alfred beams. "Have a pleasant stay."

"Yeah. Thanks."

I leave the office with two plastic keys for room eleven. As I approach, Eve unlocks the car and climbs out, glancing around nervously.

I hate that we live in a society where women see a dark parking lot as dangerous.

"You okay?" I ask her.

"Yeah." She bites her bottom lip and shrugs a little. "I listen to a lot of true crime podcasts, and a lot of them involve a seedy motel."

I'm not sure what to say to that, so I just nod. I feel like Alfred would take offense to *seedy*, but Eve is right. This place looks like it could have bedbugs.

"They only had, uh, one room left," I say, handing her one of the plastic cards. "Eleven."

I watch Eve's expression carefully as the fact that we'll be sharing a room registers.

"Oh. Okay. Good they weren't full, I guess." She looks uncertain, mostly, tapping the key against one of the flowers on her pants and gnawing on her lower lip.

I nod. "Thought the same thing." I don't mention the one-bed situation yet. I'm hoping there's a couch I can crash on. "And I promise I'm not a serial killer."

Eve's lips twitch a little. "I fear that's exactly what a serial killer would say in this situation."

Whatever expression is on my face makes her laugh. "Relax, Hunter. I trust you."

She should trust me. Trustworthy is an adjective lots of people would use to describe me.

Eve's trust feels different. I'm not sure if she means it or if she's just saying it, but I want her to mean it. I want to earn that trust, somehow.

She holds something out to me. It takes me a few seconds to realize it's a wad of cash.

"I'm not taking your money, Eve."

She moves it closer, her knuckles bumping against my ribs and then quickly retreating an inch so we're no longer touching. "It's the least I can do. You didn't let me pay for gas *or* dinner."

"I told you, I was already taking this trip. I'd have bought gas and dinner regardless of whether or not you came along, and I would have stopped for the night regardless too."

Eve raises an eyebrow. "You would have bought an extra sandwich and fries and lemonade if you were driving alone?"

I roll my eyes. "You can pay me back for your dinner, if you want. But that's it. And it can wait until we're inside. Someone's going to think we're doing a drug deal. Or that I'm paying you to have sex with me."

I'm not sure why that last sentence slips out. But, if I had to guess, I'd say that it has something to do with how having sex with Eve crossed my mind several times while we were in my car together. It just did again, when she bit her bottom lip.

Eve pockets the cash. Scoffs. "Like anyone would think *you* had to pay for sex."

Her voice has the same *duh* tone to it as when she complained I was "smart too." I think it was a compliment, and that implying I'm attractive enough to get laid without money exchanging hands is another one.

I smile as I open the trunk of my car. "Uh, thanks?"

She clears her throat. "I texted Harlow, letting her know about the traffic and that we decided to stop for the night."

I nod as I grab my duffel. The zipper clinks against the jack I didn't bother putting back into the compartment. I completely forgot about the flat tire.

This trip has been a complete clusterfuck, and I'm oddly at ease about it despite usually thriving on structure.

Eve reaches for the handle of her suitcase once I pull it out.

"I've got it," I tell her.

She keeps reaching anyway. "You've done too much already."

Too much? Buying her dinner and offering to carry her suitcase? Sounds like the bare minimum to me.

Eve's fingers brush my knuckles as she grabs the handle insistently. Reluctantly, I let go, allowing her to lift the luggage. By the time I've closed the trunk and locked the car, she's made it to the stairs that lead to the second level of the motel. Rooms one through ten are downstairs. Rooms eleven through twenty are upstairs, according to the crooked sign.

The lot's quiet now, the motorcycles gone and the remaining

spots filled with empty cars. Aside from the buzz of the lights, all I can hear is someone loudly bemoaning the 49ers' latest loss at the gas station directly across the street.

The room is exactly what I'm expecting. Generic striped carpet, beige comforter, white walls decorated with a few forgettable prints. Everything looks clean, at least. And there is a couch.

I set my duffel down on the round wooden table tucked in one corner.

Eve's looking at the bed. The *one* bed.

"I'll take the couch," I offer.

She glances at the sofa—which is a rusty-orange color with two flat pillows—then at me. Smiles. "No way you'd fit."

My sex-deprived brain delves straight into the gutter. *I'd make it fit.*

Eve's cheeks redden like other situations in which those words could be used occurred to her too. She clears her throat. "I'm fine sharing the bed." She nods to the ajar door that leads into the attached bathroom. "You can use it first."

"Okay." I grab my bag of toiletries and head into the bathroom.

This is weird. I've never spent the night with a girl without it involving sex. I've never spent the entire night with *any* girl, actually. Now that I'm no longer focused on driving or frustrated by traffic, I'm very aware of that fact.

Also, that this is Eve Driscoll, the girl I've wanted a second shot with for years.

I'm not going to make a move. She didn't sign up to share a bed with me, and I don't want to make her uncomfortable. But I'm going to be very aware that I could make a move—that we're alone in a hotel room and both single—all night, and the possibilities bode poorly for getting much sleep.

Eve's perched on the edge of the mattress when I exit the bathroom.

"It's comfy," she tells me, bouncing twice and making me smile. "Do you snore?"

"I don't think so," I answer. "Do you?"

"No. But I do roll around a lot, so I'll build a pillow wall."

"A pillow wall?" I repeat, amused.

"Yeah. A wall of pillows."

She says it like it should be obvious, and I experience this sudden flash of déjà vu, reminded of my recurring thought the night we met—that I'd never met anyone like Eve.

Almost four years later, I still haven't.

"Do you need help?" I ask.

"With what?"

"With the pillow wall."

She laughs, and the drab motel room feels brighter. "I think I can handle it, thanks."

"Okay." I walk over to my duffel, and Eve disappears into the bathroom.

I usually sleep in boxers, but that's not an option tonight. I pull on a pair of sweats and a clean T-shirt, then turn the thermostat down a few degrees. Hopefully Eve won't mind. The comforter on the bed looks thick, so I'll be sweating otherwise.

I find my charger and plug in my phone, then lie down on the mattress. Eve was right—it's surprisingly comfortable. I lie as close to the edge as possible to make sure Eve has plenty of space.

The last sound I register is the running tap as Eve gets ready for bed.

———

Persistent buzzing cuts through the haze of sleep. I fumble for where I think I left my phone, finally locating it thanks to the charge cord.

My stomach drops as soon as I see the name lit up on the screen.

Fuck.

I roll out of bed, shove my feet into my sneakers, grab a room key off the table, and then hustle outside. I close the door behind me as quietly as possible, hoping not to wake Eve, then swipe to accept the call.

"Hi, Sean." I take a seat at the top of the cement steps.

"Hunter!" my brother crows.

Fuck, fuck, fuck.

He's high. On what, I couldn't even begin to guess. It started with opioids, but I know he's sampled coke and heroin.

I press my palm flat against my forehead, forcing myself to take deep, even breaths, when all I really want to do is hurl my phone down to the cracked asphalt below and watch it shatter into a thousand unreachable pieces.

"How's it hanging, little bro?" Sean continues. "You sick of the shitty weather yet?"

At least he remembers I go to college in Washington. Last time my brother called, he was so out of it he thought I was still in high school, living at Mom and Dad's. Asked me to come pick him up at the corner convenience store where we used to stop for candy after hockey practice.

"Where are you, Sean?" I ask evenly.

Passivity is the best way to deal with him, I've learned. Too cheerful, and he tries to get me to party with him. Too angry, and he gets belligerent.

Most times, I pretend I'm a 911 operator. Poised, composed… detached. I pretend it's a stranger on the other end of the line, not my childhood hero. The funnier, more outgoing, more charming Morgan brother. The guy who helped me tie my first pair of hockey skates—hand-me-downs from him.

It fucking killed me that Sean wasn't there to see me win a championship two weeks ago. But this call—knowing rehab didn't stick, *again*—is doing even more damage.

"Sean?"

I'm so caught up in my own disappointment, it takes me too long to realize he never answered my question. That his end is dead air.

I stand and start pacing, continuing to repeat his name.

Hanging up is a gamble—Sean is a lot better at making calls than answering them—but this is a familiar part of the pattern. He calls me, then gets distracted and forgets he called me.

I repeat his name once more, then hang up. Exhale, then call him back.

No answer.

An endless stream of swears run through my head. I'm so disappointed. Mad—at Sean, and at myself, for thinking this time would be any different. Worried.

I force myself to tap the number at the top of my *Favorites* list.

"Hey, Hunter."

The forced cheerfulness in my dad's voice is worse than the undercurrent of exhaustion. He knows what this call means. I'm sure he dreaded answering, experiencing the same sick sensation that I did as soon as I saw Sean's name light up on the screen. Subconsciously, as soon as I registered the buzz. Because only one person calls me in the middle of the night.

Another thing I resent my brother for—making me be the one to break our parents' hearts over and over again. He never calls them. He always calls me.

A long time ago, I got some sick satisfaction from it. I liked that I was the person my big brother turned to for help. Almost like I was *his* hero, for once. When the phone rings now, all I feel is anger and dread.

"Hi, Dad. Sorry to wake you."

"That's all right, son. You calling from California?"

"Not quite. Car got a flat on the way and there was terrible traffic, so we stopped in Oregon for the night."

"We?" There's a rare note of curiosity in my dad's voice as we help each other prolong the inevitable. Distract each other, just for a bit, before we address why we're having this conversation at three a.m.

"Yeah." I stop pacing and rest my elbows on the metal railing. "A friend of Harlow's—Conor's girlfriend, you met her at the banquet—decided to join us. She got a ride with me."

"Does this female friend have a name?"

"Eve."

"Nice name."

My life is hockey and school. Well, was hockey. Still is school.

That's the only reason my dad is latching on to Eve, because our small talk never lasts very long before we're stuck on the big talk. He'll ask how my classes are going, how hockey is going. But he can't ask that second question anymore.

"Have you heard back from any schools yet?"

"Not yet," I lie.

I need to tell him—and my mom—the truth. But now isn't the right time for that conversation.

"How's Mom?"

"She's good. She and Kate Simpson are doing a cooking class together. We made one of the recipes tonight. It was…interesting."

I chuckle, and it releases a little of the tension humming through my body. "Edible?"

"I'd have gone to bed hungry if not for some jerky I had hidden in the garage from my last fishing trip."

"Nice one, Dad."

"Yeah. The class lasts another four weeks, so I'll have to restock this weekend."

I smile, picking at the peeling paint on the metal railing. Little bits fall the twenty or so feet to the parking lot below. "He called a few minutes ago. I tried—" My voice cracks. "I tried to get a location, but no luck."

"That's all right, son." More false cheer. "I'll swing by the usual spots."

"I'm sorry, Dad."

"Don't apologize, Hunter. None of this is your fault."

Sean won't accept any blame, though. Won't make apologies. Won't even call our parents. So I have to do it all for him. I hate the idea of my dad going to all the seediest spots in town alone, and I'm also relieved I'm hundreds of miles away. I hate that I answer the phone and indulge him, but I know I would never forgive myself if I didn't answer and he needed help.

We linger in sad silence.

"I thought maybe it stuck this time," I admit.

My dad's exhale is heavy. "Me too. Go back to sleep, kiddo. And enjoy your break. You deserve a vacation."

"Let me know…"

He understands what I'm trying to say. "I will. Night, Hunter."

"Night, Dad."

I shove my phone into my pocket and stare at the blinking *No Vacancy* sign.

The chill in the night air registers for the first time, bleeding into my beleaguered body.

I blow out one final breath, then head back to the room.

Eve's a still lump under the covers. I must have passed out before she came to bed because I have no recollection of her leaving the bathroom. Two pillows are piled between Eve and the empty spot where I was sleeping. The sight makes me smile. I hope she appreciated I took the side closest to the door in case a serial killer broke in.

I'm too restless to go back to bed. I'll just lie there, thinking. I head into the bathroom, the only separate part of the room with its own door.

Leaning against the back of the door gets old fast, so I decide to shower. Usually I shower in the morning, but this'll save some time before we hit the road. And hot water will help me decompress a little. I won't be able to fall back asleep until I get a text from my dad. Probably not after then, either.

Surprisingly, the water pressure is better here than at my bathroom off campus. I lean a hand against the damp tile and let the spray hit the top of my head, pounding my scalp and dripping down my face.

After a few minutes, I take a pump of soap from the dispenser to suds my hair and arms.

My gaze snags on a pink razor sitting on the shelf.

Eve was naked in here. Something I should *not* be thinking about before climbing back into bed with her. Two pillows aren't going to prevent me from fantasizing about all the things we could do in a bed besides sleep.

Telling myself to stop thinking about it isn't doing much either. I'm desperate for a distraction right now. More blood is rushing south. I grip my growing erection, sorely tempted to jerk off for some stress relief. But...I'll picture Eve. And it feels sleazy, pretending I'm fucking her instead of my hand while she sleeps, oblivious, on the other side of the door.

I turn the handle instead, hissing when icy water hits my abs. It feels like tiny knives are stabbing my stomach. My cock deflates some, but my balls are still throbbing.

I shut off the water and pull the shower curtain open.

There's a quiet creak, followed by a loud gasp.

My head snaps up.

Eve is standing in the doorway. Her wide eyes are fixed on my wet body, and I can actually see the color pooling in her cheeks as my nakedness registers. Her complexion will rival a tomato's soon.

"Sorry," she blurts, then spins around. Only to turn back, eyes pointedly fixed on the floor, and grab the door's handle.

It slams shut a second later.

I stare at the spot she just stood, distantly registering the *drip drip drip* as excess water rolls down my body and hits the floor of the tub.

This might make tomorrow's—technically today's—drive a little awkward.

CHAPTER NINE

EVE

EVE: I saw his thing.

HARLOW: Huh?

EVE: I SAW HIS THING.

HARLOW: Repeating the same thing in all caps
clarifies nothing, you know.

HARLOW: Especially at seven a.m.

HARLOW: There's no need for text yelling this
early in the day.

EVE: I walked in on him.

EVE: I'm mortified.

HARLOW: WHO ARE YOU TALKING ABOUT??

EVE: Now who's text yelling?

EVE: HUNTER.

EVE: Who else could I be talking about?

"You want coffee?"

The deep rumble of Hunter's voice distracts me from texting Harlow. I drop my phone guiltily. It bounces off the seat and into the cupholder, almost toppling the water bottle there.

I scramble for it, terrified he'll be able to read the all-caps messages I just sent Harlow, not relaxing until the screen is black and the device is safely tucked under my thigh.

I clear my throat, attempting some composure. "Yeah. Coffee sounds good."

"Okay." He flicks on the blinker for the drive-thru a few buildings down from the motel where we spent the night.

I continue staring straight ahead.

I can't look at Hunter. I haven't been able to look at Hunter since I got an eyeful of his giant dick.

I pretended to be asleep when he came back to bed last night, and hid in the bathroom this morning while he packed up his stuff and checked us out. My teeth have never been cleaner.

Have I imagined Hunter naked before? Yes. That night freshman year and nearly every time I've seen him since. He's a tall, strapping hockey player. Proportionally, the size of his penis makes sense.

But picturing him with a huge cock was very different from *seeing* his huge cock.

And, frankly, the timing couldn't be worse. Because I'm single. That barrier that's always been there, blocking me, Hunter, and any sort of reality, is gone. Or, it's gone on my end. He hasn't said anything to suggest he's in a relationship, but he was on a date with Holly Johnson last week.

Even if he's not dating Holly, *she's* his type. I've seen the girls who hang around the hockey team. I have big boobs that have always been popular with guys and a great ass in the right pair of jeans, but Hunter could easily pass as a Calvin Klein model. Not only because there'd be a big bulge in the boxers, but because he has abs and that cut V and strong thighs and…*fuck*, I'm thinking about his dick again.

I bite the inside of my cheek—hard—to distract myself from the flood of inappropriate thoughts.

Because of the other, more pressing reason that Dickgate couldn't have happened at a more inconvenient time: I'm stuck in a car with Hunter for another two hours and forty-three minutes, according to the GPS.

Stupid flat tire and stupid traffic. We should have pushed through, and then this never would have happened.

I'll just chug my coffee and then pretend to fall asleep for the rest of the trip, I decide.

My phone keeps buzzing under my thigh, suggesting Harlow finally woke up and figured out what I was trying to tell her. But we're stopped in the line for the drive-thru now, and I can't text Harlow about Hunter's dick while we're sitting in a car together.

Not while he's not distracted by driving, at least.

"What are you getting?"

I keep my eyes fixed on the menu. "Not sure. There are so many options."

There's a very quiet laugh to my left.

The menu has six choices: coffee, iced coffee, tea, iced tea, water, and soda. Not a vanilla soy latte—my usual order—in sight. I'm not lactose intolerant, but I switched to using alternatives after listening to a podcast about the dairy industry so that I'm not haunted by the cries of calves separated from their mothers.

"I'm, uh, sorry about last night. I was having trouble sleeping, so I—"

I wave a hand in his general direction, still studiously

avoiding eye contact. "Don't apologize. It's fine. Totally fine. I'm the one who barged in. I was half asleep and thought the bathroom door was closed because I left it that way after I used it and I—" I swallow. "I didn't, um, see anything."

Hunter chuckles at the obvious lie. He was standing—stark naked—about three feet from my face. The motel bathroom wasn't exactly spacious. Obviously, I saw *everything*.

"Aren't artists supposed to appreciate nudity?" he wonders.

"Well, walking in on you in the shower wasn't exactly the same as admiring *David*."

He's flesh and blood and muscle. Human, not carved marble.

"Ouch."

"No, I didn't mean—" My phone is buzzing again, distracting me. Harlow's definitely decoded Dickgate. "It wasn't *bad*, I just meant it wasn't the *same* as looking at art."

"Wasn't bad," Hunter muses.

I finally look at him. The longer I don't, the more obvious it is I'm avoiding eye contact. And not only are we stuck in this car together for the next two hours and forty-one minutes, we're also spending the next week in close quarters.

He's grinning. "Thought you didn't see anything?"

I feel like I have a fever. Sweat is prickling at the back of my neck and in my armpits. Good thing I applied three coats of deodorant while I was stalling in the bathroom earlier. "Can we *please* stop discussing this?"

"Yep. Sure."

He's still grinning.

I'm still hotter than a furnace.

Finally, it's our turn to order. It's a relief when Hunter rolls his window down, letting some cooler air in the car.

Hunter asks for a large coffee, black. I request an iced coffee with soy milk.

Hunter's drink appears immediately. Mine doesn't. I'm guessing the ice isn't the delay.

"What does soy milk taste like?" he asks. "I've never tried it."

"It's…I don't know. Bland. I've never drunk it plain, I just add it to my coffee. I don't like the taste of drinking it black."

"What about regular milk?"

"I feel bad about stealing it from baby cows. I listened to a podcast about the dairy industry and I'm…boycotting, I guess."

"My dad grew up on a dairy farm," Hunter tells me.

"Oh. Sorry, I didn't mean to offend—"

"You didn't offend me. I was going to say you're right—it's a tough industry. On both sides. My grandparents had to sell the farm while my dad was in college. All the cows went to slaughter and their land is a giant subdivision now."

"That's awful. I'm sorry."

My coffee appears and gets handed to Hunter. He thanks the server, then passes the coffee to me.

We're back on the highway a few minutes later. The *wide-open* highway, thankfully.

"You listen to a lot of podcasts," Hunter remarks between sips of coffee. He must be burning his mouth—there's steam curling through the tiny opening in the lid—but he appears unbothered by the temperature.

"Yeah, I do."

He nods to the stereo. "Put one on."

"What?"

"Put one on. We've got almost three hours to kill. You sketching yesterday wasn't very entertaining for me. I couldn't even tell what you were drawing."

Well, thank God for that. I had no idea he was trying to look, and I was drawing *him*. Thea said I should work on my portrait angles, and he has a really nice profile.

"I was just doodling." I unwedge my phone, ignoring all the texts from Harlow. Talking to Hunter cleared most of the awkwardness, and reading her responses is going to send me back into a spiral of embarrassment.

"Not the *poor baby cows* one, please." His smile is sheepish. "I really love ice cream."

"I still eat regular ice cream," I admit. "The dairy-free kind isn't very good." I scroll through my saved episodes, trying to judge which show Hunter might enjoy the most. "Do you want to listen to one about sports?"

I tried a football podcast hosted by two brothers last year so I'd have something to contribute when my dad talked about the Cardinals.

I'm expecting an enthusiastic response from Hunter. He plays sports—or, *a* sport—so he must like sports.

But he surprises me and says, "No. Put on something you really want to listen to."

"Why do you think I don't want to listen to sports?"

Hunter huffs a laugh as he switches lanes. "Because you're not interested in sports."

"How do you know?"

He chuckles again. "Okay. What sports do you follow?"

I sigh. "None. But I did go to a basketball game last fall. And a hockey game."

"Because you like basketball and hockey?"

"No," I admit. "I went to the basketball game because of Clayton Thomas. One of my friends had a crush on him." Hopefully Mary won't mind me throwing her under the bus. She's happily dating David now. "And I went to the hockey game because of y—" I cough, a rush of cold panic constricting my chest. "Because of, you know, the whole Harlow-and-Conor thing."

"Right."

Hunter appears oblivious to the fact that I was milliseconds away from blurting *you.*

Technically, the reason I went to a hockey game this past season was because Harlow was going to see Conor play.

The main reason I *wanted* to go to a hockey game? To see Hunter play. Because anytime anyone brought up Holt's hockey team, my first thought was always the eighteen-year-old who told me he was nervous about joining a new team. But if Hunter remembers our conversation freshman year, he's never suggested it, so I'm following his lead and pretending it never happened. He probably talked to lots of girls that night. I know he's talked to lots of girls since.

"What about a serial killer in Alaska? He would mail the coordinates of the body to the police station and that was the only way they found his victims."

C is for Crime is my favorite podcast, but I don't say so. I know Hunter said to put on what I wanted to listen to, but he's the one driving and insisting on paying for everything. Well, *almost* everything. He did grudgingly accept a twenty for my dinner.

There aren't many people I'd willingly listen to sports with, but Hunter happens to be one of them.

"Uh, sure," he answers. "Sounds…entertaining."

I can't tell if he's being genuine or simply indulging me, but I start the first episode anyway.

And when he asks me to start the second one an hour later, I find myself wishing the roads today weren't so wide open.

CHAPTER TEN

HUNTER

The rental Phillips found is right on the beach. Not the *white sands, turquoise water* sort of beach, but a craggy stretch of coastline that's currently being battered by churning gray water. Still, it's a nice view. Peaceful with an edge, like the calm before a building storm.

"Well, we made it." I state the obvious as I shut the car off.

The speakers cut out, which I'm a little disappointed by. I'm going to have to look up the podcast Eve was playing so I can find out how they wind up catching the killer. Three episodes in is a total cliffhanger.

"Yeah, we did," Eve agrees.

I glance over. She's studying the house's exterior. A smile quirks up the corners of her mouth the longer she looks. It widens when her eyes wander this way and she catches me staring at her.

I should say *something*. A comment that's meaningful or memorable, or anything that contains actual words, while we're still alone.

Eve speaks first. "Thanks, Hunter."

Every syllable is steeped in sincerity.

The genuine gratefulness in her expression makes me feel about twenty feet tall. But I really wish she'd stop thanking me. Stop acting like I did her some favor or she's some inconvenience.

That's what I should say—tell Eve I enjoyed this road trip a hell of a lot more with her than I would have alone. That I'll enjoy spring break a hell of a lot more with her here than I would have fifth-wheeling with my best friends and their girlfriends.

Before I can say a word, the front door of the rental opens. A bright flash of red flutters in the wind as Harlow jogs toward my car, waving enthusiastically.

Too late—again.

Eve pops her door open and climbs out. I do the same, more slowly.

The air is chilly and tastes like salt. Phillips was right about the weather. I can't imagine swimming in the Pacific—not without a wetsuit, at least—but the hot tub Aidan's been waxing poetic about does look enticing. I can see the steam rising from where it's tucked off one side of the patio that juts from the left side of the house.

"I'm so glad you guys finally made it!" Harlow says, flinging her arms around her best friend.

Eve's response gets lost in the wind and the wild halo of Harlow's loose hair, but her smile is bigger when Harlow steps back.

She also looks more relaxed than she has since I picked her up yesterday. The breeze has pulled some of her hair free, and the straight set of her shoulders has softened a little.

Once Harlow releases Eve, she gives me a quick squeeze too. She and Hart have only been officially dating since January, but it's hard to remember a time when she wasn't an extension of our trio. I don't know Rylan as well—not only is she a junior, but this was also her first semester on campus—since Phillips was the only guy on the team cocky enough to think that socializing with Coach's daughter was a great idea.

Speaking of Aidan, he announces his arrival outside with a loud "What the hell, Morgan? Did you decide to take the scenic route through Nevada, or something? Hit Vegas?"

I grunt when Aidan punctuates his final question with a hard slap on the back. "The only thing we 'hit' was bad traffic."

Phillips makes a face. "Lame. Hey, Eve."

Eve glances over from the whispered conversation she was having with Harlow. Based on the smirk on Harlow's face, I have a feeling Eve mentioned the whole *walking in on me naked* incident to her best friend.

Most of the awkwardness dissipated during the second leg of the drive, but I still wish it'd never happened. I've thought about being naked in front of Eve before. Never in the context of my body having just been sprayed by cold water and her being fully clothed, however.

I noticed she'd added a third pillow to the pillow wall when I went back to bed last night. I'm not sure what that meant. I've been in enough locker rooms to know that my dick is on the larger end of the scale, and every girl I've hooked up with has appreciated it. But maybe I traumatized Eve? *Wasn't bad* wasn't much of an ego boost.

"Hi, Aidan," Eve greets. "Thanks for including me. I heard you were the mastermind behind this trip."

Phillips beams proudly about receiving credit. To be fair, he did arrange most of the trip. When it relates to something he *wants* to do, Aidan's unstoppable. "No problem. We weren't going to leave you high and dry, unlike that asshole ex of yours."

Eve tenses, her smile turning forced.

Harlow and I both glare at Aidan.

"What?" he wonders, glancing back and forth between us. "Was I not supposed to know about that?"

"You were supposed to not mention it," Harlow tells him.

"Oh. Sorry—"

"It's fine," Eve interrupts. "Ben and I didn't have any spring break plans, so he didn't technically leave me 'high and dry,' but…" She shrugs, then clears her throat. "Cool place."

"Isn't it? You can see the ocean from almost every window and…" Aidan launches into an enthusiastic description of the rental's features—heavily emphasizing the hot tub—that I tune out while I unload the car.

Rylan appears, waving at me before interrupting Aidan's monologue about amenities to introduce herself to Eve.

Harlow walks over to help me unload while the three of them chat.

"Where's Hart?" I ask.

"He went for a run. I decided to stay back so I'd be here when you and Eve arrived."

I nod, unsurprised that Hart isn't taking a break from training relentlessly this week. I've kept up a workout routine, and so has Aidan. But not to the same extent as when we were in season. Conor is the only one of us who might still have a hockey career to stay in shape for.

"Well, I'm touched Hart stuck around to say hi to me," I say sarcastically.

Harlow smirks. "Guess I'm a better best friend than he is."

"Hart asked if I wanted to go running with him, but I said I had to stay here to make sure you made it," Aidan says, sauntering over. "Glad you appreciated the effort, Morgan."

I roll my eyes. "Yeah, you really went out of your way."

I haven't heard from Aidan or Conor since they left campus

on Thursday. Eve was the one telling Harlow about our delays, and presumably Harlow was passing updates along. Or my friends have unwavering faith in my ability to drive across two state lines.

Phillips waves my sarcasm away. "We both know I'm your favorite best friend anyhow."

I lift my duffel and toss it to him. "Carry that inside, and you'll at least be in the running."

Aidan heaves a sigh but he listens, heading for the house with my bag.

"I've got Eve's," Harlow says, grabbing the suitcase handle. She glances at me. "Both bathroom doors here lock, FYI."

I knew it.

"It was the middle of the night. I was tired and I—"

Harlow starts laughing, cutting me off. "No one's saying you flashed Eve on purpose, Hunter."

"And I *didn't*, for the record. I just—" I glance at where Eve is standing, talking with Rylan. "I hope I didn't make her uncomfortable. I know she's…going through a lot."

"You didn't," Harlow assures me. "Eve's tough. Honestly, it was probably good for her." She smiles. "A reminder there are other fish in the sea, you know? But without any pressure, because you're not her type."

My eyebrows furrow tight together.

Not her type? Who *is* Eve's type? Her ex, who didn't even bother making plans with her over spring break?

Harlow catches my frown and giggles. "No offense. I just meant, you're an *athlete*."

"So is Hart," I remind her, half joking and half offended by the implication that hand-eye coordination is a character flaw.

I know what Harlow means. I'm sure I've heard more shady shit than she has, and it's true that most of it has been about guys on sports teams. But we're not all like that. *I'm* not like that, which she should know.

Rylan and Eve come over, interrupting my conversation with Harlow. They offer to help carry luggage, but there's really not much. I leave my backpack in the car. Eve grabs hers, and we all head for the house.

My phone buzzes in my pocket as I walk. I hurriedly pull it out. My pulse quickens when I see the name on the screen. An update from my dad—the first one since he texted me at four a.m. to let me know he found Sean at the abandoned mini golf course.

DAD: He left twenty minutes ago.

I'm not surprised.

It's another part of the pattern. Sean relapses, he calls, he sobers up, and he disappears. A vicious, *predictable* cycle. He always relapses. I always answer. Dad always drives around until he finds him. And Sean always takes off as soon as he's sobered up.

So maybe we're all to blame, in different ways.

Mom is probably organizing the pantry or vacuuming. She cleans when she's stressed or upset about anything. And I'd bet the degree I'm about to receive that my dad sent this message on his way out the door to Pathfinder Reservoir with his tackle box and a pole.

My coping mechanism was skating circles on the ice until my cheeks were numb and my thighs burned. Did wonders for my stamina. I was known as the guy who always had more gas in the tank at the end of a game.

I would've much rather watched Sean win the state championship he talked about.

I snap a photo of the house I'm standing in front of—gray

ocean and blue sky visible in the background—and send it to my dad so he knows I made it to California. Then I slip my phone in my pocket and continue walking.

The front door is slightly ajar. I push it open wide enough for me to walk through, finding Aidan standing in the living room with a remote in one hand, raised and aimed at the flatscreen television mounted above the fireplace. There's no sign of the girls, but I can hear the chatter of voices echoing upstairs.

I glance around the first floor, letting out a low whistle. We all kicked in three hundred for this trip, which was pooled to cover groceries and the rental fee. But I have a feeling Aidan shelled out more than his fair share, based on how nice this place is.

"Check out this flatscreen," Aidan says as he flips through channels. "Perfect for watching the Kings tonight. They're playing Washington, so it should be a good game."

"Great." Sitting—and being able to stretch my legs—sounds ideal after the cramped car.

The front door opens again and Conor enters the living room. His hair and T-shirt are both soaked with sweat.

He grins when he spots me. "Hey, you're here! We weren't sure when you'd make it. Did you decide to stop in Vegas, or something?"

"Hart," Aidan says very seriously. "I already made that joke."

"What, about Vegas? It's funny, since Morgan isn't much of a gambler."

I want to grimace, but I don't. It's true; I don't have Aidan's recklessness or Conor's swagger. I don't take risks—even calculated ones. There's a reason I play defense. I like to protect what I already have, not chance losing a little while chasing more.

Most of the time, I'm fine with that. But Sean's pattern has me feeling restless. I don't love that the only unpredictable part of my life is my brother.

"Found it!" Aidan announces, Conor's infringement of his comedic material forgotten as he focuses on the commentators discussing tonight's game. "We're all set for later."

"Harlow wants to check out that bar in town," Conor says. "We probably won't catch more than the first period."

"That's cool," Aidan responds. "Rylan wants to go to Sand Bar too. That asshole at the grocery store was going on about it."

I snort, and they both look at me.

"What?" Aidan asks.

"Nothing. It just sounds like I should ask *Harlow and Rylan* what the itinerary for the week is."

Conor flips me off.

"Aww, don't worry," Aidan coos. "We'll find a girlfriend for you too, Morgan."

"Yeah." I glance out the window next to the fireplace. The yard is so huge the next house is only a speck in the distance. "This town seems like a real singles hotspot."

Conor chuckles. "We'll be your wingmen."

"Totally," Aidan agrees. "We'll get you laid this week. Although..." He glances around the living room, and then scratches the back of his neck. "You might want to go to her place. Since your sleeping arrangements leave a lot to be desired."

I snort as I stretch. My back and neck are sore from driving. "Thanks for the advice."

This place has three bedrooms. Originally, we each had a room, with Aidan and Conor sharing with their girlfriends. Then, Eve entered the equation. I'd rather sleep on the sofa than let her, but having my bedroom double as a common space does make the likelihood of me having sex this week highly unlikely.

So does Eve's presence, if I'm being honest.

I like her as much as I did freshman year. More, the longer I'm around her. She's different from anyone else I've ever met.

Any other girl I've ever dated. I noticed it the first time we spoke, and I've felt flickers of it the few times we've interacted since. I don't know how to explain or rationalize it, I just know it exists. And I know it means my celibacy streak would have continued, even if we were in Miami or Mexico or some other stereotypical spring break destination crawling with drunk college students and I had my own hotel room.

"I'm gonna go shower," Conor announces.

"Yeah, you do stink," Aidan tells him.

Conor rolls his eyes, then heads for the stairs.

I flop down on the couch doubling as my bed to watch TV with Aidan.

CHAPTER ELEVEN

EVE

"What about this top?" Rylan asks, spinning around with her arms out so we can see the shirt she's modeling from every angle.

Harlow tilts her head, considering. "Yeah, I like the green better."

"Eve?"

I set down the tube of concealer I was using to cover the dark circles under my eyes. I never fell back asleep after Dickgate, and it turns out pretending to be unconscious while actually being awake is extra exhausting.

I twist around, glancing at the maroon one-shouldered top on the bed, then at the satin halter shirt Rylan's holding up to the jeans she's wearing. A shade of green I'd call... hunter.

"Green," I say.

Rylan nods. "A consensus. Love it."

"Your clothes are so cute," Harlow says, twisting another section of her hair around the barrel of the curling iron. "Now I feel like I have nothing to wear tonight."

"You can borrow whatever," Rylan offers, nodding toward her oversized, overflowing suitcase.

"Except you wear fun colors, and fun colors make me look like I'm wearing a traffic cone on my head."

I snort a laugh. "Harlow."

"It's true!" She sets down the curling iron, grabs the top, and holds it up. "See?!"

The maroon lace *does* clash with her red hair. But it doesn't make it look *orange*.

"Go naked," I suggest.

"Helpful, Eve, thanks." She twists another section of hair, then smirks. "I'll leave that to Hunter."

"Um, *hello*? What did I miss?" Rylan glances back and forth between us. "When was Hunter naked?"

"It's a long story," I say.

"Eve walked in on Hunter in the shower last night," Harlow supplies.

"Okay, it's not *that* long of a story," I amend. "But it's one I would prefer to stop talking about. I almost died of mortification. *Multiple* times."

My traitorous best friend just laughs.

Rylan looks confused. "Why would *you* be embarrassed?"

"Because I didn't knock, and it was my fault I couldn't tell he wasn't in bed because of the pillow wall, and we don't really know each other, and I..." I shake my head and pick up my concealer again. "Just a weird part of the trip."

Rylan looks even more confused. "Pillow wall?"

"Eve's a restless sleeper," Harlow explains. "If it makes you feel any better, Hunter was worried he made you uncomfortable."

"Make me feel *better*?" I exclaim. "Harlow, that makes me feel *worse*!"

"*Relax*. I told him you enjoyed the show."

Now Rylan is laughing. Glad I could provide some pre-game amusement.

Actually, I'm *not* glad. I'd like to go back to pretending Dick-gate never happened.

"You'd better not have," I threaten.

For all her teasing, I don't think Harlow would be that bold on my behalf. She has no idea I like Hunter, and she knows I'm in a weird place right now.

I wish I was the girl who thought to say *I enjoyed the show* after accidentally seeing a hot guy naked. But no, I'm the girl who hid in the bathroom and then compared him to a Michelangelo sculpture. It was supposed to be a compliment, but I don't think it came out that way.

A loud bang rattles the door hinges, making the mirror I was using to apply my makeup bounce.

"Was the sign really necessary?" Aidan calls from the hallway.

Harlow and Rylan dissolve into giggles. They taped a *No Boys Allowed* sign on my bedroom door when we came upstairs to get ready to go out to a local bar. The boys were so busy watching hockey they didn't even notice Harlow writing on the piece of paper she found in one of the kitchen drawers. They had me sketch a hockey player at the bottom, and Rylan's contribution was drawing a red X over him.

I actually did a pretty good job of recreating Holt's jersey, if I do say so myself. Athletes aren't my usual subject matter.

"Go away, Aidan!" Rylan shouts back. "We're busy!"

There's a loud sigh on the other side of the door.

"Hayes, how much longer?" Conor's voice this time. "Do we have time to make nachos before the second period?"

"No nachos!" Harlow answers. "We'll be down in five minutes."

"We should have just made them," I hear Aidan grumble. "Forgiveness over permission and all that."

"They'll have food at the bar," Conor replies.

Receding footsteps sound, and their voices fade. I don't hear Hunter's. He must have stayed downstairs, in the living room/his bedroom. I still feel guilty about stealing his bed. I should have asked more questions about the rental the night I agreed to go, but I wasn't exactly thinking straight between the vodka and the breakup. It feels like I've inconvenienced Hunter a lot this trip, and being indebted to someone you want to impress is not a great feeling.

I finish my makeup, then stand and stretch. My muscles are stiff from sitting most of yesterday and today. I should have gone for a walk before showering.

Harlow wolf whistles as I drop my makeup bag on top of the dresser. "Damn, Eve. The surfer guys will be all over you."

"If you say so," I reply doubtfully.

Harlow keeps insisting there's a large population of eligible bachelors in this town, but I have my doubts. It's not like we're spring breaking in Cancun with two hundred other colleges.

"No, it's true," Rylan tells me. "There were *tons* of cute guys when we went to the grocery store this morning. And a bunch of them said they'd be at Sand Bar tonight."

"Assuming Aidan didn't scare them all off," Harlow adds, smirking. She glances at me. "He got a little, uh, possessive earlier."

Rylan rolls her eyes. "He's so dramatic."

But she's smiling as she says it, a soft, secret one that reminds me I'm no longer a member of the *happily in love* club. One that makes me question whether I was ever a member of that club, because I don't think that's an expression I've ever worn.

"It was sweet," Harlow states. "He's crazy about you."

Rylan tucks a piece of hair behind her ear. "He told me he loved me," she says shyly.

"Really?" Harlow squeals.

Rylan nods. "Yeah. When we were at my parents' for dinner last weekend. I was a little worried he was going to bolt after dinner with my dad. And he's so unserious most of the time, I wasn't expecting him to say it that soon. Or like, at all." She laughs. "Caught me totally off guard."

"Conor told me at SeaTac's baggage claim," Harlow says, smiling. "I had a coffee stain on my shirt and hadn't slept in twenty-four hours. I thought I was hallucinating when I first saw him." She smiles. "It was the best moment of my life."

"Well, you guys sure are making single life sound *fantastic*," I comment, spritzing my wrists with my favorite perfume.

Harlow walks up behind me and wraps her arms around my shoulders. "You're going to find your right guy, E."

I pat her arm. "I know. I'm kidding."

Sort of.

Harlow didn't love Ben. She *liked* him, but my best friend and my ex-boyfriend never moved past the friendly politeness stage that normally passes after you've known someone for more than a few weeks. I tried to force it—setting Harlow up with some of Ben's friends so we would all hang out together. Those double dates involved awkward pauses and no gains of common ground, so I gave up. And then Harlow started dating Conor, and they *fit*. And, despite my assumption that most athletes at Holt are insensitive playboys, he's a genuinely nice guy. Not just to Harlow, but welcoming to me too. I'm not sure what Ben's reaction would have been if I'd asked if Harlow could tag along on a trip he'd planned with his friends, and I hate that I'm unsure.

"Don't forget about the list," she whispers before letting me go.

Very unlikely. About the same chance as me actually *completing* the list.

"We should wingwomen Hunter too," Rylan comments, pulling her dark hair back into a ponytail. "I'm surprised he's not dating anyone."

I move my perfume bottle two inches to the right, just to look busy. "I think he is," I say, in what is hopefully a casual way.

"What?" Harlow says. "Who?"

"Holly Johnson. They were at La Bella Napoli the night Ben and I broke up."

"Oh." Harlow's curiosity has shifted to sympathy.

I shouldn't have added that last part.

"Who is Holly Johnson?" Rylan asks.

"She's a sorority girl," I answer.

Harlow makes a *rawr* noise as she shuts off and unplugs the curling iron.

"She *is*," I say, a little defensively. "I had a seminar with her freshman year, and Phi Beta Whatever was all she talked about. Stuck in my head, is all."

"I wouldn't have guessed that was Hunter's type," Rylan muses. "He's not exactly Mr. Social."

"He just takes a little longer to warm up to people," Harlow says. "I was convinced he hated me when Conor and I first started hanging out. But I think it was more his way of looking out for his friend."

I'm glad Harlow is defending Hunter. But I'm also weirdly… bothered by the realization my best friend knows him better than I do.

Rylan extracting a bottle of vodka from her giant suitcase is a welcome distraction from the strange reaction. She pulls shot glasses out next, neatly stacked and packed in a plastic bag.

"Wow, you came prepared," Harlow comments.

Rylan smiles as she carefully pours out three shots. She passes a blue glass to Harlow, a green one to me, and keeps the pink for herself.

We tap them all together, then down them in unison.

It's expensive vodka, the kind that doesn't taste like rubbing alcohol. It burns when it hits my stomach, warm numbness spreading a few seconds later.

"Let's go, ladies!" Harlow cheers, then heads for the door.

I pat my pockets to make sure I have my phone, and then follow.

"How long has it been since they came upstairs?" Rylan asks as we walk down the empty hallway toward the stairs.

"Ten minutes?" Harlow guesses.

It's been *at least* fifteen, but I don't point that out. I'm guessing Aidan will.

The sound of sports commentary is audible before we hit the first step, but the guys are gathered by the front door, not in front of the television. Aidan is tossing pieces of popcorn in his mouth, while Conor is sipping from a water bottle.

I focus on Hunter. He's showered and changed since I went upstairs to get ready. His hair is still damp, the dirty-blond shade slightly darker than usual. He's wearing jeans and a gray Henley that looks like it's constructed from the softest cotton in the world. Standing and typing on his phone, with a worried wrinkle creasing his forehead.

I linger on the last step, letting Rylan and Harlow go ahead to greet their boyfriends.

Aidan's loud joking about how long we took to get ready distracts Hunter from his phone. He shakes his head at the four-some gathered by the door before glancing at me.

And I freeze like I was caught doing something wrong beneath a bright spotlight.

Up until the recent overlap in our social spheres, my glimpses of Hunter have all been around campus. We've never interacted in this context—the *flirty outfit and vodka shots* kind of atmosphere. The closest was the school-sponsored event where we first met.

I can't tell what Hunter is thinking. If he's even noticed that the top I'm wearing is held together by four bows, exposing the center strip of my chest. This is undoubtedly the sexiest I've ever looked in front of him—I dressed this way with him in mind— and I'm...deflated that he doesn't appear to register any difference.

A gust of colder air alerts me to Rylan and Aidan's exit.

Conor is halfway out the door. "Dude. Come on."

Hunter drops the foot he had propped against the wall. Tucks his phone into his pocket. "Yeah. Ready," he says gruffly.

It's not until he moves toward the door that I register how motionless he was before. Maybe he was a *little* affected? Guys have always praised my big boobs, and they're the star of my outfit tonight.

"Eve!"

Harlow holds out her right hand—her left one is clasped with Conor's. As soon as I take it, she pulls me out the door with them. Conor pauses to lock the house, and then we follow Hunter to his car. The boys must have made a plan while we were getting ready, because Conor heads for the driver's seat and Hunter climbs into the passenger side without any discussion of the seating arrange- ments. Aidan dives into the back seat, pulling Rylan in behind him.

"This should be interesting," Harlow whispers to me, then climbs in next.

I end up with most of the seat behind Hunter. My right hip is pressed tight against the door to accommodate for the four people wedged across the back, but it's not that uncomfortable. The heady feeling of *belonging* eclipses any discomfort. I don't feel like an outsider as I stare at one of the strands of blond hair that curls against the back of Hunter's neck.

"You guys good back there?" Conor asks as we start rolling down the driveway.

"Living the dream, man," Aidan answers easily. "I'm surrounded by hot girls. Wanna sit on my lap for the ride back, Hayes?"

Conor hits the brakes.

Aidan—the only one not wearing a seat belt—flies into the back of Conor's seat. His hand hits the headrest a second before his nose.

"I was *kidding*, Hart. Jesus. I prefer brunettes." He nuzzles Rylan's neck.

"Right," Rylan drawls. "*That's* why the blonde who works in the campus coffee shop always gives you free drinks."

"I think she's just a really big hockey fan," Aidan says. "Right, Morgan?"

"I never got the impression your discounted lattes had anything to do with your subpar slap shot, Phillips," Hunter replies.

Conor laughs.

"Have fun sleeping on the floor tonight, Aidan," Harlow teases.

I'm smiling wide, which I don't realize until my cheeks start to ache a little. I've spent a decent amount of time around Conor, mostly because he spends a decent amount of time at my and Harlow's place. But the dynamic with his teammates—and Rylan —is new to me. In my experience, it's not that common to encounter friends who act like family. Aside from Harlow, my closest friend at Holt is Mary, and even with her there are times when I'm unsure what to say.

"Rylan would never make me sleep on the floor," Aidan retorts. "Because then I couldn't lick her—"

Rylan slaps a hand over his mouth. When it falls away, Aidan is grinning wide. Rylan doesn't manage to keep the smile off her face either.

Hunter clears his throat loudly. "Phillips. We talked about fucking boundaries, remember?"

"Sorry, man. I forgot you're not getting laid."

"And I forgot nothing sticks in your brain unless it's about sex."

"Not true! Hockey sticks too. Get it? Hockey sticks. Speaking of, the second period has probably started." Aidan digs his phone out of his pocket. The background is a cute photo of Rylan wearing a pink pom-pom hat. "Fuck. Halifax scored."

"Told you he would," Conor says.

That kicks off a hockey conversation full of unfamiliar names and terms that I quickly tune out. Harlow's texting her friend Landon. Rylan is snuggled against Aidan's chest while he draws circles on her knee with his free hand.

And I'm overanalyzing Aidan's comment about Hunter. Does that mean he's *not* dating Holly?

Ten minutes later, Conor pulls into a surprisingly full parking lot. I was sort of expecting a small building with a neon beer light, but this place looks bigger and busier than Gaffney's.

We're almost to the entrance of Sand Bar when my phone buzzes in my pocket.

I pull it out, and the excitement I was experiencing immediately fizzles into uneasiness.

"Go ahead," I urge Harlow, who's walking closest to me. "I'll be right in."

"Okay," she replies, then follows everyone else inside the bar.

I veer left, take a seat on a metal bench by some bushes, pull in a deep breath, and answer the call. "Hey, Dad."

"Hi, Eve."

An awkward pause ensues. We have a schedule for speaking—once a month, and always on a Tuesday at eight p.m. Since this is not a Tuesday and it's past eight, something is going on. And, knowing my dad, it's not likely to be anything good.

I clear my throat and remind him: "You called me."

"Oh, right. I just—just got home from Noah's baseball practice, and thought I'd give you a call."

My dad coaches the team. Maybe his rejection of parenthood—of me—would sting a little less if he wasn't such an involved father with his other kids. I always feel like a shitty person for thinking that—for resenting my half-siblings for their happy childhood. But emotions are rarely logical.

"How did practice go?" I ask, acting interested to alleviate a little of my own guilt.

I always ask about my half-siblings. Because it gives us something to talk about and because a petty part of me likes being the bigger person. *Let's talk about the kids you* didn't *abandon!*

"Great. Joanna found an indoor batting place in Phoenix, so we hit that a bunch this past winter. He'll be the star of the team this season."

"That's exciting."

Another beat of silence lingers.

"I just wanted to let you know...I'm not sure whether graduation will work out."

Not *sure*. After years of half-assed excuses from my father, which, pathetically, were an upgrade from his prior efforts to pretend I never existed, I'm fluent in what his hedging means.

He's not coming.

My response is a quiet "Oh."

My first test of being a braver, bolder, *better* version of myself is a complete failure.

"It's just a bad weekend for us," my father continues. "Noah has a baseball game and Lily started gymnastics, plus she's got a birthday party that Saturday. We're short-staffed at the station and they really need me on call."

I'm silent. I shouldn't be surprised, considering he's never made much of an effort to show up before. Somerville isn't exactly a short trip from Phoenix.

But I *am* surprised. It never occurred to me that my father might skip my college graduation. I thought our monthly phone call schedule meant something—was adding up to something— and that he finally cared about having some semblance of a relationship with me. He made the ten-minute drive to my high school graduation with his new wife and new baby.

I could look at a calendar and count exactly how many conversations we've had since that June. Just like I looked at a calendar and added up the amount of months I spent with Ben.

I was wrong about my dad caring. Just like I was wrong about Ben.

My dad's still talking. He sounds more cheerful than when I first answered, like telling me was an unpleasant task he's taken care of. "We'll throw a big party when you're back home," he's saying. "You can wear your cap and gown—recreate the big moment."

"Okay."

I want to say something else. I want to tell him that it's *not* okay. That I'm hurt and upset and angry. But those chaotic emotions have coalesced into a giant lump in my throat, blocking full sentences from coming out.

"Great. We can hammer out some details when we talk next. Tuesday, week after next, right?" He sounds proud, like I should be impressed he remembered the one day a month he's scheduled to check in with me.

I hate that he considers it an accomplishment. I hate myself, for allowing him to think it is one. For accepting the scraps of affection he tosses my way rather than throwing them back in his face and demanding more.

Because I'm scared *more* will revert into nothing.

"How is Ben?"

There's some twisted irony to the fact that my dad rarely asks about Ben but chooses this call to do so. He met Ben once, when he visited me in Chandler sophomore year, mostly quizzing him on New England sports teams Ben doesn't follow. Neither was that impressed by the other's contributions to the conversation.

"We broke up," I state flatly.

"Dad! Dad! You said we could take Bella for a walk" is what interrupts the noticeable pause of my father having no idea what to say. Usually, on the rare occasions he comes up, Ben is a safe topic.

"One sec, sweetheart." My dad's voice is a little muffled now, like he covered the phone with his hand.

Still, I hear Lily's next words loud and clear. "But Mom said dinner is almost ready. If we don't go now, then we won't have time before dinner and then it will be dark and then it will be bedtime and then—"

My dad folds like a cheap tent. "Okay, okay. Go put on your shoes and get Bella's leash."

A few seconds later, his voice returns to normal. "I'm sorry, Eve, but I've got to go. We'll talk Tuesday. Have fun in your classes this week."

I'm not surprised he forgot this is my spring break week.

But it does hit like another slap to the face. Another one I let land.

CHAPTER TWELVE

HUNTER

My fingers tap along to the opening chords of "Don't Stop Believing" as I study one of the vintage postcards sealed in the surface of the table. There are dozens of them—decorated with palm trees and sailboats and piers. The one half-covered by my bottle of beer shows a convertible cruising along the Pacific Coast Highway with a surfboard sticking out of the back. Blue sea and blue sky are the only backdrop.

If Eve were sitting next to me, I'd point it out to her. Ask if she's ever painted the Sound. I've never seen any of her art, and I really want to. When she was sketching in the car, she looked so peaceful. It kinda reminded me of Hart, how the ice is so obviously his happy place.

Except, with hockey, I feel like there's less mystery. Yeah, some guys are naturally more talented than others. But there's also a huge element of hard work. And that hard work consists of the same things. There's no sense of secrecy, like with the yellow sketchbook Eve was working in. Trying to guess what she would draw kept me entertained for a good hour.

Flowers, like the ones painted on her pants? Birds? Cars?

Abstract shapes? Does she consciously decide or is it like skating for her, when your muscles know exactly what to do without you making a conscious decision?

A nudge to my ribs—courtesy of Aidan's sharp elbow—makes me glance up. "Give it a go, Morgan."

"Go at what?" I ask absently.

I basically tuned him—and everyone—out ten minutes ago so I could focus on staying awake. I'm attempting not to be a wet blanket, but I'm fucking exhausted. I don't think I ever fell back asleep last night, so I'm going on about three hours of sleep.

"Hitting on Eve," Aidan answers.

That gets my attention.

I look at Eve, which I've been avoiding doing. I'm genuinely concerned I'm not going to be able to avert my eyes after a polite amount of time has passed.

The shirt she's wearing?

Fuck. Me.

That's what I imagine that shirt would say, if articles of clothing could talk. There's absolutely no way Eve's wearing a bra under it, and her tits are wrapped up like a goddamn Christmas present with a few bows on top.

And…shit, I'm staring.

I quickly glance at my smirking best friend instead. "What are you talking about, Phillips?"

"Eve's on the prowl tonight. Hart and I are taken, so you've gotta do the practice run." Aidan grins. "Pretend to pick Eve up, and then we can give her some constructive criticism."

"Stop making me sound like a jungle cat, Aidan," Eve says.

When I glance her way again—not looking can be as conspicuous as staring—Eve's cheeks are the same shade as raspberries. From embarrassment, or from the multiple rounds of shots Conor and I opted out of. He's driving and I'm having enough trouble staying awake semi-sober.

Eve seems to be studiously avoiding eye contact with me as she tells Aidan, "And a practice run is totally unnecessary. I've successfully flirted with guys *without* coaching, thank you very much."

"You've gotta be a little rusty, though," Phillips replies. "Weren't you with your loser ex for like three years?"

"Forty-one months," Eve mutters, then sips more of her drink.

It's almost empty. Between that and the shots, she's gotta be pretty buzzed by now.

Aidan's forehead furrows. "Huh?"

"Three years and five months," Rylan supplies.

Aidan rolls his eyes, then tugs on her ponytail affectionately. "Nerd alert. Anyway, as I was saying, you're rusty. A little practice never hurt anyone." He smirks. "Plus, Morgan's moves are legendary. I could use some entertainment."

I'm still five steps behind in this conversation.

When was it decided that Eve was "on the prowl" tonight? If I'd known I was going to have to sit and watch her flirt with other guys, I would've driven slower and delayed our arrival. Or stayed home and slept.

I glower at Aidan as he continues grinning at me.

I'm not *legendary* at picking up women; I'm absolute shit at it. I make meaningless small talk or resort to cliché lines I've heard teammates use over the years. The biggest problem is—and I'm aware how conceited it sounds—I've never had to work very hard at picking a woman up. No matter how little I say, no matter *what* I say, she's interested. I've never needed moves.

The irony is not lost on me that I've done a "practice run" with Eve before. Or that, under different circumstances—like the absence of our friends and her not fresh off a breakup—a chance to flirt with Eve Driscoll would be the highlight of my year.

Considering I won a national championship a couple of weeks ago, that's fucking saying something.

"I'm going to grab another drink," Eve announces, standing.

I glance at her glass. It's now empty.

Eve's seemed...off since she joined us at the table. I'm assuming it has to do with the phone call right after we arrived. Her ex, maybe? She didn't offer any information when she returned, and it's not my place to ask. Just like it's not my place to suggest she slow down on the drinks.

"Order at the left end," Harlow suggests, winking.

I glance at the bar. There's a cluster of guys standing at the left end, right by the jukebox that's blaring Journey.

Eve giggles, then heads in that direction.

I start picking at the wet label on my beer bottle. Flecks of sticky paper fall on the postcard I was studying earlier. I should order another beer. No one else seems inclined to head out anytime soon, and sipping gives me something to do. Plus, watching Eve "prowl" will be easier to stomach with a little more alcohol in my system.

Our waitress comes by a couple of minutes later, and I request a second round.

"Attaboy, Morgan!" Aidan elbows my ribs again. "Ten o'clock."

I glance in that direction. Two women are looking this way.

I drop my gaze before even registering their hair color. "Not tonight."

Phillips groans. "C'mon, man. Go get laid. I'm worried about you."

"Don't be. I'm fine."

Exhausted is more like it. Not just from the lack of sleep, but emotionally drained as well. Stuck waiting for the ticking time bomb my brother has turned into to detonate all over again.

Dealing with Sean is…well, there isn't really a coherent way to describe what it's like watching someone you love repeat the same destructive cycle over and over again.

I've never mentioned my brother to anyone at Holt. Growing up in a small town meant everyone *knew*. Coming to college was an escape from it all. A fresh start. But there are times, like now, when it would be nice to tell my best friend that I'm in a shitty mood because I got a call from my brother. For him to understand what that means without having to explain—and relive— it all.

"Leave him alone, Phillips," Conor says. Before I can feel too grateful, he adds, "Morgan probably has performance anxiety. He knows we'll all be here, watching him."

I flip Hart off.

I'm not self-conscious about flirting in front of my friends. I feel weird about hitting on someone else in front of Eve. But she clearly doesn't have the same hang-up—three of the guys at the bar are gathered around her now—and that's only exacerbating my shitty mood.

Maybe I *should* have made a move last night. Too late now, which is an unfortunate theme of my interactions with Eve.

"Wanna go play darts?" Aidan asks me.

I cover a yawn with my palm. "Maybe later, okay?"

Aidan studies me, his forehead creasing a little, before nodding. I must really look like shit, because he gives me a break rather than continue to badger me. "Yeah, okay." He turns to Rylan, who's sitting on his other side. "Dance with me, Rye."

Rylan glances around. "No one else is dancing, Aidan."

"So? More room for us. C'mon."

Rylan shakes her head. But she takes his hand and they head

for the small section of open floor between the jukebox and the pool table.

"Weird, huh?" Conor asks me as we watch Aidan twirl Rylan around.

They're both laughing. They look joyful. In love.

And I hate the little pang of jealousy that hits in the center of my chest. Hate that I resent my best friend's happiness because I'm sitting next to an empty chair.

The muscles on the right side of my neck are going stiff from the effort of not turning my head in Eve's direction.

I'm yanked out of my thoughts by a small earthquake hitting my chair. I startle, focusing on a somber Conor sitting across from me with raised eyebrows.

"Did you seriously just kick my chair?" I ask.

"Yep. What's up with you, man? You've been somewhere else since we got here."

Harlow's head turns from watching Aidan and Rylan dance, twin lines appearing between her eyes as she studies me too.

Great, everyone's worried about me.

"I'm fine," I say. "Just tired. I didn't get a great night's sleep."

I wait for Harlow to joke about the bathroom incident. But instead she asks, "Are you dating Holly Johnson?"

Hart's full attention is on me as he waits for an answer.

"What?" I respond. "No. Where did you hear that?"

"Eve mentioned she saw you guys last weekend."

Eve thinks I'm dating Holly? She must have seen us together after she literally ran into me in the hallway. That's… not ideal. That date was disastrous for reasons I didn't even realize.

"Uh, yeah. We went out. But we're definitely not dating."

Conor nods once. "Oh, right. The bad date."

"The date was bad?" Harlow sounds sympathetic. And curious. A little amused. If I had a sister, this is how I imagine she'd ask about my love life.

"It wasn't great," I say diplomatically.

"What happened?"

I exhale. "She really wanted to share a meal. Like *really* wanted to. Kept asking me about every item on the menu, even though I'd already told her twenty times I'd decided on pizza—"

Hart makes a choked coughing sound that's an obvious attempt to cover a laugh.

Harlow elbows him. "Ignore Conor."

I roll my eyes. "We just...we didn't have a lot to say to each other. Dinner was awkward, and then she wanted to hook up after. I told her I wasn't in the mood, and that went over...badly."

"You shot her down?" Hart asks.

"I wasn't a dick about it," I say defensively. "But...yeah. And she didn't take it super well. We cleared the air a little before break, but there's nothing going on there. You can tell Eve I'm not dating her."

Harlow's forehead creases with confusion. "Why would I tell Eve that?"

Crap. I fumble for some explanation that doesn't involve me caring that her best friend knows I'm single.

"Just...I'm sick of the rumor mill. I don't want her—or anyone else—spreading inaccurate information about me."

Harlow scoffs. "Hunter, I hate to break it to you, but girls are going to keep spreading inaccurate information about you. It's the plague of being popular."

I swig the last of my beer. "I'm not popular."

Harlow shakes her head, like she disagrees with me but doesn't want to bother arguing.

I'm not trying to be humble. I've always been the serious, quiet guy who rarely says or does anything remarkable. The interest in me is all secondhand. In high school, it was because of Sean. At Holt, it's because of Conor and Aidan. If I am popular, it's only by association.

I stand. "Gonna find the bathroom."

"I think they're by the entrance," Harlow tells me. "I saw them when we came in."

I nod my thanks, then head in that direction. As I walk, my eyes don't wander toward the bar once.

My willpower is pretty solid.

Sometimes, I think it's too solid.

CHAPTER THIRTEEN

EVE

I'm drunk.

I realized I was drunk two drinks ago, and I did another round of tequila shots with Finn and Hurley anyway. Now Finn has his arm slung around my shoulders as the bartender—one of their buddies, Julian—shows off his signature shaking technique.

Far as I can tell, it's identical to every other bartender's back-and-forth.

I'm having fun. Finn's arm is a warm, comforting weight, and he smells good. Like the ocean—saltwater and seaweed. Having three shaggy-haired surfers hit on me simultaneously is a new experience, and it's doing wonders for my ego. But it's also a little...weird. The easy group dynamic makes me think this isn't their first time sweet-talking a tourist.

Does one of them call dibs at some point, or are they hoping for some sort of *ménage à quatre* situation? I may be attempting to try new things, but there's no way I'm feeling *three guys at once* adventurous. I don't think I'd be able to get past the weird-ness of multiple partners to enjoy the experience. I added *sex in (semi public)* to my fuck-it list because my rather boring sex life has always taken place in a bedroom and I thought hooking up in a car or in a frat house bathroom might make it a bit more exciting, but who knows if that'll ever happen either.

Finn's fingers continue stroking my shoulder. I down another shot. Not because I'm uncomfortable, but because more alcohol should keep me from overanalyzing the situation. I have…I'll-do-the-math-when-I'm-sober days left before real adulthood kicks in. When I'm feeling claustrophobic in my cramped apartment, eating ramen for the fourth time that week, I'll be able to think back to the time I drank tequila in a bar with three strangers. YOLO, and all that jazz. Do people still say YOLO?

Since the amount of alcohol in my system has significantly affected my filter, I ask, "Do people still say YOLO?"

Finn, Hurley, and Julian all burst out laughing.

"Well, do they?" I press.

They laugh harder. I'm not sure if that's a yes or a no.

"Eve?"

I spin toward the sound of my name. Finn's arm manages to stay on my shoulders. It only falls away when I throw both of mine around Harlow.

"Harlow! Guys, this is my bestest friend in the entire world, Harlow. Harlow, this is Finn, Hurley, and Julian." I point to each guy as I introduce them, except I mix up Hurley and Julian because focusing on one spot is harder than it was a little while ago.

"Hello, gorgeous," Julian greets. "Can I get you a drink?"

"She has a boyfriend," I tell Julian. "He plays hockey and he's sitting right over there." I gesture vaguely toward where I remember the table I came from being, except my fingers end up aimed at the ceiling. Goodbye, equilibrium.

"All good," Julian says. "God and I have an agreement."

Hurley snickers.

"It's nice to meet you guys," Harlow tells the group around us. "Can I get a water, please?"

"Coming right up," Julian replies.

At the other end of the bar, a guy with a beard shouts, "I've been waiting for twenty minutes, Julian!"

"Calm your tits, Taj," Julian bellows back. "You're next."

Julian returns with a glass of ice water, then moseys down to the opposite end.

Harlow picks up the glass and holds it out to me. "Drink this."

I roll my eyes. She came over to mother me? I'm grateful, though. No way I would have let go and drunk so much tonight if Harlow weren't at this bar too. She's my safety net.

"Are you good?" Harlow asks me in a lower tone.

I beam at her. "I'm ah-mazing."

"Okay." Harlow mutters something else under her breath. All I catch is *tomorrow morning*, but that's a long time away. She smiles at Julian and Hurley, then retreats.

This time, I successfully locate our table. It's full, aside from my empty seat. Conor is tracking Harlow's progress across the bar like he's her personal bodyguard. Aidan is grinning. Rylan flashes me a thumbs-up, then mouths something I'm too tipsy to decipher.

And Hunter…Hunter is completely unreadable. He glances away when he notices I'm looking in his direction, expression entirely neutral.

Hopefully he's thinking I was right—I didn't need flirting lessons.

Not that I would have hated practicing with him.

As far as I can tell, he hasn't flirted with anyone tonight. Every time I've looked at the table, he's been sitting there with some assortment of his—our?—friends.

I guess he is dating Holly. Lucky girl.

I refocus on the bar, taking a long sip from the water Harlow ordered for me. My stomach gurgles as the cold liquid trickles through my system. We ordered pizza for dinner, but I only ate a couple of slices before heading up to shower and get ready for tonight.

They have food here, but I've blazed by the munchy stage of inebriation and headed straight into the spins. The thought of eating right now makes me feel nauseous.

My phone buzzes in my pocket. I take another sip of water, then pull it out. New messages litter the screen. There's a series of texts from Harlow, ending with one announcing she was coming over to check on me. Another one from Ben, suggesting I call him. And one from my mother.

MOM: *Stop expecting him to change, Eve.*

The tips of my fingers go white on the sides of the screen. I scoff, then forcefully shove my phone back into the pocket of my jeans.

I never learn. Not when it comes to my dad—and not when it comes to my mom.

She resents him for never taking any responsibility when it comes to me. And she resents me for wanting a relationship with my father despite him never taking any responsibility.

Obviously, she was going to find out he was skipping my graduation when he never showed up. I figured telling her right away would rip the metaphorical Band-Aid off, so I texted her after I hung up with my dad. That was a mistake. Now, I'm dealing with the double-whammy of my parents' disregard—my dad's dismissiveness and my mom's diatribe.

"Are you okay?" Finn asks.

"I'm *great*." I reach for the glass Julian keeps refilling instead of the water Harlow ordered and down another sip of the drink that tastes sweet and slightly smoky.

"Come help me pick out a song, then." He slings his arm around my shoulders again and steers me toward the jukebox in the corner.

I go willingly, letting Finn support most of my weight. It feels nice to lean on someone. To not have to think about where I'm headed.

He selects Etta James's "I Just Want to Make Love to You."

I snort a laugh as the opening lyrics start to play. "Is this your move?"

Finn grins. He's smiled most of the hour I've known him. He seems like a genuine, goofy guy—the laid-back type of person you expect lives in a sleepy town, is buddies with the local bartender, and surfs as much as he can.

Nonchalant, whereas I've always been very chalant. *Is chalant a word?*

"Is it working?" Finn asks, before I can voice the question aloud.

"Not really," I answer truthfully.

I find Finn objectively attractive. But I'm not attracted *to* him. Not in the *butterflies in my belly, nervous blurting* kind of way, at least. Maybe it's the numbing haze of alcohol.

Finn laughs in response to my candor rather than taking offense, which makes me like him a little more. "Then, no. It's not my move."

"Surf lessons?" I suggest, taking over on scrolling through the jukebox selections. Give up when the motion makes me feel queasy again. I'll just let Etta do her thing.

"Do you want to learn how to surf?" Finn asks. His eyes dance mischievously.

"Nope." I pop the P for emphasis. "I've watched too many shark documentaries with Harlow. The ocean is theirs. And chlorine is bad for hair, so I avoid pools too. I would swim in a lake, but I don't think you can surf in a lake. Right?"

The way Finn is looking at me—entertained and clearly interested—should affect me. Not many guys have found my babbling charming.

He laughs again, cheeks still stretched in a wide smile. "Right. So, no. Surf lessons aren't my move either."

I swallow the bizarre urge to ask him to stop grinning at me. It feels…superficial, like he's smiling just to smile and it doesn't have anything to do with *me*.

"What's your move, then?" I ask.

Rather than reply, Finn kisses me.

It's…nice. His lips are a little chapped, but warm. He tastes like lime and salt and still smells like the ocean.

But kissing him is like drinking water. Like reality trickling in and ruining the fantasy. The tease of his tongue and the ridge of his erection against my stomach feel distant, somehow. There's no answering pulse of heat. It's like I'm watching a pair of strangers kiss in a movie, not experiencing any sensations firsthand.

I *am* numb.

Finn pulls back a few inches and smiles again. His eyes are half-lidded, his expression a little dopey. "Wanna get out of here?"

I swallow hard, then shake my head.

He groans quietly. "You're killing me, gorgeous. *That* move always works."

A laugh spills out.

Finn's grin grows. "That's more like it."

"I'm sorry," I say, then mentally chastise myself for apologizing. I don't owe him anything. "I just—I just got out of a serious relationship, and I'm not ready to move on—that way—yet."

Finn stops smiling, but he doesn't look that upset. He nods. "I get it. Love's complicated. He's clearly not over you either."

I frown at him, then glance around like Ben could have possibly appeared inside Sand Bar in the past few minutes. "What? Who?"

"The blond dude who's looked like he wants to punch me all night. That's your ex, right?"

Hunter, I realize. Finn's talking about Hunter.

My eyes seek him out as soon as I think his name. Hunter's head isn't turned this way. He's saying something that has Rylan laughing so hard she's covering her face with her hands. I'm immediately hit by a pang of envy that leaves me breathless. I could be sitting at that table, talking to Hunter. Listening to whatever he said that was so funny. Glimpsing another one of his rare smiles. What am I doing over here, proving I can still flirt and considering having sex with a stranger I'll never see again?

Reluctantly, my gaze leaves Hunter and returns to Finn. "Uh, no. He's not my ex. He's just...we're friends."

Are we friends? I'm not really sure. I don't know if I can handle being friends with Hunter, since he's the one person I seem incapable of staying numb around. He makes me *feel*, and that sounds like a good thing. It can be a scary and unpleasant thing too. And the more I get used to being around Hunter—to him offering to carry my bag or asking me questions about my favorite podcast between episodes—the more I'll mourn his absence. In my experience, loss hurts a little less when you expect it.

"Well, your 'friend' wants to fuck you, gorgeous," Finn comments. "Not that I blame him."

He winks—the guy's as drunk as I am, I guess. No way is he reading Hunter right.

Finn grabs a pen from a signed receipt off the nearest table and scrawls a series of numbers on my palm. "In case you change your mind."

I watch him walk back toward Hurley and Julian. I've already been replaced. There are two other girls doing shots with the group of guys and lapping up their generous attention.

My phone buzzes in my pocket again, but I don't pull it out. It's either my mom or Ben, and I don't feel like hearing from either of them.

I relax against the wall and blow out a long, unsteady breath, wondering what it's like to feel prioritized and irreplaceable and hoping, one day, I'll find out.

CHAPTER FOURTEEN

HUNTER

As soon as we step outside of the bar, Eve recoils. "What's that smell?" she asks, sounding aghast.

"California," Aidan proclaims proudly. "You see, when it's not raining all the time, you can really smell the sea—"

"I don't feel good," Eve interrupts.

"Drinking my body weight in alcohol always makes me a little queasy too," Aidan tells her cheerfully.

Eve groans.

She's drunk. *Wasted* would be more accurate. I'm impressed she's vertical right now.

After Eve stumbled back to our table—minus the guy who'd been drooling all over her for the past hour, thank God—there was a group consensus that it was time to head out.

"Do you want more water—oh, shit." Harlow hurries after Eve, who's made an abrupt beeline toward the bushes that line the parking lot.

"I'll grab her some water." Rylan heads back inside.

Aidan, Conor, and I stand around awkwardly, listening to Eve's heaves and the low murmur of Harlow's voice.

"Really takes you back to freshman year, huh?" Aidan says. "Remember the Beer Olympics?"

"Yeah, because Morgan and I weren't the ones puking in the yard," Conor replies.

"Whatever. I participated in twice as many events as you two. Good sportsmanship. Plus, the whole team got trashed. Pretty sure every plant on the property got christened."

Conor sighs.

I make a face.

We live in that house now.

Thankfully, Aidan ends his trip down memory lane there. "We still on for surfing tomorrow morning?"

He talked me and Conor into a morning surf session while we were watching hockey earlier.

"I'm in," I say.

I had two beers. Not enough to wake up with a hangover, although it's late enough I'll still be tired tomorrow unless I sleep most of the morning.

"Yeah. Me too," Conor adds.

He's the only one of us who's completely sober. Harlow tried to talk him into getting a beer when we arrived, but he refused.

"Great." Aidan rubs his hands together excitedly. "I was scoping out the boards in the garage earlier and—you need help, Rye?"

Rylan's back, carefully balancing a plastic cup of water. She glances at Harlow and Eve. "I think we're good," she replies before continuing toward them.

Eve's still bent over, so I can't see more than her silhouette. This parking lot could use some better lighting. All the streetlights line the opposite edge of the lot, closer to the road.

"How many shots did she have?" Aidan wonders. "Four? Five?"

"A lot," Conor says. "I knew those surfer guys were bad news."

I barely avoid nodding along in agreement. Hart's pissed because they checked Harlow out when she went over to check on Eve. *I* have no good reason to hate the bartender and his buddies.

"Come on, she looked like she was having fun," Aidan comments. "Eve's in way better shape than you were after breaking up with Harlow."

"Yeah, because I was in love with her."

"Eve dated that asshole for three years. She must have been in love with him."

My gaze falls to the ground. I scrutinize a crack in the pavement, lifting my hand to rub at the back of my neck.

Frustration balloons, making my chest feel too tight. Eve's single, and she's ten feet away from me, and she's still completely untouchable. Even if I were skilled at making moves, which I'm not, she's obviously in no shape to start anything new. And by the time she is, we'll probably have graduated.

Meaning I'll have missed my shot…again.

Eve shuffles out of the shadows, flanked by Rylan and Harlow, drinking from the glass Rylan got her.

She lowers the cup, wrinkles her nose, then turns and dumps the rest of the water on the bush she vomited behind. "Sorry," she says to the plant, very seriously.

Aidan snorts a laugh.

Rylan glares at him, and Aidan immediately shuts up. I mouth *tamed stallion* at Conor, and he coughs to cover his chuckle.

"I'm tired," Eve announces, sinking down onto the curb. She rests her chin on her knees, the same way she did when I was changing the tire yesterday.

She looks as tired as I feel. Sad, and lost, too, which makes me want to punch whoever put that expression on her face. I was watching bar guy closely—well, as close as I could without being entirely obvious—and she seemed into him. Smiling and laughing and never looking uncomfortable.

Harlow digs a pack of gum out of her purse and hands a piece to her best friend. "Can you pull the car up here?" she asks Conor. Glances at Eve. "I'm not sure she's in any shape to walk."

"I've got it." The words are out of my mouth before I've thought them through. Before Conor has even responded to Harlow's request.

I crouch down next to Eve. She turns her head toward me, blinking drowsily. Smiles. "Hey, Hunter."

"Hi, Eve. You want a ride to the car?"

She tilts her head, considering the offer. "How far is it?"

"Pretty far."

I don't even remember where Conor parked. But since the walk from the bar to the bushes wore her out, I'm guessing it's an accurate assessment.

"Okay." Eve yawns. "Ride, please."

A silly flutter of nerves appears as I tuck one arm under Eve's knees and curl the other behind her back, lifting her from the curb. It's the same anticipatory rush I get right before I step on the ice during a game. The same anticipatory rush I *used* to get right before I stepped on the ice during a game, rather.

A unique burst of excitement and adrenaline I wasn't expecting to experience again. Ever, anywhere, let alone in a dim parking lot carrying a drunk girl.

Eve yawns again before her head turns into my chest, nestling naturally into the hollow of my throat.

"You smell good," she murmurs against my neck.

The words linger in the air. She smells like mint, and I can feel it tingle against my skin.

Eve's voice has the soft slur of too much alcohol and being

half asleep. She's close to passing out completely. I doubt she even knows what she's saying right now.

"You keep helping me."

The soft sound of her voice startles me. I thought she was too drunk and sleepy to continue a conversation. "You're welcome."

Her answering laugh ends in a sigh. "I messed up again."

I'm not sure what she's talking about, exactly, but I figure "Everyone makes mistakes, Eve" is a safe answer.

"But the same one? That's intensity."

"Insanity," I correct.

She laughs again, but this one sounds sad. "Right. Insanity. I never learn. He doesn't want me."

She's in love with another guy.

"He's an idiot."

Eve exhales. "Yeah."

She sounds unconvinced, and I'm not sure what else to say.

I don't know any details about her breakup, but after forty-one months together, it must have been big. You don't casually call it quits after that long. I don't want to seem insensitive, but I do want to tell her to move on and forget about the dick. I'm sure as hell not going to suggest she give him another chance.

I doubt it matters *what* I say. The odds of Eve remembering this conversation seem extremely low.

"Is chalant a word?" she asks suddenly.

"Chalant? Uh, no. I don't think so."

"I knew you'd know the answer," Eve says confidently.

It's another one of those statements I'm unsure is a compliment or not. She's not being sarcastic, despite the fact my reply wasn't exactly *definitive.*

"There's a lot of shit I don't know, Eve."

Specifically, what the hell to do around her.

"I'm trying to be nonchalant," she tells me. "Instead of chalant, if that was a real word."

"Caring isn't a bad thing."

Her whispered "It feels like it is" is so low I wouldn't have heard it if her mouth wasn't right by my ear.

And I have this sudden, epiphanic moment where my attraction to Eve becomes more tangible. Because I know exactly what she means. I may pretend I'm a 911 operator when I'm on the phone with Sean, but that apathy collapses as soon as the call ends. There have been so many fucking times when I've wished I could shut that flow of turbulent emotion off, the same way you turn a faucet or flick off a light. Because it's useless and unnecessary and Sean doesn't want it. Doesn't *feel* it, so why should I?

I glance down at Eve, nestled against my chest. Her eyes are closed, her breathing even. She's asleep.

We're almost at Conor's car.

"You parked *so* far away," I hear Harlow bemoan behind me.

"Not really." Hart sounds amused, not annoyed, and there's no one else he'd be using that tone with. He doesn't drink during the season, so I've witnessed Conor around plenty of tipsy peers. His patience level usually hovers at zero.

"Easy for you to say," Harlow replies. "*I'm* the one wearing heels."

Now that Eve's stopped talking, I can hear them clacking on the asphalt. I've honestly never understood why women wear heels. Walking on sticks can't possibly be comfortable, as evidenced by Harlow's complaining.

"Heels don't make the car any farther away," Conor tells her. "Honestly, this says a lot about your slacking with training, Hayes."

Harlow huffs. "Maybe I'd be in better shape if my coach didn't get so distracted."

Conor is training Harlow for a marathon she's running this summer. It's a fundraiser for an organization that works to prevent drunk driving, which is how Harlow's parents were tragically killed when she was in high school. I know Conor is hoping to run it with her, but it's another piece of his future that will get decided by the draft.

"Maybe your coach would get less distracted if you stopped training in spandex outfits that show off your tits and ass."

"They're *aerodynamic*, Conor. Mr. Focused can't handle a sports bra and some leggings?"

"Not if you're wearing them," Hart says seriously.

I speed up my steps, guessing their conversation is going to become increasingly R-rated.

Hart's SUV is locked, and I don't have a free hand to open a door anyway. So I just stand next to the car, holding Eve.

Hart and Harlow arrive next, Harlow beaming brightly as she clings to Conor's back.

And, looking at them, I'm relieved.

Even when Aidan was at risk of not graduating, I was never really worried about his future. Not because he has a trust fund, although money never hurts, obviously. Because Phillips is adaptable. He makes himself at home around anyone, in any situation.

Conor is rigid. He has one plan. One way of doing things. One mindset. There's a real possibility he won't make it to the pros, and I can't picture him doing anything else except playing hockey. I don't think I could do anything to cushion the blow of that not happening. Neither could Phillips. Or Coach. I know Conor's protective of his mom and contentious with his dad.

I'm a lot less worried about Conor's future, watching Harlow slide off his back. She wobbles in her heels, clutching at Hart's shirt tightly for support, only a few inches shorter than him with the added height. "I love you."

"Love you t—" They're kissing before Conor gets the last word out.

I avert my gaze, deciding being the single one amidst happy couples is about as bad as being sober in a crowd of drunks.

"—could have asked!"

"Harlow and Eve didn't *have to ask*!"

Aidan and Rylan loudly announce their arrival. At least the bickering separates Hart and Harlow.

Phillips sighs when he reaches us, then glances between me and Conor. "When did you two get so chivalrous?"

"Harlow's feet hurt," Conor explains.

"I've always been chivalrous," I add. "Remember when your car stopped working and I chauffeured you around for a month?"

Aidan scoffs. "It was not a month."

Eve groans against my chest. Hopefully just a reaction to Phillips's loud voice and not an indication she's going to throw up again.

I catch Conor's eye and nod toward the locked car.

"Oh, shit. Yeah. Sorry." He digs the keys out of his pocket and the SUV's lights flash.

Aidan picks Rylan up and deposits her two feet closer to the car, right next to the door. "There ya go, babe."

Rylan rolls her eyes, but she's fighting a smile as she climbs in the back seat.

"I've got her," Harlow tells me, appearing at my side.

I set Eve down carefully, making sure her Converse-clad feet are under her before dropping my arm. She groans again, resting heavily on Harlow as she guides her best friend into the car.

I climb into the front seat, and Conor starts driving.

CHAPTER FIFTEEN

EVE

A sledgehammer is battering my brain when I wake up.

I groan, pulling the extra pillow over my face to block out some of the sunlight streaming in through the windows.

"She's alive."

I groan again before shifting the pillow off my face and sitting up. I squint in the direction of Harlow's voice. I find her sitting in the armchair in the corner, legs tucked under her and red hair pulled back in a messy ponytail.

"What are you doing in here?"

Each word I speak worsens the reverberations in my skull. *Why* did I drink so much last night?

A whiny voice whispers the answer. *My life is falling apart.*

"Your life is not falling apart," Harlow says.

Oh. That whiny voice was *my* voice.

"Well…it's been better."

She nods sympathetically, ceding that point. "Is this about Ben…or about something else?"

I blow out a long breath, then wince when the exhale worsens my head's throbbing. "It's not *not* about Ben. But more…the future I'd planned with him than Ben specifically. I mean, yeah, I miss him. But—he pushed the first domino, and now the whole line is falling down. I planned *everything* with him, and now it feels like that's all just…gone."

"I know the cell service here is spotty, but I think we would have heard if New York City was no longer standing."

I roll my eyes, and regret that movement too. Not moving *at all* seems like the best strategy until I swallow some painkillers. "You know what I mean."

Harlow nods. "Yeah. I do. But I'm serious. New York's still there. Everything you planned—it's still there. You don't need him, Eve. You're brave and smart and talented and brilliant, and New York has been your dream for as long as I've known you. Keep chasing it."

My throat thickens. "Thanks, H. I'm sorry I was such a mess last night."

My memory of the bar is fuzzy, which is probably for the best. I raise my hand, squinting at the faded black marks written on my palm. I have a vague recollection of doing shots with surfers. This is Julian's number. No, Finn. Finn was the one I kissed.

I kissed a guy who wasn't Ben.

I wait for the rush of guilt to appear. It doesn't, which surprises me. Not that I *should* feel guilty, but I thought I *would*. We were together for a long time. I'm not sure if the lack of shame makes me heartless or means I'm healing.

"Don't worry about it," Harlow replies, pulling me back to the present.

"How—how bad was I?"

Harlow waves a hand. "You were just a little tipsy."

My stomach sinks. I know my best friend well enough to see straight through that causal phrasing. Plus, I've never had this bad a headache from being *a little tipsy*. "How bad, Harlow?"

She grimaces. "Hunter had to carry you to the car."

Mortification sweeps through me, making me feel dizzy. "*What?*"

"It was very sweet, actually. After you threw up in the bushes, he picked you—"

"After I *what?*" I blurt, horrified.

Now that she's bringing it up, I do have some vague recollection of my throat burning. I've *never* thrown up for any reason except a stomach bug.

Fuck. I *vomited* in front of *Hunter Morgan*. This is worse than the time I asked Peter Jenkins to the eighth grade semi-formal with toilet paper stuck to my shoe.

"I'm never leaving this bed," I announce, then lie down and pull the pillow back over my face.

"Nuh-uh." Harlow grabs the pillow, and then my arm, forcibly pulling me away from the mattress. "You need coffee, and Gatorade, and breakfast. Then, you can go back to bed if you want."

"Just let me hide in here," I plead.

Harlow holds firm, tugging me out of my room, into the hallway, and down in the direction of the bathroom. She drops her hand once we reach the doorway. "You have five minutes to pee and wash your face. Also, I'd suggest brushing your teeth. I tried to help you last night, but I think you mostly just swallowed the toothpaste."

I glance down, noticing what I'm wearing for the first time. The jeans and skimpy top I put on last night were replaced by my favorite pair of cotton sleep shorts and the NYU hoodie I ordered online last year, thinking it would help me look like a local when I move to Manhattan.

Warmth expands in my chest. My life might be falling apart, but I have the best friend in the entire world.

I fling my arms around Harlow's neck, nearly toppling her even though she has several inches on me. "I'm sorry I was a drunken disaster last night. Thank you for taking care of me."

She squeezes me back. "Always. Too bad Sand Bar didn't have karaoke."

I groan. Ever since she heard me singing in the shower once, Harlow has tried to talk me into singing in public. She's right; last night I would have been drunk enough to do it.

"Girl-on-girl action before breakfast? Spring break is the *best*."

Harlow flips Aidan off as he saunters past us, tugging a sweatshirt over his bed head.

He laughs, then calls, "Nice to see you vertical, Eve," over one shoulder.

My cheeks burn as I head into the bathroom and close the door.

I look like hell. I'm not sure that's an accurate description, actually, because hell is supposedly red and fiery. I look pale and pasty. Tangled hair, sickly pallor, and dark circles stare back at me in the mirror.

Bad decisions, Eve, I tell my reflection.

I brush my teeth—twice—before washing my face. I scrub so hard my complexion is splotchy after rinsing. It's an improvement to my appearance, sadly. I pee, wash my hands, and then pull my hair back into a ponytail with the elastic on my wrist. There's a bottle of painkillers in the medicine cabinet. I swallow one before stepping back into the hallway, feeling marginally more human.

Harlow's still in the hallway, but she's not alone. In fact, I can barely see my best friend past the guy she's playing tonsil hockey with.

An ache echoes in the center of my chest.

I've witnessed Harlow around plenty of guys. She's that effortless combination of gorgeous and cool, the girl who always knows what to say and how to act. That attracts a lot of male attention. I've watched her interact with the opposite sex with amusement and a little envy at how easy she made flirting look. Even happily committed to Ben, I envied that allure. Wondered what it would be like to have guys tripping over themselves to talk to you. To be near you.

Ben made me happy. He made me feel secure and supported. But he never made me feel *wanted*. I never *needed* him, not in the way Conor and Harlow's tight embrace suggests.

Seeing Harlow with Conor, I feel like a voyeur. They're so *bright* together, happiness emanating like beams radiating from the sun.

Harlow has never looked that lit up with anyone else.

Ben and I weren't that bright. At most, we were a dim glow, like one of those energy-saving lightbulbs. Content and unremarkable.

I clear my throat. "Get a room, guys."

I hear Harlow laugh before Conor moves to the side. He glances at my best friend. Smiles. "We would've, but my girlfriend spent the night in yours."

Harlow smacks his bicep.

Guilt floods me. I assumed Harlow was in my bedroom waiting for me to wake up, not that she'd spent all night in that armchair.

"Shit. I'm *so* sorry—"

Harlow cuts me off. "Don't apologize again. And—" She glances at Conor. "Don't feel bad for him. He got laid *and* got to hog the whole bed last night."

"I'm not a bed hog," Conor protests. "I'm just taller. It's not my fault I take up more space than you do."

Harlow rolls her eyes before grabbing my hand and pulling me toward the stairs.

Rylan's standing at the stove cooking eggs when I enter the kitchen. Aidan's draped over her, his chin on her shoulder and his arms wrapped around her waist.

Another ache appears. Going on a trip with two madly in love couples fresh off a breakup was not my best idea. Not only are there the constant reminders of my single status, there are also the frequent examples that my relationship lacked more than I realized.

"Hey! Morning!" Rylan says when she spots me. "Want some eggs?"

I nod. "Yes, please."

There's a pot of coffee sitting out on the counter. I hunt through the cabinets until I find a mug, filling it nearly to the brim before taking a seat at the kitchen table. Even black, it's the best thing I've tasted. Rich and hot and invigorating.

Harlow plops a blue bottle of Gatorade down in front of me. "Drink this too."

"Thanks, Mom."

She pats the top of my head before taking the seat next to mine.

I'm in the middle of twisting the top off the Gatorade when the patio door opens and Hunter walks in. I figured he was still asleep in the living room, but he looks like he's been up for hours.

And he's...shirtless.

My body temperature instantly rockets ten degrees warmer.

As slutty as it makes me sound, my focus was...lower during Dickgate. I got a glimpse of the rest of his body—enough to tell that he's muscular *everywhere*—but it was not an opportunity to really take it all in.

Heat crawls up my spine and blasts the back of my neck as I

stare. Broad shoulders. Bulging biceps. Solid pecs. Stacked abs. There's a thin line of golden hair that disappears into the elastic waistband of his black basketball shorts. And it's framed by a defined V that points directly at what I know is a huge penis. A golden Adonis, sweaty and in the same room as me.

If Harlow's to be believed—and I can't think of a single reason why she would make it up—I was pressed up against that impressive physique last night. And not only did I not get to enjoy it, I have absolutely no memory of it happening.

My cheeks burn as hot as the rest of my body as I focus every ounce of my attention on twisting the plastic lid off the Gatorade.

He's just a guy. He's just a guy. He's just a guy. The chant does nothing to cool me off.

I hear the low rumble of Hunter's voice as he says something to Conor, who's manning the toaster. All I catch is "six miles."

He just ran *six miles*?

Jesus. No wonder his muscles have muscles. I'd probably pass out after one mile. Definitely pass out today.

Aidan folds his large frame into the seat across from me. He's every bit as tall and muscular as Hunter is, but I've never felt the slightest spark of attraction toward him. Not even when he was single and known as the *good time guy* on campus. Same with Conor. He's ridiculously attractive, but I spoke in full, normal sentences the first time he showed up at our house, back when Harlow was insistent that she had no interest in the campus "Hartbreaker."

Realizing I'm not harboring a secret fantasy about just *any* hockey player should be reassuring. But I wish this awareness *wasn't* specific to Hunter. Wish I'd felt a fraction of this sensation last night with Julian. I mean, Finn.

I didn't just remember Hunter's name after our first conversation. I recall our entire interaction, years later.

I rub my temple, praying the painkillers will kick in soon.

Aidan gives me a sympathetic grin across the table. "How ya feeling?"

I sip some Gatorade, then more coffee. "Like there's a construction crew working on my brain and the rest of my body got run over by an eighteen-wheeler. Sorry about last night, guys."

I make it a group apology, careful not to look toward where Hunter's voice was coming from last. Aside from Harlow, he's who I feel most indebted to. And Harlow and I have years of history between us. We've laughed and cried together. We spent the night on the bathroom floor together after one party sophomore year. I feel bad she had to help me last night, but we don't have the same uneven dynamic that exists between me and Hunter. He didn't sign up to carry the drunk girl who stole his bedroom to the car because she got too wasted to walk.

Shit, that sounds bad. I don't drink very often, which was one reason last night turned into such a disaster. I have no clue what my alcohol tolerance is, and by the time I realized I was past it, I was *way* past it. Too past it to consider consequences.

"Don't sweat it," Aidan says. "We've all been there."

I doubt he's ever thrown up in front of a secret crush, but I appreciate Aidan's effort to make me feel better.

"When we get back to campus, you can brag that you drank three hockey players under the table," he adds.

I reach for my mug of coffee again. "Yeah, I'll add that to my résumé. Thanks."

"Bon appétit." Rylan sets a steaming pan of eggs on the table.

"Ooh la la," Aidan says, in the worst imitation of a French accent I've ever heard. He pulls Rylan into his lap.

"I still need to get forks and plates," she tells him, struggling to stand.

"Hart! Morgan! Plates and forks!" Aidan calls, not letting go.

"*You* could get them," Rylan suggests.

Aidan smirks at his girlfriend. "Nah. I'm comfortable."

Conor approaches with a stack of plates. The top one has several pieces of buttered toast piled on it. He takes a seat on the other side of Harlow.

Hunter sits down last, a cluster of forks in one hand that clink when he sets them on the table. He has a shirt on now, but it's the athletic kind that's made from a fabric that clings like a second skin. So I can basically still see all his muscles.

Stop staring.

"You gonna be ready to go after breakfast?" Aidan asks Hunter.

He reaches for a piece of toast. "Uh-huh."

"Go where?" Rylan asks.

"We're surfing," Aidan replies in an enthusiastic volume that worsens my headache.

"Oh. Right."

"You *sure* you don't want to try it?"

"Very sure."

Aidan sighs. "Harlow? Eve?"

"I'm good," Harlow says.

"Me too," I answer. "Not feeling super athletic today."

Truthfully, surfing would sound fun if I wasn't so hungover. I've never tried it before. But the mere thought of rocking waves is making me feel nauseous. And I *refuse* to risk throwing up in front of Hunter again.

Conor has his phone out now, researching beaches nearby for their surfing expedition. It sounds like Harlow and Rylan are planning to tag along for a walk on the beach, and I'll probably do the same.

Walking on the sand sounds safe, and I can bring my sketchbook. I'm sure the scenery will be stunning. A closer look at what's essentially our backyard here.

"You sleep okay?"

I choke a little on my breakfast as Hunter's question registers. Glance up to confirm he's speaking to me and then hastily swallow. Once, to clear the eggs. Again, because it suddenly feels like my throat is stuffed with cotton.

I can actually feel my pulse quickening. Goose bumps rise on my arms under my hoodie. I sat in a car with Hunter for—eleven hours? Twelve? I can't remember exactly how long our trip ended up taking with all the delays. But these weird reactions should have worn off by now. I should have developed some immunity to those blue eyes by now.

"Like the dead," I say. "I guess the secret cure to insomnia is tequila shots."

Great job, Eve. Keep reminding him how drunk and disastrous you were.

I clear my throat and add, "Uh, you?"

"Yeah, I slept well."

What a nice, *normal* answer.

"No three-a.m. shower?"

God, what am I doing? Teasing him? Attempting to flirt? Running through a highlight reel of my most embarrassing moments?

"No three-a.m. shower," Hunter confirms. The corners of his eyes are crinkled a tiny bit, like he's fighting a smile.

I hope he loses.

But before I can find out, Conor passes his phone to him. "What do you think of this place?"

Hunter takes the phone. "Why are you asking me?"

"Because you have more common sense than Phillips, and this is where he's suggesting."

"Fuck you, Hart," Aidan says. "I'm also the only one with *surfing experience*."

Conor rolls his eyes, waiting for Hunter's assessment.

Aidan glances at Hunter too. "What do you think, Morgan?"

I think most people would assume Conor is the leader of any group he's part of. He was the hockey team's captain. He's the guy on campus everyone knows—the one girls want to be with and guys want to be. He has that presence people take note of.

But I've noticed, since we arrived, that Hunter gets looked to a lot. Or maybe I'm just projecting, because *I* look to him a lot.

"Yeah, that spot seems good to me," Hunter says.

"Great." Conor takes his phone back, and then he and Aidan start discussing wetsuits. I guess some came with the rental.

Hunter doesn't strike up our conversation again. But he does glance at me once, catch me staring at him, and smile.

And that full smile does more to cure my headache than those painkillers did.

CHAPTER SIXTEEN

HUNTER

Wind whistles in my ears as I stare out at the water. The salty air blows my hair straight back and out of my face, which is actually convenient. I need a haircut. I kind of let it grow out once we hit the playoffs, more out of laziness than any sort of superstition. It's reached that annoying length where it falls into my eyes half the time.

"Morgan! C'mere!"

I turn away from the ocean and toward Aidan. He's spent the past fifteen minutes rubbing wax on the boards, supposedly so it's easier to stand up. I appreciate the effort, but the repetitive motion is not very entertaining to watch. When I offered to help, he told me he had some special technique that couldn't be taught.

I think he's just enjoying being the "expert."

The girls only stuck around for a few minutes, then set off on a walk. They're three distant dots down the beach at this point. I can make out Harlow's red hair and Rylan's pink hat. But the figure I squint at is the one walking closest to the cliffs. Eve's staring up, but I can't make out her expression from here.

"Ready for the demonstration?" Aidan asks.

"Uh, sure," I answer.

Conor looks equally cautious.

It's not exactly sunbathing weather. It's not *cold* out—I'd guess the temperature is hovering in the fifties—but it's definitely not warm enough for swimming to sound appealing. We're all wearing wetsuits, so I'm not worried about hypothermia, but I *am* worried this won't be a pleasant experience.

We basically have the beach to ourselves. One older couple passed us by shortly after we arrived, and a middle-aged woman walking a Lab is approaching from the direction of the parking lot. If this really *is* some surfing hidden gem—like the article on Conor's phone claimed—we came at the wrong time.

Aidan stands. "Okay, I waxed all the boards. So, if you can't get up, it's your fault, not the board's. Make sure you've got the leash around your ankle." Phillips wraps the black Velcro band around his ankle and then lies down flat on the surfboard. It must be about seven feet long, because it's got more than a few inches on him. He slides closer to the back, head raised and back arched. "This is how you should paddle out. And this—" He suddenly leaps up to balance on the board. "Is how you should pop up to catch a wave."

I glance at Hart, who's studying Phillips's movements closely. Conor's crazy competitive, and Aidan has done this before, so I'm most likely going to be the only one bobbing out there like a buoy.

Phillips demonstrates how to stand on the board a few more times, then tells us to try it ourselves.

The pretend paddling part is easy. The whole *push up into standing with your arms out and knees bent* aspect? Way harder. And this is on flat, solid ground. I doubt it is going to be any easier in the ocean.

"Let's go!" Aidan is still as enthusiastic as he was when he proposed this outing yesterday. Aside from the hot tub, it's the most animated I've seen him this entire trip.

For Phillips, I'll fall on my ass in the ocean.

Aidan's already claimed his board. I grab one of the remaining two, Conor takes the other, and we walk toward the ocean.

I haven't been swimming since some trips to the pool last summer. The salt water is chilly enough to numb my feet almost instantly. I'm unsure if that's a good or a bad thing, but I continue battling the surf after Conor and Aidan.

The slight resistance of waves rolling into shore stops at about waist level. Deep enough to climb on the board and switch to paddling. Both Aidan and Conor do, so I follow their lead.

At first, it's fine. The farther we go out, the more my shoulders tire. Whatever weight exercises I've been doing don't strengthen these muscles, I guess. I attempt to adjust, and there's a sharp twinge in my shoulder. I slow down a little.

And then Aidan suddenly stops and sits up on his board, letting his feet dangle in the water. He slicks his hair back and out of his face, then glances back and me and Hart. "Isn't this *awesome?*"

I stop paddling too. My arms feel better as soon as I relax my muscles, but my shoulder still twinges.

It's peaceful, I'll admit. All you can hear this far out are the sounds of the sea. Seagulls cawing and wind blowing and the rhythm of water lapping against the boards. Any noises from the shore—voices or cars—are too distant to hear from here.

Conor paddles a little closer to us, then sits up too. He twists to look back toward the beach, appearing surprised by how far we came.

I am too. Makes me feel a little better about my sore arms.

"Most shark attacks involve surfers," Conor says casually.

"Sharks have shitty eyesight, and a human lying on a board looks just like a seal from way down there." He nods at the textured surface of the water stretching around us.

I sit up. "What a *fun* fact, Hart."

He shrugs. "Harlow and I watched a Shark Week special a couple of weeks ago. It was pretty cool."

"It would be cooler if you didn't bring it up while we were in shark-infested waters," I tell him.

Aidan shrugs. "I don't think there are any sharks around here."

"Right. Why would they be in the *ocean*, where they live?" I ask sarcastically.

Conor laughs.

I glance around. There are no shark fins in sight, at least. "What do we do now?"

"Uh…" Aidan looks toward the horizon. "Wait for some waves?"

The water around us isn't completely flat, but I wouldn't say anything resembling a wave is anywhere in the immediate vicinity of our current location.

"Wait how long?" Conor questions.

"Until a wave comes. You can't control nature, Hart."

"How many times have you surfed, exactly?"

Aidan blows out an irritated sigh. "More times than you!"

"Well, yeah. I've *never* been surfing."

"Does this even count as surfing?" I wonder. "We're just floating, waiting for a shark to attack."

"If one does, punch it in the nose," Hart advises.

"What if I miss and my hand goes right in its mouth?" I wonder. "Is that still a deterrent, or helpful for the shark?"

"Guys," Phillips whines. "Don't be assholes and ruin this for me."

Conor grins. "So we're just supposed to sit here in silence?"

"*Yes*," Aidan answers emphatically.

"*You're* going to sit here in silence?"

I share Conor's skepticism. Aidan is—by far—the chattiest of the three of us. I can't recall a time where we just sat quietly together. Even watching sports, he talks a lot.

Aidan huffs. "I'm meditating."

If Hart hadn't brought up sharks, I'd probably be enjoying this experience more. My feet have adjusted to the water temperature, so sitting here is mostly enjoyable.

"Maybe we should go a little farther out," Aidan suggests.

"You lasted three minutes, Phillips," Conor tells him.

And then we all start paddling again.

———

When we get back to the car, I check my phone and discover I have a missed call from my mom.

"I'll be right back," I mutter distractedly, leaving my board with Conor and Aidan and wandering farther down the sidewalk before anyone replies.

My mom answers on the second ring. "Hi, honey."

My "Hi" is cautious.

I haven't talked to her since Friday night's unfortunate events, just my dad.

Sean's relapses have always hit my mom the hardest. My dad and I have gotten…accustomed to it in some ways, I guess. But my mom, she gives Sean a clean slate every time. Acts like each setback is a fresh failure and a fresh start.

"I'm sorry to bother you while you're on your break."

"You're not bothering me, Mom. Is—is everything okay?

"Everything's fine," she tells me. "I was just calling about hotels."

"Hotels?" I echo.

"Yes. For graduation. The spot we stayed when we dropped you off freshman year—I can't believe that was almost four years ago—was so far from campus. Are there better options closer? Where are your friends' families staying?"

Relief she's not calling because something is wrong mixes with bitter recollection of how that trip ended, stalling my response.

"Oh. Uh. Yeah, there are closer options. They'll be more expensive, though."

My parents both work in education. My dad is the superintendent for the elementary school, and my mom is a third-grade teacher. Having my parents both work at my school embarrassed me as a kid. As an adult, I think it's kind of cute they carpool and eat lunch together.

Their choice of careers means money has always been tight. My grandparents gave my dad a portion of the money they made from the sale of their farm, but I believe Sean's multiple rehab stints have blown through a large chunk of that. One of the reasons I chose Holt, aside from its location meaning I could escape my brother's shadow, was that they offered me a full academic scholarship.

"It's your graduation, honey. I'm not concerned about the cost."

I swallow. "Okay. I'll ask around. Send you some options."

"Great, thank you. Are you having fun on your break?"

"Yeah. I just went surfing, actually."

"I hope you were careful, Hunter."

"I was," I assure her. "Made it back to shore in one piece."

"Good." A relieved sigh follows. I'm supposed to be the son

she doesn't have to worry about. "Well, I won't keep you. Have fun with your friends. I love you, Hunter."

"Love you too," I reply, then hang up and start back toward Conor's SUV.

Everyone else is already in the car. It's the same seating arrangement as last night. Hart in the driver's seat and Phillips in the back with the girls. We took Conor's car again today because it's a little roomier than mine, plus I'm hoping the spare will make it back to Washington.

"Everything okay?" Conor asks as I climb in.

"Yeah. Just my mom."

Hart nods.

I catch the look he gives Aidan a few seconds later. I haven't talked about my family very much. It's always felt strange to exclude Sean and hard to include him. And neither Conor nor Aidan talked about theirs, so it felt less noticeable. But that's shifted, a little, in the past few months.

After Harlow's parents passed away, the close family friends she moved in with also happen to be Conor's father, stepmother, and half brother. Harlow and Conor's relationship seems to have been a tentative bridge to Conor communicating with family he was totally estranged from. His dad came to a few of our final games.

And Aidan's relationship with Rylan seems to have allowed him to move past the fucked-up dynamic with his brother—who's engaged to Aidan's ex. His parents were there to watch us win the championship, which I know meant a lot to Phillips.

So I'm the only one still hiding skeletons.

"We good to go?" Conor asks, turning on the engine.

"One sec," Rylan replies. "I can't find my seat belt."

"Pretty sure I'm sitting on it," Aidan tells her.

Some muttered curses follow as they rearrange in the back.

I glance in the rearview mirror.

Eve's on the far side, behind Conor. The yellow sketchpad she was drawing in on the drive here is clutched to her chest, a pencil poking through the spiral. Her hair is pulled back in two braids, which I find fucking adorable. And there's more color in her face than there was at breakfast this morning.

Her gaze flickers from the back seat window to meet mine—like she can feel my eyes on her.

She smiles.

I smile back.

And when I glance out the windshield, it seems like the sunshine peeking through the clouds just got a little brighter.

CHAPTER SEVENTEEN

EVE

I'm snuggled into the couch cushions, listening to the logs in the fireplace crackle and sketching the beach we visited this morning, when I hear a low "Hey."

Still not immune. The sound of Hunter's deep voice has my steady heart rate immediately quickening.

I clear my throat before replying, "Hey."

"Cool if I chill in here?" Hunter asks.

He's standing at the opposite end of the couch, looming over me like the rocky cliffs I was admiring earlier. Beautiful and rugged and untouchable.

I fake a cough to…I don't know why. Act casual, I guess? "Yeah, of course."

Technically, I'm in his bedroom. I should be the one asking permission to enter.

Hunter nods once, then takes a seat a couple of feet away. Not as far away as he *could* sit, but not right next to me either. A polite distance, in a huge room, and it still feels like he's stealing more than his fair share of oxygen. I'm breathing fast, yet I can't seem to pull enough air in.

Air that smells like him. The same scent as his car, except a more concentrated form. My brain isn't working fast enough to identify a single component, distracted by the giddiness that appears whenever we're in close proximity.

Ben always used the same cologne—a vanilla-and-tobacco scent that I secretly hated. I bought him different brands as gifts, but he never strayed from his favorite. It became a joke, almost, the unopened bottles sitting unused on his dresser. The final bottle I gave Ben, I told him, "I thought this would look good with the rest of the set."

Looking back, it's not funny. It's another example of a time I hid my true feelings, like with my dad last night. And a premonition of how my relationship with Ben would end. There were always limits to what we'd do for each other. He never changed his cologne. I feigned interest in the films he enjoyed. I don't know if we ever compromised. If our interests overlapped, great. If they didn't, we'd each do our own thing. And there's a very thin line between healthy boundaries and creating distance.

I glance at Hunter's profile. He's interlocked his hands behind his head as he stares at the muted television. Hockey is on. I thought the game the guys were watching before dinner ended. But either it's still going on or another team is playing now.

The jerseys on ice disappear, replaced by a commercial for a fast-food restaurant.

"You didn't feel like hot-tubbing?" I ask Hunter.

That was tonight's after-dinner activity. Aidan suggested it. He, Rylan, Harlow, and Conor are all out there, laughing and playing music.

One corner of Hunter's mouth lifts an inch. "Nah," he replies, glancing over. "What are you drawing?"

"Uh, the beach we went to."

"Can I see?"

I hold my sketchpad toward him. As soon as it's gripped in his hand, my stomach starts performing an acrobatic routine. My teeth worry against my lower lip.

If he flips back a few pages, he'll see the drawing I did of him in the car. Sadly, I'm not sure that would be the *most* embarrassed I've been around Hunter. But it would be a close second.

Hunter doesn't flip through the pages. He just stares at the sheet it's open to. *Stares*, like he's really looking, not just taking an obligatory glance. Long enough for me to feel *very* self-conscious.

I roll the pencil between my fingers nervously. Chew my lip until I'm worried I'll break skin. Clear my throat. "It's not finished. I was just—"

"You drew this? Just now, after dinner? You just sat down and drew *this*?"

"Um, yes?"

"Wow. Fuck. I mean, you're good. You're really talented, Eve."

"Thanks," I say softly. My stomach is a riot of butterflies right now.

He's still studying my drawing.

It's not my best work. It's not even completed. But Hunter is looking at it like he's genuinely impressed.

Compliments are always nice. But something about Hunter's praise hits differently. It feels…earned? Like he wouldn't say something he didn't mean.

A few seconds later, he hands my sketchbook back. "I draw a mean stick figure, you know."

I smile. "Oh, yeah?"

"Yep. I use a ruler to make sure that all the arms and legs are the same length. My first-grade teacher was so impressed by my technique that my family portrait was picked for the spot of honor above the whiteboard."

"Whoa."

Hunter nods somberly. "I know."

"Were there a lot of stick figures in the portrait?" I ask, then shake my head. "Sorry. That was a really weird way to ask about your family."

He props a socked foot on the coffee table. "All good." His knee bounces once before he continues. "And uh, not really. Just me, my parents, and my brother."

"Your mom and dad are still together?"

"Yeah. They're kinda like those guys." He nods toward the commotion coming from the patio. "Lovey-dovey. Grossed me out as a kid, but now…it's nice."

I would have guessed that Hunter comes from a traditional family. He has that settled ease I associate with a more stable home situation than I experienced. A mom who baked cookies after school and a dad who built a swing set in the backyard one weekend.

Hunter lifts his arm and rotates his shoulder a couple of times. "Think I messed my shoulder up paddling out earlier," he says.

It's a casual comment. But it also occurs to me that he's deftly steering the subject away from his family.

"How was surfing otherwise?" I ask.

"I would have rather walked on the beach," Hunter replies. His expression turns wry. "Don't tell Aidan."

"I won't," I assure him.

"The water wasn't warm and Hart spent most of the time talking about this shark documentary he watched with Harlow. I guess surfers often get mistaken for seals." He rotates his shoulder again. "I hadn't swum in a while and stopped lifting regularly after the season ended."

"Well, you've still got a six-pack."

For a few seconds, I'm able to pretend that thought stayed in my head.

But when my eyes meet Hunter's blue ones, the corners are crinkled from his grin. "Thought you didn't see anything?"

There's no chance I'm not bright red. "I wasn't—I was talking about this morning. When you were, um, shirtless."

I don't think clarifying that made things better. That might have made things worse. Essentially, I've admitted to checking him out multiple times.

He nods, still grinning.

And, despite my embarrassment, I'm a little proud. Even around Conor and Aidan, I haven't seen Hunter smile that wide.

Since I'm already blushing, I figure the next words can't hurt. "Harlow mentioned that you had to carry me to the car last night. Thank you. And, uh, sorry. That you had to. Not my finest moment."

"No thanks necessary," he tells me.

Hunter says that like any guy would think to carry his best friend's girlfriend's best friend after she'd downed too many tequila shots. When, in my experience, *college guys* and *chivalrous* are not three words that are used in conjunction with each other.

I glance down at the drawing in my lap. Wriggle my toes inside my striped fuzzy socks. I want to keep talking with him, but I don't know what to say next.

The giddiness isn't evaporating. It's rolling over me in endless waves, like I'm standing at the edge of the ocean I was drawing and water keeps kissing the shore.

I'm alone with Hunter Morgan. I'm alone with Hunter Morgan. I'm alone with Hunter Morgan.

Maybe if I repeat it enough times, the shock value will start to wear off and I'll think of something witty to say.

"Can I ask you a random question?" he asks suddenly.

I glance over. "Yeah. Sure."

"Where are your folks staying for graduation?" He rubs his shoulder again. "That's why my mom called earlier. She's trying to make plans and thinks the hotel they stayed at before is too far from campus."

A question he could have asked the group when he climbed in the car. Instead he's asking only me, now.

"I think my mom is staying at the Westin in Loughton. And my dad…he's not coming. He called to tell me last night. But the Westin's nice. About fifteen minutes from campus, and not that pricey. They probably raised rates for graduation, but hopefully not too much. I'd suggest it to your mom."

I can *feel* Hunter's eyes on me, but I don't look over. I roll my pencil between my fingers, pretending to focus on my drawing.

"I'm really sorry, Eve."

I nod, then tuck a piece of hair behind my ear. "Thanks. It shouldn't have been…" I exhale, then relax deeper into the couch, letting the sketchbook slide off my lap. "My dad and me…it's one of those situations that's always sucked. I accepted it sucked a long time ago, and it's just gone through different degrees of suckiness since. So, I shouldn't have been surprised, but I was."

"I know exactly what you mean."

The sentence is earnest. There's no hesitation. No uncomfortable edge to Hunter's tone.

It compels me to continue talking. "That's why I drank so much last night. But I promise it was a one-time thing. You won't need to employ any more heroics this trip. I'll get over it. It's just a silly ceremony, anyway."

"It's a ceremony celebrating four years of hard work. It's not silly."

His matter-of-fact statement cuts deep. It's what I was hoping my mom would say, I realize. I needed some acknowledgment that I have a right to be disappointed my father won't be there to see me graduate college. It's a moment that will mean something to me. And I wanted it to be a moment that meant something to him too.

I nod jerkily. "Yeah. You're right. But I promise I'm done being a disaster."

"I promise I've never thought you were a disaster, Eve."

The soft sincerity in Hunter's voice is not helping the *secret crush* situation.

I thought that was the point of crushes—they're rooted in fantasy. They're an escape from reality and its inevitable disappointments. They're based on tiny, enticing glimpses of someone, not the full, flawed picture. But each longer look I get at Hunter only makes me like him more.

I glance at the television. The hockey game is back on, colorful jerseys darting around on the ice.

"Do you miss playing hockey?" I ask.

"Yeah." When I sneak a peek at him, Hunter's staring at the screen. "But it had to end sometime, and it couldn't have ended any better than it did."

"Will you, uh, explain it to me?" I ask.

I feel his eyes on me, but keep mine straight ahead. "Hockey?"

"Uh-huh. I've only been to one game, and I didn't figure out much aside from it being a good thing when the blue jerseys scored."

Hunter doesn't reply right away. When I muster the courage to glance over, he's studying me instead of the game. Almost like he's testing my true level of interest.

I must pass, because he holds out a hand. "Can I use that?"

I flip to a fresh page before handing my sketchbook and pencil over.

"Okay, so—" He draws a huge oval on the page, slashing a line down the center and two more on either side of it. "Here's the rink. Red line and two blue lines. Goals are here and here." Hunter adds two X's to each end of the oval. "Each team is allowed six players on the ice at a time, one being the goalie. Two defensemen, who guard their end of the rink and assist the goalie in preventing the other team from scoring."

"That's what you play, right?" *Played*, I guess, but he doesn't correct me.

Hunter nods. "Right. Then there are the two wingers and the center, who are on offense. Their main purpose is to score goals for their team, but when they're past the blue line and in the opposing team's zone, the defensemen will typically come down to assist. Just like the other team's wingers and center will hang back and help play defense in certain situations. Players follow the puck, for the most part. If it's by your goal, you're focused on getting it as far away as possible. If it's by the other team's goal, you're trying to get it in the goal. Doesn't matter your position, as much."

"That's why all the players are gathered in the same spot?" I gesture at the screen, where there's currently a clump of mixed jerseys.

"Yeah. To prevent a goal, you have to be close to the puck. To score a goal, you have to be close to the puck. Half those guys are trying to get it closer to the pipes, the rest are trying to send it in the opposite direction."

"Makes sense," I say, and I'm not even lying.

Sports have always been this elusive clump of rules and jargon and chants that, frankly, I've had no interest in trying to decipher. My sudden interest absolutely has something to do with Hunter, but I'm also glancing between his drawing and the screen, attempting to figure out which players are defensemen and which are the wingers and center. The goalie, at least, I can identify easily.

"Okay, what else? Uh, there are three periods. Twenty minutes apiece. And these"—he adds five circles to his drawing, one in the very center and two toward each end—"are the face-off circles. Whenever there's a stoppage of play, that's how the game resumes. One of the refs drops the puck, and whoever is playing center for each team fights for possession." He glances at me. "Still with me?"

"Uh-huh. I think I followed."

"You sure?" He passes me my sketchbook and pencil back. "I've never actually explained hockey to anyone before. As my first pupil, you owe it to me to tell me if I suck."

"You can give me a pop quiz later, if you want."

He smiles and glances at the screen. It's back to ads. "We should go over penalties and offsides and icing first. Overtime rules, for extra credit."

I can't tell if he's kidding or not.

Hunter is complicated. It's not a bad thing, just noticeable. The guys I've dated have been endearing and open and…simple. There was no puzzle to decipher. Never any sign of the quiet intensity that radiates from Hunter like a forcefield.

I noticed it the first time we met, and it's just as compelling now.

And for some reason, this moment is when I decide to finally say, "You probably don't remember, but we met freshman year.

At one of those first-week mixers. The very first night on campus."

Hunter's hand stalls in the midst of adjusting the pillow under his arm, and immediate regret swamps me.

I've debated bringing that night up every single time I've seen him since. But I've always talked myself out of it, convinced it was weird or unnecessary or would result in the awkward pause I'm experiencing now. Now that the words are out, I can tell they were a mistake.

Of course he doesn't remember. It was a ten-minute interaction nearly four years ago. And I've just put Hunter in the uncomfortable position of admitting how forgettable I am or else feigning remembrance of a meaningless moment.

"Are you guys seriously sitting on the *couch* instead of in the *hot tub*?" Aidan's booming voice fills the living room, cutting through the heavy silence.

I've never been more relieved for an interruption.

I glance over one shoulder, spotting Aidan in the kitchen rummaging through the fridge. "I, um, forgot my suit."

I wasn't expecting to swim in the ocean, and Harlow didn't mention a hot tub. Which is probably for the best, because I have a strong feeling sitting in a hot tub with two couples would *really* feel like fifth-wheeling.

"Did you tell Rylan? She basically brought her entire closet. I'm sure she has an extra."

I can't think of a tactful way to tell Aidan that my boobs are twice the size of his girlfriend's, and that bikinis aren't exactly a *one size fits all* situation, so I just respond with a vague "Maybe."

And then, before Aidan can exit and leave me and Hunter alone, I stand and stretch. "I'll come outside in a little bit. I just have to use the bathroom first."

I flee before Aidan or Hunter can say a word.

The rest of this trip, I'm *triple*-guessing before opening my mouth.

Especially around Hunter.

CHAPTER EIGHTEEN

HUNTER

FRESHMAN YEAR

"Where to next?" Aidan Phillips asks.

The group of girls clustered around him immediately chime in with suggestions, all vying for my new teammate's attention.

I tune out the chatter as I shove my hands deeper into my pockets, staring at the front yard littered with red plastic cups. So far, college parties seem pretty similar to high school ones. Less supervision, I guess, but same games. Partying has never been my scene, but I'm trying to fit in. This isn't Casper. When I started high school, Sean had already paved the way. Holt is a fresh start in every sense. All that the strangers clustered around know about me is that I play hockey.

And the only reason they know that much is because Aidan has been talking loudly enough about the team for everyone in a twenty-foot radius to hear. He's been bragging we'll be raising a championship trophy before we graduate.

Unlikely, but not impossible.

Aidan's high school stats are decent. I looked his up—along with those of the other freshmen on the team—but if we have any shot at improving Holt's historically horrible ranking, it'll be because of Conor Hart. I haven't met him yet, and there's a good chance I'll be starstruck when I do. The guy is insanely talented. He should be playing at Boston College or Minnesota or some other DI program that's basically a straight shot to the pros.

I'm not sure if Conor has arrived on campus yet. If he has, he's kept a low profile. Pretty much everyone who Aidan has talked to has asked if Conor Hart is here, and no one appears to have actually met the guy yet.

The porch railing shifts as someone claims the spot next to me, jarring me from my thoughts.

"Hey. I'm Sarah."

I glance over at the girl who's leaning beside me, summoning a smile so I don't come off as a total dick. "Hey. Hunter."

"Nice to meet you, Hunter." She tilts her mostly empty beer bottle toward me, and I tap my mostly full one against it.

"You too, Sarah."

"Where are you from?" she asks.

"Wyoming."

"So, like, cowboys?"

I've worn a cowboy hat exactly once in my life, when I visited my grandparents' ranch before it sold. The kids I grew up with wore hoodies and sneakers, not chaps and boots.

But I nod, because that's obviously the answer she's looking for. "Yeah, sure."

She smiles. "Yeehaw."

We tap bottles again. This time Sarah sways a little closer, her bare arm brushing mine. She's wearing a top that teases the lacy strap of her bra, and a suggestive smile that makes it fairly obvious she's flirting with me.

Jemma—my high school girlfriend—broke up with me at the start of the summer. I think she would have ended things sooner if I wasn't her date to senior prom.

I wasn't in love with Jemma, but it does feel strange to realize our lives are entirely separate now. And that the main reason Jemma broke up with me is as far away as she is.

My phone buzzes in my pocket. I pull it out, flashing an apologetic look at Sarah before answering the call. "Hey."

"Hey, man," my roommate replies. "You still coming to this thing? It's kinda lame, but there are tons of people here. Plus free food."

My stomach grumbles. The lines in the dining hall were ridiculous, and free food sounds a lot better than warm beer.

"Yeah, I'll be there," I say. "Student center, right?"

"Right. Hurry up, yeah?"

"Yeah. I'm leaving now." I hang up with Clayton, tell Sarah I have to head out, and then walk over to Aidan.

"Hey, Morgan!" His full attention lands on me, ignoring the people trying to gain a scrap of it.

I wasn't sure we'd hit it off. In the two hours I've known Aidan, he's mostly cracked jokes, downed drinks, or flirted with the many girls who have hit on him. He's from Los Angeles, and he has that privileged, flashy aura about him that makes me think his parents didn't immediately turn around after dropping him off so they didn't have to spend money on another hotel stay.

"Hey. I'm headed out."

"Better offer?"

"Uh…" I can't tell if he's kidding or actually offended. "My roommate. He's at this thing on campus, and I told him I'd stop by. I gotta live with the guy, so…"

Aidan nods. "I get it. Probably gonna bounce soon too. There's this party on Lake with senior girls."

"Right. Have, um, fun."

He winks. "I will."

"'Kay. I'll see you at the meeting, I guess?"

We have our first team meeting with Holt's head coach, Coach Keller, next week.

Aidan nods again, then shoves his hands into his pockets. "Or we could grab lunch tomorrow? I found this cool burrito place online. It's just the next town over. Loughton?"

My meal plan is already paid for. I have some money saved from the summer, but the responsible thing to do would be to save it and opt for the free lunch.

But there's no sign of Aidan's earlier bluster now. He seems unsure, like he's worried I *will* say no.

"That sounds great," I tell him.

His face lights up. "Yeah?"

"Yeah. Just text me."

"All right, I will. See ya, Morgan."

"Later, Phillips."

Aidan's expression brightens even more when I use his last name. He holds out a fist for me to tap, then pounds my back twice.

We exchange a grin before I walk down the porch stairs and in the direction of campus. Most of the upperclassmen live in the houses on the periphery of campus, like the place I just left.

I pass a few giggling groups of students headed off campus. No one else appears to be going to the student center. But Clayton was right, when I walk in the lower level, it's packed with freshmen who opted for the school-sponsored version of a welcome party. Crowded enough that I can't spot Clayton, which is surprising. Guy's on the basketball team and well over six feet.

I slide my phone out of my pocket to shoot him a quick text letting him know I'm here, then veer in the direction of the buffet tables lining one wall to get some food. It's pretty picked over at this point—the event started two hours ago—but I grab a bag of potato chips. There's a colorful display of Jell-O cups that I move toward next.

My mom is a terrible cook. She can't be trusted to boil water without evaporating most of it. Since my dad, brother, and I are hardly culinary geniuses ourselves, we learned to make specific snack requests to supplement meals and keep from starving. My dad always requested jerky, Sean was obsessed with Cheez-Its, and I asked for Jell-O. Not the most filling choice, but I love the taste of it.

"That's brave."

I glance past the Jell-O tower at the end of the table. There's a girl leaning against the wall, right next to a poster advertising the club fair tomorrow afternoon.

Pink rushes into her cheeks when she realizes I'm looking at her.

"Brave?" I echo.

"Just—I've been standing here for like fifty minutes, and no one's taken one of those. So yeah, you seem brave."

I smile. "It seems safer than the cheese plate. Who knows how long that's been sitting out."

"Yeah, that hasn't been super popular either. The Oreos went fastest." She nods at a large plate that's empty aside from a few black crumbs.

"I love Jell-O," I inform her.

The girl's nose wrinkles, crinkling her freckles. "I've never tried it. I'm not sure which is less appealing—the neon color or the way it...jiggles."

I laugh. Her honesty is refreshing. She's the first person I've met at Holt who doesn't seem to be putting on any sort of act seeking approval.

"It tastes good."

She sucks in a deep breath, like she's preparing for some Herculean task. "Okay. I'll try it."

"Yeah?"

"Uh-huh." She shoves away from the wall and takes a couple of steps closer. Her forehead furrows as she scans the three flavor options.

While she deliberates, I study her. She's really pretty, which I've never thought about a girl before. Usually they're categorized as *cute* or *hot* in my head. But this girl—I should ask for her name—is *pretty*.

She's on the petite side. At six-two, I'm roughly a foot taller than her, although her hair—loose and a little wild—makes up some of the difference. She's tan from the summer, her bare arms several shades darker than her white T-shirt. The Beatles' logo is on the front. There's another strip of skin visible between her shirt's hem and the waistband of her jean shorts that my gaze keeps getting drawn to. She also has an amazing rack.

She selects lime, glancing over a split second after I've averted my eyes from her boobs.

I set the strawberry I picked down so I can hold out a hand. "I'm Hunter."

She smiles, swapping the cup to her left palm so she can shake mine. "Hey. I'm Eve."

I'm already second-guessing the formal handshake—she's not a professor or a coach—but it's too late to drop my hand now.

There's a weird lurch in my stomach—like missing a step descending stairs—when her smaller fingers fold around mine. There's a blue stain on her pointer finger. Paint?

My hold lingers longer than is polite or necessary. "Eve, huh? Too bad Jell-O doesn't have an apple flavor."

Eve rolls her eyes, but she's smiling. "Clever, Hunter. I didn't ask if you liked guns."

I'm smiling too. "I don't. I'm a pacifist."

"Really?"

"No. I play hockey."

"I don't know anything about sports," Eve says, almost apologetically.

"I don't know anything about theology," I reply. "I only knew about Eve and the apple from a Christmas pageant in middle school."

She frowns. "What does the Garden of Eden have to do with Christmas?"

"Nothing, I'm pretty sure. I think it was an interpretive adaptation. Creative liberties were taken."

Eve laughs and shakes her head. "Does Holt have a good hockey team?"

"We're Division III."

She points to herself. "Knows nothing, remember?"

"Right. Well, there are three divisions in college sports. Division I is the best; Division III is last. And Holt…Holt isn't exactly at the top of the bottom. So no, Holt doesn't have a good hockey team. That'll hopefully change this season." I try to project the same confidence Aidan was radiating on the porch.

There's a mental component to every athletic activity. Mindset matters. Also, I kind of want to impress Eve.

"Because you'll be on the team?"

I grin at her teasing tone. "Nah. I'm not that player. Wasn't even sure I'd play in college. There's another freshman on the team who has some serious hype. Assuming he lives up to it, things could turn around. We'll see. It's been a while since I joined a new team, and it's hard to judge how everyone will gel before we start playing together. Honestly, I'm nervous about it.

But it would be pretty cool to be part of the team that wins when everyone expects them to lose."

"Prove people wrong instead of right."

There's a flash of understanding between us that makes me think Eve might be speaking from personal experience. That she has been underestimated or underappreciated before. "Exactly."

"Well, good luck."

"Thanks."

She smiles again, but this one looks more unsure. Her teeth sink into her bottom lip, then suck it inside her mouth. All I can think about is doing the same.

I want to kiss Eve—badly. I also want to keep talking with her. Learn her last name. Find out what the stain on her hand is. Ask if she wants to meet in the dining hall for an actual meal sometime.

There's an open table in the opposite corner of the room.

Before I can suggest we go sit, my phone buzzes in my pocket. It keeps buzzing, so someone is calling me.

I pull it out, expecting Clayton. But *Sean* is flashing on the screen instead.

My appetite disappears, squashed by a ball of dread. He's supposed to be at work.

"Sorry," I say to Eve. "I've got to take this. I'll be right back."

"Oh. Okay." She tucks one of her curls behind her ear. "No problem."

I give her one last apologetic smile before turning and heading for the nearest door. I answer Sean's call halfway across the room, but it's too loud to hear anything.

Although, when I get outside, I realize it's not just loud on my end. It's as noisy on his.

"Sean? What's going on?"

"I didn't mean for it to happen, okay? You'll tell them I didn't mean for it to happen?"

I take a seat on one of the metal benches, dropping the chips and Jell-O down beside me. The Jell-O promptly rolls right off the edge, landing on the brick walkway with a *splat*.

He's high. And he's definitely not at work.

And I'm so mad—so fucking furious—at my brother, that I can't even find words.

Six months. He's been sober for six months. Living at home, showing up for his job at one of the fast-food joints in town, even reconnecting with some of his friends who still live in Casper. He was gaining weight. Going for runs. Sleeping normally, aside from his night shifts.

My mom was worried about leaving him to move me into Holt. My dad and I convinced her it was fine, that Sean was completely recovered and wouldn't relapse.

We were wrong. All that progress—all the stress and worry and small steps forward—is gone. Slithered down the drain back to rock bottom.

Sean is talking, but I'm still spiraling.

This isn't like the other times. I'm in Washington, and I'm not supposed to return to Wyoming until Thanksgiving. I won't be there to see the cycle start all over again, and I'm relieved. I feel so *guilty* for how relieved I am. Sean makes his problems everyone's problems, and I've never had any form of escape from it before.

"Hunter!"

"What?" I snap back.

"Are you listening?"

"No, Sean, I'm not. I don't know why you called me, but you need to deal with whatever the fuck it is before Mom and Dad get home. If you still have pills, flush them down the damn toilet. Call your sponsor and—"

"One of the neighbors called the cops. They're arresting me. I can't do shit. I need you to call Mom and Dad, so they're not worried where I am when they get home."

He thinks *that's* what they'll be worried about?

"You got arrested? You're in jail? How do you have your cell phone?"

"They sent Officer Peterson." One of Dad's fishing buddies. "He let me use my cell, but he's taking it now. I gotta go."

The call disconnects before I can ask any more questions.

I stare straight ahead at Holt's brick library in utter disbelief. I'm sitting and still, but it feels like a seismic shift is happening beneath my feet.

I thought all of this was in the past. I committed to Holt because I wanted a fresh start where no one knew me as Sean Morgan's little brother, and because I thought I could leave. That the days of Sean stealing cash and disappearing for twenty-four hours and calling me to confess were over.

I call my mom, because I'm not sure what else to do. My dad's the one driving. They're probably only an hour or two away from Casper by now. They left as soon as all of my belongings were moved into my dorm room.

She answers on the second ring. "Hey, honey. I wasn't expecting to hear from you tonight. Is everything okay?"

My left hand clenches into a fist, nails biting into my palm deep enough to break skin. "With me, yeah. But Sean called."

"Oh." She says a lot with that single syllable.

And I know my mom is experiencing the same sinking sensation that's making me feel nauseous.

"He got arrested. Detective Peterson was at the house with

him. I—I don't know any details, but he sounded—he sounded like…before."

"Okay." She sounds years older than when she answered the phone, like all the emotion has been leached out of her voice. I can hear my dad in the background, asking what's going on.

"I'm so sorry, Mom. I know you were worried about leaving—"

She interrupts. "None of this is your fault, Hunter. *None* of it."

My dad's questions die off in the background as he realizes why I'm calling.

"Let me… Let me know if I can do anything, and what happened, and—"

"I will," my mom interrupts. "I'll update you in the morning, but there's nothing you can do, honey. I've got to call the station now. Good night. I love you."

I think my "Love you too" is spoken to dead air. She's already hung up to start dealing with Sean's mess.

I drop my phone in my lap, then drop my head in my hands. *Fuck.* I feel like I've aged a few years too.

At least ten minutes pass before I stand. Clayton has texted, but I don't check the messages. I toss my dented Jell-O in the trash, grab the chips, and head back inside.

I was outside for even longer than I realized, because the formerly crowded room is basically empty. College staff are clearing the last of the food away. A few clusters of students are standing around, but none of them are Eve.

"Hunter!"

I turn to see Clayton ambling this way. "What the hell happened to you?"

"I, uh…" I rake a hand through my hair, glancing around again. Still no sign of her. "I had a phone call. You didn't meet a girl named Eve tonight, did you?"

"Nope," Clayton answers cheerfully, oblivious to the way my stomach is sinking all over again. I guess tonight is going to be full of disappointments. "You met a chick already? Impressive, man. Hasn't even been twenty-four hours."

He gives me a cheeky smile. I can't muster a matching grin.

If Clayton thinks he ended up with some suave player as a roommate, he'll figure out the truth soon enough. I wasn't very smooth with Eve, but I enjoyed talking to her.

My very first night of college, and Sean couldn't resist fucking it up.

"Come on, Hunter." Clayton bumps his shoulder against mine. "Paul down the hall from us is having a little get-together. I told him we'd stop by. Maybe your mystery girl will be there."

I nod. "Maybe."

But with my luck tonight, probably not.

CHAPTER NINETEEN

HUNTER

Shadows recede across white plaster as the sun rises. I continue staring at the ceiling as the light spreads, same as I have for the past hour.

You probably don't remember.

You probably don't remember.

You probably don't remember.

Those four words echo endlessly in my head.

I froze as soon as she said them.

Listening to them on a loop, I nearly start laughing out loud.

I lost track of how many times I thought about meeting Eve freshman year a long time ago. The next time I saw her—in the dining hall a couple of weeks later—she was holding hands with a guy wearing a Star Wars shirt, beaming at him like he'd hung the damn moon.

I found out, after Conor started dating Eve's best friend, that his name was Ben. Harlow mentioned once that they met at a Freshman Week event—maybe the same one Eve and I did.

I didn't think *Eve* remembered talking to *me*. And I certainly wasn't expecting her to bring it up last night. Does it mean something that she did, or was she just reminiscing? Thinking back to the start of college since we were discussing its end?

Uncertainty is my least favorite feeling.

Do I pretend she never said anything? Let her continue thinking I don't remember? Do I admit I would have asked her out if she'd still been there when I got back? Do I ask her out now?

She made out with one of the guys hitting on her in the bar. And it sounded like she left the bar because she was upset about her dad not coming to graduation, not her ex. But she's been single for a week, and was with her ex for *years*.

Bottom line: I never thought I'd have a second chance with her. I'm terrified of fucking it up somehow.

There's also the tiny issue that we're graduating in a couple of months. Eve is planning to move to New York. I got into Columbia, but the only reason I applied was because they have one of the top political science programs in the country and my advisor recommended I at least consider it. Not because it was a school I was seriously considering. But I *could*. Could chase a girl I've never even kissed to the opposite side of the country.

I groan, punch my pillow, and sit up. Yawn. I'm tired, yet I can't sleep.

I roll out of bed and pull on a pair of running shorts. It feels weird to sleep in just my boxer briefs, in what is technically the living room, so I've been wearing a shirt to bed too.

Well, you've still got a six-pack.

I smile automatically, recalling Eve's blush after she blurted that out. On second thought, maybe I should stop wearing shirts altogether.

I use the bathroom off the kitchen, grab a bottle of water from the fridge, and then step outside. It feels warmer today, but the sky is overcast. Clouds above threaten rain, and so does the dampness hovering in the air.

I jog down the driveway, hoping any showers will hold off but not really caring if I stay dry or not.

Rain can be nice. Peaceful. I've gotten accustomed to a lot of it, living in Somerville. One item on a long list of things I'll miss wherever I move next.

The route I run takes me about forty-five minutes. Just long enough to listen to another episode of the murder podcast Eve put on in the car. They still haven't caught the killer by the end, which I'm disappointed by. Something to look forward to when I run tomorrow, I guess.

Hart is in the kitchen, brewing coffee, when I get back to the house.

He looks me over. It didn't actually start raining, but my shirt is damp from mugginess and sweat. "Shit, man. You already went running?"

"Yeah." I grab more water out of the fridge and gulp it down. "Couldn't sleep."

"Sorry, man. I feel bad you got stuck on the sofa."

"Don't. It's fine. It wasn't the couch."

Conor swipes his keys off the counter. "Wanna go for a drive? We're out of eggs and bread. I told Harlow I'd run to the store."

"Sure." I drain the rest of my glass, and then follow Conor out to his car.

He fiddles with the stereo while I snap my seat belt on, then reverses past my SUV.

"So…you wanna talk about it?" he asks once we're driving down the street.

"Talk about what?"

"Whatever's been bumming you out lately."

I blow out a long breath. "I've gotta decide what I'm doing next year."

"What do you mean? I thought you were waiting to hear back from grad schools."

"Yeah. I heard back. And now I have to decide where to go."

A complicated decision that's only gotten more challenging since Sean relapsed *again*.

"How many options do you have?"

"Ten," I answer.

"*Ten*? Jesus. How many schools did you apply to?"

"Ten."

Hart whistles. "Damn, man. Congrats."

"Yeah. Thanks."

"When do you have to decide by?"

"April fifteenth."

"That's still weeks away."

"I know, but what's gonna change between now and then? I just need to…choose. And…I should pick UW."

"University of Wyoming? Why?"

"It's close to my parents."

I still feel guilty for coming to Holt for college. Who knows what I could have done to help Sean the past four years, but at least I would have been there for my mom and dad. They lost Sean to drugs, and I moved a thousand miles away.

"They ask you to move back?"

Conor's tone is careful, same as I am when we discuss his family. He's obviously assumed I wouldn't move home because things are so great. Probably because I'm making UW sound like a death sentence, not an opportunity. Because no matter how much I want to support my parents—and I do—it's hard not to see returning to Wyoming as a regression. I may pick up every time

Sean calls, but that doesn't mean I don't resent him for needing to call in the first place. Moving back there will be stepping into quicksand. I'll get sucked back in to all of Sean's shit.

"No," I answer. "They wouldn't ask. That's the problem. They'd tell me to go wherever I want to go."

And if I do that, they'll be the ones stuck with Sean's selfishness.

Conor exhales as he brakes at a stoplight. One of a few this town has, I'm betting. I couldn't believe the number of people at Sand Bar, since this town seems smaller than Somerville. "Well, if it makes you feel any better, your future looks more solid than mine."

"Bullshit. You're gonna get drafted, Hart."

He shrugs a shoulder before stepping on the gas again. "Do you know how many free agents have gotten drafted in the past ten years? The odds aren't exactly in my favor."

"Fuck the odds, man. What were the chances we'd win a national championship?"

"Exactly. Maybe I used up my one miracle already."

"I don't think it works that way. Everyone loves an underdog."

"Right. And no one liked Gretzky or Orr or Howe or—"

"None of those guys started out as household names, Hart. They put in the work, just like you have. Just like you will. Not a single thing you could have done more this season."

"Not one, huh?"

I know exactly what he's referring to. "I was wrong about Harlow, okay?"

"No. You were right, about me getting distracted. What you didn't realize—and me neither—I wanted her more than that championship. I love her more than I love hockey."

"Wow." Coming from Conor, there's no stronger declaration. The guy eats, sleeps, and breathes hockey. There's dedication and obsession, and then there's Hart on the ice.

I had a good idea how he felt about Harlow. But I've never heard him lay it out in such stark terms. Never heard him sound so *sure*.

Hart chuckles. "Yeah. That's part of why I'm so stressed about the draft. The uncertainty isn't just fucking with my future. It's messing with Harlow's too."

"She knows that's nothing you can control. And she's crazy about you. You guys will figure it out."

"I hope so. I don't know—I don't know what I'd do if..." He sighs. "There are oceans all over the fucking place, you know? Covers seventy-one percent of the planet. What if she gets a job in the fucking Arctic, studying seals or something?"

I snicker. Which makes me a shitty friend, because Hart sounds genuinely tortured by the possibility. "Well, if that happens and you don't get drafted, you can go with her. Living in an igloo would be cool."

Pun intended.

Conor snorts. "An igloo makes me feel a *lot* better about everything. Thanks."

I grin. "Anytime."

He parks and shuts off the car. "You'll be there, right? If I do make it?"

"Wouldn't miss it for the world," I assure him. "I'll even skip class."

Hart grins. He and Phillips made fun of me for not missing Friday's lecture. "Attaboy."

It starts sprinkling as we cross the asphalt, headed for the supermarket's automatic doors.

"I'm so damn sick of the rain," Conor grouses.

"Maybe you'll get drafted to Florida," I say. "Solid team, sunny, and plenty of ocean for Harlow."

"Yeah, except she actually *loves* the rain."

"Dude, now you're just being difficult," I say as I grab one of the metal shopping carts. "No place is perfect."

"Says the guy bummed out because ten grad schools are begging for him to attend."

"No one's begging," I mutter.

Most of them did offer me pretty generous scholarships, though, so point taken. Options are a luxury.

"Doritos are on sale. Sweet. Cool Ranch?"

"Sure. Grab 'em." I continue down the aisle, stopping in front of the baking section to study the Jell-O mix flavor options. They have lime, so I grab a box and toss it in the cart.

Conor groans, then tosses a bag of chips on top. "Seriously?"

"Have you ever even tried it?" I challenge.

A grunt is Hart's only reply.

We grab two loaves of multigrain and some bananas before heading toward the checkout. I pause in the refrigerated section to pick up a container of soy milk. Eve drank her coffee black yesterday.

Conor's eyebrows lift. "Since when do you drink soy milk?"

I ignore the question. "Is that everything?"

Hart scans the contents of the shopping cart. "I think so—aw, shit. We still need eggs."

"'Kay. I'll grab a carton. Get in line."

There's only one register open, and five people waiting to check out.

"And get Phillips more blue Gatorade!" Conor calls after me.

I roll my eyes as I head back toward the drink section. I don't get why he indulges Aidan's weird obsessions but makes fun of mine.

They're out of blue Gatorade on the shelf, so I have to convince one of the yawning employees to grab a case from the stockroom in the back. By the time I make it back to the register, Conor is second in line to check out. I'm glad he stayed, because there are at least ten people waiting behind him. I have to squeeze past them all—knocking a packet of gum off the shelf—to stick the Gatorade under the cart.

Phillips owes me.

I pick the gum up, go to set it back, and then just toss it in the cart. My stomach is growling from the combination of exercise and no food, so that'll give me something to chew on until we get back to the rental.

The drizzle is coming down faster when we exit. Luckily it's a short trip across the parking lot.

I help load the back of Hart's car as quickly as possible, grab my gum, and climb in the front. Water droplets are coasting down my hair and soaking my shoulders, reminding me again that I need a haircut.

Conor runs the cart back to the entrance. By the time he returns, his gray Holt Hockey T-shirt looks black.

"Smart, to run early," he comments, flipping the wipers to their highest speed. "I'm going to have to wait until later."

"We could go surfing again," I suggest.

"Fuck no," Hart replies instantly. "And don't you dare suggest that to Phillips."

I laugh. "He was talking about bowling this week too."

"I'm good with that," Conor says as he pulls out of the parking lot. "Hayes and I haven't been since, uh, you know."

I do know. He went bowling with Harlow, one of her friends, and Clayton last semester, which set off a series of unfortunate events that put me smack-dab in the middle between my first friend at Holt and one of my closest friends. I know Hart feels bad about that, but Clayton wasn't entirely innocent either.

"Did you consider asking Harlow out sooner? Like, sophomore year, after she broke up with Williams?"

Bringing up Harlow's past with one of our teammates is a risky decision. But it's the closest comparison I can come up with for my current situation. Harlow and Jack dated for a couple of months, not three years, so I'm not sure it's much of one, but I'm sorta desperate for advice.

Conor looks more confused than annoyed about the question.

"No," he finally answers. "I wish I had. Wish that we'd had more guaranteed time together. And I know it makes me a hypocrite, but I hate the thought of her being with anyone else."

I'm well aware of that last part. There's a hole the size of Conor's fist in his bedroom wall that our landlord is going to throw a fit about when we move out.

"But I wasn't ready," he continues. "I needed to grow up. Figure some shit out."

"Yeah, that makes sense."

"Why are you asking?"

"Just…timing, I guess. We're so close to the end of college. I keep thinking about ways some things might have worked out differently."

"Is this related to your recent interest in dating?"

"A little. I thought I'd meet someone, at some point. Not everyone blinks twice and realizes their soulmate is the girl they spent the past three years avoiding, you know."

"That's not *exactly* how it happened," Conor says wryly.

"You get what I mean, though."

He exhales. "Yeah. I do."

You probably don't remember.

I sigh too, in response to the echo of Eve's voice in my head. "Even if I met someone soon, it'd be shitty timing with graduation coming up."

Rather than agree, like I'm expecting, Conor laughs. "Morgan, there's no ideal time to fall in love. It just fucking happens, and then you've got to figure the rest out."

CHAPTER TWENTY

EVE

The Bowl-a-Rama is completely empty when we walk inside. And silent, aside from the eighties pop song playing.

"Huh," Aidan says, glancing around. "Guess this spot is another hidden gem."

Harlow snorts as she pulls her hood down. It's pouring out today, making any outdoor activity unpleasant, which is why bowling was suggested.

I glance at Hunter. He's nodding along to something Rylan is saying to him.

I haven't had a chance to talk to him today—not that I'm sure what I would say, aside from thanking him for the soy milk that mysteriously appeared in the fridge. Harlow knows my preference for it too, but Conor said Hunter was the one who went grocery shopping with him. He was in the shower when I ate breakfast, and didn't reappear downstairs until we were all ready to leave and head here.

Hopefully, he's forgotten about my comment last night—

along with the range of other ways I've embarrassed myself in front of him recently—and some streak of me acting calm, cool, and collected around him is about to begin.

Given that I have a complete lack of coordination when it comes to anything athletic, I kind of doubt it.

The middle-aged man behind the counter—wearing a yellow polyester shirt with *Frank* stitched on the front pocket—looks understandably thrilled to have some customers.

"Where are ya folks visiting from?" Frank asks around the toothpick sticking out one corner of his mouth.

"Somerville," Conor answers.

"Never heard of it."

"It's in Washington," Harlow adds.

"I've heard of Seattle."

Harlow shrugs. "Sure, close enough."

"Write down your shoe sizes here." Frank flips over one of the flyers advertising the Bowl-a-Rama's hours and shoves it across the counter along with a dull pencil. We take turns writing. "How many lanes?"

Conor and Harlow exchange a look.

"Boys versus girls?" she says.

"Just one lane," Conor tells Frank.

He frowns before typing something on the keyboard in front of him. Frank probably assumed we'd take up two lanes. Possibly three.

I was thinking the same. Hoping we'd be going at the same time, rather than sitting around and watching each other bowl.

What if I fall on my ass? Or don't hit a single pin? Or—

"Come on, ladies." Harlow hooks one elbow with mine, grabbing Rylan with the other. "Time to strategize."

She pulls us to lane six, the only one with a lit screen.

"What about our shoes?" I ask.

Not that I'm looking forward to putting on the ugly sneakers, but Frank seems like he'd be a stickler for rules.

"The boys will bring them over," Rylan answers as she takes a seat on the right side of the lane.

Harlow sinks down next to her. I take the last chair.

"Okay." Harlow claps her hands together. "Team name, guys. What are we thinking?"

"Pin Pals?" Rylan suggests.

"Ooh, that's cute," Harlow comments. "E?"

"Livin' on a Spare?"

Harlow beams. "Damn. Look at you, coming through with the bowling lingo."

"It was written on one of the posters behind the counter," I admit.

Rylan laughs. "Still counts. It's catchy."

Harlow glances over one shoulder at the huddle of Hunter, Aidan, and Conor waiting for Frank to grab our shoes. "I guarantee the boys are going to come up with something dirty."

"Agreed," Rylan says. "Like Three Fingers Fit or Bowls Deep."

Harlow laughs so hard she starts coughing. "Damn. You and Aidan are so perfect for each other."

Rylan sticks her tongue out. "Bitch."

Harlow's still giggling.

I peek at the counter. The boys are walking this way, laces dangling from both hands.

"Guys, we're running out of time," I say.

"You're right, you're right." Harlow sobers. "Alley Cats?"

"Ball Busters?" Rylan adds.

"Split it up, ladies!" Aidan calls, dropping the shoes he's

carrying on the floor. Hunter and Conor do the same. "We're ready to kick your asses."

Rylan flips him off. "Good luck."

Unless she and Harlow are Olympic-level bowlers, no luck will be necessary. I certainly won't be the one carrying the team.

I find my size in the shoe pile and slip them on. "Split is a bowling term, right?" I whisper to Harlow as I tie the laces.

"Yeah," she replies. "When you knock down pins in the middle and leave some standing on both sides so that—"

"What about Split or Swallow?" I ask.

"*Evelyn Jane*," Harlow mock-scolds me. "I fear I've been a terrible influence on you."

"You *have*, Harlow Cara."

She smirks and bumps my shoulder before turning to whisper to Rylan.

Rylan hoots a few seconds later. "It's perfect!" She leans past Harlow to flash me a thumbs-up.

I finish knotting my laces and glance at the guys. Aidan and Hunter are slouched on the plastic seats. Conor's standing with a ball already in hand. "Ladies first," he says, winking at Harlow.

"You go first," she whispers to Rylan.

Rylan nods seriously. "And I'm not supposed to aim toward the center, right?"

"I mean, aim toward the center. But it'll veer, so don't *actually* aim toward the center," Harlow replies.

Rylan looks to me. "Am I crazy, or did that make no sense?"

"It made no sense," I assure her, increasingly nervous about my own turn.

"Rye! Bowl!" Aidan bellows. "You already had your secret strategy session."

Rylan rolls her eyes before she stands and walks toward the lane.

"Wait, what's your team name?" Aidan asks. "Gotta put it on the board."

"Split or Swallow," Rylan replies primly.

Aidan makes a choked sound, then coughs. Conor's chuckling. Hunter's only reaction is to lift his eyebrows a little.

"I knew you were going to make it dirty," Aidan says.

"I knew *you* were going to make it dirty," Rylan replies. "And Eve was the one who came up with it."

Aidan tips an imaginary cap to me. I smile, then check my buzzing phone.

It's a call from my mom. I silence it, then shove my phone away.

When I glance up, Hunter's looking this way. I break eye contact quickly, focusing on Rylan setting up to bowl.

"Your name's too long to fit, babe," Aidan says. He's perched in the chair behind the small computer that controls the screen. "Wanna be Swallow or SOS?"

"SOS," we all say in unison.

Aidan keys in our team name.

Rylan rolls the first ball.

The green ball veers left, left, and then ends its roll down the lane in the gutter. Her second roll takes the same unfortunate path.

I relax a little. It doesn't bode well for our chances of winning, but it means my poor performance will stand out a little less.

"That's okay," Aidan says, clapping encouragingly. "You know what they say."

I glance at Harlow. "What do they say?"

Harlow laughs. "You're either good at bowling—or good in bed."

"Oh." I laugh too.

"But—" She glances at Conor, who's up next. His ball stays

straight, smashing into the first row and sending all the pins flying. Aidan cheers loudly as *Strike* flashes across the screen. "It's bullshit," Harlow finishes.

"Lucky you," I tease.

"You're up, Hayes," Conor says, returning to his seat.

Harlow stands and carefully selects a purple ball from the rack. Squints up at the screen. "You guys are KD?"

"Knuckles Deep," Aidan explains.

"I was close," Rylan says.

I grin as Harlow walks to the line at the top of the lane, staring intently at the pins that have been reset in a triangle formation.

"Spread your feet, Hayes," Conor calls. "And remember to keep your arm straight."

Hunter groans. "*Seriously*, Hart? She's on the other fucking team."

"You didn't lecture Phillips," Conor retorts.

"Because I wasn't *coaching*," Aidan interjects. "I was being supportive in the face of adversity."

Harlow bowls a strike.

Rylan and I put Aidan and Hunter's celebration to shame, chanting Harlow's name as she returns to our side of the plastic seating section. Conor is grinning; his teammates are scowling.

"Don't be sore losers," Rylan calls. "I know my dad's coaching stats. You guys have had practice."

"Not this season. We're national fucking champions!" Aidan cheers as he stands to take his turn.

He doesn't manage a strike, but he does knock all the pins down during his turn. Since Rylan didn't hit any, the boys are back ahead.

The last time I went bowling was Amelia Holloway's twelfth birthday party. Meaning I have little to no confidence in my ability to contribute to the team. I was never the kid who got picked first during gym class or made any significant contributions during dodgeball, and that was not when I was playing against three athletes.

But I stand determined to hit *something*. Maybe I'll visualize a photo of my dad's face to help motivate me. More of the hurt has faded, leaving pure anger behind.

Everyone's watching me. The attention feels brighter than a spotlight as I stand and head for the rack filled with bowling balls of different sizes and shapes. Why are there so many options and why do they all look different? I should have paid closer attention to which balls Rylan and Harlow selected.

"Hey, Phillips, didn't you say you wanted to get snacks?" Hunter asks suddenly.

"Yes. You know I'm always hungry," Aidan replies.

"Let's go. Hart can monitor the girls for any cheating."

"Hey!" Rylan protests. "I rolled *two* gutter balls, and you're accusing us of cheating?"

"Hart might let them cheat," Aidan muses. "He's clearly handed *his* balls over to Harlow."

"She's never had to *ask* me to carry her," Conor retorts.

I have no idea what that means, but Aidan seems to. He grimaces before glancing at Hunter. "Snacks?"

"Snacks," Hunter agrees, standing.

"Anyone else want anything?" Aidan asks, giving Conor a look that makes him grin.

I obviously missed something. I shake my head no, and so do Conor and Harlow.

Rylan stands. "I'll see what the options are."

My gaze drops back to the rack of balls. At least I'll have less of an audience for my first attempt. The spotlight has dimmed.

"Try the medium first."

Hunter's voice registers a half second before his proximity

does. He's only a few inches away. Close enough to touch. Close enough to hear the startled breath I suck in.

"And aim for the pin to the left of the center," he adds. His knuckles graze my hand, hanging limply by my side, as he passes me and follows Aidan toward the concessions.

My mom loves candles. She always used to light them for dinner and it was my job to extinguish them after we finished eating. Before I lowered the snuffer, I'd stick a finger in the flame for a few seconds to see what it was like.

That's how the aftermath of Hunter's touch feels. Like a lick of fire, warm enough to feel but not hot enough to burn.

I grab a medium ball and glance over my shoulder. Rylan, Aidan, and Hunter are over by the snack counter, conversing with Frank. Harlow and Conor are both on their phones. Texting each other, probably.

I no longer have an audience.

My tensed shoulders relax, registering that. And something else occurs to me. Not only did Hunter do exactly what he chastised Conor for—helping the opposing team—he also caused a distraction.

Maybe it wasn't intentional. Maybe *he* was hungry.

"You good, E?"

I startle at the sound of Harlow's voice, almost dropping the heavy ball on my foot.

"Yep," I reply, walking to the top of the lane. I focus on the center pin nearest me, then shift my gaze one to the left. Squint toward it, swing the ball back, and relax my curled fingers so it slips free from my grip.

Watch, heart racing, as it rolls, rolls, *rolls* down the wooden lane. It's on the *lane*, not in the gutter. It collides with the left side at an unimpressive velocity, but it tips one. One that tips another and another and another. Six fall in total.

"Yes, Eve!" Harlow cheers.

Conor's smiling too.

So am I, even though the second ball I roll follows the same path and doesn't add any more pins to my total tally.

When the rest of our group returns from the concession stand a few minutes later, Hunter's hands are empty.

CHAPTER TWENTY-ONE

HUNTER

I groan and roll over, realizing my mistake a second too late. I plant a palm on the rug just in time to keep my face from colliding with the floor instead, sighing and sitting up on the couch. I check the time on my phone.

Two thirty-seven a.m.

No missed calls.

This is Sean's pattern, though. The first stumble has the quickest recovery. I probably won't hear from him for another couple of weeks. Maybe even a month. But there's always another fall after the first call, and knowing that's coming feels like being followed around by a storm cloud.

I run my hands through my hair, wide-awake in the middle of the night. Stand, stretch, and then head toward the kitchen. Flick on the light above the kitchen sink and stare out the window for a good minute before heading into the bathroom. I piss, wash my hands, grimace at the dark circles under my eyes in the mirror, and then head back into the kitchen.

The fridge door is open, a pair of bare, smooth legs visible beneath the shiny silver.

I recognize the striped fuzzy socks.

"Hey."

Eve stumbles back a step, straight into the kitchen island. The fridge door swings open, the handle hitting the stove with a low thud.

Wide eyes meet mine as she yanks a pair of headphones off. "*Shit*. You scared me," Eve says, lifting one hand and pressing her chest like she's trying to physically slow her heart rate. "I thought the light got left on by accident."

I clear my throat and force my eyes to stay on hers. No way is she wearing a bra under her T-shirt. "Sorry."

"Don't apologize. It's my fault for walking around wearing these." She pulls her phone out of the waistband of her shorts and sets it on the island along with the headphones she had on. "I couldn't sleep, so I started listening to the latest *C is for Crime* episode. It released at midnight."

She's walking around listening to a serial killer podcast in the middle of the night? No wonder she's jumpy.

That also means… "They're not all out yet?"

"Nope. They release weekly. Episode nine just came out."

"Damnit. I'm already on episode eight."

"Episode eight—you kept listening to it?" Eve sounds stunned.

"Yeah, I wanted to know how they caught him. Right now, my money's on the postal worker guy. I've been listening to it on my runs this week." I walk toward the fridge and glance inside. "What were you getting?"

"Huh?"

"In the fridge. What were you getting?"

"Oh. Uh, something to drink." Eve's standing close enough I can feel the warmth radiating from her body. Or maybe that's just mine overheating, reacting to how close she is. Either way, it's fucking distracting.

"Your options are water or blue Gatorade," I tell her.

"What's with all the blue Gatorade?"

"Ask Aidan. It's his favorite flavor."

Eve reaches past me to grab a bottle of water, her wrist grazing my bicep, and my cock immediately starts to harden. *Perfect.* Hiding a boner is *really* easy when you're only wearing boxers.

My gaze snags on the green glob on the top shelf of the fridge. Since we couldn't find any smaller cups, we decided to make the Jell-O shots in a square baking dish.

"You ever try it?"

Eve pauses in the middle of twisting the top off the water bottle. "What?"

"Jell-O. Did you ever try it?"

Her lips move, but nothing comes out. "I—you…" She coughs. "You remember?"

"'Course I do. You picked lime. Did you ever try it?"

Eve hesitates before shaking her head. "No."

I grab the pan off the shelf. It barely wobbles. It's set. "Wanna?"

"*Now?*"

I glance at the clock. Two forty-nine a.m. "It's not even three. You know there are spring breakers in a nightclub doing tequila shots right now."

Eve makes a face. "I'm off tequila for a while."

I smirk. "We used vodka."

"Okay." She exhales. "Yeah, I'll try it."

"Yeah?"

"Gotta see what all the hype is about, right?"

I scrutinize the dish. Aidan and I didn't discuss how we'd serve the shots. Usually they're already portioned in little cups.

"Okay." I grab a knife out of the drawer and rip a piece of paper towel in two.

Eve watches me cut two squares with an amused look on her face. One piece almost hits the counter during the transfer to the makeshift plate, but I manage to save it.

I pick one up, then gesture for Eve to do the same.

She does, still looking like she's on the cusp of laughter. The wobbly squares do look ridiculous jiggling in our palms.

"Ready?" I ask.

"Yeah. Cheers."

"To what?"

She tilts her head, studying me. "What?"

"What are we cheers-ing to? You're supposed to say cheers to…something."

Eve shrugs. "I don't know. I always just say cheers. You pick."

"All right." I think for a few seconds. "Cheers to…fifth wheels."

She laughs and nods. "To fifth wheels. Unnecessary but…"

"Decorative?" I suggest.

Eve laughs again before downing her shot.

I take mine too, scrutinizing Eve's reaction closely. She chews furiously, nose scrunching a little before she swallows.

"What'd you think?" I ask.

"Taste wasn't terrible. But consistency?" She makes a face. "Not my favorite."

"Fair," I tell her, pulling the plastic back over the pan.

Eve doesn't move as I place it back in the fridge.

"I was thinking of going in the hot tub," she says suddenly. "After I got a drink."

And *that's* not going to keep all my blood from heading south.

"Oh, yeah?" My voice does not sound normal *at all*. More like I sucked on a balloon recently.

I was still processing Eve's revelation that she recalled our first conversation at the time, but I clearly remember her telling Aidan she didn't pack a bathing suit. Meaning she's intending to go in the hot tub *without* one.

She sips some water. "Yeah. Then I can add it to my fuck-it list."

"Your *what* list?" I ask, immediately intrigued by the name.

The paper sleeve on the water bottle crinkles as she plays with it. "Last semester, I wrote this senior year bucket list. Stuff I wanted to do before the end of college. After I broke up with Ben, Harlow renamed it my fuck-it list. All those things you think *fuck it* before doing, you know?"

"Yeah. I know." My tone has turned husky, because I'm thinking about all the *fuck it* things I'd like to do with—to—Eve.

"I'm trying to…I don't know. Be braver, for myself. Be enough, on my own. I don't need Ben to move to New York to move there myself. I don't need my dad to come to graduation for it to be an accomplishment. I know that, but I'm trying to prove it. So whenever I do something that's outside my comfort zone but I tried anyway, I cross it off my list. I added bowling." A soft rip sounds, as she tears the paper sleeve off. "Thank you for that, by the way."

"I didn't do anything."

"Yeah, you did," she says softly.

I am so, *so* fucked, I realize. Fucked worse than I thought I was. It's the same sudden jolt of shock as when I glanced back after paddling on the surfboard and realized how far from shore I was.

I'm no longer thinking about sliding my hands up Eve's shirt or tugging her sleep shorts down.

I'm thinking about how Eve looked happier and more confident each time she picked up a bowling ball. And that I'd listen to Aidan deliberate between pretzels and potato chips for hours if it led to that outcome.

Eve drains the rest of her water bottle and tosses it in the recycling. "The hot tub is on, right?"

"Should be, but I'll check." I walk toward the door that leads to the patio, unlock it, and step outside. Hopefully some fresh air will clear my head. Calm down my cock.

It's cool out, but the temperature feels much closer to spring than winter. Walking on the pavers is the worst part, since they're chilled and hard against my bare feet. The cover is off, so it's immediately obvious the tub is on. Steam curls into the air, creating a mist that hovers over the surface of the bubbling water. Jets are on too.

Soft steps alert me to Eve's presence. She followed me out here.

"It's on," I state unnecessarily. She can see the steam too.

"I didn't bring a bathing suit. I thought it'd be too cold to swim in the ocean and I didn't know about the hot tub."

I know doesn't seem like the right response, so I ask, "Do you want to borrow my trunks?"

Eve laughs. The light, happy sound drifts away in the night air, dissipating the same way the rising steam is. "No, thanks. I just, um, if you wanted to go in too… Sorry. I'm making it weird. I've never had a guy friend. Not that I'm assuming we're friends, but—"

"We're friends," I interrupt.

Do I want more? Yes. But I'm not sure if Eve is ready for more. And I'd rather have her as a friend than revert to saying hi to her in passing once a month. I enjoy being around her. It's never been *only* about attraction with Eve.

She smiles, and it's one that has my stomach muscles clenching. Eve spins one finger. "Turn around."

I raise an eyebrow.

Eve spins her finger more insistently.

I rotate so I'm facing shingles. She's not seriously going to—the unmistakable rustle of fabric reaches my ears over the thud of my pounding heart.

Yeah, she is. She's taking off her clothes and climbing in a hot tub while I'm standing ten feet away. Because we're *friends*.

I'm friends with girls. Holt doesn't have a women's hockey team, but the women's basketball team is often in the weight or cardio rooms before or after us. There are girls in my major or my classes who I'll study with.

And none of those situations have given me any preparation for how to act now.

I can hear her padding across the pavers. Followed by a quiet *slosh* as water's displaced.

"Okay. You can turn around."

I clench my jaw before glancing over my shoulder.

Eve's in the hot tub. From here, all I can see is her dark head bobbing. But the T-shirt and shorts she was wearing as pajamas are draped over the arm of one of the Adirondack chairs surrounding the fire pit we roasted marshmallows in last night.

I have two options. Tell Eve I'm tired and head inside, or stay out here and torture myself.

"Are you, uh, coming in?" she asks. Her voice is tentative, unsure of the answer.

Most people would call me reliable. I'm not sure Eve would. The first time we met, I left. She doesn't know the why. Doesn't know about Sean. And if we're going to be *friends*, I want her to know I'm a friend who sticks around.

"Yeah. I'm coming in."

I watch my reply register on Eve's face. She bites her bottom lip, but it doesn't entirely hide her smile.

"Someone has to protect you from serial killers," I add.

She laughs again. A happy sound I'm quickly becoming addicted to.

I shuck my T-shirt off, dropping it on the same chair her clothes are draped on.

There are a couple of stairs on one side of the hot tub to make it easier to climb into. I bypass them, hoisting myself up the side opposite Eve and sinking into the water.

Damn. I kinda get what Phillips has been going on about. I've never been in a hot tub before, and it's *nice*. Especially now, when everything around it is dark and still and quiet. The cool night air is the perfect contrast to the hot water, and the jets are massaging the knots in my shoulder. It's still a little sore from surfing.

"Not bad, huh?" Eve asks.

"Not bad at all," I agree, tilting my head back to study the sky.

Between the steam and the churning jets distorting the surface, I can't see anything beneath the water. But yeah, that's where I looked first. Focusing on the full moon seems safer.

"Sometimes I think about how the sky stays the same," Eve comments.

I glance at her, and she's mimicking my posture. Head back, eyes up. Her dark hair fans out around her shoulders.

"What do you mean?"

"Everyone who's ever lived has existed beneath the same sun and the same moon. The sky stays the same, while the world around us changes. It's weird to think about."

"Art stays the same too," I comment. "Once it's created."

Eve glances at me, and it feels like the invisible molecules in the air around us are shifting. Pulling us closer together.

"Yeah, it does," she agrees. "Your stick figures are kicking around somewhere."

I laugh, flicking my fingers against the water. "My parents' attic, probably."

Eve smiles, then tips her head back to stare at the sky again.

It's peaceful, the only sound the bubbling jets, and, if I really focus, the distant roar of the ocean.

I let the silence stretch for a few minutes before I ask, "What else is on your *fuck it* list?"

"Not much," she answers quickly. Too quickly.

"C'mon, Eve. Tell me one thing."

She bites her bottom lip.

I wait, hoping she'll trust me.

"I want to visit Paris one day. I've never left the country. I'd never even left *Arizona* until I was eighteen and came to Holt."

"Where in Arizona did you grow up?" I ask.

"Chandler. It's a suburb outside Phoenix."

"You liked it?"

"Chandler? Yeah, it was nice." She shrugs a shoulder, sending fresh ripples this way.

I think I catch a flash of a curve, and quickly lift my gaze. "You don't sound sure."

"I'm not. It's home…and it's also my least favorite place in the world."

I wait, hoping she'll continue.

A few seconds later, she does. "My mom got pregnant with me when she was sixteen. Her parents kicked her out, and my dad —my dad had no interest in being a dad. I think I would have left town. But my mom stayed. She got an apartment ten minutes away from the house she grew up in, went to cosmetology school, and started cutting hair. I grew up within walking distance of my grandparents', but we never visited them and they never visited us. And I met my dad for the first time when I was in second grade. He came to my school for a fire safety demonstration—he's a firefighter. I didn't even know he was my dad at the time. I'll never forget the expression on his face when he saw me. Like he'd seen a ghost. I look a lot like my mom."

"Shit, Eve. That's—"

"Fucked up? Yeah, I know. The people who were supposed to support my mom abandoned her. Acted like she—like *we*—didn't exist. It was brave of her, to make it hard for them by not disappearing the way they wanted her to. But it was confusing as a kid. Coming to Holt was the first time it felt like I had a fresh start."

Something we have in common, I realize. And maybe an explanation for the immediate sense of connection I felt. That first night of college, most people were defining their new identity.

Eve and I were embracing the mystery.

"You have a relationship with your dad now?"

"Depends how you define *relationship*, I guess." Her smile is brittle. Fragile, like a facade cracking around the edges. She sinks a couple of inches lower in the tub. "Where did you grow up?"

"Wyoming. The soy milk capital of the world."

Eve laughs. "I owe you another thank-you for the carton in the fridge."

"You don't *owe* me anything, Eve." My tone is a little too intense for the topic of soy milk, but I mean the words.

"Thank you, Hunter."

I hold her gaze. "You're welcome, Eve."

She blinks first. "What's Wyoming like?"

"It's big. You leave town, and there's all this empty land around. So much open space, it's easy to forget how huge the rest of the world is. Nothing terribly exciting ever happened in Casper.

The views of the mountains are pretty crazy. There are tons of trails for biking or running. Lots of fishing spots. We'd go snowmobiling in the winter. And the aquatic center next to the town rink had two waterslides, so we'd go down those after hockey practice in elementary school."

It feels good to reminisce about those early years. Back when I was a kid whose only concern was whether his mom had remembered to get Jell-O at the store. Before my brother morphed into someone unrecognizable and altered our family forever. Sean twisted my perception of Casper, same as Eve's dad and grandparents affected her feelings toward her hometown.

"Will you move back?" she asks.

I exhale. "I don't know. I got into UW—University of Wyoming—so it's an option. I've never had a place I pictured ending up after college, like you with New York. I just figured something would make sense when I got to this point, and it…it kinda snuck up on me, I guess."

The same way the end of spring break did. Tomorrow's Saturday—our last day here. Classes resume Monday, and April 15th will continue creeping closer.

"Time flies when it's always raining," Eve says.

I smile. "You sound like Hart."

"I know. It drives Harlow crazy. She loves the rain. Water in any form, really."

"They're good together," I state. "Harlow and Conor. I wasn't sure at first, but they fit."

Eve nods. "Yeah, they do. Weather preferences aside."

I smile again. Or maybe I never stopped. "Speaking of couples, Harlow mentioned she heard I was dating Holly Johnson."

Eve's chewing on her lower lip again. "Oh, really?"

I almost laugh at the feigned casualness in her tone. Eve might be a talented artist, but she's not a great actress. She's obviously wondering whether Harlow named a source.

"Uh-huh." I rub a hand along my jaw. My skin's damp from the steam. "I went out with her once, that night I ran into you at La Bella Napoli. But I haven't gone out with her again, and I'm not going to. I'm not dating her."

"Good."

I'm not sure who's more surprised by Eve's reply—her or me.

Her cheeks flush scarlet. "I wasn't, um, I just meant, if you're not going out with her because you don't want to go out with her, then that's…good." Eve tilts her head back, her throat working furiously. "*Wow*, those Jell-O shots were strong."

I laugh, then reluctantly lift my arms out of the warm water. "I should head back to bed. Aidan was talking about leaving at seven."

After some research on swells, Phillips decided our shitty surfing experience was because we went to the beach too late in the day. And somehow, he talked me and Hart into going again. Tomorrow's our last chance.

"Be careful," she says.

"Of sharks?"

"No. I mean, yes, I saw the same documentary with Harlow and they *do* mistake surfers for seals sometimes, but I was more meaning your…shoulder."

"Oh. Right." I forgot I mentioned it to her, and I'm taken aback that Eve remembered. "It's not bothering me much anymore."

She nods. "Good."

I stand to climb out. The water level hits just below my waist. And Eve's eyes do *not* stay on mine. They trail down, lower and lower, which is what I was hoping would happen. When she walked in on me in the shower, it was sudden and unexpected. I couldn't get a good read on her reaction before she shut the door. But now, she's looking deliberately at my soaked boxers. Looking like she likes what she sees.

"Good night, Eve."

Her eyes dart up to meet mine, fresh color flooding her face. "Night, Hunter."

I vault over the edge and walk to the chair, using my T-shirt as a temporary towel to dry off a little before I head inside.

I glance back at Eve once, when I reach the door. She's in the same spot, staring up at the sky that doesn't change.

Tonight, it felt like we did.

And I hope we'll *keep* changing.

CHAPTER TWENTY-TWO

EVE

"Home sweet home," Harlow announces as Conor brakes in front of our house.

I cover a yawn with the back of my hand, then rub at my gritty eyes. I dozed off and on during the drive back to Holt.

We made the most of our final night of spring break. I don't think anyone went to bed before two a.m. last night, and we left at nine to arrive back at campus at a decent hour.

I drove back with Conor and Harlow, while Rylan and Aidan went in Hunter's car. Harlow suggested it—saying it made the most sense since she and I were headed back to the same place. And, as much as I love my best friend, I had to fight the urge to say we could keep the same seating arrangement. I wanted more time with Hunter.

I haven't had a chance to talk to him alone since we went hot-tubbing in the middle of the night, and it bothers me how it feels like the end of a chapter. Like I lost something I was never even certain I had.

He's single. Hunter Morgan—who I've had a crush on for as

long as I've known him—told me he was single while we were barely clothed in a hot tub.

And what did I do? I froze. I blurted out "Good" and then something absurd about Jell-O shots.

I *panicked*. Because the possibility of kissing Hunter—of more than kissing Hunter—was nothing like the reality of kissing Finn. It would have mattered. It would have meant something. Not just in Calaveras, where we were two fifth wheels. In Somerville, too, where the distance between us feels more than physical. There's a reason our paths rarely cross on campus.

"Eve!"

Based on the tone of Harlow's voice, it's not the first time she's said my name.

"Yeah?" I reply, covering another yawn.

"I was asking if you were awake, but I think I got my answer. You know what they say—it was a good spring break if you come home sleep-deprived."

"Do people say that?" Conor muses. "Because I've never heard that phrase before."

Harlow smacks his arm. "Are you saying it wasn't a good spring break, Hart?"

"Not saying that at all, Hayes. Especially last night. I might owe Morgan an apology, because the Jell-O shots were pretty good."

The mention of Hunter's name wakes me up more than Harlow calling mine did.

I had *four* Jell-O shots last night, solely because Hunter smiled every time I took one.

My liver is going to need a *long* hiatus after spring break. But even drinking too much feels like it was part of the experience. I don't often allow myself to make mistakes outside of art. On a canvas, it's called creativity. In life, it has consequences. Some necessary, some scary.

For the first time in—ever, maybe, I feel like I seized some moments.

In one week, I changed more than I have in months. Maybe years. Since the adjustment of coming to college, I've spent most of the time looking ahead to graduation. I've viewed moving to New York as the "official" start to my life, and I'm belatedly realizing how often that mindset resulted in me playing it safe. In placing limits on myself.

I stuff my sketchbook into the backpack resting in the footwell, then pop the door open. "Thanks for driving, Conor."

"No problem, Eve. Glad you came."

"Thanks," I say, touched by the comment he didn't have to make.

"I'll be inside in a bit," Harlow tells me.

"Okay." I grab my suitcase out of the trunk of Conor's car, and then start toward our little house.

It hits me, stepping inside, that this is likely the final time I'll come back here after any extended time away. That was our last break before graduation.

I shut the door behind me, leaving it unlocked so Harlow doesn't have to use her key. Hang up my winter coat, which I only wore so I wouldn't have to pack or carry it. It's nearly sixty in Somerville today, making spring feel well on its way.

My room has the stale feel of stagnancy when I enter it. I leave my suitcase by the end of my bed. Walk over to my window, unlock it, and crack it open a couple of inches, allowing some fresh air to seep inside. Slowly, I spin and survey my bedroom. The drawings and posters on the walls. The heap of clothes I sorted through packing for spring break. The stack of New York guidebooks on my dresser.

I head over to my desk. Open the top left drawer.

Last year's Christmas card from my dad is on the very top.

I tear it in half. Tear the halves in half. Over and over again, until the paper rectangle is nothing more than a pile of scraps on the bottom of the drawer. Then, I shut the drawer again. I don't feel better or worse, but I do feel different. Almost like…I didn't realize I could do that. It never occurred to me to rip that card up when I received it.

Calmly, I lay my suitcase down on the floor and unzip it. There are a few clean items, but it's mostly filled with laundry. Midway through sorting whites and colors, my mom calls.

It's the third time she's called since our brief text exchange about my dad missing my graduation. I've ignored every one, because I assumed that's why she was calling and because discussing my father with her never ends well.

I blow out a long breath, emptying my lungs, before leaning back against my bedframe and answering. "Hi, Mom."

"'Sorry, Mom' would be a more fitting greeting, Eve. You didn't answer a single phone call this week. I had half a mind to call campus."

"I wasn't on campus. It was my spring break week, remember?"

The pause on the other end of the line tells me my mom did not, in fact, remember. She's not as checked out as my dad, but she's not entirely checked in, either. She has two other kids to look after, and I'm off living on my own.

And she never went to college. Never experienced a spring break. Never had a model for what parenting an adult child was supposed to look like.

"I'm sorry I worried you," I mutter, adding another T-shirt to the pile of darks.

"Did you have a nice break?" The question is followed by the distant hum of a hair dryer and a crinkle of foil. The busy soundtrack to my childhood.

I'm not surprised she's calling me from the salon between clients. It gives her an easy excuse to hang up when we inevitably start arguing about something. And tracks with the brisk efficiency my mom prides herself on.

"Yeah," I answer. "It was really fun. I went on a road trip with Harlow and her—with Harlow and some other friends. To northern California."

Harlow's the only friend from Holt my mom knows—or has met. Harlow made quite the impression on my mother while we were moving into the dorms by telling her she swims on a regular basis. My mom sends her some special shampoo that's supposed to protect hair from chlorine now.

"That sounds nice."

"Yeah, it was. We were right on the beach, so the scenery was beautiful. I'll send you a few photos."

"Please do. Did Ben go as well?"

"No. He, uh, we broke up, actually." I hold my breath, waiting for her response.

"That's… I'm sorry, honey."

Honestly, I was never sure how my mom felt about Ben. After they met for the first time, she told me he *took direction well*. To this day, I don't know if that was a compliment or an insult. But I think it skewed negative, since my mom values independence. Ten years together, and she hasn't married John. I know he's asked, because there was an engagement ring on her dresser the first time I came home from Holt.

"Thanks," I tell her. "I'm fine."

I say the words because they're expected, but they're also true. I *am* fine.

"You were together for a long time. Do you think you'll work things out?"

"Nope" is all I offer in response, hoping she hears the heavy undertone of *I don't want to talk about it.*

"Is he still moving to New York?"

"No," I say tightly. "He's not."

She sighs. "Eve, I really think that—"

"I know what you *really think*, Mom. But I've made up *my* mind, about *my* life."

She exhales again, frustration evident in the sound. "I'm not telling you not to pursue art, Eve. But you could paint just as easily in Chandler as you could in New York. It's so far and expensive and—"

"Did you only call to give me another lecture? Because I heard your concerns the first hundred times."

A pause, as she deliberates how hard to push. I've always said I would move to New York after college, and she's always tried to talk me out of it. There's a new urgency on her end, as graduation ticks closer. And a new determination on mine, now that I'm moving solo.

She lets the subject drop. "I called to check on you. I know you're upset about your father—"

"I'm not," I lie. "I saw it coming, just like you said. I was just letting you know, in case *you* thought he'd changed."

"I learned that lesson a long time ago, Eve."

I toss another balled-up T-shirt atop the colors, grimacing when it topples the entire pile.

I get why my mom hates my dad. He completely ignored my existence. The first child support check didn't come until I was nine. My mom never deposited it, even though she needed the money. Having me ruined her relationship with her parents, and her plans for the future, while my dad's life didn't change at all.

I hate him for that.

But also… He's my dad. The only one I have. I like John, but we've never had the sort of relationship where I view him as a father figure. No matter how many mistakes my dad has made, I'd rather suffer through the occasional, sports-centered phone call than never have any communication with him at all. I want to have *some* idea of who he is, rather than just this blank void in my life.

I haven't forgotten or forgiven the past. But I don't feel I have to, to talk to him once a month.

Or, I *didn't*. After our last conversation, I'm tempted to end any effort. I'll have to decide by Tuesday, when he's supposed to call.

I play with the zipper on my suitcase. "I should go, Mom. Classes start back up tomorrow morning, and I've got a stack of laundry to do."

"Okay." She hesitates, and I know what's coming before she speaks. She can't help herself. "Just think about moving home at first, all right? New York isn't going anywhere. You could save some money, and think things through a little more."

My mom thinks my life-long dream of living in New York is an idea I *haven't thought through.*

I wish she'd try to see my perspective on things. With my dad, and with my art. Understand that I have to learn lessons too. That Chandler doesn't have the museums or the galleries or the opportunities or the excitement of New York. But practicality is her way of expressing love. It's what worked for her. She's worried about me in a strange city, and I can't resent her for that.

"Yeah," I say. "I will."

"Okay. I love you, Eve," she tells me, and then hangs up.

A sentiment she only expresses after we've argued about something. Almost like an explanation.

I'm telling you to move home *because I love you.*

I'm telling you to give up on your father *because I love you.*

I know she does. I just hate how those three words feel like a reminder of the ways I've inconvenienced her—and continue to. She made so many sacrifices for me, because that's what a good parent is supposed to do. And a dutiful daughter would have majored in something practical, not art, and have a job offer waiting in a reasonably priced city.

I put on some Arctic Monkeys to drown out my mother's worried voice in my head, then haul my dirty laundry down the hall to the washer. It only works after you kick the bottom left corner twice, a trick it took me and Harlow three weeks to figure out. We should leave a note for the next tenants.

Once the washer starts spinning, I head into the kitchen. There's no sign of Harlow, so she must still be outside with Conor.

I make myself a peanut butter and jelly sandwich—food options are limited since most of what's in the fridge has expired —and return to my room.

It's a mess from my hasty packing last week, so I clean up a little while "Fluorescent Adolescent" blares.

Halfway through organizing my desk, I sigh and pick up my phone. Typing out the text to my mom only takes a few seconds.

EVE: I love you too.

CHAPTER TWENTY-THREE

HUNTER

I drum my fingers against the side of the table, take a bite of the turkey wrap I made for lunch, and then resume staring at my phone.

I asked Conor for Eve's number before he left for class this morning, claiming she'd left a phone charger in my car. Except… she didn't, so I have no clue *what* to text her.

So far, all I have is *Hey*. Which is a solid, predictable start, but not very memorable. I could suggest grabbing coffee, I guess, but that seems too…basic. I'm hoping she'll fall in love with me, not encourage her thing for soy milk.

We're not sleeping under the same roof anymore. Holt's campus is small, but there's no guarantee I'll randomly run into Eve anytime soon. I want—need—to make a move, I just don't know the right one.

I've been attracted to Eve ever since we first met, and I think a part of me thought I'd overhyped that moment in my head. Built her up as the dream girl who got away. Wanted her because I thought I'd never have her.

Maybe all of that was true. But the past week around Eve

confirmed that anything—everything—I felt the night we met is still there.

I want her to know how much I wish that night had ended differently. How much I wish several recent nights had ended differently.

I add *Eve* to the new message so it now reads: *Hey, Eve.*

Not much of an improvement.

Before I can come up with anything else to add, my phone lights up with a call from my mom.

"Hey, Mom," I answer, then take another bite of my wrap.

I texted her the name of the hotel Eve suggested a few days ago, but haven't spoken to her since returning to campus.

"Hi, honey." I relax some when her voice sounds chipper. "How was the rest of your break?"

"It was great. The rental Aidan found was really nice, right on the water, so we hung out there most of the time. We went bowling, on a rainy day. Nothing too crazy, but it was nice to get away for a bit."

"Nothing too crazy is what moms love to hear," she tells me. "I'm glad you had fun, Hunter."

"Yeah, me too." I clear my throat. "How are…how are things there?"

"Oh, we're doing fine. This weekend warmed up some, so I did some gardening. Your father went fishing and had a lot of luck, so we had your grandparents over for dinner."

"Tell him about the size of the trout," I hear my dad say.

"You can tell him when you talk to him," my mom replies.

I smile, realizing they're on their lunch break together. "That sounds nice, Mom." I fiddle with the tortilla of my wrap, debating on whether to ask the next question. But I don't trust my mom to bring it up if there is something to say. "Anything from Sean?"

"No, we haven't heard from him. I tried calling last week. No answer."

I blow out a long breath, relieved and also annoyed. Sean tends to disappear after a relapse, like our worry is driving him away. Alarm he only adds to, by taking off.

"I told him to stop calling you."

"Mom…"

"No, Hunter. It isn't fair to you. If he wants help, he can call us."

I don't argue with her. Mostly because Sean has proven over and over again that he'll do whatever the hell he wants. He was always stubborn and contrarian, but it's ten times worse when he's on…whatever his drug of choice happens to be that night.

"How are your classes going?" she asks, in an obvious attempt to change the subject from my brother.

"They're good," I answer. "Busy. I have a lot of work to do on my thesis. But home stretch, you know."

"Anything from grad schools yet?" There's a hint of concern in my mom's voice, and I realize she's stressed I didn't get in anywhere.

I rub at my shoulder. Driving all day yesterday and a second surfing trip didn't help the spot I strained. "Uh, yeah. I got in."

"Got in? Where?" She sounds thrilled, and I immediately feel like an asshole for keeping the news from her.

"Everywhere I applied. Stanford, Princeton, Yale, Columbia, Rochester, Washington University, Ohio State, Northwestern, UPenn, and UW."

"Hunter! That is *incredible*. Wow! Congratulations, honey. *He got in everywhere he applied*," I hear her whisper to my dad. "Your dad says congratulations too. Oh, Hunter, we're *so* proud of you."

I have to clear my throat before I can speak. "Thanks, Mom. Tell Dad thanks too."

It feels really good to make my parents proud. Yet I can't help but think mine is the second college graduation they should be attending. Sean had offers, before everything careened out of control. In comparison to him, anything I achieve looks impressive.

"Do you know what one you're picking?"

She asks the question so easily. So simply, like there *should* be a choice.

"No." I lean back in the chair, bouncing my knee. "I just… I kinda wish I hadn't applied to so many places. Having so many options…I'm not sure where to go."

"Is there an advisor you can talk to?"

"Yeah, I'm meeting with him tomorrow to go over the options. From an academic perspective. But I—I'm also picking the place I'll live for the next two years."

"You're young, honey. Wherever you end up, it'll be a new experience. Hopefully a good one, but if not, it's only two years. Think about how quickly college has gone by, and that was twice as long."

"Yeah." I pause. "UW would be a little familiar."

"Hunter. I know very little about political science programs. But I do know UW is not the most competitive program on that list."

"Rankings aren't everything, Mom."

But they do matter. Competitive schools attract top professors and lead to opportunities and connections that other universities can't provide.

"Honey, your dad and I will support whatever you decide. But make sure you're deciding for *you*, not anyone else."

"I feel like I should be close to home, with everything that's going on with Sean again," I confess.

It feels good to say it aloud. It's still a weight, but it's a little less suffocating.

My mom exhales. "I'm not going to lie to you, Hunter. Things with your brother are…hard. We've gone through the same cycle so many times it's starting to feel like an endless loop. But you being closer to home won't change that. In fact, it would only make things harder for me and your father, knowing that you shrunk your dreams. And if Sean were in a better place, he'd tell you the same thing. Make sure you're considering all that too, all right?"

"Yeah, I will."

I know Professor Hayden isn't going to suggest I choose UW during our meeting tomorrow. And…part of me doesn't want to pick UW for the same reason I feel like I should.

I don't know where the line is when I let Sean go. I could block his number, prevent him from calling me. Cut off all contact. Snip all ties. He's isolated himself from our family in nearly every way. Even during the rare stretches of sobriety, the easy dynamic that characterized my childhood is gone. It's awkward, being around my brother. We don't banter or share any inside jokes. It's stiff.

Sean's made his choices, and maybe I've reached my limit on allowing his to affect mine.

"I have to get back to the classroom," my mom says. "Let us know how your meeting with your advisor goes, okay?"

"Yeah, I will. Love you, Mom. Say bye to Dad."

"I will. And I love you too, Hunter."

I end the call and take another bite of my turkey wrap. Conor enters the kitchen while I'm chewing.

"Hey," he greets, dropping his backpack on the floor with a heavy thump.

I swallow. "Hey. You done with classes for the day?"

Hart scoffs. "I can't believe you haven't memorized my class schedule yet, Morgan. It's on the damn fridge."

I roll my eyes. I know Conor found Aidan's insistence we all post our schedules on the fridge as silly as I did, but I can't deny that it has come in handy before. Saves a text.

"Yeah, I'm done for the day," he continues. "Came home for some food, and then I'm headed to Harlow's to study."

"*To study*, huh? Is that what the kids are calling it these days?"

Hart flips me off before opening the fridge.

"It's not a euphemism. I've got a paper due Thursday, and Hayes has an exam on Friday. Plus, she's going home this weekend, so studying seemed like the best shot at spending time together this week."

"You going home with her?" I ask.

Hart sets some leftover chicken on the table, and then takes the chair across from mine. "No. She's going to see Landon's band play."

"Oh." Realization dawns.

"Yeah."

Ever since the mystery of why Conor inexplicably avoided Harlow was solved, I've had a lot more sympathy toward Hart about the whole situation. If my dad left my mom and had a family—another son—I'd definitely carry some resentment about it. Avoid any reminders of the situation. I don't envy Harlow's spot smack in the middle either.

But, as far as I can tell, they haven't allowed it to mess with their relationship.

"That…going okay?" I ask carefully.

"About the same." He shrugs a shoulder. "Landon still thinks Harlow is just a fling for me."

"He doesn't know you very well, then."

"No," Conor agrees. "He doesn't."

"Sorry, man."

Hart nods. "I knew what I was getting into. Wouldn't change a damn thing." He swallows some water. "Hey, did Eve reply about the charger?"

"Huh?"

"Eve's charger, that she left in your car. I can bring it when I head over there."

Oh. *Oh.* Shit.

I clear my throat. "Right. It wasn't hers, it turns out."

"Oh." Conor frowns. "Weird."

He appears puzzled, not suspicious. Then again, why would he assume I was lying about a phone charger?

I finish off my lunch, then stick my plate in the dishwasher. "I'll see you later. I'm headed to the library to work on my thesis."

"Have fun."

Writing a thesis is a requirement for all political science majors. Not for English, which is Hart's major.

"Yeah, thanks." I match his sarcasm.

"I told you to major in English, dude. Then we could have had all our classes together."

"You mean, the language I already speak? Pass."

Conor throws a balled-up napkin at me as I head for the doorway. "It's the study of literature and how it relates to culture and history, you dick."

"You missed, Hart," I call over one shoulder. "Stick to hockey."

CHAPTER TWENTY-FOUR

EVE

"We'll wrap up today's critiques with Eve's project," Professor Alday announces. "Jayden, we'll start with you on Thursday."

The guy on my left nods as I pick up my canvas and head for the easel at the front of the room.

My steps drag with dread.

Critiques are my least favorite part of art classes. I understand their purpose, that skills have to be assessed to provide feedback and encourage improvement. But it feels very vulnerable, listening to others interpret or analyze your art, and Professor Alday is famous for his candor with students. It's why this course —the most difficult painting class Holt offers—only has seven students enrolled.

Professor Alday is already frowning as he appraises the painting I finished late last night. It's the same one I was working on right before break—a little girl and her father.

The prompt for this assignment was a place that you used to visit in the past, but can no longer go. Most of my peers painted landscapes of previous hometowns, which I would argue was a loose interpretation of the assignment. Those are places they *could* go back to, they just *haven't*.

Whether or not I answer my father's call later, I'll never get to be the little girl with a dad.

"You should work with watercolors more often, Eve. Excellent technique."

I smile, pleasantly surprised by the praise. But my smile fades as he continues talking.

"But I don't quite see how you captured the prompt. The happiness of a father and child is hardly the bittersweet sentimentality I was looking for."

"How do you know they're happy?" I ask.

"Because that is the viewpoint you've created here. The way the father is looking at the child, keeping a careful eye on her. The background, a house that is messy and lived-in. You are crafting clues for the viewer, and none of them evoke the wistfulness I was looking for in this project. I'd like you to redo it, please."

I blink at him, momentarily stunned. I've *never* been asked to redo a project before. This was some of Professor Alday's milder feedback, but even his harsh criticism has ended with a grade for the original work I handed in.

"What's more *wistful* than time?" I argue. "This is supposed to be a memory from the past. You can remember memories, but you can't return to them. The moment is gone forever."

"Art isn't supposed to require an explanation, Eve. You have to tell us how to feel without saying a word. Perhaps you were conflicted, and that came through in the piece. Give some more thought to what you're wanting to say before you tackle this assignment again. You have two weeks to turn in another interpretation of the prompt." Professor Alday glances at the clock. "That's all for today. Enjoy your afternoons, everyone."

Not likely, I think, as I retrieve my canvas and trudge down the hallway to my private studio. I stash the watercolor painting as far back as it'll fit, then grab my backpack from the corner and relock the room.

Mae Wilkins, whose room is two doors down from mine, is locking her studio space at the same time. She glances up as I approach, shooting me a sympathetic smile. "Seems like Alday had a shitty break."

I huff a laugh. "Yeah."

"For what it's worth, I thought yours was really great."

"Thanks. Yours too. I'll see you Thursday."

"See you, Eve," she calls after me.

Rather than head home, I decide to go to the library to work on an essay for my Poetics of Narrative class. I've been putting it off because the prompt makes no sense, but it's due next week. And I'll be more productive in the library than in my bed.

I decide to get a coffee on the way. A treat, for having to redo a project I already spent many hours on.

A small, small part of me acknowledges that Professor Alday was right about one thing. I didn't know what I wanted that painting to say. I *was* conflicted about it, same as I am about my current relationship with my dad.

Fifteen feet from the student center, I regret the choice to stop for a coffee.

Ben's leaning against one of the brick pillars, watching me approach. He smiles when he sees me.

My smile back is tentative.

I don't believe this is a coincidence. He's met me here after my Advanced Painting class before.

I never responded to any of the texts he sent over break. And I knew, as soon as I was back on campus, that there was a chance of seeing him. But right now, I'm *really* not in the mood.

"Hey," Ben greets.

"Hey," I echo, keeping my hands shoved deep in my jacket pockets.

"You getting coffee?" he asks hopefully.

I glance at the door that leads into the campus coffee shop. "Yeah. You?"

"Yep. I've been editing footage for a few hours. Needed a break."

"Funny timing," I comment dryly.

Ben walks ahead to open the door for me. When I pass him, I notice the tips of his ears are pink.

It's warmer inside—almost stifling—so I unzip my fleece and fiddle with the strap of my backpack as Ben and I join the line in front of the pastry display case.

"How was your break?" he asks as we wait.

"It was good," I answer. "Great, actually. Was nice to go somewhere."

Ben nods, visibly unsure what to do with that information. We don't usually discuss our breaks from school. We either spent them together or spoke so frequently during them it felt like we did.

"Where exactly did you go?"

"Calaveras," I reply.

"Never heard of it."

I hadn't either, but my voice is a touch defensive as I say, "It's beautiful. Right on the Pacific."

"Guess I'm partial to the Atlantic," Ben tells me.

I glance at the line. Still two people ahead of us. "Right. How was Maine?"

"It was fine." Ben averts his gaze, looking at the chalk whiteboard instead of at me.

I was expecting a more verbose answer. In the past, he's told me about his family and his friends and his friends' families. And the latest with the lobster shack, although I get why he's not mentioning that now.

An awkward pause lingers as I try to come up with something else to say. I'm not sure when we stopped having meaningful conversations with each other, but I think it predated our breakup.

"They have blueberry muffins" is the best I can come up with.

Ben loves blueberry muffins.

"Oh. Great," he says.

What feels like hours later, we reach the front of the line. Ben orders a cappuccino, and then the blonde girl at the register looks to me.

I wonder if she's the one who gives Aidan free drinks, and smile at the memory of him bickering with Rylan.

I wonder if she's ever given Hunter a free drink, and frown before ordering a soy latte.

"Are you paying together or separately?" the cashier asks.

Ben hesitates.

"Separately," I say, handing her my student ID to swipe.

Ben doesn't argue. Not the way he would when I offered to pay while we were together. And it's a stupid thing to be bothered by—I should be relieved, assuming that means he's accepted we're over—but I immediately think of the way Hunter refused to let me pay for a single thing on our road trip when we've never been together. I don't get the sense he grew up with money when he was talking about his hometown, either.

Once we've paid, we move down to the end of the counter, past the whistling espresso machine.

Thankfully, my drink is ready first. I grab one of the paper sleeves and slide it around the cup. "I'll see you—"

"Can we talk, Eve? Just for a minute."

"I have an essay to write…" I hedge.

"It won't take long. I promise."

In the time I hesitate, Ben's drink arrives. He swipes it off the counter, shoots me a pleading look, and heads toward an empty table.

I sigh and follow him. Take a seat. Cross my legs. Tap my foot against the side of my backpack, fighting the urge to stand and hustle out of here.

Ben's tearing open a sugar packet and pouring it in slowly.

"So…what's up?" I ask, hoping to hurry things along.

Ben exhales and snaps his lid on before he leans forward. "All right. Here it is. I, uh, I had sex with Rowan over spring break."

I stare at him, totally taken aback. A hundred tries, and I wouldn't have guessed those were going to be the next words out of Ben's mouth.

The longer I stay silent, the more color leeches from his face.

"Say something, Eve. Please."

"I—I don't know what to say," I admit.

Ben rubs at his face with the palm not cupped around his coffee. "I'm *so* sorry."

More words finally form. "You don't need to apologize. We're not together. You didn't cheat."

"It felt like cheating."

I say nothing. I didn't feel like I was cheating when I kissed Finn. Or when I repeatedly checked Hunter out. Does that make me a terrible person? Did my father's abandonment break something in me, so that I move on too quickly in other relationships to avoid attachment or disappointment?

Maybe I'm listening to too many psychology podcasts. That's what I would have majored in, if not art.

Ben rests his elbows on the table. "It was my last night at home. You hadn't responded to my texts and we were both drinking and it just…happened."

"I *really* don't need details, Ben."

He winces. "Yeah. Right. I just—I wanted you to know it wasn't planned. And it didn't mean anything."

I scoff at that. "Of course it meant something. She's your best friend."

"I—I know. But I've never thought of her that way. I swear. When we were together, I never even considered—"

"We're *not* together, Ben."

"That's your choice. Not mine."

My spine stiffens. "'I'm not sure we're forever.' Your words. Not mine."

Another wince. "I didn't mean it, Eve. I was worried about how you were going to react to me moving home, and I just—it came out all wrong. I already told you that."

"I don't care how it came out. It did, and we're done."

Ben looks down at the table. "You don't miss…us?"

I'm honest. "Not the way that I should."

That became glaringly obvious when I was in Calaveras. Rylan and Aidan…Harlow and Conor…*that's* how couples in love are supposed to act around each other. Ben and I were never like that.

Ben doesn't bother to hide the hurt on his face. "And Rowan? You don't care that it happened?"

I exhale. "You really want to know how I feel about it?"

He nods.

"I'm…relieved. I'm glad that you moved on."

Ben sighs. "Fuck."

He sounds resigned, not mad, but I still feel obligated to say, "You asked."

"Yeah. I know I did."

I take a sip of my coffee. The two girls at the table next to ours are whispering and looking toward the register, and I follow their gaze.

Harlow, Conor, and Hunter are standing in line.

Harlow and Conor are talking to each other.

Hunter *was* looking this way. He glances back at the chalkboard as soon as he realizes my head turned.

Fuck.

Last night, when I couldn't fall asleep, I thought about what I'd say to Hunter if I ran into him on campus this week. Ask how the drive back went or how his shoulder is or if he'd decided about grad school. If that went well, suggest we hang out sometime.

I *hoped* I'd run into Hunter.

But Hunter showing up now, when I got roped into having coffee with my ex? Far from ideal.

Harlow glances this way a few seconds later. She smiles when she spots me, but it fades into a questioning look when she sees Ben seated across from me. She says something to Conor and then heads this way. Conor waves as Harlow weaves around tables. I wave back, and the two nosy girls whip their heads in my direction.

I forgot, when we were in California, that Conor is a campus celebrity.

But then I hear one of the girls whisper Hunter's name, and realize maybe they were staring at a different hockey player. Unsurprisingly, that makes me feel about as great as picturing him with the pretty blonde cashier did. The pretty blonde cashier who's *also* staring at Hunter.

Harlow's arrival distracts me.

"Saw you over here. Just wanted to say hi." Harlow tucks a piece of hair behind one ear, raising her eyebrows at me before glancing at Ben. "Hey, Ben." Her tone is cooler than it was when she was talking to me.

"Hi, Harlow." Ben's fingers tap nervously against the side of his coffee. "Good break?"

"Yeah, it was great. Yours?"

"Um, good, yeah."

I snort. I can't help it. Some of the shock is fading. I *am* relieved that Ben had sex with someone else. It's ridiculous, because I don't need his permission, but I feel like that gives me free rein to do the same, sans guilt.

I'm also…miffed. He tells me breaking up was a mistake right before leaving, and then hooks up with his childhood bestie? Talk about mixed messages.

Harlow hears the snort and shoots me a questioning look.

Later, I mouth at her.

She nods. "See you at home, E."

"I'm not her favorite person, huh?" Ben says as Harlow heads back to the line without saying another word to him.

Conor is watching her. Hunter's staring straight ahead, and it causes this strange spasm in my stomach. Maybe that's my answer—we're back on campus and we're back to being barely acquaintances.

"She's my best friend," I reply. "And you blindsided me, Ben."

"I know. And I'm so sorry about that. Truly, I am. Changing my mind about New York—it had nothing to do with you, Eve."

I nod.

I know it didn't. And that's the problem. He wasn't willing to move to New York for me after he changed his mind about film school. Just like I wasn't willing to move to Maine for him, even though I could waitress and paint in a small town just as easily— more easily, probably—as I could in Manhattan.

And Ben knew that.

Knew it so certainly he didn't even bother asking me to.

CHAPTER TWENTY-FIVE

HUNTER

Gaffney's is packed. It's *always* packed, but Tuesdays— when wings and pints are offered at half price—are extra chaotic.

There are perks to being a member of a championship-winning sports team, though.

"Go ahead, man," some guy I've never seen before says, stepping aside so I can take his spot at the bar. "Awesome season."

I give him an appreciative nod before stepping up to the counter. The varnished wood is worn in spots, scratched in others.

A blonde appears with a white rag in hand, swiping up a spill someone left behind. I recognize her. Her name is Stacey, according to the name tag attached to her cleavage.

She recognizes me too. "Hey, Hunter."

"Hey. Pint of IPA, please."

I already finished my first beer, and usually that's my limit on school nights. But Phillips drove us in his fire engine–colored truck, and I had a long day, so I'm making an exception. Plus, they're half price, so it's basically like drinking one.

"Coming right up," Stacey says.

She reappears with a fresh beer less than a minute later.

"Conor still with the redhead?" Stacey asks as she slides it to me.

"Yep," I answer.

Not the first time I've been asked about Hart's relationship status today, and I'm guessing it won't be the last. His nickname on campus is "Hart-breaker." And honestly, it doesn't have much to do with his last name.

Stacey makes a face, then glances toward the group of my teammates. "Guys' night?"

"I guess."

Neither Rylan nor Harlow are here. And last I heard Jack Williams was dating someone, but his girlfriend isn't at Gaffney's either.

"What about you?"

I take a sip of my drink, then fish a five out of my wallet. "What about me?"

Stacey smirks. "Are you single, Hunter?"

"Thanks for the beer," I say, then walk off without waiting for my change. Hopefully she prefers a two-dollar tip to an answer.

Most of the hockey team is clustered around Gaffney's largest table. I prop a hip against one of the chairs and sip on my cold beer, watching the sports commentators on the television above the bar. It's too loud to hear what they're saying, but I scan the subtitles. They're discussing Opening Day, which is Thursday.

"'Sup, Morgan?"

Robby's voice registers a half second before he appears next to me, also holding a pint.

"Not much," I say, glancing away from the screen. "You? How was…Kentucky?"

Sampson grins. "Awesome. I'd ask how yours was, but

Phillips already filled me in. Jealous you guys surfed. I've always wanted to try."

"Don't," I advise. "My shoulder is still fucked up."

Robby punches my left arm. "This one?"

I roll my eyes as I sip more beer.

"You bummed break is over? You seem more serious than your usual serious self."

I snort at his observation. "Stressful day."

"How come?"

"Just a long meeting with my advisor."

I spent two hours in Professor Hayden's office this afternoon, going over my grad school options. I'm glad I talked to my mom beforehand, because it was a lot easier to discuss all my options after admitting my hesitations to her. But still, I have to make a final decision, and there's no obvious choice.

"Ah. Endless praise must suck."

"Fuck off, Sampson."

Robby laughs. "Dude, it's not a secret. You're the only guy on the team who got academic honors every damn semester."

"Yeah, yeah. And I thought *that* was the hard part."

"Tell me about it." Robby groans. "I thought the last weeks before graduation were supposed to be the *easiest* of college."

I snort. "Who the hell told you that?"

"Wishful thinking, I guess. I already finished all my major requirements. Diploma's just a fucking formality at this point, right?"

"I guess."

Robby got a job as a market research analyst, so he knows exactly what his post-grad life will look like.

I've had four years to get used to the idea, but it's bizarre to realize college will just be...*over*, and soon. No more nights at Gaffney's. No more living with Conor and Aidan. Somerville is the only town I've lived in aside from Casper. It's become a second home.

Holt doesn't have any graduate schools. Staying past senior year was never a possibility. But it's unsettling to realize how close to the end we really are.

"Hey! I thought you couldn't make it."

I glance in the direction of Conor's voice.

He's hugging Harlow. I can't see her face, but Harlow's red hair is easily identifiable.

And…Harlow didn't show up alone. Standing a foot away from her is Eve. She's smiling as she watches Conor and Harlow embrace.

My first instinct is avoidance. "Wanna play pool?" I ask Robby.

"Yeah, sure," he agrees. "Just let me grab another beer. I'll meet you over there."

I nod, then start weaving through the busy bar toward the pool table.

There are a couple of guys standing around it, but they move away as soon as they see me coming.

"All yours, man," one says.

"You guys can play too," I offer.

"Nah, nah. We're good," the same guy says. His eyes are on Robby, who's appeared with a green bottle in hand. Not surprised he enjoyed the same fast service I did.

Robby glances at the wide-eyed guys, then grins at me.

More perks. They're juniors. Or maybe even sophomores. Gaffney's is pretty liberal with its carding policy. As in, it doesn't really have one. College kids keep this place in business.

These younger guys are staring at us like we're gods and they're mere mortals, and I kind of want to tell them that getting older isn't all it's cracked up to be.

"You break first," Robby says. He's already racked up the balls.

I sneak a look at the team's table.

Aidan's hugging Eve. He lets her go and glances around, possibly looking for me. The three of us usually stick together at these things. The whole team is tight, but Conor, Aidan, and I are known as a unit.

Was walking off as soon as Eve showed up childish? Absolutely. I should have said hi to her, at least.

But I'm pissed. Not *at* her, but around her.

I didn't realize how badly I wanted that shot with her. Didn't realize how much hope I'd let accumulate last week.

Not until I saw her sitting with her ex on a coffee date earlier. She had every right to meet him. I thought she needed more time, and maybe space, and so I didn't flat-out tell her how I felt.

And disappointment sucks. Especially *this* type of disappointment.

If we'd lost the championship, it would have felt awful. But I would have known I did everything I could.

I didn't do everything I could, with Eve.

So I need to scowl and sulk and hit something. Expel some of that disappointment. Be selfish, for once, rather than pretend everything's fine.

Robby's distracted, chatting with a brunette who came over to squeeze into one of the booths lining the wall past the pool table.

I shake my head before breaking the balls. I sink the 4 ball into a pocket, then call out, "You're stripes."

Robby hands the girl her phone, then ambles toward me wearing a shit-eating grin to take his turn.

Playing pool with Sampson is a decent distraction. By the time the game ends—I win—my beer glass is empty and I'm ready to go.

Robby's chatting with the brunette again, so I head over to Aidan to let him know I'm done for the night. The walk from here back to our place isn't bad, and I could use some fresh air and silence.

There's no sign of Conor, Harlow, or Eve by our usual table, so they must have moved to another section of the bar.

Aidan's by the television, talking to one of the juniors, Jake Brennan. They caused quite the scene right before the championship game, but they seem to be on good terms again now. Phillips has always been more forgiving than Hart, who holds a grudge better than anyone I've ever met.

Aidan frowns when I tell him I'm leaving. "It's not even nine."

"I know. I'm not feeling great."

Not a lie. I feel like shit. *Cowardly* shit.

Phillips pulls his keys out of his pocket. "I'll drive you."

"You don't need to do that. I'll walk home."

"I'm driving you, man. Let's go."

"What about Hart?"

"Harlow's here, and she drove. She'll drop him, or he'll stay at her place. No biggie. Come on."

Aidan seems determined to drive me, so I stop arguing.

I follow him out of Gaffney's, inhaling a deep breath of damp air. It's warmer than it's been since the very start of senior year, another reminder of May's rapid approach.

One upside of its color: Aidan's truck is always easy to spot. My SUV—which is currently at a local mechanic getting a new tire put on—is practically camouflage by comparison.

"Do you think I could run a place like that?" Phillips asks.

I glance over, confused by the question, but Aidan's eyes are on the road as he pulls out of the parking lot. And it's too dim in the car for me to see much of his expression. "A place like what? Gaffney's?"

"Yeah." His fingers tighten on the wheel briefly. "I have the money to invest in something, and I have—well, I *will* have—a business degree. There's this waitress who works at Gaffney's, Zara, who wants to open a brewery. She actually does it—brews beer. I've tried a couple, they're good…" He clears his throat. "So, you think I'd be any good at it?"

"I think you'd be great at it," I tell him.

Another vehicle's headlights flash through the cab, revealing the smile on Aidan's face. "Yeah?"

"Yeah. I mean, you've basically spent the past four years researching the industry."

He guffaws. "True. Plus, it'll really piss off my parents if I spend my trust fund on a bar."

I've never met Aidan's parents, which says a lot about his relationship with them. And about them, period. Aidan's a really difficult person to piss off, and he could become best friends with a brick wall.

"Where would you open it?" I ask.

"Seattle, probably. There's no way I'm moving back to LA, and Rye—it's serious with her. I don't want to do long distance. Seattle is far enough away I can do my own thing—work, I guess—during the week, but we could still see each other on the weekends."

"That sounds perfect, man. If there's anything I can do to help make it happen, let me know."

"You could come buy a beer, when we open."

"I'll be there, Phillips."

Aidan laughs. "Nah, I'm kidding. First round would be on the house. Friends and family discount. I might make Hart pay, though, depending on the size of his rookie contract."

I smile, then tentatively ask, "You think he'll make it?"

It's a topic we've never discussed. I've talked to Conor about his dream directly, and I'm sure Aidan has too. But he and I never have.

"He deserves to."

"He does," I agree.

"If I'd missed that goal in the championship—if we'd *lost* the fucking championship…"

"I know. But you didn't. We didn't. There's nothing else we could have done. Nothing else we *can* do."

Which is the toughest part. Knowing a bunch of guys in suits are picking apart Hart's stats in a conference room, deliberating whether or not to give him a chance.

"He'll be fine, if he doesn't make it," Aidan tells me. He sounds like he's reassuring himself, as much as me. "His grades are almost as good as yours. And he has Harlow in his corner now. They're so in love it's ridiculous. They'll probably get married before our five-year reunion."

"Five years? I'd guess three. And *ridiculous* is rich, coming from the guy who spent most of spring break kissing his girlfriend in a hot tub."

Phillips grins. "I have no regrets about that. But I am sorry you got stuck as the odd man out. I remember what hanging out with Hart was like after he and Harlow got together. Never meant to make you feel that way."

"Don't worry about it, man. I'm happy for you. And Hart. Yeah, the dynamic is definitely different, but that's life. Things change."

"It worked out well, having Eve there," Aidan comments.

I glance out the window. We're almost home. "Yeah. It did."

"It's Robby's birthday next Sunday," Aidan says, flicking on a blinker to turn down our street. "That's what I was talking to

Brennan about. We were thinking of throwing a party here? I'll run it past Hart, but good with you?"

"Yep," I reply. "Sounds good. Let me know what I can do."

"Will do."

"Thanks for the ride," I say as Aidan pulls into our driveway.

"No problem." He nods, popping his door open. "You feel like watching something?"

I deliberate as we walk toward the front steps. I'm tired, but I doubt I'll actually fall asleep this early. And if I did, I'd probably wake up in the middle of the night. "I'm good for an hour or so."

Phillips grins as we head inside. Which means I doubt I'll get to bed before midnight.

CHAPTER TWENTY-SIX

EVE

"*Please* come," Mary pleads.

"I don't know," I hedge, poking at a tomato with my fork. "Won't it be…weird?"

Mary shakes her head emphatically. "It won't be weird. You said you and Ben are on good terms."

"We're…" I drop my fork and sigh. "We're not on *bad* terms. But we're…it's different now."

"I know," Mary says sympathetically. "But that doesn't mean—"

"Hey, babe. Eve." David Morrison takes the seat next to Mary, kissing her cheek before stealing a potato chip from her plate.

"Hi, David," I greet.

Mary elbows her boyfriend when he steals another chip from her plate. "Go get your own lunch."

"Can't. I've got class in—" David checks his watch. "Eight minutes."

"I was just telling Eve about the plan for Saturday night."

"Oh, yeah? Cool. Should be fun."

"And Eve should come, right?" Mary presses.

David glances at me. "Uh, yep. Definitely."

His response isn't very convincing. But I can't tell if it's because David doesn't care whether I go or not or because he thinks Ben *will* care. I'm friendly with David, more so since he and Mary started dating, but he's definitely Ben's friend, not mine.

David looks at his watch again, curses, and then stands. "I gotta run. See you later, babe." He kisses Mary, then nods toward me. "Nice to see you, Eve."

I muster a smile. "Yeah, you too."

As soon as David walks away, Mary leans forward. "See?"

"Uh-huh. He's *obviously* missed me at movie nights."

Mary rolls her eyes. "Well, *I* want you there. We haven't hung out since before break."

"We're hanging out right now," I point out.

"We're eating lunch. I'm talking about sneaking cheap wine into the theater and listening to the guys go on about film angles while we pretend to care about anything except the shirtless-guy scenes."

My smile comes naturally this time. So does a twinge of nostalgia. "I'll think about it."

"Promise?"

"Promise," I say, then take a bite of salad.

"Hey! I thought that was you."

Rylan appears out of nowhere, stopping right beside our table and smiling at me.

"Hi!" I reply, standing to give her a quick hug. "How are you?"

I haven't seen Rylan since we left California. Seeing her now is an unexpected reminder that spring break happened. As this week has gone by, that trip has felt further and further away.

"Good," she answers cheerfully. "Just grabbing lunch."

"Do you want to sit with us?" I offer.

"I'd love to, but I can't. I have class in a few minutes. It's at the worst time, but at least the professor lets students bring food. Hunter's saving my spot in line. I just saw you and wanted to say hi."

I glance toward the two cash registers. I recognize Hunter's broad shoulders immediately. He's turned, talking to the girl in line behind him.

My stomach lurches unpleasantly when I recognize Holly Johnson. Is she why he disappeared at Gaffney's on Tuesday? The main reason I tagged along when Harlow said she was going to meet Conor at the local bar was because I thought Hunter would be there. And he was, allegedly, although I never saw him. For a guy who made a point of telling me he was single, he lost interest awfully fast.

"I didn't realize you and Hunter had a class together."

Rylan nods. "Some of my credits from BU didn't transfer, so I'm having to retake a few courses outside of my major. I sort of avoided Hunter at first, when I realized he was on the hockey team, but you know how that ended. Thank God, because he's the main reason I'm passing the class." She smiles, then glances at Mary. "Hi! I'm Rylan."

"Oh, sorry," I say, belatedly realizing I never made introductions. "Mary, this is Rylan. Rylan, Mary."

Mary smiles back at Rylan. "Nice to meet you. Are you talking about *Hunter Morgan*?"

Something about the awed way Mary emphasizes Hunter's name makes me want to scowl. I didn't realize her interest in athletes extended beyond basketball players.

"Sure am," Rylan replies. "Do you know him?"

Mary shakes her head. "No. He just…he lived on my floor freshman year. I've kinda had a crush on him ever since."

"You have a boyfriend," I remind Mary.

"I can still look," she retorts.

"I thought you swore off athletes after Clayton Thomas."

Rylan laughs. "Hunter's nothing like the guys on the basketball team. Eve knows."

Mary looks to me, eyebrows raised. As much as I like Rylan, I start to wish she'd never come over here.

Rylan glances toward the café. "I've gotta go. I'll text you, Eve." She smiles at Mary, then hurries back toward the cash registers.

I pick up my soda. "Did you see—"

"What did 'Eve knows' mean?"

Guess we're sticking with this topic.

I shrug, then take a sip. "He's a nice guy."

"Which you know because…"

"What does it matter?"

"I just didn't know you hung out with that crowd."

"What crowd?" I question.

"*That crowd*. The popular jocks."

"Um, *you're* the one who went bowling with Clayton Thomas and Conor Hart."

Mary waves a dismissive hand in my direction. "Yeah, only because you talked Harlow into setting it up. I didn't know *you* knew those guys. Or *Hunter Morgan*."

"Stop saying his name like that."

"Like what?"

"Like he's some type of celebrity."

"Um, what school do you go to? He *is* a celebrity on campus."

I make a vague sound and shove a large bite of salad into my mouth. We've been friends since sophomore year, and I have never heard Mary mention Hunter's name before. And, frankly, this timing couldn't be worse.

"So, how do you know?" she persists.

"Know what?"

"You said you know Hunter isn't a jerk. How do you know?"

I sigh. "Because we spent spring break together, and he was perfectly nice the entire time."

Since then, though…

I shove the thought far away. He *was* nice to me while we were stuck on vacation together. And a few conversations didn't mean he needed to hurry over to say hi to me at Gaffney's. It's possible he never even realized I was there. But I *wanted* him to notice I was there.

Mary gasps. "You *did*?"

"Yeah. I told you Harlow invited me."

"Yeah. *Harlow*. You didn't mention anyone else."

"Oh. Well…" I take another bite of salad. "Conor and his friends were there too."

"And?"

"And Rylan. She's dating one of Conor's teammates."

"*Details*, Eve. What did you guys do? Let me live vicariously."

"Uh, let's see. I got drunk off tequila shots, kissed a surfer named Finn, and then threw up in the bushes in front of everyone. How's that for details?"

"Oh, Eve." Mary's curiosity has morphed into sympathy.

"Yeah. It's fine. I'd had a shitty few days and needed to blow off some steam. I'm all good now."

She glances down and plays with her chips, clearly contemplating saying something.

"Spit it out," I tell her.

"Are you—do you—is there a chance you and Ben will get back together?"

"No," I answer firmly.

"Maine isn't that far from New York. You guys could make it work."

"It's not a question of geography. It's…we weren't right together."

"What are you talking about? You guys were perfect together."

"No." I shake my head. "We weren't."

If Ben told David what happened with Rowan, it doesn't seem like he mentioned it to Mary. I doubt Mary would be asking at all if she knew that Ben mourned our breakup by sleeping with his best friend.

Mary bites her bottom lip. "Are you sure you're not just saying that because you're…upset about everything?"

"I'm sure," I assure her. "I'm—I'm not *in love* with him, Mary. And honestly, I'm not sure if I ever really was. I loved him, but not the way I should have. I never got giddy around Ben. I never lay awake at night and replayed our conversations. When we broke up, my first thought was about New York and how *our* plan had become *my* plan."

Mary bites her bottom lip. "I just want you to be happy, Eve. I understand things feel different now, after what happened, but think about this weekend, okay? We only have so much time left, and you never know. Maybe things will work out if you spend more time together."

I nod, because that's simpler than telling Mary the reason I'm certain Ben and I will never get back together.

The reason I'm second-guessing if I've ever been in love.

The reason that's following Rylan out of the café.

CHAPTER TWENTY-SEVEN

HUNTER

Aidan and Conor are both sitting in the kitchen when I walk inside.

"Finally!" Aidan crows when he spots me. He squints at the schedules on the fridge. "Diplomacy, Crisis, and War in the Modern Era ended two hours ago. Where have you been?"

"I was in the library," I answer, pulling a container of leftover pasta out of the fridge. "I just came home for some dinner and my laptop charger, then I'm headed back."

"The library?" Aidan looks aghast. Prior to his tutoring arrangement, I'm pretty sure he had no clue where the library was located on campus. "It's *Friday night*."

"Yeah, and I've got to turn in my thesis presentation on Tuesday."

"Yeah, and that leaves Monday to get it done."

I snort as the microwave beeps, pulling my steaming pasta out. "You sure you only failed the one class, Phillips?"

Aidan flips me off as I blow on a bite. "I *un*failed, dick. Come on. The lacrosse team won their first game of the season earlier. They're throwing a party at Willis's tonight."

"Good for them."

"Good for *us*. When was the last time we all went to a party together?"

"The Thursday before break," I reply.

Conor rolls his eyes. "That was a rhetorical question, Morgan."

"How about you come tonight, and then I won't make fun of you for spending the weekend in the library?" Aidan suggests.

"You and Hart go," I tell him. "Bring your girlfriends."

"Harlow went home for the weekend, and Rylan has a family thing with her parents."

"Ah, right."

I forgot Conor mentioned Harlow was leaving this weekend, and Rylan's unavailability explains Aidan's availability.

"Don't be like that, man. Hart and I are offering to be your wingmen. When was the last time you got laid?"

I continue shoving pasta into my mouth, hoping Aidan will have moved on to another topic by the time I finish dinner.

"Rylan said Holly was flirting with you in the café yesterday," he says.

I hide a grimace. Getting stuck in a conversation with Holly while Rylan went over to chat with Eve was uncomfortable for multiple reasons. Holly *was* flirty while returning my notes, and I don't know why, because I thought we were in agreement after our disastrous date. Also, Rylan leaving me in line to say hi to Eve meant *I* couldn't leave the line to say hi to Eve and try to make up for avoiding her at Gaffney's.

Aidan and Conor are both staring at me expectantly, waiting for some sort of a reply.

I like Rylan and Harlow, consider them both friends, but a definite downside of hanging out with them is that they remember —and share—details my friends wouldn't know otherwise.

"I'll find out if she's going to be at Willis's tonight," Phillips decides.

"Don't," I tell Aidan around a mouthful of penne.

He sighs and sets his phone down. "Rylan said one of her roommates—Chloe, I think—is single."

"Dude, she's a junior," Conor says.

"So?" Aidan challenges. "What's wrong with being a junior?"

I swallow the last bite of pasta and set the empty glass container in the sink. They can do the dishes while they play matchmaker. "If I get enough done tonight, I'll go out with you guys tomorrow night. But because you're my best friends. Not because I want you to find me a girlfriend."

Hart frowns. "I thought you wanted a relationship. Isn't that why you went out with Holly?"

I can't explain to Conor that I lost interest in dating Holly—in dating anyone—as soon as Eve ran into me in the hallway and the words *My boyfriend and I just broke up* left her mouth. Or I could, I guess, if I wanted pity stares and for my best friends to physically drag me out tonight.

"I've got other priorities right now," I say instead. "Have fun at the lax party."

I head upstairs for my laptop charger, and then back outside without stopping in the kitchen. Hart's persistent and Phillips is stubborn. Chances are, they'd lasso me into going out with them.

I *do* need to get this presentation finished, but the main reason I'm avoiding going out tonight is that I'm simply not in the mood. I still feel strange about things with Eve.

At some point soon, I need to get over my disappointment. I got past missing my chance with Eve once—sort of. I'll get over it again—for good this time.

Unsurprisingly, the parking lot closest to the library is practically empty. Fridays—particularly Friday nights—are not the most popular time to hang out in the library.

I prefer it like this. You don't have to go up to one of the quiet floors to be able to focus. The first floor, where normal noise level is allowed, is almost completely silent.

I walk through the lobby, pausing to fill up my water bottle at the fountain, and then turn left. The windows at the far end overlook the main quad of campus, lit up by the lamps that line the brick walkways. It's very collegiate-looking. And, call me a nerd, but I've always loved school. I like learning new things and I like the challenge of applying that knowledge to different situations.

Once I near the windows I start scanning the tables, looking for a spot to sit.

My steps slow as soon as I spot her. I blink rapidly, like I might possibly be imagining the sight.

She's at the table I usually choose, right past the Greek mythology section. I took a classical mythology course sophomore year and had to write a paper on Hades. Since the books all weighed a ridiculous amount, sitting nearby made sense. It's farther away from most of the traffic on the first floor on busier days and has a clear view out the windows, so sitting there has stuck.

I swallow and swerve in that direction.

Eve doesn't see me coming. She's focused on her laptop, lips moving silently as she scans the screen open in front of her. She's wearing glasses, which I've never seen her wear before.

Every time I see Eve, I notice something different about her appearance. Even after this past week, when I got to steal a lot of looks. Today, in addition to the glasses, it's the green ribbon tying together the end of her braid.

She still doesn't glance up when I reach the table, so I tap the chair across from her.

Eve jumps, her elbow nearly spilling her water bottle all over the keyboard.

"Sorry," I say.

I'm apologizing for more than startling her.

This time, she doesn't tell me not to.

"Hi." Eve sits up straight. Her tongue swipes her lower lip, wetting it nervously. She lifts one hand and tugs on the end of the ribbon in her hair. It flutters to the table.

She says nothing else.

My grip on the chair back tightens. "Hey. Can I sit with you?"

Eve glances at the sea of empty tables surrounding us. "There are lots of other options."

The tightness in her tone is new. Eve sounds…*angry*. Angry at *me*. I've never even heard Eve annoyed before.

Absurdly, it makes me want to smile. Because Eve and I haven't spoken since spring break. So, if she's mad at me, she's bothered by that.

I rest my elbows on the back of the chair, leaning a little closer. "I don't want other options, Eve."

She blushes. And fuck, if I haven't missed that sight. Her cheeks weren't pink when she was getting coffee with Ben.

"You can sit. But I have a lot to get done."

I pull the chair out. "I have a lot to get done too."

She watches me get settled, opening my laptop and plugging in the charger.

"Cute glasses," I comment, pulling out the folder that has my notes.

Eve reaches up and fiddles with them. "They're for blue light," she explains. "I get headaches after looking at screens. Although…" She glances at the computer. "I think it might be the work giving me a headache, not the screen."

"What are you working on?"

"An essay for my Poetics of Narrative class. My advisor wouldn't let me take only art classes, and it sounded interesting. Interpretive."

"Is it?"

Her nose wrinkles, lifting her glasses a little. "I guess? The discussions are interesting, but this was the prompt for our first paper, and it's worth *half* of our final grade." She shoves a sheet toward me, sounding stressed.

"'Analyze the significance of a pivotal turning point in a story and compare it in three different literary works, exploring its impact in contrasting narrative forms,'" I read aloud. "What the fuck does *contrasting narrative forms* mean?"

"I don't know. I met with the professor, but left more confused. And if *you* can't figure it out, then I'm really screwed."

I smile. "What does that mean?"

"It means you're *smart*, Mr. I Got In To Every School I Applied To."

"You're smart, Eve. And you're the one who's actually taking the class."

"If only that was helpful." She takes the paper back. "What are you working on?"

"My senior thesis presentation. It's due Tuesday."

"What's your thesis about?"

"The impact criminalizing Schedule II substances has on government policy and public perception."

"Wow. Big topic."

"Yeah," I agree. "It is."

Eve doesn't ask why I chose it, which I'm grateful for. I'm not sure I'd lie to her, but I don't feel like discussing Sean either.

She refocuses on her work. I follow her studious lead, reviewing slides and making changes. I'm about three-quarters through my presentation when I hear Eve swear under her breath.

I glance up. "Something wrong?"

She's scowling at the screen. "My laptop died and I forgot to bring a charger." She pushes her glasses to the top of her head and then rubs her eyes.

"You can borrow mine," I offer. I've been here an hour, so my computer will last a while if I unplug.

"No, it's fine. I need a break anyway. I'll finish it tomorrow."

I can't think of a single reason to ask her to stay, aside from that I want her to. But she probably has plans with Ben. If Harlow's out of town, she has their place to herself.

I shove thoughts of what that could mean far, far away.

Eve shuts her laptop. Exhales, before she asks, "Why did you sit here, Hunter?"

She sounds angry again.

"Because I wanted to," I answer honestly.

"*Why* did you want to?" she presses.

"Why did you get back together with him?" I retort.

The irritation bleeds out of Eve's expression. She blinks rapidly. "What?"

"Your ex. *Ben*. Aren't you back together with him?"

"I—no. *No*. Why would you think that?"

No. That might be my new favorite word.

Relief hits me like a cascade of falling bricks. "I saw you getting coffee with him on Monday. You guys looked... I just assumed..."

"I ran into him on my *way* to get a coffee. He asked to talk and I couldn't think of a good excuse not to fast enough, and then...we're definitely not—he wanted to tell me he had sex with someone else over break." She shakes her head.

More relief hits. And then her words fully register.

"He had sex with someone else over break?"

"Yep." Eve plays with the ribbon on the table. "Sure didn't

waste any time. Guess I'm not the only one who thought our sex life was boring." She blushes, then glances around at the empty tables surrounding us to make sure no one else is in earshot. "Or maybe I'm just bad at it."

"You're not bad at sex."

Eve raises one eyebrow. "How do *you* know?"

"Because you're bad at bowling."

She laughs. Loudly enough that if anyone was in earshot, they would have looked this way.

"That's mean." She's smiling as she says it.

I shrug. "I don't make the rules."

"You had four strikes. Does that mean you're bad in bed?"

"Every rule has its exceptions."

Eve tilts her head, shooting me a teasing smile. "Or you just want to think so."

"Wanna find out?"

I hold my breath, waiting for her reply.

"Yes."

I changed my mind.

That's my new favorite word.

CHAPTER TWENTY-EIGHT

EVE

There's a knock on the door while I'm toweling off.

Crap. He's early again. Or—I glance at the alarm clock on my bedside table—exactly on time.

I keep digging through the drawer in a frantic quest for the black lace thong that's the sexiest underwear I own. I finally locate them with a triumphant "Aha!" that dims to a vehement "Ow!" when my victory dance ends with a stubbed toe.

Another knock, and I'm naked except for a scrap of lace. Which is actually *more* than I need to be wearing for what's about to happen, but I'm not brave enough to answer the door in my towel—or underwear. With my luck, Mr. Goodman would be out in his yard with his dog.

I grab the sweats and oversize T-shirt I wore to bed last night off my comforter and yank them on. Not the most enticing outfit, but I don't have time to pick out anything else. Shaving *every-where* took too long.

I toss a heap of laundry into the closet, slam the door closed, and then hustle down the hallway.

I'm breathing heavily when I yank the front door open, then

stop breathing entirely, the full weight of this moment slamming into me like an avalanche.

I'm about to have sex with Hunter Morgan. If my freshman year–self could see me now.

"Hey." Hunter's smile is almost…shy, as he shoves his hands into his pockets. He's changed since leaving the library, into sweats and a hoodie with *Holt Hockey* written on the front. His hair glints in the porch light, damp even though it's not raining for once.

"Hey," I breathe.

We stare at each other, and I wonder how many times he's done this before. I know very little about Hunter's dating-slash-hookup history in college, which seems extremely unfair since he knows all of mine. *I'm* a nervous mess, but I was expecting him to take the lead here. To act like showing up at a girl's house for sex is a normal Friday for him.

Hunter raises a hand to rub the back of his neck, tugging his hoodie up a few inches. My mouth goes dry as I focus on that strip of exposed skin. On the glimpse of his obliques and the line of golden hair that disappears into the waistband of his sweats. My gaze moves lower, to the bulge below the waistband, the glimpses of his penis I got in the shower and the hot tub flashing in my mind like a neon sign.

Heat pools, low in my stomach, settling right between my thighs. My breasts feel heavy and achy, reminding me I ran out of time to put a bra on. My breasts are big enough to make that obvious, even if my nipples weren't hardened to horny peaks.

"Can I come in?" Hunter asks.

Warmth floods my cheeks when I realize I've just been standing and staring at him. "Oh, yeah. Come in." I take a step back, holding the door open as wide as the hinges will allow.

He chuckles. A rough sound that sends another bolt of heat surging through me.

I inhale deeply as he passes. He smells very masculine, mixed with a whiff of laundry detergent, and I think that plus his wet hair means his stop at home involved showering and putting on clean clothes.

That consideration triples the nerves.

I shut and lock the front door, then spin around to face him. Hunter's standing by the bookcase, studying the painting hanging next to it. "Did you paint this?" he asks, not looking away from the wall.

I swallow before walking over. "Uh, yeah. It's supposed to be my mom's hair salon."

The painting is a collection of colorful shampoo bottles, mixed with few spiky cacti and one candle. All sights I associate with home. Before she could afford to rent a chair at a salon, my mom used to see clients in our apartment. Most days when I came home from school, there was a woman sitting in our living room getting highlights or her bangs trimmed. And since we didn't have a yard, my mom would buy me plants. Succulents, and then cacti, when it became obvious I have whatever the opposite of a green thumb is.

"Do you want anything to drink?" I offer.

He's still staring at my painting, and I feel as self-conscious as I did when he was looking at my sketch in the living room of the rental.

"Sure, water sounds good."

"Coming right up." I head into the kitchen, and Hunter follows me.

The bowl of yogurt and granola I made before realizing I didn't have time to eat *and* shower is sitting out on the counter. I forgot to stick it in the fridge before hustling to the bathroom.

"Late dinner?" Hunter asks, spotting it.

"Just a snack," I say, grabbing a glass out of the cabinet and filling it with water before setting it down in front of him.

"Thanks." He glances at the bowl. "You gonna eat?"

"Oh. No. I'm good." I grab the bowl and stick it in the fridge.

When I turn back around, Hunter is watching me. "You can eat, Eve. I'm not in a rush."

Yeah, there's *no way* I'll be able to stand here and eat while he's a few feet away. When we're about to have sex.

"I'm good. I just brushed my teeth."

One corner of his mouth kicks up in that almost-smile that he flashes a lot more freely than a full one. "I like the taste of yogurt and granola."

My cheeks burn. Based on the way Hunter's lips move a half inch higher, he noticed my blush.

My pulse picks up, hammering wildly in my fingertips and especially in that wet, secret spot, and it'll be a miracle if I make it through tonight without having a heart attack. I'm freaking out just from the suggestion that Hunter's going to find out what I *taste* like. That he's going to kiss me soon.

I want this. I want this so badly it feels like I'm living in a hallucination of some wild fantasy that's far removed from reality. And I'm scared. Terrified, actually, that I won't be what Hunter expects.

"I'm not hungry," I manage to say.

"Okay." He picks up the glass of water I poured and drains it in one sip.

I watch the cords of his throat work as he swallows, mesmerized by the smooth motion.

I find Hunter fascinating. I always have. He's a puzzle I haven't solved. One I don't have most of the pieces to. Everything I learn about him prompts more questions.

The empty glass lands on the counter with a soft tap, and then he's walking toward me.

Before I can speak, before I can become more nervous than I already am, he's cupping my jaw with one hand. Sweeping a calloused thumb across my cheek and sliding his fingers into my hair. And then, his warm mouth is covering mine with a perfect pressure it feels like I've waited an eternity to experience.

I've spent an embarrassing—and guilt-inducing, before my breakup—amount of time wondering what kissing Hunter might be like. Considering I can't stand near the guy without worrying about self-combustion, it seemed like a dangerous prospect.

Turns out it is.

This *is what a first kiss is supposed to feel like*, some distant corner of my mind decides.

And I no longer have anything to feel guilty about. For the first time since that awful night at La Bella Napoli, I'm *thrilled* about being single. That gaping terror of being alone doesn't feel big or scary. It's freeing, like I shed a weight I didn't realize I was carrying.

Maybe because I've never felt so safe.

Hunter makes a deep, sexy groan in the back of his throat when I start kissing him back. It vibrates on my tongue, sending shivers dancing down my spine as I press closer to him and seek out more contact.

My overwhelmed brain isn't doing a great job of remembering any make-out tips. I give up quickly, attempting to mimic Hunter instead.

He's an *excellent* kisser. Right angle, perfect amount of tongue. When he tugs my lower lip between his teeth, I moan so loudly I shock myself.

What feels like a full smile curls against my lips, and I'm annoyed our mouths are so close I missed it.

His hands land on my hips, squeezing once. "Where's your bedroom, Eve?"

"This—this way." I break out of his light hold, stumbling down the hallway like I'm failing a sobriety test.

I am drunk. Just not on any substance. On him.

I'm still nervous. *Very* nervous. But it's now mixed with an overdose of lust and anticipation, which is an intoxicating combination.

He kisses me again in my bedroom, and I stumble back against my dresser. Hard wood is literally the only reason I'm staying vertical.

"Mint's good too," he tells me when our lips separate for a necessary breath.

I'm blushing again, even though him tasting my mouth is no longer a hypothetical. His eyes dance as he looks at my red cheeks, more animated than I've ever seen them. Darkened with amusement and—I hope—arousal.

Our eyes hold for a few seconds, the entertainment in his slowing and then going still. "You're sure you want to do this?"

He's really asking. It's not an empty offer. If I said no, I'm positive Hunter would walk away and never mention this night again.

But I don't have to think about my answer. "I really want to do this."

Hunter nods, something that looks remarkably like relief flashing across his handsome face before I'm spun around and tossed onto the comforter. *Tossed.* He picks me up like I weigh nothing and I land, sprawled on the soft mattress, a second later.

My heart is beating so fast I'm not even sure there are separate beats. It feels like one endless pulse pumping adrenaline through my body.

I'm still registering the sudden change in position when he

tugs my sweatpants down. One firm yank, and they're a ball of fabric on the floor.

I gasp when a gust of cooler air hits the wet spot on my underwear—lace isn't known for its absorbance—and clamp my thighs together.

Hunter instantly hesitates.

I open my knees a few inches, gnawing on the inside of my cheek as a wave of self-consciousness swallows me. He can't see everything, but he can see *a lot*, and spread out half naked in front of your crush is a very vulnerable position to be in.

Hunter swallows twice before speaking. He's not touching me, just staring. "You still good?"

"Yeah. Good." In a humiliating turn of events, my voice cracks. Right between the *Go* and the *od*, an abyss I wish I could disappear into. If he had any questions about my limited sexual experience, I think this is answering them. I clear my throat. "Just a little cold."

"Cold, huh?"

Hunter's hand lands on my bent knee, thumb tracing circles, and tiny shockwaves dance across the surface of my skin.

His palm slides higher. Higher. *Higher*, until he's toying with the flimsy scrap of lace sitting on my right hip. He hooks it with one finger, then reverses course back down my thigh.

The left side hangs on for a few seconds, then slips too.

His jaw tightens when another wave of cool air hits wetness, letting me know I'm naked from the waist down. That's his only reaction as he pulls my thong down to my toes, and I'm not sure if that's a good or a bad thing.

The charged atmosphere between us crackles with a new intensity as my underwear join my sweatpants.

I should say something. Like *I showed you mine, now show me yours* or *Need me to talk you through it?* Something teasing and sexy. But I've never been *that girl*. The one who always knows what to do or say. The one who's seductive and smooth.

So I simply look up at him, my mouth so dry I doubt I could speak anyway.

"Eve…" He utters my name like a prayer, tone a little reverent and a lot awed, and some of the self-consciousness recedes.

My legs widen another few inches, my calf no longer blocking my view of his crotch. The bulge is bigger than it was when I checked his dick out earlier, and seeing that reaction helps my confidence too.

"It's short for Evelyn," I whisper.

He half smiles again. "Yeah?"

"Yeah," I reply, resenting the side of his mouth that stays flat. I want to see his full grin.

"Hunter isn't short for anything," he tells me.

A surprised laugh bursts out. "I figured."

He nods, half smile still in place, and then his head ducks down.

I don't realize what he's doing until the first swipe of his tongue parts my slit.

"Fuck" slips through my surprised lips, because it feels *good*. His fingers dig into my upper right thigh, holding me spread wide, his other hand lifting my left leg and resting it on his broad shoulder. His tongue circles my opening with teasing licks, then his lips close around my clit and suck.

I swear again—a *lot* louder. The sudden assault of pleasure is startling. It feels like I'm floating, my only anchor the spots buzzing from his touch. The familiar surroundings of my bedroom are a blur of color, the sparks skittering across my vision otherworldly.

This is what it's supposed to feel like? Oral sex has never been unpleasant, but it has mostly felt like wet lapping. A nudge of pleasure that faded quickly. Not the inferno that's blazing now.

Hunter's tongue is stroking with the same skilled focus he kissed my mouth with, and I realize… I'm not going to have to fake an orgasm.

I'm *fighting* to keep the pressure from shattering, because I want to memorize how this peak feels before I fall. It's a shimmering bubble I want to remain in forever.

Hunter's grip on my thigh relaxes, his mouth moving higher and his fingers filling former emptiness. My back arches when he starts to fuck me with two fingers, my inner muscles clutching at them greedily.

I only last three pumps before losing the battle. I come calling his name, strong convulsions wracking my entire body as my toes flex and my fingers fist the comforter so tightly my knuckles turn white.

It doesn't stop. Doesn't fade after a few seconds. The waves of bliss don't disappear until my muscles are shaking and my throat feels raw. Even then, I can still feel the faint echo of pleasure in lingering twitches.

I'm still panting, still stunned, when Hunter raises his head. His lips and chin are glossy with the evidence of my arousal. He smirks at my slack expression, running a tongue along his bottom lip before resting a knee on the bed. The mattress beside my hip dips as he joins me, springs squeaking softly.

"Still cold?" he asks casually.

I manage a "No" between pants as he sprawls out beside me, fully clothed. "Um, thanks."

When I gather enough energy to glance over, he's smiling at the ceiling. "You're welcome."

Well, aren't we polite.

I'm waiting for him to make another move, but he seems content to relax on my bed.

I wasn't expecting him to go down on me. If I'd known he was planning to, I would have told him not to bother, since it's always ended with disappointment and embarrassment on both sides. I thought we'd come in here, have sex, and then he'd leave.

Be brave, Eve.

I sit up, which is harder than it's ever been before. My muscles are languid and loose, completely uncooperative. My limbs feel like limp, overcooked noodles. I could have just woken up from a coma.

Hunter's head rolls to look at me, his blue eyes alert and assessing. They darken to near-navy as I straddle his hips, the ridge of his erection reigniting the needy ache he just alleviated.

"Do you have a condom?" I ask.

He nods. "In my pocket." His hands grasp the hem of my shirt and lift, skimming my ribs so the fabric bunches beneath my boobs. "Take this off."

His voice is low and husky, yet still manages to sound author-itative.

I yank my shirt the rest of the way off. As soon as it's gone, Hunter cups my breasts in his broad hands.

I lean into his touch. The swells that have often seemed too large settle perfectly in his palms. His thumbs play with the points of my nipples, managing to make the throb feel better and worse.

"They look even better like this than they did in that Beatles shirt," he says.

I smile, glance at my shirt, and then frown. There's no logo on it.

"Not tonight. Freshman year."

I stare at him sprawled on my mattress, stunned. "You've been thinking about my boobs for four years?"

"Not *just* your tits. But yeah."

I reach into his pocket, propelled by a fresh sense of this urgency. This *need* is new to me. It's a desperation that's deeper than physical desire.

The heat of his skin sears through the pocket's thin fabric. Hunter's thigh is hard and firm, thick muscles tensing beneath my touch as my fingers close around a foil packet.

I've never put a condom on a guy before, even though I've never had sex without one. That's what happens when you're raised by a single mother who got pregnant at sixteen, I guess. When it comes to sex, I've never felt like there was such a thing as *too careful*. I've thought *Was that worth getting pregnant over?* after sex. Tracked my cycle so I knew exactly which days I was ovulating. I have plenty of unhealthy hang-ups about physical intimacy—maybe emotional intimacy too—that I try to ignore most of the time.

But I've never been less aware of them than I am right now. Rolling the condom over Hunter's dick has nothing to do with safe sex. I want to touch him this intimately. To memorize the shape of what's about to be inside of me.

I scoot backward so I'm sitting on his thighs. My grip on the foil packet is getting sweaty, so I drop the condom on my comforter and use both hands to work the elastic waistbands of his boxers and sweats down his hips.

Some of my courage withers when I get my first glimpse of his bare erection.

I saw his size before, during Dickgate. But that was a quick peek in a motel bathroom's shitty lighting. And he wasn't hard.

I reach out slowly, trailing my fingers along the soft skin pulled so taut it looks shiny. The tip *is* shiny, flushed an angry purplish red.

This is *for me. Because of me.*

Hunter grunts when I fist the flared head, pre-cum smearing my palm.

"I know this sounds like a porn line," I start, and his eyebrows lift with interest. "But are you *sure* it's going to fit? Because I'm…not."

His chest rumbles with a low laugh. "Yeah. It's going to fit."

"You don't sound worried."

He smirks. "I'm not."

"Well, *I* am. I have a *really* low pain tolerance." My first time hurt like hell, and Dean Ackerman's dick was half the size of Hunter's.

But I pick up the condom and tear the wrapper open, because that isn't enough of a deterrent. Because I trust Hunter.

He groans when I roll the condom down the thick length of his erection. I can feel the raised vein pulsing through the thin layer of latex.

"I'm going to try to make this last," he tells me as he sits up. "But it's been a while."

Talking takes me a minute, because he's just yanked his hoodie off. His blond hair is boyishly mussed, but his body is all man.

I know hockey is a physical sport. Know athletes work hard to keep their bodies in peak condition. But I've never been on a bed with someone in this sort of shape, and it… Honestly, it's a massive turn-on. There's some primal part of me that loves how *masculine* Hunter looks. How soft his hardness makes me feel. How safe his strength makes me feel.

"How long?" I ask, a little breathlessly, as I shift onto the mattress so Hunter can pull his sweats the rest of the way down.

"November."

"*November?*" He hasn't had sex since *last year*? I thought he was going to say a few weeks, at most.

"I was focused on hockey," he tells me, tossing his sweatpants on the floor. "This season was our last chance to win a championship."

"That's a lot of dedication," I comment.

"I'm a dedicated guy." A strange shadow passes across his face after he says it.

I'm distracted by him moving over me. We're both completely naked, and I start moaning from the first glide of his cock through the slickness between my thighs.

All thoughts of possible pain disappear as he teases me, only giving me an inch or two at a time before withdrawing. *I'm* the one wriggling and begging, trying to lift my hips and take him deeper.

His hands move from massaging my breasts to squeezing my hips. And then move lower, cupping my thighs, lifting my legs up, and then shifting me so that I'm basically folded in half. The center of my body is on full display to him.

"Can you take me like this?" he asks.

I nod quickly—I'd agree to any position right now—and he chuckles.

And then he thrusts, the burn of my leg muscles stretching fading in comparison to the way my pussy is parting to accommodate him. It's not pleasant, but he was right. It doesn't hurt. And my body is adjusting, widening with each tiny pulse of his hips as he works his way inside. He hits a spot that makes me gasp, already knowing my body better than I do.

I slept with two guys in high school. One, I dated for a few months. The other was a drunken fumbling at a party the summer before I left for Holt. Then, I met Ben, and at some point I concluded I'd had sex for the last first time.

I've always enjoyed sex, aside from my first time.

But I'm realizing I've never been *fucked* before.

And I'm learning that sex can be more than *enjoyable*.

It can be this maelstrom of sensation—electricity and desperation and feeling like you might *die* if it stops. A flood of feelings that fills you up so there's no space for anything else. No thoughts. No fears. No worries. No dreams.

The one thing I'm aware of right now—not my name, not any fears of getting pregnant, not any insecurity about how I compare to other girls he's been with—is that I was right about Hunter.

Whatever unconscious draw that's existed since the first moment I saw him? *I was right.*

Reality is supposed to be subpar to fantasy.

But I'm worried Hunter just ruined me for anyone else.

CHAPTER TWENTY-NINE

HUNTER

I wake up confused.

Confused why I'm wearing sweatpants when I normally sleep in my boxers. Confused why there's someone in my bed. Confused why my alarm is going off and the room is dark.

I squint at the source of light, my stomach sinking and my confusion clearing when I get a good look at the phone screen.

I'm in Eve's bed. And it's not my alarm going off.

I roll off her mattress as quickly and as quietly as I can. Eve shifts but doesn't seem to wake up. I grab my phone and hustle down the hallway into the living room, answering the call as I sink down on the couch.

"Hello?" I croak, reaching over to turn on a lamp and then rubbing at my tired eyes.

"Hey, little brother."

It's silent in the background, for once. But that only makes the happy hike in his words more obvious. Makes the false cheer that's chemically induced sound louder.

"Where are you, Sean?" I ask.

"Home," he answers simply.

Last I knew, he was renting an apartment a town over from Casper. But I say, "And where's that?" because I'm not even sure if he still lives there.

"I didn't call you so that you'd call Dad, Hunter."

"Then why did you call?"

"Just to say hi," he tells me cheerfully.

"You called to say hi in the middle of the night, while you're *high*? What the fuck, Sean?"

"I wasn't sure if you'd pick up any other time."

Because he only ever calls me when he's high.

"I always pick up. I always fucking *pick up*. And then I have to call Dad, wake him up and worry him, just so that I know you're not lying in a ditch somewhere with a needle in your arm!"

There's a pause. Then, "I stopped doing heroin."

I scoff. Rake a hand through my hair. "But you kept doing something else. You have no fucking clue what it's been like, Sean. For me. For Mom and Dad. How fucking selfish can you be, putting us through the same shit over and over and over again?"

My brother is silent as I rant.

I never *talk* during these brief conversations. They're mostly me asking questions, trying to assess what's happening and how I should respond before he hangs up. But if Sean is telling the truth about being home—and I'm choosing to believe him because I don't know what else to do at this point—then he doesn't need to be dragged out of some shady situation. He's not on the cusp of another poor decision he needs to be pulled away from. He's as safe as he can be in one of these situations, and I finally have the opportunity to speak.

Or maybe I've just given up on rescuing him.

"Don't fucking call me high again."

I toss my phone onto the cushion next to me without bothering to hang up, breathing heavily. My heart is pounding like I just got back from a hard run.

I pinch the bridge of my nose as I release a long exhale. My eyes feel hot; my throat thick.

"Are you okay?"

My head snaps up. Eve's hovering at the end of the hallway, the heel of one foot propped against her ankle casually, like she's prepared to stand in that spot for a while.

"Not really," I answer honestly.

She nods like that was the response she expected.

And oddly, that's the reaction I wanted. I'm accustomed to always being the guy people expect to be okay. I'm on time and I'm prepared and I'm capable and I don't fall apart. It's freeing to admit that's not always the case. And even more of a relief not to have the exposure of cracks be met with surprise that they exist.

"Want some tea?" Eve asks.

"Uh, sure."

She nods, then disappears into the kitchen. I collapse back against the soft pillows, glancing at my phone. It landed screen down, so I flip it over. The call has ended.

Sean hung up.

I thought going off on him would make me feel better. But I don't. I feel worse, actually.

Eve returns a minute later, carrying two steaming mugs. She passes me one that smells like peppermint.

"Thank you," I tell her.

"No problem." She sits, cross-legged, on the opposite side of the couch, leaving a couple of feet between us. Blows on her tea. "Woke up and thought maybe you snuck out on me."

"I wouldn't do that. I just—"

"It's fine, Hunter. I was kidding." Eve takes a hasty sip of her tea, then winces. "I'm gonna get some ice."

She hops up before I can offer to get it for her, returning a minute later with a cup full of frozen cubes. She plops two in her mug, then offers it to me.

I take one, then stare at the rapidly melting blob bobbing on the surface. "My brother is a drug addict."

A sentence I've never said aloud before. I've never talked about Sean with anyone at Holt, and everyone back home already knew everything. Hard to keep something like that a secret in a small town.

"It started in high school, with oxy. He broke his leg playing hockey. Had a rough recovery and too much downtime. It was all downhill from there. With school, with sports, with drugs. I barely recognize him anymore."

"I'm so sorry, Hunter."

I try a sip of the tea. It's good. Minty.

"I grew up known as Sean Morgan's little brother. I was always trying to be exactly like him. Dress like him, which was easy wearing his hand-me-downs. Act like him. Sean was popular and smart and charming and a hell of a hockey player. He's the only reason I started playing." My eyes remain on my mug, rolling the ceramic cylinder between my palms. "My parents and I have done interventions. They've paid for rehab three times. Nothing sticks. It's like knocking on a front door and no one's home. He…he only calls me when he's high, in the middle of the night. I should probably stop answering, but…"

"But he's your brother."

I glance at Eve. She's holding her mug, knees tucked up under her chin now. She looks sad—and sympathetic—but there's no sign of the pity I'm greeted by every time I go home. "Yeah, exactly. But he's my brother."

"I'm sorry, Hunter," she tells me again.

I get that helpless feeling of not knowing what to say. There's no easy response to hard situations.

"Thanks."

She doesn't break eye contact. Neither do I.

"Do you have any siblings?" I ask.

Her lips twist in a grimace so slight I almost miss it. "Uh… yeah."

"You don't sound sure."

Eve plays with the string attached to her tea bag. "My dad and his wife have two kids. My mom and her boyfriend had a baby right before I left for college. Her boyfriend, John, has a daughter from a previous relationship that he has full custody of. So I have four siblings, I guess, but I sort of feel like an only child. I'm not close with any of them. In age or…otherwise."

"I'm sorry, Eve."

"Yeah. It sucks, sometimes." She leans forward and tilts her mug toward mine. "Cheers to messy families."

For some reason, I'm certain she's thinking about the last time we did a *cheers*.

It makes me smile, a feat that's normally impossible after a call from Sean. "To messy families." There's a soft clink when the ceramic connects. "Sorry for waking you up."

"You didn't. I'm having to redo a painting project, so I've been in the studio really late the past few nights. I'm on a wacky sleep schedule."

I glance at the painting by the bookcase. She's *really* good. I don't know shit about art. But Eve's work is striking. Creative and compelling. The sort of sight that stops you in your tracks.

"Why are you redoing a project?"

"It didn't turn out right the first time. I was…indecisive."

I nod, then drain the rest of my tea and grab my phone. "I should, uh, probably get going. Since I'm already up."

Before falling asleep, I set my alarm for seven. Neither Aidan nor Conor were home when I stopped by after the library before coming here. They must have gone to the lax party, so I doubt either of them will be up early, but I'd rather not have to explain where I spent the night.

I'm not ready to tell them about Eve. I don't even know what there is to tell. We're graduating in a matter of weeks. I haven't decided where I'll be headed in the fall. And it feels massively presumptuous to ask Eve if she's open to a long-distance relationship after one night together. Now that I know she's not back together with her ex, that they're not *going* to get back together, it feels like I have a little more time.

Eve nods too, setting her mug on the coffee table right next to a stack of marine biology textbooks. "Right. Yeah, of course."

I hook a thumb in the direction of her bedroom. "Just going to grab my sweatshirt."

"I think it's by my desk," she says before heading into the kitchen with our empty mugs.

Eve turned a lamp on when she got up. The bed—and our jumbled clothes—are bathed by a soft glow as I grab my sweatshirt off the floor and tug it on.

Her sketchbook is sitting on top of her desk, open to a clean page. I grab a pen out of the cup on her desk and scribble my number on the blank sheet. I have Eve's number from Conor, but since I never texted her, she doesn't have mine.

When I return to the living room, she's waiting by the doorway that leads to their front door. Foot propped against her ankle again.

"So, what's the verdict?" I ask, sticking my hands in the front pocket of my hoodie.

Her forehead wrinkles. "Verdict?"

"You know. Am I good at bowling and sex?"

"Oh." She huffs the syllable, then rolls her eyes.

I know the answer. She came three times. And she doesn't have to admit it. I just enjoy teasing her.

I reach out, running my thumb along her jaw before tilting her chin up.

When Eve's eyes meet mine, they're surprised. I think she expected me to rush out of here after Sean's call.

I'm still in a weird headspace from it, honestly. A little startled by my own behavior. By the realization that I have a breaking point. And not just with my brother.

Eve holds the power to wreck me, and I'm fairly certain she has no idea.

Like now, when she bites her bottom lip.

My thumb moves higher, pulling it free from her teeth.

"I think about kissing you every damn time you do that," I confess.

Her eyes widen. And then she tilts her head. Bites her lip again.

"Do it," she whispers.

It's been a long time since I kissed a girl *just* to kiss her. There's usually an expectation of something else to come later. But this—now—I just *want* to kiss her. And it feels like I finally can. So I do.

We're both breathing heavily when we break apart.

Some of her hair has fallen out of the bun it was pulled back in.

I tuck a rogue strand behind her ear. "Which game did you go to last season?"

"Uh…" She thinks. "I don't remember the name of the other team. They had gray jerseys on, I think?"

Rochester State or Olympia, then. I can look up how I played in those games later.

"You had two assists."

I still, wondering if I accidentally spoke aloud. How else would Eve know why I'm wondering? If I'd known she was there, it probably would have been my best performance of the season.

"I mean, I think it was two."

Her cheeks are red again.

And this thing between us? It doesn't feel anywhere close to over.

CHAPTER THIRTY

EVE

It's strange how much your perception of a place can change. How a place can look the same, but you feel so different.

I stare at the exterior of the apartment building where Ben lives with David and one other friend, fiddling with the bracelets on my left wrist.

I've been here hundreds of times before, but this is my first visit post-breakup.

Mary texted me this morning, once again begging me to come to the movie with her tonight. And I—fresh off the high of the most incredible sex I'd ever experienced and filled with a confidence that I could conquer anything—agreed.

I miss my friend. And being around Ben sounded easier after what happened with Hunter last night. We've both been with other people. And Ben hasn't attempted to contact me since our conversation on Monday.

More than *easy*, seeing Ben felt like an opportunity for growth. A chance to show myself I'm strong enough to recover from losing someone.

I didn't answer my dad's call on Tuesday. This feels like a second step in the same direction.

I dry my sweaty palms on my favorite pair of jeans and blow out a long breath before starting up the concrete walk. I've never noticed before, but the path to the front door is more cracks than solid cement.

My stomach grumbles, reminding me I skipped lunch and haven't had dinner yet. I was in the studio most of the day, finishing my new painting for Professor Alday.

I buzz the button for 3A, and a male voice answers with a "Yeah" seconds later.

It's hard to tell with the static, but I think it's Devon, Ben's third roommate.

"Hey, it's Eve."

More static, then the click of the door to my right unlocking. I grab the handle before it locks again.

Warm welcome.

The elevator in here only works half the time, so I head for the stairs. My mind wanders to Hunter as I climb the three flights, partly because I'm reminded of him every time the seam of my jeans rubs against my underwear.

The sex was good. So, *so* good.

But the emotional connection—talking to Hunter on my couch in the middle of the night—is the main reason he's filled my head all day. When he was talking about his brother, I got the sense that it's not a topic he discusses very often. I've never heard Harlow— or Conor or Aidan—ever mention Hunter's brother. It seems possible that they…don't know.

And if Hunter confided in me about something his best friends aren't aware of, that's a lot more than the one-night stand I crossed off my fuck-it list this morning.

I knew I felt that way about Hunter. Attraction has always been one of many feelings I have for him.

Last night, I expected the sex to seem…practiced. For him to be the popular jock who knew exactly what to do and say.

But it felt real, and not just for me. For him too.

I reach 3A, blowing out a long breath before knocking once.

David opens the door. "Oh. Hey, Eve."

"Hi, David."

"Thought you were the pizza." He turns and heads into what I know is the kitchen, leaving the door open.

Okay, then.

I have no idea what details Ben did—or didn't—share with his friends about our breakup, but it seems like they were selective. David or Devon have never been effusively affectionate toward me, but we used to exchange more than just a few syllables when I came over, at least.

Tonight is feeling increasingly like a mistake. But I'm already here, so I step inside, shut the door behind me, and follow David into the kitchen.

"Eve!" Mary hurtles into my arms as soon as she spots me, smelling strongly of tequila.

My stomach turns. My memory of that night at Sand Bar is still a little hazy, but my nose does not have any positive associations with the smoky scent of alcohol.

"I'm so glad you came!" she adds, bouncing back to beam at me.

I return Mary's wide smile, not surprised she's already started drinking. Ben and David like to discuss a director's style and filmography before going to see a movie, and their conversations tend to make the film itself seem riveting by comparison.

"Me too," I reply, unsure if it's a lie.

"Ben's in his room," she tells me. "Grabbing his laptop. He wanted to show David something."

I nod, taking a seat on the stool next to her so I feel like less of an imposter standing in the center of the room. David's leaning against the counter next to the sink, scrolling on his phone, presumably waiting for Ben to come back. There's no sign of Devon, but he only participated in these outings sporadically. I have more sympathy for the "fifth wheel" situation he was in after being in that position myself.

There's a box of donuts open on the counter. I recognize Holey Moley's logo on the side.

"Help yourself," Mary urges. "I got them for you."

I thank her and grab a chocolate glazed.

So damn good.

"Want a drink?" Mary asks me, gesturing toward the three bottles on the counter.

"Is there something besides tequila?" I ask, squinting at the labels between bites.

"What's wrong with tequila?"

"Spring break," I remind her.

"*Oh*. Right. There's vodka?"

"That's perfect."

"What does tequila have to do with spring break?" David asks, glancing up from his phone.

Now he decides to be chatty.

"Eve had a little too much fun," Mary replies, winking at me.

"Oh, yeah. Ben mentioned you were partying with Harlow Hayes," David says, then looks back down at his phone.

His cavalier comment pisses me off for two reasons.

One, it means that Ben was definitely sparse in details shared about our breakup. Because Ben dropping the bomb that he'd changed his whole future without consulting me and Harlow jumping in to make sure I didn't spend spring break depressed and alone is not what I'd describe as *partying*.

Two, there's definitely some judgment of my best friend in David's tone, which I suspect might be a sore ego about how poorly his date with her went. I'm offended on Harlow's behalf—and Mary's, who is sitting right here.

Mary scowls at her boyfriend. "Eve isn't allowed to have fun?"

Ben walks into the kitchen with his laptop tucked under one arm before David can respond. He glances around, taking in me holding a half-eaten donut, Mary as she glares at David, and David's sheepish expression.

He clears his throat before speaking. "Hey, Eve."

I don't echo the greeting. "You told David I spent spring break *partying*?"

Ben grimaces a little, moving the laptop under his other arm as he takes another step into the kitchen. "Well, I said you were *probably* partying."

"That's such a stereotype," Mary says. "The athletes on campus aren't the only ones who party. And they won a national championship."

Ben frowns. "Wait, what?"

"You think Eve was partying just because she spent break with half the hockey team? It's not your business anymore, Ben!"

Gratitude for Mary's defense is eclipsed by dread when I get a glimpse of the incredulous look on Ben's face. "You spent spring break with *half the hockey team*?"

"No. I mean, yes, some of the guys were there. Not half the team. But *you're* not in any fucking position to judge how *I* spent break, right, Ben?"

He winces, but recovers quickly. "You let me feel guilty about Rowan when you moved on just as fast?"

"Rowan?" David asks, confirming my assumption that Ben withheld some relevant information. "What does Rowan have to do with anything?"

I ignore David. Ben can share details later. "I let you feel guilty? I let you feel *guilty*, Ben? I told you that I was *relieved*. How the fuck is that letting you feel guilty?"

At least he has the sense to look shame-faced. "I—I wasn't sure if you were just saying that. We were together for three years, Eve. We were going to live together."

"All past tense, Ben! Everything's different now!"

"I know! I know it is! I know I fucked everything up!" He throws his hands up in the air. "That means I can't be upset you spent break with a bunch of other guys?"

I blow out a frustrated breath. *That's* exactly *what it means*, hovers on the tip of my tongue.

But Ben looks hurt, not just mad, and I can't make the words come out. "I went on a trip with Harlow and her boyfriend and some of Conor's friends because it was that or sit alone on the couch for a week. You can feel however you want, Ben, but what I do or who I do it with isn't any of your fucking business anymore." I glance at Mary. "This was a mistake. I'll, uh, I'll text you later."

I spin and head for the door.

Three steps down the hallway, I hear Mary call my name.

"Are you okay?" she asks as soon as I turn around.

"Yeah. I'm fine." Surprisingly, I mean it. I'm annoyed by Ben's behavior, but not at Ben. It feels like I've moved on, and now I'm waiting for him to catch up. "Sorry to bail like that, I just—"

"No, I get it. I'm sorry I pushed this. I missed the way things were, but things change, right? Even if you guys had stayed together, everything would have been different after graduation anyway."

The sky doesn't change. If Hunter were here, I'd say it aloud. It'd probably coax a half smile out of him.

"It's not your fault," I tell Mary. "I think Ben needed to hear it was over again."

"He really slept with Rowan?"

I nod.

Mary shakes her head. "If I'd known, I never would have—"

"I know," I assure her.

"I heard there's a party on Oak. You wanna go?"

I do, actually, but I glance at the apartment door. "What about the movie night?"

David isn't my favorite person right now, but I think his treatment of me tonight was mostly driven by loyalty to Ben. And I've spent enough time around him and Mary to tell he adores her. I'm not interested in allowing my drama to affect their relationship.

"I'll survive without seeing the movie with the ten-word title I can't even remember. Plus, I'm mad at David. He was a jerk to you."

I open my mouth to speak at the same time the door swings open. David appears.

He gives me a hasty, apologetic look, and then focuses on his girlfriend. "Mary."

"What?" she snaps.

"I'm sorry, okay? Really sorry. I shouldn't have gotten involved or said any of that stuff." He glances at me. "I didn't mean to stir anything up, Eve. I just—I know Ben has been really broken up about you guys, and I… I was trying to look out for him. Maybe even get you to see you made a mistake. But you're always welcome here, regardless of what's going on with you and Ben."

"Thanks, David," I tell him.

He nods, then glances at Mary. "Will you come back inside? Please? We can watch whatever you want."

Mary looks to me, clearly torn about what to do.

"We can hang out next weekend," I say, solving her dilemma.

"You're sure?" Mary questions, still uncertain. She clearly feels badly about staying behind.

I give her a quick hug. "Positive. Have a good night, guys."

Then, I start down the familiar carpeted stairs for what I'm certain will be the final time.

CHAPTER THIRTY-ONE

EVE

Parties are loud. *Especially* loud when you're alone and everyone around you is shouting. I've never shown up to a party solo before, which was the whole point of coming tonight.

After leaving Ben's, I went home. Ate dinner, and then—instead of yanking on sweats and flopping on the couch—I put on my sexy bow top and walked to Oak Street, only a few blocks from my house. Mary didn't mention a specific address for the party, but I didn't need one. It was pretty obvious where it was taking place.

Now I'm inside, clutching a cup of beer that's mostly foam and second-guessing this impulsive *Fuck it* decision.

Mary was busy. Harlow doesn't get back until tomorrow. Most of my other friends are either connected to Ben or peers I'm only friendly during classes with, like Mae. Not people I can picture playing beer pong with.

It's noisy and crowded and I know absolutely no one. Which is ridiculous, considering the total size of Holt's student population. But if any of the faces around me don't belong to total strangers, it's too hard to recognize anyone in the dim lighting.

I manage to push my way through the packed kitchen and out into the backyard. I suck in greedy gulps of fresh air, then start coughing when I accidentally swallow a cloud of sweet smoke.

"Want some?" A lit joint appears to my left.

I cough again, waving a hand in front of my face to circulate some fresh air. "No, thanks. I'm good."

"Suit yourself." The joint disappears.

I glance at the guy next to me. He's towering—more than a foot taller than me even though he's slouched against the shingles. All I can see is his profile as he stares ahead at the group playing a drinking game in the backyard.

Another cloud of smoke drifts toward me. This time, I hold my breath until it drifts past.

"You a freshman?"

I should be offended by that assumption, I think. I'm not old enough that being mistaken for eighteen is a compliment. It's more of a testament to my sad social status.

"Nope. Senior."

"Really?" There's surprise in his voice, and it sounds louder, like he's looking this way, but I don't glance at him to confirm.

"Really."

"That's cool. I'm Gates."

Instead of a joint, a hand appears in my vision. I shake the offered hand, meeting his eyes this time. "Eve."

"Wanna go upstairs, Eve?" Gates asks as soon as our hands separate.

I choke a little on nothing except my own spit. I'm startled... and a little flattered. No one has ever made hooking up sound like such a simple, straightforward transaction before.

Gates is waiting for an answer.

"Uh...I'm sort of seeing someone."

He nods, then raises the joint to his mouth. "Where is he?"

A male voice interrupts before I have to come up with an answer. "Stop hoarding the good shit over here, man."

One of the guys who was part of the drinking game is approaching us. And surprisingly, he's the first person I recognize at this party.

It's Clayton Thomas.

I'm assuming that means Gates is on the basketball team, both from their familiarity and his height.

Clayton takes the joint from Gates, and then glances at me. "Oh. Hey, Eve."

My surprise at recognizing Clayton has nothing on my shock about *him* recognizing *me*. We've only been introduced once, months ago.

I clear my throat. "Hi, Clayton."

Gates glances between us. "You two know each other?"

"I'm going to find a bathroom," I say, before Clayton can reply. Honestly, I have no clue what he'd say. "See you guys later."

Pushing back into the house is harder than shoving my way out was. I finally make it inside, trying to remember what little of the layout I noticed on the trip in and which way will most likely lead to a bathroom. I make it to the hallway and decide to ask the two girls standing by the doorway. One of them tells me to head just past the stairs.

A few minutes later, I locate the bathroom…and the line of eight girls waiting to use it.

I lean back against the white, blank wall—I'm guessing guys live here—and pull out my phone to check the time.

Only to discover that my phone is dead. Crap. I usually charge it overnight, but I was distracted last night. And I blasted music while I was working in the studio all day, not paying attention to the battery percentage.

I was planning to call a campus cab to get back home. The walk isn't far, but it's one I'd rather not do alone and late at night. Plus it makes me uneasy to be at a party where I know no one and not have a phone.

But there's nothing I can do about that now.

Thanks to my useless phone, I have no clue how long it takes me to make it into the bathroom. But it's eventually my turn. After I pee and wash my hands, I'm faced with the dilemma of what to do next.

I decide to shove my way toward the front door. Not to leave, necessarily, but there's a spacious front porch with a swing that seems like a less claustrophobic place to hang out.

There are a decent number of people out here already. I pass a couple making out on the swing and a group of three girls whispering before perching on the railing and leaning back against the side of the house, resting my feet on one of the porch caps. I stare over the bushes at the street, watching the stream of students still arriving to the party.

I sip some of the warm beer in my cup, then make a face.

"Want something else?"

I glance up quickly. Clayton is approaching, his own red cup dangling from his fingers.

"I'm good," I say, surprised to see him again. "Uh, thanks."

He nods, stopping a couple of feet away. "You here with anyone?"

I chew on the inside of my cheek. "Um…"

I'm not sure why he's asking. And I listen to too many true crime podcasts to think admitting you're alone is a smart idea.

"I'm not asking for me," Clayton adds.

I tilt my head, even more confused. Then, I realize what he means. "Oh. Gates seemed, um, nice. But I don't think we're… compatible."

Clayton tips his head back and laughs. A genuine, deep one that makes me feel more at ease around him. "If I were you, I'd stay the fuck away from Gates. From all of my teammates, actually. They're not..." He shakes his head. "I'm asking for Morgan."

I sit up straight. "Hunter?"

"Yeah. I'm not that tight with the hockey guys anymore due to some, uh, unfortunate events." He scratches his jaw.

I swallow an apology, knowing exactly what he's referring to. Unfortunate events I encouraged, convincing Harlow to leave Gaffney's with Clayton to make Conor jealous.

"But I was freshman roommates with Morgan," Clayton continues. "And he *is* a good guy. He also talked about an Eve he met back then. That was you, right? I've never met any other chick here with that name."

"Um..." I'm so stunned Hunter mentioned me to his roommate, words aren't forming easily. And almost as surprised Clayton remembered Hunter mentioned me.

"Look." Clayton takes a step closer. "I fucked up, getting involved with Hart's girl. Nothing actually happened, which I'm guessing you know since you're friends with Harlow. Morgan took Hart's side, which I get. Respect, even. Like I said, he's a good guy. But I saw you here, and I just thought..." He shrugs. "We're graduating next month. YOLO, you know. I'm assuming you're single if you're here solo, so I'm *suggesting* you shoot a shot with Morgan." He gives me a boyish grin. "Call me Cupid."

I blink at Clayton. When I impulsively decided to come here tonight, I wasn't sure what to expect. No chance I ever would have guessed *this* taking place.

"I didn't know anyone else still said YOLO," I say.

Clayton laughs again.

"Thomas. Where's the other keg?"

Clayton glances over his shoulder. A tall guy with some scruff who I'm assuming is also on the basketball team has appeared.

"Garage. I'll help you grab it," he replies. "See you, Eve."

"Bye, Clayton."

I relax back against the shingles as Clayton disappears, replaying what he just told me and taking a few more tentative sips of my beer. I'm feeling more relaxed about being here, all of a sudden. No one on the porch is looking at me like I'm an outsider. They're either absorbed in conversation or looking at their phones. And...*I'm* not worried about being an outsider. Maybe that's the secret to belonging. You'll never feel included so long as *you* see yourself as other.

I alternate between people-watching and stealing looks up at the stars. It's a clear, warm night.

At least, warm in comparison to recent nights. I doubt it's over sixty right now.

I'm debating who to ask to borrow their phone to call a cab— the girl leaning against the railing with friends, or the guy sitting on the swing texting—when I spot a familiar figure walking up the front path.

I've abandoned the idea that I'll gain immunity to the sight of him. I've gotten used to the giddiness. It's almost addictive, the sudden spurt of awareness as soon as his presence registers. Colors seem brighter. Sounds louder. Air warmer.

Right now, it's mixed with a heady amount of surprise.

I stare, my heart rate steadily increasing, as Hunter climbs the three steps that lead up to the porch. He gets stopped immediately, first by a couple of guys and then by the group of girls. Both times, he glances my way during the conversations, as if he's checking I'm still in the same spot.

My eyes don't waver from him the whole time. Staring I might feel self-conscious about, in other circumstances, but it feels right in this one. It's almost like we're having a silent, private conversation. Almost like he has the same mysterious draw to me that I have to him.

Hunter says something to the girl I was considering asking if I could borrow her phone, then continues my way.

Porch boards creak underfoot as he approaches, perching on the railing right next to my feet.

"Hey." I speak first, my voice stronger than I expected it to be.

I thought I'd feel shy the next time we saw each other. But all I'm experiencing right now is happiness. I'm really, really happy that he's here.

"Hey," he replies. "I have a few fantasies involving that top, you know."

I glance down at my skimpy shirt, then back at Hunter. "It didn't seem like you noticed it before."

Our trip to Sand Bar wasn't that long ago, but it feels like an eternity.

One corner of his mouth curves up. "I've got a good poker face, Eve. Doesn't mean I miss anything." He reaches out, twisting the laces of my Converse around his thumb. One of his fingers brushes my ankle, sending shockwaves across my skin. "You having fun?"

"More, now."

"Good answer." Hunter reaches out with his other hand, taking the cup I'm holding. He sniffs the cup's contents. "I've never seen you drink beer."

"It took me ten minutes to fight my way to the keg. No way was I looking for anything else."

"Want me to get you—crap." The laces he was playing with unknotted.

Hunter lifts my cup, clutching it between his teeth so his hands are free, and deftly reties the knot.

It's hotter than watching him change a tire was. Because he's not looking after his car; he's taking care of me.

I slip off the railing and close the short distance between us. People are staring at us—at Hunter, rather—and that would normally make me uncomfortable. But his attention on me is too consuming. It's like blinders, blocking out everything else I'd normally be aware of.

"Did Clayton tell you I was here?" I ask.

"Mm-hmm." I'm standing close, but he tugs me even closer until I'm standing between his spread thighs. His hands slip under the hem of my shirt, palming my lower back possessively. More shivers dance along my nerve endings, raising goose bumps on my skin.

"You told him about me," I state.

Since Hunter's half sitting, leaning against the railing, the height difference between us is several inches shorter. Blue eyes hold my gaze as he nods. "Yeah. I did."

I smile. "I like that you did that. I like that you're here."

"I would have been here sooner, if *you'd* texted me." His tone is teasing. But there's an unspoken question in it too.

"I wanted to add this to my fuck-it list. I'd never gone to a party alone before. Also, I don't have your number."

His thumb draws a tiny circle on my back. "Yeah, you do. I wrote it on your sketchbook before I left last night. It's on your desk."

"Oh. I, uh, I didn't see it."

I'm pretty sure I dumped a load of clean laundry on my desk, actually. I need to clean my room again.

"I should've just texted you. I got your number from Conor, but I wasn't sure what to say."

His honesty is refreshing. It's reassuring to realize I'm not the only uncertain one.

"'Hi, Eve. It's Hunter' would have worked," I tell him.

He chuckles. "Yeah. I was attempting to come up with something a *little* more memorable than that."

He was honest; I decide to be the same. "*Anything* you sent me would have been memorable, Hunter."

"That's good to know." The corners of his eyes crinkle as he smiles. His hands are still roaming my lower back, the sensation distracting enough that I have to force myself to focus. "You want something else to drink?"

I glance at the cup I abandoned by my former spot. "I think I'm good. I mostly was just sipping to look busy since I showed up alone and my phone is dead."

He frowns. "You came to a party without a phone?"

"I didn't realize it was dead until I got here, but yeah. I usually charge it overnight, but…"

Some of the concern evaporates from his expression. Worry for *me*, I realize. "So it was my fault?"

"Pretty much. If you were bad in bed, I'd have remembered to charge it."

He laughs. It's tenfold the thrill of a full smile, like a straight shot of adrenaline. "So your lack of a working phone means you're admitting I'm good in bed?"

I'm blushing, no doubt about it.

And I'm no longer embarrassed by my flushed cheeks. I don't care if Hunter knows he's affecting me. "You know you are."

Hunter smiles. "It's still nice to hear."

"It was the best sex I've ever had," I admit.

He no longer looks amused.

Oftentimes, Hunter appears detached. Not superior or uninterested, but remote. Hard to entertain. Hard to reach. Hard to affect.

I'm not sure I'll ever become accustomed to how it feels to have his full attention. And it was one thing to know that I can affect Hunter's body. But having power over his feelings? His emotions?

It's a rush like none I've ever experienced before.

I bite my bottom lip, recalling what he said last night, and his eyes track the motion. "Did you want to stay?"

Hunter shakes his head. "I just came to see you."

I lift a hand and run my thumb across his eyebrow. The one with the thin white scar. When I smooth the short hairs, it's almost invisible, but I can feel the raised line. "Take me home?"

He nods immediately. His blue eyes appear especially bright as he straightens, hands dropping from my waist. He takes one of my hands before heading toward the stairs, interlocking our fingers together.

Several heads turn as we cross the porch, but I keep my attention on Hunter slightly ahead.

We descend the stairs and walk along the driveway. I glance to the right, toward the garage.

Clayton's height is easy to spot. He's standing, talking with two girls. When we make eye contact, he lifts his cup in a silent salute.

Thank you, I mouth.

CHAPTER THIRTY-TWO

EVE

I t takes us less than five minutes to reach Hunter's SUV parked down the street. Most people walked to the party. This entire neighborhood is rentals where students live, and most of the street seems to be at Clayton's, judging by all the dark windows of the houses we walk past.

A streetlight flickers overhead, buzzing softly. Aside from the sound, the road is silent. We're far enough from the party that all the noise has faded.

Hunter opens the car door for me.

"You bit your lower lip" is his only explanation before he kisses me.

We make out until my head is spinning.

And I'm glad he's the one driving, not me, because I'm still dizzy when I climb inside his green SUV a few minutes later. Relaxing against the soft leather seat feels familiar, like embracing an old friend.

I run my tongue back and forth along the undersides of my upper teeth, watching Hunter walk around the front of the car, backlit by the quiet street. My blood buzzes with impatience, wanting to touch him again.

An idea forms in my head. The kind of thought that's occurred to me before, but I never would have dared to actually *do*.

Hunter had fantasies about this top? I lay awake on a motel mattress, wondering what he would have done if I'd been bold enough to step into that shower with him and sink to my knees.

Once he's in the car but before he's started the engine, I lean over the center console. Fist his shirt and kiss him again, the warm press of his lips alarmingly addictive.

It's never long enough, no matter how many seconds our mouths stay pressed together before separating for essential breaths.

My hands move down his chest, relying on feel to find my way since my face is too close to his to see anything south of his shoulders.

He groans my name when I palm his erection through his pants, squeezing the impressive bulge.

I bite his bottom lip, then suck it in my mouth.

A strangled-sounding "Holy shit" interrupts the whir of the zipper sliding down.

"I want to do something else on my fuck-it list tonight," I inform him, fisting his erection and tugging it free from his boxer briefs.

Hunter glances down, watching my hand move back and forth. I can't see his lap very well in the limited light, which makes this feel more illicit. I'm relying on feel, more than sight.

In the past twenty-four hours, I forgot how huge his dick is. How thick and firm and *male*.

"You feel that?" he whispers roughly. "Feel how fucking hard I get for you, Eve?"

It feels like the most natural thing in the world—leaning lower and letting him fill my mouth. *Necessary*, like I'm doing this for me as much as for him. I suck him as deep as I dare, tightening my grip on the base as I let everything except the flared tip slip back out. I flick his slit before tracing the rim with my tongue.

Hunter grunts, and it feels like his erection swells even more. His thigh muscles tense, thickening beneath the hand I have braced on his thigh.

I lower my head again, surprised by how much I enjoy swallowing his shape. The head hits the back of my throat, and I don't even flinch. I swallow again, feeling the rub that tells me how deep he is, and breathe through my nose as I continue to suck.

A flash of movement registers as Hunter's hand moves. For a split second, I'm concerned I did something wrong or unwanted and he's trying to push me off. But his fingers thread through my hair, tugging at the curls gently. Encouragingly.

My hand squeezes around the inches my mouth can't reach before slipping lower. There's only a little trimmed hair to search through. It rasps against my fingers as I cup his balls. My other hand slips under his shirt's hem, exploring the firm, hot skin of his stomach. Hunter's abs bunch beneath my palm as another sexy groan spills out of his mouth.

The aching pulse between my thighs gives an especially insistent throb. I wanted this. But I wasn't expecting it to feel so good for *me*.

"Eve," he says. "I'm going to—"

I can't say anything intelligible around the mouthful of his cock, but I understand exactly what he's warning.

And I reply by suctioning harder. Either Hunter understands the silent encouragement or he isn't able to hold off any longer.

A few seconds later, spurts of hot, salty liquid fill my mouth and coat my tongue. I don't gag; I swallow. And swallow. And *swallow* again, what seems to be an endless supply of cum.

Pride and desire are the predominant emotions humming through me as I shove up straight, swiping the back of my hand across my mouth.

My thighs squeeze tight together as I study Hunter, head tilted back and hair disheveled. He must have been running a hand through it while I was going down on him, because it was flatter before we climbed in the car. His expression is a little dazed, his shoulders rising and falling fast.

Headlights sweep across the interior of the SUV as another car drives down the opposite side of the street.

The ordinary sight is startling.

I forgot the world was bigger than me and him. Hunter has this incredible ability to make me forget everything except him. To turn my surroundings into a blur and my brain blissfully blank.

"That was on your list?"

The sound of his deep, husky voice makes me blush.

"Fooling around in a car? Yeah."

Technically *fooling around anywhere that's not a bed*, but close enough. I added it this morning.

"I don't think it counts as fooling around if only one of us got off."

My pulse quickens at the implication. But my voice is shockingly calm as I casually reply, "None of the guys I fooled around with in high school shared that philosophy."

I feel powerful and confident right now, and it feels good. The last time I wore this top, I was literally falling-down drunk. I want Hunter to see me sexy and carefree, not only vulnerable and unsure.

Just like last night, I barely register I'm moving before I'm already in a new spot. Hunter's pulled me effortlessly to his side of the car, his expression dark as his hand slides up my thigh.

"Do me a favor," he says conversationally.

My "Yeah?" sounds breathless, since his palm is under my skirt now.

"Don't ever fucking mention another guy touching you to me again. Got it?"

Oh.

Fuck.

The flint in his tone. The fire in his eyes. The fierceness in his expression. And the fucking cherry on top? Two of his talented fingers tugging my underwear to the side and slipping inside of me.

I fall forward like I was pushed, barely having the foresight to raise my hands in time.

If I ever had a chance in hell of not falling for Hunter Morgan, he just eviscerated it.

My eyes flutter as his fingers stroke. My thighs tremble in response to the expanding onslaught of pleasure, struggling to stay tensed and upright. I'm drunk on desire, the edges of my vision turning blurry as I press my face against his neck and inhale deeply.

"That feels really…" The final syllable falls off a cliff as his thumb rubs devastatingly close to the bundle of nerves that are begging for his touch. "Good," I croak, not quite managing to keep the disappointment out of my tone.

"Oh, yeah?" I can hear the smile in Hunter's voice. Feel it in the charged air around us, draped like a cozy blanket.

I'm getting off in a parked car on a public street, and I feel special. Safe and cherished.

"Please," I plead, turning my head and pressing my lips against his collarbone.

He smells so *good*, a scent I can only describe as Hunter. My tongue darts out for a taste.

Hunter pinches my swollen clit.

I gasp, my knees giving way. Now I can feel the firm length of his dick pressed against the inside of my thigh, the hot skin still damp from my mouth.

For the first time, I'm tempted to have sex without a condom.

His thumb makes another wider circle, avoiding the sensitive spot that's throbbing for—and from—his touch.

"Please," I beg again, kissing a line up his neck and along his jaw until I reach the corner of his mouth.

Hunter angles his head so his lips meet mine. His tongue teases the seam before it slips inside, mimicking the way his fingers are moving between my legs. I moan at the dual intrusion and spread my thighs a little wider, allowing him easier access.

"You taste like me," he murmurs against my mouth.

It takes a few seconds for my frazzled brain to register his meaning. When the realization hits, so does a fresh wave of warmth.

I whimper, shifting my hips and trying to bear down on his hand harder. That has the unintended effect of thrusting my boobs right in Hunter's face. It's impossible to wear a bra with this top, and I watch Hunter register I'm not wearing one. His hand flexes against my thigh before his mouth lands on my left breast, biting the raised point of my nipple through the flimsy fabric.

I cry out so loudly I'm genuinely concerned that if anyone's home on this block, they might call the few cops that make up Somerville's police department.

Hunter's smirk is lethal when he leans back. He looks devilishly, devastatingly gorgeous as his fingers continue to torture me.

"Did you hear me, Eve?"

It hits me like a flash of lightning, what he's waiting for me to say.

"I heard you." I lean closer, brushing my lips across his before adding, "I'm not thinking about anyone else."

There's more I could say. Like how I *never* think about anyone else when I'm with him. That he's the one guy I've never forgotten. That everything about him has been branded in my memory like an invisible tattoo. That maybe I *did* meet my soulmate at eighteen.

Hunter rubs my clit again, and I can't focus on anything else.

This time, he doesn't stop. He continues to put pressure on the perfect places. Pleasure builds to an unbearable point, then combusts in an explosive surge that rushes through my entire body. My inner muscles clench around his fingers as waves of release roll over me. Just like last night, it lasts for a while.

I collapse against his chest, breathing heavily, listening to his heartbeat. It sounds as wild as my own.

I thought I'd experienced lust before.

But it wasn't like this.

I thought I'd fallen in love before.

But now, I'm not so sure.

I thought New York must be the most magical place in the whole world. But if you asked me to define that location right now?

I'd say it's wherever Hunter is.

CHAPTER THIRTY-THREE

HUNTER

"**M**ORGAN!" Aidan shouts. "Hurry up, dude! You've been in there forever!"

"This was a bad idea," Eve whispers.

"Nah. It was a *great* idea." I grin, working my hand faster. She's tight and slick, the steam swirling around our bodies making everything slippery.

I can't get enough. No matter how many times I touch Eve, or kiss her, or fuck her, I can't get enough. Sex has always been good. Well, aside from the first few times when I had no clue what I was doing. But that still felt good. It never felt like *this*, though.

It's the first time I've let loose in...ever? Maybe because there's no goal. No game to win or result to achieve. So much of discipline is working toward something.

With Eve, I just exist. Enjoy.

She moans my name, tilting her head back against the white tile as her pussy flutters around my fingers.

"MORGAN!"

Eve's closed eyes fly open.

I'm going to kill Aidan. He and Conor were both out when Eve and I got back here last night. We had sex twice before falling asleep, and I convinced her to take a shower with me before she headed home.

"Fuck off, Phillips," I yell back.

What is he even doing up so early? It's not even nine.

"Dude, I know you're backed up, but can you *not* schedule your solo session during our once-a-week ice time? You've been in there forever!"

Eve covers her mouth, but I can tell she's laughing from the way her shoulders are shaking. Definitely murdering my best friend later.

And…shit. That explains why Aidan is up. It's Sunday.

"Just go ahead without me," I call out. "I'll meet you there."

"What?" Aidan replies. I can't tell if he can't hear me or is questioning what I said, and I'm not exactly in a position to move closer to the door. Two of my fingers are inside Eve.

"He's still in there?" Conor's voice joins the conversation.

I swear under my breath.

Eve's cheeks are bright red. From arousal or the hot water or amusement.

"Bad idea," she whispers. "There's no way I'm going to be able to come again now."

She *really* shouldn't have said that.

"Don't challenge an athlete."

Eve rolls her eyes. "You're technically retired—*oh fuck*."

I curl my fingers, and she slips an inch, grasping wildly at the wet tile. I hook her knee over my left hip, spreading her open wider, then circle her clit with my thumb.

She's moaning like crazy now, so I kiss her in case the spray of water isn't loud enough to cover the sound.

Eve arches her back, trying to take my fingers deeper. If I had another condom in here, I'd push into her. But I don't, and we haven't had the protection or exclusivity talk yet, so I've used one every time.

Less than a minute later, she's coming.

As we towel off, I stare at her.

The first time I saw Eve, I thought she was pretty. And she is. Stunning, actually. But there's something mystical about her appearance. I have her face memorized. If I had any drawing talent, I could sketch it perfectly. But I'm still noticing new details too, and it's not for lack of attention previously. I look at Eve every chance I get.

"What?" she asks, flipping her hair over one shoulder. Her eyes still have that sated, sleepy look I'm learning is part of her post-orgasm expression.

"Nothing."

"You're staring."

"I know."

Because Eve, wrapped in a navy towel with my initials on it—part of a set my grandparents had monogrammed as a graduation gift—after spending the night in my bed? That's a sight I want to remember.

She wrinkles her nose a little. "You're pretty good for my ego, Hunter."

Before I can reply, Eve heads into the hallway.

At first, I think it's fine that I didn't remind her my room-mates-slash-teammates-slash-best friends don't have many boundaries and are probably waiting for me to leave the bathroom so they can make fun of me for masturbating in here.

Then, I hear "Finally! Get your ass dressed and—" followed by a beat of silence and then a thud that sounds a lot like hockey skates hitting hardwood.

Eve has already hustled into my bedroom across the hall by the time I step out in a cloud of steam.

They're standing at the opposite end of the hallway, at the top of the stairs. Far enough away they probably can't see the hickey Eve left on my neck. Close enough there's no way they missed I'm the second person leaving the bathroom.

"Thanks for the privacy," I drawl dryly.

"I, uh, I—" It's one of the rare occasions I've seen Aidan speechless. "I thought you were jerking off."

"Yeah. We heard."

Aidan exchanges a look with Conor. I can't get a read on Hart's expression at all. I care about his reaction more than Aidan's, simply because he's dating Eve's best friend.

"You coming this morning?" Conor asks.

"Since we're out of hot water, I'm assuming he already did," Aidan quips.

I flip Phillips off before replying to Conor. "Yeah. I'll meet you guys there."

I catch Hart's nod before I continue into my bedroom.

Aidan calls, "You broke your own bathroom rule!" after me.

Eve is already dressed. All she has with her are her clothes from last night—a sinfully short skirt and the shirt with the bows. Untying each of those was every bit as spectacular as I thought it would be, and I already want to do it all over again.

"You wanna borrow something to wear?" I ask her.

"I'm fine," she tells me, toweling her hair. "I'll change at home."

"Sorry about the guys," I say, wrenching open the top drawer of my dresser and pulling clothes out. "I should have warned you that they'd probably be loitering out in the hallway."

"It's fine." She fiddles with the towel, running her finger over the embroidered letters. "Do you, uh, think they'll say anything?"

I can't tell from her tone what she wants the answer to be, so my reply is just as careful. "Aidan talks a lot. Conor talks to Harlow a lot."

Both facts she already knows.

Eve nods in agreement. "Right."

I still can't tell what she's thinking.

"I'm not trying to hide anything, Eve."

She hangs the towel on the back of my desk chair. "I'm moving to New York soon."

My forehead furrows. "I know."

"Does that, uh, bother you?"

"No," I state, then yank on a pair of sweatpants so I'm not stark naked.

I'm not him. I think it, but I don't say it, because I don't want our relationship to have anything to do with her ex.

"Does it bother *you*, that I don't know where I'll be moving?" I ask.

"No. I just—I—" She smiles ruefully. "I'd have an easier time thinking straight if you put a shirt on."

My phone starts buzzing on my dresser. It's Aidan calling.

"Hello?" I answer, holding the phone tight to my ear as I tug a shirt on and wink at Eve.

She blushes, and a little of the tightness in my chest eases.

I never had the *Are we in a relationship?* talk with Jemma, which is where I think my conversation with Eve was headed. Jemma just started calling me her boyfriend after we'd hung out a few times, and I went along with it.

Aidan's repeating my name.

"I'm here, sorry," I say.

"I said, I forgot my stick. Should be leaning right by the door. Can you grab it on your way?"

"Yeah, no problem."

"Cool. Thanks. See you soon."

"See you soon," I echo, then lower the phone. "Aidan forgot his stick," I explain to Eve.

"You should go skate with your friends," she tells me. "We can, um, talk later?"

I scan her expression, trying to tell if she means it. "You sure?"

Eve nods.

Maybe that's *not* where our talk was headed, and I'm oddly disappointed by that.

We had sex for the first time on Friday night; it's Sunday morning now. It's not like we've been hooking up for months without labels.

But it doesn't feel like things with Eve started a day and a half ago. It feels like they started four years ago, and I've been waiting for her ever since.

I've known all along that she just got out of a relationship. That she's planning to move to New York in a matter of weeks.

I also knew those two things would complicate any relation-ship between us, and I kissed her anyway.

"Got everything?" I ask, keeping my tone light as I pocket my keys.

"Yeah," she answers. "And I can walk home, so you can head straight to the rink."

Eve is nice. She's a genuinely kind, thoughtful person. And the problem with being around nice people is you can't tell when they're being nice or when they're making excuses.

Like right now, I can't tell if Eve's motivation is me missing time skating with my best friends or if she would *rather* walk.

"Let me drive you home, Eve," I say.

I was the one who suggested we come back to my place

instead of hers last night, so I feel responsible for getting her home.

"We can stop for donuts at Holey Moley," I offer.

When we were in California, Eve and Harlow were loudly proclaiming their love for the local spot.

Eve immediately perks up. "Yeah?"

I hide a smile. "Uh-huh. I've never been, so I—"

"You've *never* been to Holey Moley? How is that possible?"

I shrug. "I want something sweet, I have Jell-O."

"Okay, well, we're rectifying that immediately. Come on. I'll explain the flavors on the way."

I grab my phone, then follow Eve toward the stairs.

CHAPTER THIRTY-FOUR

EVE

Harlow breezes through the front door while I'm staring at my sketchbook. "Hey!"

"Hey!" I call back.

She's home early.

Except, I check the time on my phone and realize she's not. I've been sitting on the couch, memorizing Hunter's phone number, for hours. How ironic that I teased him last night for admitting he didn't know what to text me. Now, I'm facing the same dilemma.

This morning's drive from his house to mine wasn't awkward. We stopped for donuts—Hunter ran in since I wasn't exactly dressed for breakfast—and then he dropped me off before continuing to the rink. It felt normal. Natural, like a routine.

Routines take time to form, though. And I—we—don't have a lot of time.

Now that Conor and Aidan know about us, I need to tell Harlow. And she's going to have questions—questions I seriously fumbled with Hunter this morning.

"How was your weekend?" Harlow plops down on the opposite end of the couch, tucking her feet up under her.

"Uh, good. How was yours?"

She nods enthusiastically. "Really nice. Allison and I got our nails done." She waves her pale blue fingernails in my direction. "And Landon's gig went great. The band's really improving."

"That's great."

Harlow reaches out and snags one of the donuts out of the box I carried over to the couch.

My best friend hums happily as she chews. "They'd better have donuts as good as Holey Moley's wherever the hell I end up moving next month."

"They definitely have donuts this good in New York, so you'll have to come visit me," I say.

"You know I will," she replies, licking some chocolate frosting off her finger.

"Any updates on when *wherever the hell* is getting figured out?"

Harlow shakes her head. "I've applied for a few positions, but haven't heard back from any of them. The Garrisons said I can stay with them whenever, for however long I want. But... I'm really waiting on Conor."

"When is the draft?"

That detail didn't come up during Hunter's hockey explanation.

"End of June," Harlow answers.

"And...if he doesn't get drafted?" I ask tentatively.

She exhales. "No clue. It's his big dream, you know? Like New York for you. I'm not worried he won't be able to find a job doing something else. But I am worried what not making it might do to him. To us. I did decide—I'm going to follow him."

"You are?" I'm surprised, and I know it comes through in my voice.

Harlow's independent and opinionated and passionate about marine biology. I assumed she'd prioritize her career, and they'd do long distance.

"Yeah. Wherever he gets drafted, I'll go. If he doesn't get drafted, we'll figure it out then."

"Wow."

"You think I'm crazy," she surmises.

"No, I don't." I'm a little envious of her certainty, actually. Of *how* certain she is, even in the midst of uncertainty. That's a scary leap of faith, no matter how much you love someone. "I think it's romantic. But I figured you'd go on some crazy expedition to see seals in Antarctica or survey salmon in Alaska."

Harlow half smiles. "Maybe I will, one day. But right now, this is what it feels like I should do."

"Maybe Conor will get drafted to the Rangers or the Islanders, and we'll end up in the same city."

She applauds. "Look at you, knowing the team names. Part of your New York research?"

"Sort of," I say.

Truthfully, I looked up tickets yesterday morning, after Hunter left, as part of some fantasy he might visit me in the city and we could go see a hockey game together. He pays attention to my art. Listens to the podcast I recommended. I wanted to reciprocate in some way, to show interest in something that's important to him.

"I haven't mentioned it to the Garrisons," Harlow says, playing with a tassel on the corner of one of the pillows. "They're supportive of our relationship—well, supportive-ish, counting Landon—but it's still weird. Talking about Conor with them, discussing them with Conor, it's like being the negotiator between two countries at war.

That's dramatic, I know, but being stuck in the middle is—" She stops talking and pulls her phone out of her pocket. "Speaking of Conor. One sec, I'm just going to let him know I'm—"

Shocking both of us, I reach out and pluck Harlow's phone out of her hand.

She stares at me, arm and eyebrows both raised.

"I had sex with Hunter. Two—no three—times. More, if you count oral."

Silence.

"You heard me, right?" I don't see how she possibly couldn't have, she's sitting two feet away, but the quiet is making me twitchy.

Harlow stares at me for thirty seconds—I start counting—before saying, "Hunter *Morgan*?"

"Do you know any other guys named Hunter?" I ask dryly.

"Well, no. But I thought maybe *you* did."

"Well, I don't."

"I—wow. I'm—how? When? How?"

"How, like positions? Because we tried some I don't know the names for."

Harlow laughs. "No, I mean how did it happen. Did you run into him at a party or—"

"No. He was at the library on Friday night. I went to work on that awful poetry essay, and he showed up, and he asked to sit with me, and then it just…happened."

"In the library?"

"*In* the library? No! People—people do that?"

Harlow nods, smiling, and the blowjob in the car no longer seems quite as adventurous.

"Um, well, no. We did it here?"

"*Here*, here? Like on this couch?"

"No. In my bedroom. Have you had sex—actually, never mind. I don't want to know. We had sex in my bedroom."

"You and Hunter."

"Yeah. Me and Hunter."

"Wow. That's big, Eve. I mean, you hadn't since…"

I know what she's alluding to while trying to avoid saying Ben's name.

"It was big," I agree. "Because it was Hunter."

Harlow's forehead wrinkles. "What do you mean?"

"Do you remember where you went, the first night of college?"

She looks even more confused, but she answers, "Yeah. Some party off campus. I think it was on Fore Street."

"Do you remember where I went, the first night of college?"

"One of the Freshman Week events, right? You went to a bunch of those."

"Yeah." I nod. "I went to all of them, because I met a guy the first night and I was hoping to run into him again. Instead, I kept seeing Ben. And the next time I saw Hunter, he was with half the hockey team and I was dating Ben."

"Wait." Harlow leans closer. "You met Hunter Morgan the first night at Holt?"

I nod.

"And you've—"

"Had a secret crush on him ever since? Pretty much."

"Holy shit. Why did you never tell me?"

I play with the spiral of my sketchbook. "I thought it was silly. Who has one conversation with a guy and then gets butterflies around him for the next four years? It was like admiring a movie star. The chance of it ever happening seemed so unrealistic. It was just a fun fantasy to think about sometimes. But then, you and

Conor started dating, and Ben and I broke up, and he was there over spring break, and—"

"Did something happen over spring break?"

"No. But I said something about freshman year and then he told me he remembered it too and then there was this moment in the hot tub when he told me he wasn't dating Holly and—"

"Wait, wait." Harlow flaps her hands at me. "When were you guys in the hot tub? I thought you forgot a suit?"

I sink down on the couch and cover my face with my hands. "It was late at night. And forget the hot tub. Now I—"

Harlow's phone starts buzzing in its spot on the coffee table where I set it after stealing it. Conor, again.

She glances at her vibrating phone, then at me. "You don't want me to tell Conor about you and Hunter?"

I bite the inside of my cheek. "Uh, not exactly. I didn't want Conor to tell *you* about me and Hunter. Not before I did, at least."

She lifts her eyebrows again, waiting for more of an explanation.

"He, uh, saw me walk out of the bathroom this morning."

Harlow tilts her head. "I thought you said this happened Friday night."

"Yeah. It did. And then it happened *again* last night."

She smirks. "Get it, girl."

I smile, then admit, "I don't know what to do now."

Instantly, Harlow's expression shifts to her protective, pissed-off one. "Did he do something?"

"*No.* It's what *I* did. Or didn't do, maybe. I don't know."

She frowns. "What are you talking about?"

"After Conor and Aidan saw us this morning, it was a little weird. No one else knew about us, before, and it was…I don't know. I could just enjoy it, and not think about what anything meant. But then I started thinking, and I… I don't know. I freaked out a little. It feels like this thing with Hunter has been coming for a long time, but it also feels like this whirlwind and graduation is coming and I'm just…overwhelmed. He's *very* overwhelming. When I'm with him, everything else matters less."

"That's not a bad thing, E."

"I know it's not. It's just…scary." I chew on the inside of my cheek. "I don't know how he feels. If *he* wants a relationship."

I think I finally understand why it's called *falling in love*. Because a lot of it is outside of your control, governed by conjectural forces like chemistry and chance. But there's also a moment when you *jump*, I'm learning. When you make a conscious choice to pursue love and risk heartbreak. I'm standing at those crossroads now, realizing I've never jumped before.

"Ask him," Harlow suggests, sounding like she's trying very hard not to add a *duh* at the end.

I roll my eyes. "You know that's easier said than done."

"Yeah, I do. But I also promise you it's better than not knowing." She nudges my knee. "I'm going to make some dinner, because I have a feeling all you've eaten today is donuts. And then, we're getting dressed and going out."

Harlow stands and heads for the kitchen.

"Going out where?" I call after her.

"You'll see!" she shouts back.

I glance at Hunter's number again. I'd rather talk to him in person.

After Harlow's mysterious destination, I'll ask her to drop me at his house, I decide.

CHAPTER THIRTY-FIVE

HUNTER

I firmly believe skating across wide-open ice is the closest sensation to flying anyone can experience.

The rush of cool air makes my eyes water and the strain of hustling so hard has my quads burning. But I keep skating, losing track of how many times I've circled the rink, as I chase that feeling of freedom.

By the time my strokes slow, I'm breathing hard and soaked with sweat.

I'm not sure I'll be able to walk tomorrow. My muscles are literally trembling. I doubt I've ever skated this much in a single day before. I practiced with Conor and Aidan earlier—Phillips spent most of the time teasing me about causing "Somerville's first draught" with my "selfish showering habits."

I went to the library to finish working on my thesis presentation, and then I came back to the rink to skate solo for a bit before heading home.

"I see Hart is keeping a real close eye on that key."

I stop in front of the away bench, sending a spray of shavings across the blue line. Conor only left me the key because he had a study session to get to and I was the last one in the showers earlier. But Coach is kidding—I think. His rare humor is hard to decipher.

"Hi, Coach. You're here late."

"So are you," Coach Keller replies.

I shrug. "You going to kick me out?"

"You going to tell me why you're skating faster than you ever did during practice?"

I crack a small smile. "More room on the ice now than there was during practice."

"I suppose that's true." He rests his elbows on the plastic partition separating the bench from the ice. "Do you want to talk about it?"

"Talk about what?"

"Whatever has you here."

I have a lot of respect for Coach. He's one of the main reasons I chose Holt.

I didn't come here chasing a hockey career, like Conor did. I knew the past four seasons would be the final four I ever played competitive hockey, and I wanted to do it as part of a program that I was proud to be associated with. Despite Holt's mediocre reputation when it came to winning, it had everything else I was looking for.

Or maybe *because* of its mediocre reputation when it came to winning. If you ask me, how you lose says a lot more about you than how you win.

But my relationship with Coach has never extended very far off the ice. I was never the flashy star—Conor—or the trouble-maker—Aidan—that required any extra attention. I was reliable and responsible, and we never became very close as a result.

I glance at the new championship banner hanging from the rafters, then at Coach. "I think better here."

He nods. "And what are you thinking about?"

"I've, uh, I've got to decide what to do with the rest of my life."

It's a cop-out of an answer. I mean, yeah, I have to decide that. Eve is the main reason I'm here skating like a madman, though. But broaching girl troubles with Coach seems like a real leap from our previous exchanges.

"Is that all?"

I catch one of Coach's rare smiles before looking down at the ice.

I skate a little closer, leaning a hip against the boards. Now that I've stopped moving, I'm exhausted. My trembling muscles feel like lead.

"Nothing's as permanent as it seems, Morgan. You're young. You're allowed to make mistakes. Change your mind. You're starting a new chapter, but it won't be the last one."

"I just…" I move my left skate forward and back, deepening a groove in the ice. "I like getting things right on the first try, I guess."

Coach chuckles. "Don't we all."

I clear my throat. "Have you ever gotten something you really wanted? I mean, *really* wanted? Not a good grade or a pair of new skates, but something super important. Life-changing. Or, gotten close to getting it, and realized how scary actually getting it would be? Like, you wanted it, but you also liked wanting it because as long as you didn't have it, you could never lose it? Did that make any sense?"

He glances up at the banner. "Yes."

"I'm not talking about hockey."

"I'm not either, Morgan."

"Oh. Right. Well, she—"

Coach's expression doesn't change when I let the pronoun slip. "Go on."

"She might—she might finally be mine. And I always thought if there was ever an opening, I'd have the balls to make a move. But now I'm…sort of…choking."

"Because you're scared of losing her?"

I nod.

He sighs. "I'm a hockey coach, Morgan, not a relationship expert. But the way I see it, if you don't fight, you'll definitely lose her. And if you do fight, you might lose her or you might not. Which odds do you want?"

"I'm not much of a gambler."

Which Coach knows, after coaching me for four years. I pick the reliable play over the risky one, every time.

Coach looks up at the banner again. "Winning that championship was the third best day of my life. Second best was when I married my wife. And the top spot will always be getting to hold my little girl for the first time. Most terrified I've ever been in my life." He tugs the brim of his Holt Hockey cap lower. "Do you know how I found out my daughter was dating one of my players?"

"Uh…"

Is this a trick question? Discussing the morning we discovered Aidan had snuck into our coach's daughter's room was high on my topics to never bring up with Coach Keller.

"Phillips was never a rule follower. But he wanted that win for Hart. If I'd found out about him and Rylan any other way, I would have doubted his intentions. I would have smelled the bullshit of him showing up in a tie on my doorstep asking permission to date my daughter a mile away. But him jeopardizing the entire team? That made a damn impression. Opportunities don't fall into your lap, Morgan. You have to make them happen."

"So, you're telling me to go for it?"

"I'm saying you miss a hundred percent of the shots you don't take, Hunter."

His use of my first name draws me up short. Coach always calls us by our last names. I wasn't even sure he *knew* my first name.

He's right.

I want Eve; there's no question about that. And I hope she feels the same way about me, but it won't change how I feel. I have nothing to lose, except my heart, and I think I already handed that over to her.

"Thanks, Coach," I say.

He nods. "Good luck, Morgan. I'll see you at the dinner."

I nod back, pretending like I hadn't totally forgotten about that. When he turns to leave, I add, "Coach?"

He glances back, one eyebrow raised. "Yes?"

"Aidan is one of the best people I know. He would die for her. I know she's your daughter, but if you're worried…don't be."

Coach chuckles a little. "You're a good man, Morgan."

I watch him head for the lobby that serves as the rink's main exit. For some reason, this moment feels like the end of hockey. I thought it would be raising the championship trophy after that final game. But that was a team event. A celebration, mostly, because we won. This, talking to Coach in an empty rink, felt more final.

I skate slowly to the door that leads to the tunnel. Back in the locker room, I shower and change for the second time today. Before leaving, I also empty out my locker, shoving all the gear and clothing into my hockey bag.

I don't know the exact date they're melting the ice, but I know it's coming up soon. And this should get washed anyway.

It's pitch-black out when I leave the rink. There's a pang of nostalgia as I walk to my car. During the season, leaving at this hour was a regular occurrence.

Rather than drive straight home, I head toward Eve's. I could call or text her, but this feels like a conversation we should have in person. She hasn't called or texted me, despite now knowing she has my number, but I shove that concern to the back of my head.

When I get to Eve's house, the driveway is empty and all the windows are dark. No one's home.

I swallow my disappointment and continue to my place, which is the total opposite of empty. I have to park halfway down the street, since my usual spot is taken by what I think is Robby's black Jeep. Even this far down the block, I can hear the music.

What the hell is—*shit*. It's Sunday. It's Robby's birthday. Why didn't Conor or Aidan mention it when we were at the rink this morning?

I'm guessing the answer is they were distracted by what happened before our weekly practice, same as I was.

I swear under my breath as I walk toward the front door, a heavy bag of smelly hockey equipment slung over one shoulder.

As soon as I step inside, there's a loud chorus of my name. The entire team is here, plus a lot of other people. The only shout I acknowledge is Robby's, clapping him on the back and wishing him a happy birthday.

I sneak upstairs as soon as I can, depositing the bag in my room and changing into jeans before heading back downstairs.

Aidan and Conor are in the kitchen. So's Robby. He's talking with Jake Brennan. It sounds like they're discussing Brennan's twenty-first.

"Your days of delinquency are almost over." Robby knocks his cup with Jake's so hard that some of the beer in his sloshes over the rim and into the one Jake is holding.

Jake grins. "Dunno about that."

Robby grins back, then notices me. "Where are your Jell-O shots, Morgan?"

"Didn't make any," I say.

"What?" Conor asks, glancing over from his spot by the stove. "Why?"

"No one else likes them."

Conor's frown deepens. "You do."

"Well, it's not my birthday."

"Can you make some now?" Aidan asks. His expression is uncharacteristically somber. For anytime, let alone at a party.

"Yeah, but it takes a couple of hours to set."

Aidan shrugs. "I'm not going anywhere."

"You live here, Phillips."

"Exactly. You want some of Morgan's famous Jell-O shots, Sampson?"

"Hell yeah!" Robby calls back.

"Fine." I open the cabinet that contains my extra stash and pull out boxes of cherry and lime.

Conor shifts to the left so I can boil the water on the stove. "Wasn't sure you'd make it," he says in a low voice that I can barely make out over the commotion in the kitchen.

"I forgot," I admit. "You guys didn't mention it this morning."

"Because you never forget shit."

I watch the bubbles form on the bottom of the saucepan. "I know."

Rylan appears, setting an empty can by the sink before walking over to me. "Hey, Hunter! I was wondering where you were."

"Here," I say, returning her hug. "Just making Jell-O shots."

"Can I help?" she offers.

"Sure. Cups are in the drawer. Vodka's in the cabinet above the fridge. Grab a mixing bowl too."

Rylan nods. "Got it."

She returns with the items a minute later. "Is Harlow coming?" she asks Conor. "I haven't seen her."

Conor shrugs, then scratches his jaw. "I'm not sure." He also glances at me.

"You're not sure?" Rylan asks, confused.

"She went home for the weekend," Hart says. "I forgot to mention it before she left, and she didn't answer when I called earlier. I texted her about it, but she might still be driving. Or back, and busy with Eve." He slants another look at me.

"Invite Eve too!" Rylan suggests. "I haven't hung out with her since spring break."

Conor makes a vague "Uh-huh" sound.

"Jell-O shots, huh? Should have known I'd find you over here, Morgan."

I glance at Jack Williams, a smile appearing automatically. I've always liked Williams. Oftentimes—and especially at parties like this—we were the twin pillars of reason when guys would suggest streaking across campus or breaking into the rink to skate suicides.

We haven't hung out much since the season ended. We've never socialized much outside of hockey. Jack and Harlow dated sophomore year, and Conor is…Conor.

"Hey, man," I greet. "They'll be ready in a bit."

"No rush." Williams props a hip against the counter. "How've you been?"

"Not bad."

"You pick a grad school yet?" he asks.

Jack and I were the two guys doing homework on the bus to

away games. He's from LA, like Aidan, and working for his dad's accounting company after graduation.

"He's still busy weighing his *many* offers," Conor says.

I roll my eyes. "Not that many."

"Morgan got into every fucking school he applied to," Hart brags.

"What? I didn't know that!" Aidan interjects. "Did they send you something I can put on the fridge?"

I laugh and shake my head. "A couple of schools sent welcome packets, yeah."

Including University of Pennsylvania, which is the program I'm leaning toward. It's one of the top in the country, and Philadelphia is a cool city. For many reasons, including its proximity to New York.

The water's boiling. I grab a potholder and pass the pan to Rylan, who carefully mixes it with the Jell-O powder and then adds the vodka.

Aidan's busy rearranging the papers on the fridge so there's an open spot for my grad school decision. And fuck if that doesn't make me feel as sentimental as clearing out my locker did.

"Is Kylie here?" I ask Jack.

Jack shakes his head. "Nah, we broke up. End of senior year is a tough time to start a relationship, especially if you're not headed to the same place. She got a job offer in Chicago…and that was pretty much it."

I nod, attempting to ignore how similar his words sound to my own situation. "Sorry, man."

"S'okay. It was amicable. But thanks."

"Yay! You made it!" Rylan abandons the Jell-O shots halfway through pouring the mixture into the tiny cups, setting the pan on the counter and then shoving her way toward Harlow, who's appeared in the doorway that leads from the front hall.

"Hey!" Harlow hugs Rylan back, mouthing something at Conor that makes him grin.

Harlow smiles back. Then, she glances at me, and I immediately tense.

She knows about me and Eve. I can just tell.

And then Eve herself appears and steals all of my attention. She stops beside Harlow, looking around the packed kitchen with wide eyes. It doesn't seem like she knew there was a party, and there's a spark of hope in my chest when I realize that means she likely came to see *me*.

Rylan pulls Eve into a hug. Harlow moves deeper into the kitchen.

"Hey, Hart's girl," Brennan greets. He's leaning against the wall at that end of the kitchen, next to Robby.

Next to me, Conor nods approvingly at the address.

I'm pretty sure Harlow rolls her eyes before saying hi to Jake.

Jake straightens and steps closer to the girls, holding a hand out to Eve. "Hey, I'm Jake. We've never met before." He smirks. "I'd remember."

My jaw clenches tight as I watch Eve shake Brennan's hand.

I can feel eyes on me. Conor and Aidan, I'm guessing, but I don't glance around to confirm.

My fuse is long. I don't lose my temper.

Eve and Jake are still talking.

There's enough activity in the kitchen that I can't hear everything they're saying. But I hear him offer to get her a drink, followed by Eve's "I'm okay, thanks" clear as a bell.

Brennan acts all disappointed, flashing her the grin I've seen succeed many times before and rattling off some different options in a cajoling tone.

Harlow's looking at me now too.

And my fuse *was* long, because I'm pretty damn close to losing it. He says something else, and it burns down to nothing.

"She said *no*, Brennan."

A beat of total silence follows. My voice was louder—flintier—than I intended, cutting through the conversations in the kitchen and leaving complete quiet in its wake. I don't say anything else. I don't soften my tone or cut the tension with a joke.

And I hold Jake's gaze as he stares at me, eyebrows raised.

Surprisingly, he breaks eye contact before me. I've seen Brennan go head-to-head with plenty of guys on the team before, and it's rare he's the one to back down first. It's usually me and Williams pulling them apart to break things up.

"Sorry," he tells Eve. "I didn't know you and Morgan were together."

I don't correct Jake's assumption. Neither does Eve. She says something to Brennan I can't hear, and then starts weaving her way around the people in the kitchen. Toward me.

People are talking again. Most of them are also staring this way. The worst offenders are Harlow, Conor, Rylan, and Aidan, who aren't even bothering to be surreptitious about it.

"Hey," she greets, slipping in next to me.

"Hey," I echo, scanning her expression.

"I didn't mean to crash your party."

"You aren't. I would have invited you if I'd remembered it was happening." I reach up and rub the back of my neck. "And I meant to text you, when I got home, but there was the party and I accidentally left my phone upstairs and—"

Eve cuts me off by rising up on her tiptoes and kissing me.

Distantly, I'm aware of commotion. Cheering. But mostly, I'm focused on Eve. The tiny moan she makes when I suck on her tongue and the way she leans into me like *close* isn't close enough.

And how it feels like I finally got the girl.

CHAPTER THIRTY-SIX

EVE

I'm in an excellent mood leaving the art building. Professor Alday just praised my redo of his assignment as "raw" and "haunting."

I painted the same scene as before. The background was still my mom's old apartment. But it was dusk, the end of the day. The shadows took me forever, but the final effect was worth it. And I flipped the man and his daughter, so you could see the vacancy in his expression and the disappointment in hers.

Painting it was oddly cathartic, and I'm fairly certain it'll earn me an A.

I also have a text from Hunter, asking if he can come over, so I have sex with my boyfriend to look forward to when I get home.

We snuck upstairs from Robby's birthday party last weekend for a long conversation and some fooling around, and I left the hockey house as a girlfriend.

Hunter Morgan is my boyfriend.

Sometimes, I just say that sentence to myself. As some reminder that life works in mysterious ways. And to experience the giddiness all over again.

There's a group of guys with a video camera off to the left of the path, so I skirt toward the right on my way to the student center. I'm meeting Mary for lunch before heading home.

"Hey, Eve."

I do a double take at the guy wearing a Sea Dogs cap. "Ben. Hi. I didn't realize…" I glance at the other guys, recognizing David too. He gives me a small wave. The other guys are friends of Ben's I've met before but don't know very well, so I just smile at them. "Film project?"

"Yep." Ben shoves his baseball hat higher to scratch at his forehead. "Final one, actually. Hard to believe."

I nod in agreement. "I'm sure it'll be great."

"Thanks, Eve. You're…good?"

I nod. "I'm good. You?"

"Yeah, all right. I, uh, rented a place in Portland. Not a bad commute to my folks', and I'll have my own space."

"That's great, Ben. Congrats."

He kicks a pebble on the path. "Thanks."

I glance at the other guys. They're all fiddling with the equipment, acting busy, but they're definitely within earshot. "Could I, uh, could I talk to you for a minute? Alone?"

"Yeah, of course." Ben nods toward a bench ahead. "There?"

"Sure," I say, and we start walking together.

I breathe deeply, pulling in a lungful of fresh air. It's a beautiful day, clear and warm and the dictionary definition of spring.

"Everything okay?" Ben asks as soon as we're a little ways from his friends. "Did something happen with your mom? Your dad?"

"No. I mean, my mom's worried about me moving and my dad isn't coming to graduation, but…I'll be fine."

"You'll be more than fine. You'll thrive in New York, Eve," Ben tells me. "I never doubted that."

It feels like he did, but I appreciate the endorsement now. "Thank you."

"And your dad is an asshole."

I laugh. Ben doesn't swear very often, so it's always entertaining when he does. "Yeah. He is."

"All he wanted to talk about was sports. Typical jock."

I run my tongue along the backs of my teeth, tempted to grimace. Not the best intro to telling my ex I'm dating an athlete.

I clear my throat. "What I wanted to talk to you about doesn't have to do with my parents. I wanted to let you know that I'm, um, seeing someone."

No reaction this time.

Ben's expression appears purposefully blank. I'm not even sure if he's blinking.

"Oh," he finally states.

I gnaw on the inside of my cheek. "I wasn't sure if you would want to know. But it's a small campus and I know you might see us together or hear something, and so I just—I wanted you to hear it from me."

Ben nods once. "Who is he?"

"Hunter Morgan."

"I don't know him."

"Yeah, I figured. He's, um, he's friends with Conor. He's on the hockey team."

"Oh." Now Ben's expression *is* purposefully blank. "Is it serious?"

"Yes."

He glances down briefly, then makes eye contact again. "Okay. Thanks for telling me."

"Yeah, of course. I... I should go. I'm getting lunch with Mary."

He nods again. "Have fun."

I smile before turning, but only make it a couple of steps before Ben says my name.

I swallow, then spin back around to face him.

Ben's staring at the ground, but he glances up when I say, "Yeah?"

"Hunter's a good guy? He treats you well?"

I swallow again, this time to clear the lump in my throat. "Yes—yeah. He's…really good."

Ben nods. "Good."

"You—you talk to Rowan lately?" I ask tentatively.

He shakes his head. "No. Not since…"

"You should call her," I suggest softly.

"Yeah. Maybe. See you, Eve."

"Bye, Ben."

When I walk away from him this time, it feels like closure.

Hunter's bicep bunches as he runs a hand through his hair. "I need a haircut."

"I can do it," I offer. "My mom taught me the basics."

"Nah, it's fine. There's a barber in Loughton I've gone to before. Just haven't been that way recently."

"A barber?" I scoff. "Do you not trust me?"

"Of course I trust you. I'm also pretty comfortable, so…"

I sit up. My muscles still feel like jelly from the multiple orgasms, but I'm excited by the idea of getting to do something for him for once. "Get dressed. I won't be able to focus if you're naked."

Hunter grins as I climb out of bed and pull on some clothes and go in search of supplies.

When I return to my room with a comb, towel, and the

sharpest pair of scissors I could find, Hunter is dressed and seated in the chair at my desk.

I smile approvingly before laying the towel on his shoulders and tucking it into the collar of his T-shirt. I'll have to vacuum the floor later, but that should keep most of the hair contained.

"You wanted a mohawk, right?"

Hunter laughs, but there's a hint of nerves in the sound. "Eve…"

"Relax. I know what I'm doing."

He's got the big dinner celebrating the championship this weekend. No matter how funny fucking with his hair could be, I wouldn't do that to him.

"Just a trim, yeah?" I check.

"Yeah. It keeps falling into my eyes."

I noticed. And I'll miss watching his arm muscles flex when he runs his hand through his hair constantly.

It's hair. It'll grow back. But…I'm not sure I'll get to see it.

I comb a section and start cutting.

Hunter's quiet and still—the perfect client.

So of course my mind starts racing.

"I, uh, ran into Ben earlier."

"Oh" is the extent of Hunter's response. His only reaction is to stay completely still.

I wish I'd mentioned this when I could look at his face, at least.

I chew on the inside of my cheek as I trim another section. "I told him about us. I wasn't sure if I should or not, but I happened to see him and it seemed—I don't know? Respectful."

"What did he say?"

"Not much. It wasn't really about what he said, more for me. Part of moving on."

Hunter hesitates before asking, "Have you moved on?"

"From Ben? Of course. I'm dating you, remember?"

"You were with him for a long time, Eve."

I finish the final section in the back and then round the chair to face him. "I know. And part of the reason we were together for so long was because I thought it was supposed to feel like that. Always looking ahead, not really enjoying the present."

Hunter's expression is serious, brows knit together the same way they do when he's reading or concentrating hard on something.

"It's different with you," I tell him.

Hunter runs his fingers through the longer section of hair I haven't reached yet. "So you're not using me as a rebound to get over Ben before you meet a sculptor in New York?"

I bite my bottom lip to hide my smile. "A sculptor?"

There's a slight ruddiness to Hunter's cheeks. "You know, a guy who's more your type."

I shove away from the desk I was leaning against and take a seat on his lap. Hunter's hands fall to my hips automatically as I straddle him. "*You're* my type, Hunter. I don't remember the night we met in some vague sense. I remember it well, because I've thought about it a lot. Because I've always been attracted to you. Because I've never thought of you as a rebound. Ben was basically my rebound from *you*. If, you know, ten-minute conversations counted as relationships."

One corner of his mouth kicks up an inch. I poke the dimple that appears in his cheek, and it deepens.

"Sean called me that night. That's why I left—why it took me so long to come back. By the time I did, you were gone."

"I should have waited longer."

"I should have tracked you down. The first few weeks of school were crazy, and the next time I saw you you were holding hands with Ben. I thought I'd missed my shot."

"You didn't," I whisper.

Relief is obvious in Hunter's expression, but there's still some worry lingering. He exhales. "I'm planning to pick Penn, Eve. I had a long talk with my parents last night, and…as much as I wish the world didn't work this way, I'll have a lot more opportunities if I choose a more prestigious school than UW. I wish I could do something for Sean, but I can't, and it's selfish, but I can't sit around and wait for him to relapse again."

I smooth the crease on his forehead with one finger. "I think Penn is a great choice, Hunter. It's a great school. Philadelphia is supposed to be really nice."

"It's not New York."

"Well, nowhere else *can* be."

Beneath my palms, Hunter's chest heaves with a heavy exhale. "You would consider long distance?"

"Yeah. Short distance seems to be going well."

He smiles briefly. "I'm serious, Eve."

"So am I. I want you, Hunter. I want you when you're right in front of me and I'll want you just as much when we're in different states." I circle my hips on his lap. "Maybe even more, because I'll be missing *this* too."

One corner of his mouth curves up again, creasing a comma in his cheek. "Good to know you mostly want me for my dick."

The dick that's rapidly growing, right between my spread thighs, putting pressure on the perfect spot.

"It *was* love at first sight in the motel bathroom," I admit.

Hunter laughs as his hands roam higher. I moan when he reaches my tits, rubbing my nipples into aching points in seconds. We had sex less than an hour ago, but I'm desperate for more.

"We should take another road trip," he tells me. "Stop at a hotel with a big shower and no pillow wall."

"That sounds perfect," I murmur.

My arms wind around his neck—dislodging the towel, which falls to the floor—as I grind harder against his erection, but it isn't just torture for him.

I pull back far enough so that I can run a hand down the firm muscles of his stomach and into the waistband of his joggers. Hunter grunts when I fist the base and tug his cock free from the confines of the fabric, the elastic waistband easily giving way.

He's fully hard, the fat tip already leaking pre-cum.

Hunter grins. "I guess getting dressed was a waste of time."

I almost fall as I stand, the sudden rush of lust making my limbs heavy and my reflexes sluggish. I catch myself with one hand on the desk, toppling my yellow sketchpad. I'm too impatient to pick it up, my fumbling fingers busy trying to find my waistband.

Hunter is stroking himself, gaze hooded and heavy with lust as he watches me attempt to undress. He looks so sexy, fully dressed with the evidence of his desire on display.

A few wriggles later, my pants are a pool of cotton around my ankles. I jerk my underwear down, not bothering with my shirt, and then return to Hunter's lap.

We both groan at how much better it feels skin to skin.

Hunter's hands land on my waist, moving me back a couple of inches. At first, I think he's trying to take his pants all the way off. Then, I realize he's reaching into his pocket.

I stare at the foil packet in his hand.

"Don't put it on."

He stills. "What?"

"Don't wear one."

"It's not a big deal to me, Eve. Now, or ever."

"It *is* a big deal to me," I tell him. "It felt like I couldn't be too careful, because of my mom."

Hunter nods. "I get it, Eve. And I'd never—"

I press a finger to his lips. "That's not what I mean. I've never had sex without one before. And I don't want you to wear one. I want to feel you. There are other, um, protections in place. So we could, if *you* want to."

"Eve." His voice is soft and achingly intimate. My room has never felt so tiny. "You don't have to prove anything to me."

"That's not what this is. I promise. I want to…I want *you*."

Hunter holds my gaze like he's trying to read the truth there. Then he drops the condom and reaches for me, pulling me right on top of his cock.

"Go slowly, or else there's no way I'm going to last…*fuck*." The last word is strangled, his grip on my hips tightening more with every inch I take between my thighs.

"It feels different?" I ask.

His Adam's apple bobs with a swallow. "Yeah," he replies hoarsely.

"Have you done it like this…before?"

An involuntary question I regret asking as soon as I catch the subtle grimace on his face.

"Never mind," I add quickly.

That will teach me to bring up the past during sex. And considering I dated someone else for years while we attended the same school, I have no right to be upset that he's been with other people.

But emotions are rarely rational.

"It was high school, Eve," he tells me. "I barely knew what I was doing."

"You don't have to explain," I say, but I do feel better knowing that it was a while ago.

"I will. If you want to know something, ask me."

I can feel his balls beneath my ass. He's fully seated, and I'm pretty sure I can feel that thick vein pulsing inside of me. I clench my inner muscles, and the cords of his neck flex.

"Not that fucking slow, Eve."

"You should have been more specific," I tease, running a finger down the bridge of his nose.

"You're so fucking tight. And wet. I can feel it dripping out of you."

My inner muscles spasm again, this time unintentionally.

"Fuck. You fit me perfectly."

He's playing dirty. And the pressure is too much. I *need* the delicious friction of his cock moving inside of me. Need it more than air.

I lift up until only the tip is lodged inside of me. Then rise even higher, so I'm entirely empty.

Hunter wasn't kidding. His dick is soaked with the evidence of my desire.

I grab the base and watch, transfixed, as it slides back inside of me. When I glance at Hunter, he's watching too. That makes it even hotter, somehow, both of us staring as my body spreads to take him.

This angle is different. He feels *huge*, and he hits some deep spot that has white dancing across my vision. I'm so full it feels like he's invaded my entire body. Turned me entirely into his.

I repeat the up and down motion over and over again. I'm barely hanging on, so close to coming but wanting this to last forever.

I love when Hunter takes control, but I feel *powerful* in this position. This big, strong man is focused on nothing except each thrust of my hips.

Hunter says my name through gritted teeth.

I hear the warning in it. He's giving me one final chance to change my mind.

But it's already made up. I brace my right hand against his rigid abdomen, bearing down as hard as I can.

I see his release appear. But I also *feel* it. His cock thickens and jerks, and then there's a seeping of warmth that I somehow distinguish from the other heat.

I reach between our bodies, feeling the stretch of my body and the stickiness trickling out, before moving higher and rubbing some of Hunter's cum around my clit.

He releases a rough groan when he realizes what I'm doing, and that sound sends me flying over the edge.

I'm coming so hard I can feel the convulsions ripping through my body.

Hunter can feel them too. He grips my hips, taking over thrusting, and draws out my orgasm even longer.

When I collapse against his chest, he's still inside of me. We're as connected as two people can be.

"Best haircut ever," he whispers into my neck.

And I almost whisper three different words back to him.

CHAPTER THIRTY-SEVEN

HUNTER

A distant door slams. "Eve! You home?"

I roll on my back and rub at my eyes. Beside me, Eve stirs.

"Eve?" a voice—Harlow's—calls again.

Eve yawns, covering her mouth with one hand. "Yeah! One sec," she shouts.

She rolls toward me, tucking both hands under her cheek. "We fell asleep."

"Yeah," I say, scrubbing my face with one palm.

Not surprising. I just came harder than I ever have in my life.

When I suggested going bareback to Jemma, it was because some high school buddies were talking about how much better sex felt without a condom. Honestly, I'm not sure I noticed much of a difference. It felt good, but it always did.

With Eve, it was incomparable. Not just physically, although feeling her pussy without a latex barrier had me worried I wasn't going to last *one* stroke, but because of the level of intimacy she trusted me with.

She smiles. "You wore me out."

I chuckle. "You wore me out. I haven't napped since I was a little kid. Everyone else would pass out on the way home after away games, and I'd be awake with the coaches."

"Sean would sleep?"

It's the first time Eve has mentioned my brother since she found out he existed. And I appreciate the way she does it, letting me reminisce about Sean without having to talk about his struggles.

"Yeah, he could fall asleep whenever, wherever. I was always jealous of that."

She smiles again. "Do you want to stay for dinner?"

"I'm supposed to get burritos with Conor and Aidan at…" I crane my neck to see the clock on her dresser. "Five minutes ago. I should go."

That explains why my phone keeps buzzing. Surprised it didn't wake me up before Harlow did.

I sit up, running my hands through my hair.

"Shit." Eve sits up too.

I glance over at her, alarmed.

"I didn't finish your hair."

I laugh, relieved. "I didn't mind."

"You can't leave it like that. Get dressed. It won't take long."

"Uh-huh." This is basically exactly how my last haircut—which ended with us back in her bed—started.

Eve's busy pulling clothes on, so I stretch and stand too.

"I'm making pasta," Harlow shouts. "Want some?"

"Yes, please!" Eve calls back.

I walk over to the pile of my clothes. I pull on my pants, then reach down to pick up my shirt. Beneath it, Eve's sketchbook is lying open on the floor.

I stare at it. "What's this?"

"What's what—oh." She stops next to me, rolling the waistband of her sweatpants. "I told you that you were my type."

She's acting casual, but her cheeks are pink. She's embarrassed.

I'm…stunned.

I reach down to pick up the sketchbook, studying it more closely.

The resemblance is uncanny. Every detail of the interior of my car is exact. It's like I'm staring at a photo of myself driving.

"I know we weren't…anything, so maybe it's weird. But, in my defense, it was draw you or draw the highway, so—"

"I love it, Eve. Can I keep it?"

A wrinkle appears between her eyes. "Um, sure."

I swipe a hand through my hair so I can keep staring at it. Aside from a silly caricature at a state fair, no one has ever *drawn* me before.

It feels a lot more intimate than snapping a photograph. I trace the pencil strokes that created this likeness to me, feeling honored. Art is an important part of Eve's world. Her taking the time to sketch me—to include me in that part in some way—feels special.

"Sit," she tells me, nodding toward her desk chair. "I have to fix your hair."

That distracts me from the drawing.

"*Fix* it?"

I haven't looked in the mirror since she started cutting earlier. I won't be mad if she snipped a section too short, but I will have to figure out a time to see a barber before the team dinner on Saturday night.

She smirks. "Finish it. The front just needs a trim."

I release a subtle sigh of relief.

Not subtle enough, because Eve smacks my shoulder before

picking up the comb and scissors again. "I didn't mess up your hair!"

"I didn't say you did. But I really don't have time, Eve, I've got to go."

Conor and Aidan will understand my tardiness. If they don't, I'll remind them how often they've gotten "delayed" in the past few months. But I'm normally on time, so they're probably worried—and hungry.

"It won't take long," she tells me, picking up the towel that got knocked to the floor during sex and tucking it back into my T-shirt.

"It's already taken an hour."

She blushes, and it's beautiful. "Don't distract me this time."

"You sat in my lap," I remind her, taking a seat. I leave the drawing propped on my knee, so I can keep looking at it.

Eve rolls her eyes before she starts snipping again. I stay silent and still, both so I can't be accused of distracting and so I end up with an even cut.

A few minutes later, she steps back and tilts her head. Then nods. "Okay, you're good." She picks the makeup mirror off her desk and hands it to me.

My haircut looks the same, just an inch shorter. Perfectly straight and even.

"Thank you."

"You're welcome." Eve smiles before walking over to the bed and grabbing my Holt Hockey hoodie. I think she's making sure I don't forget it, but she yanks it over her head instead.

It never occurred to me that having a girl wear my clothes would be sexy. In high school, varsity players on the football team were each assigned a cheerleader. The tradition was they'd wear their player's jersey at school on game days. Even though I was dating one of them, I always thought the tradition was a little weird. Maybe because that was when things with Sean were getting really bad and everything else seemed superficial in comparison.

But Eve? Wearing my sweatshirt? It affects me a hell of a lot more than her lip-biting.

"I was wearing that," I say as she saunters back toward me.

"Sorry," she says, not sounding remorseful at all.

I shake my head before grasping the hoodie's drawstrings and pulling her in for a kiss. "That's my favorite sweatshirt. It still has the fleece lining."

She smiles. "I noticed. It smells like you too. I *really* like it."

I realize I'm never going to see this sweatshirt again—unless Eve is wearing it. But I play along. "If I let you keep it, what are you going to give me?"

"What do you want?" Eve whispers.

"I want—"

"Eve?"

We both startle at the sound of Harlow's voice. It's close—coming directly from the other side of the door.

Eve reaches for the door handle. "Yeah?"

"Everything okay? You usually—oh." The door swings open.

"Hey, Harlow," I say.

She smiles. Glances at Eve, focusing on the sweatshirt she's wearing. Her smile widens. "Hey, guys. Sorry to interrupt. There wasn't a sock on the doorknob."

Eve snorts.

She also flushes a brilliant shade of red.

"I'll text you later," I tell Eve.

I give her a quick peck—no tongue because Harlow is still standing and beaming at us—and smile when I feel her lips curve up against mine.

"See ya, Harlow," I say before heading down the hallway toward the front door.

"Bye, Hunter," she calls after me.

Before I'm out of earshot, I hear Harlow tell Eve, "Nice sweatshirt."

———

Conor and Aidan are—predictably—pissed.

I jogged the whole way home from Eve's, and neither of them appears to appreciate the effort.

To be fair, I'm twenty-five minutes late.

"*Finally*," Hart grumbles.

"My stomach ate itself half an hour ago," Phillips informs me.

"Sorry. I got distracted."

Aidan squints at me. "There's something different about you."

I nod. "Eve cut my hair."

"No, that's not it. It's…" He snaps his fingers. "You lost your punctuality."

Conor laughs.

"You're an asshole," I say. "I take back my apology. *And* I'm sitting shotgun."

Aidan grumbles about the lack of foot room in the back seat the whole walk to Conor's car.

"So, where were you?" he asks as he reverses out of our driveway.

"At Eve's. Getting a haircut." Among other things.

Conor scowls. "Are you kidding me? We could have picked you up there, and I could have seen Harlow."

"And my knees wouldn't be under my chin right now," Aidan pipes in with from the back.

"I didn't think of that. I fell asleep and lost track of time."

"You *fell asleep* during sex?" Aidan sounds horrified.

"No," I correct quickly. "It was after."

"How long after? That doesn't say much about your stamina, Morgan."

"My stamina? I'm not—my stamina is fine."

Aidan whistles. "*Fine*? Yikes."

Conor is silently shaking with laughter in the driver's seat.

"I can't believe I'm explaining this to you, but it was after the third round, okay? My stamina is fucking fantastic."

"Speaking of, where's your grad school thingy?"

"*Speaking of*? How is that a speaking of?" I question.

"I don't know. We were just talking about you and I thought of it. You never stuck anything on the fridge."

I shake my head, torn between exasperation and amusement. I spend a lot of time in that state around Aidan.

"I was waiting until I picked a school."

"And?"

"I'm going to Penn."

It's the first time I've said that aloud so definitively. It sounds right. And it feels amazing to have made a decision.

"Congrats, man," Conor says. "That's an awesome school."

"Penn's in Philadelphia, right?" Aidan asks.

"Yeah," I confirm.

"Sweet. I love cheesesteaks."

"You love all food," Conor corrects.

"Well, my stomach knows it was supposed to be eating a burrito by now, so yeah."

Conor parks outside of our favorite Mexican restaurant, and we all pile out of the car.

Before I can even shut my car door, Aidan's pulling me in for a hug and pounding my back. "I'm proud of you, Morgan. All those hours in the library paid off. And, you got the girl."

I told Conor and Aidan about meeting Eve freshman year fully expecting them to tease me about it for the foreseeable future. But they surprised me. Phillips said he knew I was a secret romantic. Hart said he clocked my interest in Eve as soon as I put soy milk in the grocery cart.

"Thanks, Phillips."

"Try to work on the whole tardiness thing though, 'kay?"

I roll my eyes and shove him away. "Take your own advice. I was late *once*. You're *always* ten minutes behind."

"Going to have to side with Morgan on this one," Conor says, rounding the front of his car and walking toward us.

Aidan rolls his eyes. "Yeah, yeah, Captain."

I sling my arms around my best friends' shoulders and steer them toward the restaurant.

CHAPTER THIRTY-EIGHT

EVE

A pillow lands on my face right as the rookie FBI agent is headed to a remote cabin to track down the suspected killer. I drop the paperback, yank out my headphones, and glare at a grinning Harlow.

"Ever try knocking?" I ask.

"I *did* try knocking. And calling your name. Get worse headphones."

I roll my eyes and sit up. "Where are you headed?"

"Grocery store. We're out of limes and bagels. You need anything?"

"I'm good, thanks."

"Okay. Conor's coming over. Can you let him in if he shows up before I get back?"

"Yeah, of course."

"We're just planning to watch a movie, if you want to join us. Or invite Hunter."

I glance at my charging laptop. I switched to reading when it died. Before it did, I was looking at apartments in New York.

"I might," I answer. "But Hunter's busy. He had some department honors dinner tonight." I smile. "He gets a little plaque and everything."

The corners of Harlow's mouth turn up a little. "You look happy, E."

"I am."

Almost alarmingly so. The sort of bliss that is almost scary, because it feels like life can only go downhill from here.

Harlow smiles again, then taps my doorframe. "Okay. I'll be back soon."

"Okay," I reply before she disappears down the hallway.

I look at my laptop again, then heave a sigh and open it. I've always been excited about moving to New York one day. But *one day* has suddenly snuck up to seem imminent, and now I actually have to make plans. Sign a lease. Submit job applications. Still exciting. Also stressful.

I switch my music to play on the living room speaker rather than through my headphones, head bobbing to a pop playlist as I browse apartment listings. I lose track of time until the doorbell rings.

Must be Conor.

I slide off my bed and pad down the hallway to answer the door, pausing to plug my phone in before that battery dies too.

Conor gives me a lopsided smile when I open it. "Hey, Eve."

"Hey. Harlow isn't back yet." I step aside so he can enter.

"No problem." He heads for the couch.

The music I was playing cuts out abruptly, replaced by a quieter buzzing as my phone vibrates on the coffee table.

"Your, uh, dad is calling," Conor tells me.

"Let it go to voicemail," I tell him, then glance at the clock on the wall. Eight p.m. exactly.

I'm not sure if my dad calling at our usual time means he's truly trying to reach me or he's too set in his ways to adjust. We always schedule our next conversation at the end of the last one. Since I didn't answer his most recent call, that date hasn't been chosen. Part of me was expecting him to wait a full month to try me again.

"I've never heard you mention your dad before," Conor comments.

"Yeah…we're not close. He basically abandoned me and my mom, and now he has a new family with someone else."

"Sounds familiar."

"Oh. Uh, right," I say awkwardly.

I don't know all the details about Conor's family, but Harlow has filled me in on enough to know the story shares some similarities to my situation.

Although, from what she's told me, Conor's dad has regrets. He genuinely wanted a relationship with his oldest kid, even before they had Harlow in common.

I don't think my dad could say the same. I think he grew up, had more children, and realized pretending he didn't have a third kid was a shitty decision. He checks in out of guilt or to ease his own conscience, not because he wants to know me.

"Do you usually pick up?" Conor asks.

I exhale. "Yeah. We talk sports for a few minutes, and I ask about his other kids."

"I didn't know you were a sports fan."

"I'm not."

"Ah," Conor realizes.

"Yeah. For a while, I thought some pointless small talk with my dad was better than never talking to him at all. But recently, I'm reassessing. I want to make it a little less *easy* for him, I guess." I bite my bottom lip. "Does that make me a terrible person?"

Conor chuckles. "You're definitely asking the wrong person. I didn't—well, I made my dad's life hell every chance I got. Yelled at him, refused to talk to him, locked myself in a room to avoid him. I was so *mad* at him. So fucking furious, there was this angry haze that I couldn't see past. I looked at my dad, and all I saw was red. But…he never gave up. Never stopped inviting me for holidays or sending birthday cards. And I have regrets for how I handled it, so I'm definitely not recommending you do this. Your dad *should* show he cares, though. Whether or not you answer, he should keep calling."

"He's not coming to my graduation," I admit. "He told me the last time we talked, and I haven't answered since. Not that he's tried very hard. One—well, now two calls."

"I'm sorry, Eve. That sucks."

"Yeah, it does," I agree. "But at least now I know where we stand. Or where we don't, rather. That our phone calls were as meaningless as the conversations themselves."

"My dad came to my high school graduation. But Landon was playing 'Pomp and Circumstance' with the school band, so I was never really sure if he showed up for me. And next month, he'll be there, but…"

"But Harlow is graduating too," I finish.

Conor nods. "Exactly. Most of the time, I think I'm better off not knowing his exact motivations. Sometimes…not knowing feels like the worst thing in the world."

I nod too, understanding exactly what he means. "Well, if you and Harlow get married, you know he'll be at the wedding."

He laughs. "Yeah. When."

"What?"

"*When* Harlow and I get married."

I smile. "Since we're bonding, I feel like I should apologize."

He frowns. "For what?"

"I might have strongly encouraged Harlow to leave Gaffney's

with Clayton Thomas at the end of last semester. In my defense, all I knew about you was that you were a fuckboy player and that you broke my best friend's heart on her birthday, but still. I saw your face after she left with him, and I've felt bad about it ever since. So, sorry."

Conor mostly looks amused. "Fuckboy player, huh? I should have you pitch me to some team managers."

"Most art professors allow talking, so people in my classes gossip a lot," I inform him. "And I was just trying to be a good friend."

"You don't owe me an apology, Eve. Was I thrilled about it at the time? No. But it was my own fault, and I deserved that kick in the ass."

I nod. "Maybe lay off Clayton, then?"

"Thomas?" Conor's focus sharpens, and I'm immediately intimidated. I feel bad for the guys who have to face off against him on the ice. "Did he ask you to say something?"

"*No*," I say quickly, worried I'm making the situation worse. "He—I just ran into him at a party."

Conor raises an eyebrow. "I didn't know you hung out with the basketball team."

"I didn't—don't. It was…well, I'm trying to experience some new things before graduation. Go out of my comfort zone a little."

Conor nods.

"Anyway, I happened to see Clayton there and it was obvious he felt bad about the whole thing. He, uh, he was roommates with Hunter freshman year."

Conor's head is tilted, studying me. "I know."

"Right. Of course you do. I just…he gave me a little push with Hunter. And I'd like to return the favor in some way."

"I didn't tell the team to shut out Thomas."

"But they all did, because they knew how you felt about him."

Conor nods. "Me and Thomas will never be buddies. But I'll make sure the boys know they can ease up there. Best I can do."

"Thanks."

He's still studying me. "I didn't mean to make Hunter pick sides."

"You knew he'd pick yours, though."

"Yeah, I did," he agrees. "Like I know he'd pick yours. I've never seen him like this. All…" He smiles. "He was almost a half hour late for dinner the other night. That's literally never happened before. You're good for him, Eve. Get him to let loose a little and take things less seriously. So, in exchange for me doing Thomas a solid, don't break my best friend's heart, okay?"

"I won't," I assure him. "And you'd better not either, Hart-breaker."

Conor shakes his head. "Fuck. That made it all the way to the art building?"

I smile. "I told you, art students gossip a lot."

The front door opens. "Hey, I'm back!" Harlow's voice calls. "Just have to grab the rest of the bags from the car."

"Leave the bags, Hayes," Conor says, standing. "I'll grab them."

As he passes me, he adds a quiet "I won't."

CHAPTER THIRTY-NINE

HUNTER

I'm frowning in the mirror, attempting to knot my tie properly, when my phone buzzes in the pocket of my slacks.

I pull it out. "Hey, Mom," I greet cheerfully.

"Hunter."

Something's wrong. I hear it in her voice as soon as she says my name.

"What's going on?" I ask, yanking the tie off.

"It's Sean. He…honey, he overdosed. His landlord found him when he went to collect rent. And Sean—" Her voice collapses in a sob. "Sean was unresponsive, so his landlord called 911. Your father and I just got to the hospital. We're waiting to talk to the doctors."

The room around me is spinning, all the familiar surroundings a ceaseless blur of color.

He didn't call me.

That's my first thought. My brother got high and didn't call me.

Because I told him not to.

"Fuck," I breathe.

For once, my mom doesn't chastise me for language. She hiccups, hiccups like she's been crying hard for a long time.

"I'll be there. I'm leaving now and I'll…I'll be there."

"Hunter, there's nothing you can do. I'm here and your dad is here and we'll make sure the doctors do everything they can."

"I need to be there. I need to see him."

He could die. My brother could die—could already be dead.

I hated seeing Sean pale and underweight. But I would take that now, would take it and feel grateful he had a heartbeat.

"You have two weeks of college left, Hunter. Classes and exams. *There's nothing you can do here*. I called because I knew you'd want to know. Not so you'd drop everything and drive seventeen hours. I already—" Her voice breaks. "I already have one son to worry about. Don't make me worry about you too."

I'm breathing too fast. Hyperventilating, maybe. But I force my inhales to slow because she's right. She doesn't need to worry about me right now.

"You'll update me?"

"As soon as I hear something," she assures me.

"Okay. Love you, Mom."

"I love you too, Hunter."

She hangs up.

I stand frozen for a few seconds, then tear out of my room. All of a sudden, it seems too small. I need to be outside. I need to be moving. I need to be somewhere else, where the walls aren't collapsing.

I bang on Conor's door.

"One sec!" he calls. It feels like an eternity until he opens the door, tie loose and jacket off. "Dude, I'm almost—" Conor frowns. "What's wrong?"

"I've gotta go."

"What? Go? Go where?"

The rest of Conor's words get lost in the rush of blood whooshing through my ears.

I pass Aidan's empty bedroom. He already left to pick up Rylan. Conor and I were going to carpool with Harlow and Eve.

Eve…

Fuck. Not only am I going to miss the team dinner, I'm skipping out on what was essentially our first official date.

But I'm in no fucking shape for it. I won't be able to sit and smile and wonder if I'll be able to sense the moment I lose my brother. And I don't want to have to explain why I'm in such a state right now.

I just need to *move*.

I'm almost to the stairs when Conor grabs my arm, pulling me up short and spinning me to face him. His face is pale, his expression drawn and worried. "What the fuck is going on, Morgan?"

"I can't—I can't get into it right now. Just…tell Eve I'm sorry. And that I'll make it up to her."

I try to jerk my arm away, but Conor's hold tightens. "Hunter, you're seriously freaking me out. What could possibly be more important than taking the girl you seem crazy about to celebrate the championship we won?"

"I'm not in the mood to talk, Hart."

He scans my face. "Promise me if I let go, you're not about to go do something stupid."

"I'm not the one who did something stupid."

Hart's grip doesn't loosen.

"I'm fine. I mean, I'm not. And I'll explain why later. But right now, I just really need to get the hell out of here. I'll be back later tonight."

His hand finally drops. "Okay. Call me if you need anything, all right?"

I nod, then pound down the stairs.

My keys were already in my pocket in case Conor wanted me to drive. I reverse out of my usual spot, a little of the tightness in my chest easing as I accelerate down the road.

Ten minutes later, I'm doing eighty along I-5.

If Sean isn't okay, I'm going to blame myself. I'm going to wonder if he didn't call because I told him not to. I'm going to wonder whether he'd be okay if he'd called.

I'm sick with the possibility. There's no anger or resentment, how I normally feel after one of Sean's relapses. None of the exhaustion either. I'm so jacked up my hands are trembling.

I tighten my grip on the steering wheel, making sure the wheels stay straight in my lane.

As I drive, I let myself think about the memories I usually avoid.

Sean and I were inseparable as kids. That changed a little as we got older. I became the annoying little brother tagging along. But he was always there when I needed him. For girl advice, for a ride to a party, for a trip to the rink. Even after all the distance his addiction created, I can't imagine my life without him.

I didn't think he'd show up for the championship game, but I hoped.

I didn't think he'd come to graduation with my parents, but I hoped.

And hope is really dangerous. Because it assumes anything can be fixed, and some things are too final to be resuscitated.

I didn't realize how much I relied on hope—on the belief Sean would be okay one day—until now.

You can't *hope* someone comes back from the dead.

I've always kept it together after Sean called. I swallowed my disappointment and resentment and fear, and I kept going.

But I'm realizing I never considered how badly it could end. I'd rather Sean call me in the middle of the night for the rest of my life than never call again.

I told him not to call.

That guilt is suffocating.

A torturous hour later, my mom calls. The car swerves a little as I rush to answer.

"He's awake."

The flood of relief is like a first breath after being held underwater. I'm gasping. Reeling. But so, *so* relieved it's staggering.

"They're running a bunch of tests, and we're waiting to talk to another doctor. But the nurse said he's stable. Out of the woods. Oh, honey, here's the doctor now. I'll give you another update as soon as I can."

"Okay," I say before she hangs up.

My voice sounds hoarse, like I was screaming.

I kind of want to. The relief is mixing with all the other chaotic emotions churning inside of me, and I need some sort of outlet.

I take the next exit, then merge back onto the highway headed in the direction I came from. Toward Somerville. The dinner is more than halfway over, so showing up now will just be a distraction.

And I feel better than when my mom first called, but not by much. Attending a celebration is one of the last things I feel like doing right now.

Rather than heading straight home, I drive to the rink. Skating's never failed to make me feel better.

I still have the key from the last time Hart left it with me. And I realize why he never asked for it back when I step inside.

They melted the ice.

I've never been in here this far past the season. The rink is basically boarded up. The only lights on are the emergency ones, illuminating the giant slab of cement that's replaced the smooth stretch of white.

Another reminder of how quickly things can change.

CHAPTER FORTY

EVE

I tear the strip of tape off the canvas slowly, balling it up and tossing it in the trash. Right as I'm dabbing my paintbrush in linseed oil to start on the lower half, there's a knock on the door.

I freeze, a cold fist of fear tightening around my windpipe. When I got here fifteen minutes ago, the entire building was silent and empty. The exact solitude I was craving to worry about Hunter. But now, the silence seems menacing.

"Eve? You in there?"

I recognize his voice and relax.

Then tense again, because I have no idea what him taking off earlier means. Hunter *doesn't* take off. He shows up.

Conor was clearly worried about him. Harlow had to talk him into going to the event celebrating the championship that the team won. That was almost as concerning as Hunter's choice not to go.

"Eve?" Hunter says again.

I slide off my stool and walk to the door.

When I open it, Hunter has one hand braced on the doorframe, right next to the plaque with my name on it.

He looks…devastated. His eyes are red-rimmed and his hair

is a chaotic mess that looks like it's had hands run through it repeatedly. He's wearing a dress shirt and slacks, but no tie or jacket. Like he started getting ready for tonight and suddenly stopped.

"Sean overdosed," he states before I can say a word.

I clap a hand to my mouth. "Oh my God. Is he…okay?"

"He's awake. My mom called a little while ago with that update. But when she first called…" He swallows. "They found him unconscious."

"I'm so sorry. Is there anything I can do?"

Hunter shakes his head, then glances down. "Nothing I can do either. My mom told me not to come, and I just—" He blows out a long breath. "I feel so fucking helpless."

I step into Hunter's chest, wrapping my arms around his waist.

He hugs me back instantly, like he needs the contact. "I drove around for a while. Then I went to the rink for…habit, I guess. Skating helps when I'm upset. But they melted the ice. I was leaving campus and it occurred to me you might be here." He exhales. "Glad I was right."

"Painting helps when I'm upset," I tell him.

His arms tighten around me. "I know. I'm so sorry about earlier. I would have called or texted to explain but I just—I was in shock."

"Don't apologize. I was just worried about you. I knew you wouldn't miss the dinner unless it was important."

Hunter rests his chin on the top of my head.

And we just stand like that, holding each other.

"I told him not to call."

"Sean?" I question.

"Yeah. The last time we talked. It was this endless cycle, it seemed like, and I thought that maybe me cutting him off might help. Like talking to me meant something and stopping might be some type of wake-up call." He scoffs. "As if."

"He's sick, Hunter. Addiction is a disease. And it's not because of anything you did or didn't do. You were trying to help him. And deep down, he knows that."

Hunter lifts his chin and tilts mine up. His blue eyes scan my face like he's never seen it before.

"You look beautiful, Eve."

I changed out of the dress I was wearing for the dinner after Conor showed up without Hunter. But I didn't touch my hair or makeup, because both took a while.

"Thanks," I whisper.

The kiss starts out sweet. Gentle and purposeful and safe. Then, something shifts. It becomes more raw. Less disciplined.

Tension hums through Hunter's rigid muscles.

He's holding back, I realize.

Has he always held back?

When we've had sex, it's been a perfectly choreographed dance. I've followed his lead, and each step has felt completely right. Even the times I've initiated intimacy, he's seized control in some way.

It doesn't seem like Hunter is following a plan right now. Part of his world was just upended, and he's still reeling. Still coming to terms with how close he came to losing his brother.

He came here for comfort, and he's never sought me out in that way before. When he told me about Sean, it was because we were already together when his brother called. And with every-thing else, he's so *solid*. Disciplined and capable. He's the person you go to for help, not the one who seeks it out.

"I'm not breakable," I whisper, running my palms down the sculpted planes of his chest. Even through the starched cotton of his button-down, I can feel the energy buzzing beneath taut skin.

"You can be rough. You can lean on me. I'm not going anywhere."

I mean the last part in the emotional sense, not the physical one. Because I am going somewhere, and he is too.

A topic we've avoided talking about, aside from his decision about Penn.

Amidst all the big and scary feelings I have for Hunter, discussing our lives after graduation feels especially big and scary. I molded most of my relationship with Ben around the future. I was attracted to his interest in living in New York, to the joint life I saw there together.

With Hunter, it doesn't feel like a factor. I never expected—thought—that we would end up in the same place post-graduation.

And I fell in love with him anyway.

I'm in love with him.

Hunter exhales, and a little of the tension releases too. "I didn't come here for sex, Eve."

My right hand moves lower. "You're hard."

"Well, yeah." His voice is rough. "Happens a lot around you. Especially when I'm kissing you."

His lips land on mine again.

This time, it doesn't start out sweet. Immediately, there's the same unrestrained intensity.

I kiss him back just as passionately, to the soundtrack of my racing heart and ragged breaths.

I've never felt less in control. It's thrilling…and terrifying. It feels like I *am* falling.

His hand settles on the waistband of my shorts, then slips inside.

"Fuck, Eve. You're so wet."

My head falls back from the first brush of his fingers along my underwear. The hit of pleasure is so sudden and powerful it's almost dizzying. All thoughts flee from my mind, smooth like sand after a wave washed the grains flat.

"You've turned me into a sex addict," I tell him.

It's true. I had no idea this level of physical desire—of *need*—existed.

"Well"—the tone of Hunter's voice is wry—"there are worse things to be addicted to."

"Right." Mine is apologetic. I didn't mean to remind him about Sean. "There are."

Hunter tugs on one of my curls with his other hand. He touches my hair a lot, I've noticed. I've started wearing it down more often, hoping he will. "As long as it's just with me."

He's teasing, a little, but he's also serious.

And I'm *very* serious when I reply, "It is."

Too serious, maybe. Now that I've realized I love Hunter, it feels like maybe that's stamped on my forehead or something. Obvious in *some* way, when I look at him.

"You ever have sex on campus before?" he asks me.

Until now, the concept had not really occurred to me. My world narrows to Hunter when we're in the same place. I completely forgot that we're in a school building. In my broom closet with a door that locks, but still.

"*No*," I answer, in a way that suggests it should have been obvious. I may be trying to be more impulsive and adventurous, but I'm still a rule-follower at heart. "Have—have you?"

"No." His lips move to my neck, sucking gently on the skin there. I'll have a hickey in the morning. "Is it on your list?"

"I could add it."

His pelvis presses into mine, the hard, hot ridge of his erection nudging my inner thigh.

I tug his button-down out of his waistband, impatiently

pulling the buttons open until his chest is exposed. I drag my fingernails down his pecs and over his abs, running a teasing finger back and forth along his waistband once I reach it.

His hands land on the backs of my thighs, erasing all the distance between our lower bodies. I whimper, the pulse between my thighs a second rapid heartbeat.

I squeeze them tight together as I rise on my tippy-toes. My tongue swipes along the curve of his collarbone, then I scrape my teeth on the same spot.

"I can handle it, Hunter."

His fingers bite into the backs of my legs so hard I'll probably have bruises. "Tell me if it's too rough."

"I will," I promise.

He releases me and then spins me around, pressing a palm flat on my back until I'm bent over the stool I sit on to paint. My hair falls over my shoulders, partially covering my face.

I can't see Hunter, and that makes the quick tug of him pulling my shorts and underwear down especially erotic.

I gasp, feeling the cool air hit the wetness that's gathered. I clench around nothing, trying to alleviate a little of the ache.

I barely register the feel of his cock at my entrance before he thrusts without any hesitation, filling me with one stroke. He drags his dick out slowly, so slow I can feel every ridge, and then fills me fast again.

Arousal flows through me like an endless cascade of water.

I'm pinned in place, the press of the stool against my stomach all that's keeping me from collapsing. I have no leverage in this position. I'm entirely at Hunter's mercy. He's controlling everything—the angle, the speed, the depth.

And I love it. I'm completely relaxed, letting him use my body however he wants and enjoying every second.

He pulls out and flips me on my back. I arch so the stool

doesn't dig into my spine, and Hunter's heated gaze lands on my breasts. He yanks my shirt up and the left cup of my bra down until my breast pops free. He palms it, rolling my nipple between two fingers.

I suck in a sharp breath, then cry out when he thrusts inside of me again.

I tighten my inner muscles around his erection, trying to keep him inside of me. My legs wrap around his waist too.

"Fuck, Eve." His cock twitches inside of me and his hips rock harder into mine.

His hands roam all over my body. All the spots that aren't normally sensitive—my ribs, my shoulders, my hips—come alive under his touch.

"More," I beg.

His arm circles my lower back, lifting my pelvis higher and forcing my thighs to open wider.

I moan when he slips even deeper, almost orgasming from that alone.

"This fucking view. Look at you."

I'm looking at *him*. Watching his muscles work to fuck me.

He rubs at my clit, and sparks of light dance across my vision. "Your pussy is so tight. It feels like you're trying to suck the cum right out of me."

I was barely holding it together *before* he started talking dirty. Now, I'm a breath away from nirvana.

Hunter reaches toward the palette I left out, running his finger through the smear of green.

I crane my neck to watch as he draws a heart on my stomach with the paint. He adds two lines on each side, then several angles and a circle.

And I laugh, realizing they're stick figures.

"Impressive," I pant.

"Told you I was talented."

His hand slides lower, smearing some of the paint, pulling my knee up higher. He hits a deeper spot, and it pushes me past the peak.

He covers my mouth when I start to convulse, which is when I remember that we're in a *school building*.

He also pumps faster, the pace quick enough I can hear the collision of our skin as sweat builds between our bodies. My thighs quiver and my toes curl and my vision blurs.

Hunter kisses me. It's a messy, wet tangle of tongues, both of us distracted by the pulse of pleasure. I bite his lower lip, and he moans in response.

"I can feel you coming," I tell him.

The flood of warmth has become one of my favorite parts of sex. It feels like more than usual, already seeping out of me as he continues to thrust lazily. My inner thighs are slick with it.

He groans my name like a prayer.

I don't let those three little words slip out.

But they're right there, waiting, on the tip of my tongue.

CHAPTER FORTY-ONE

HUNTER

AIDAN: Ordering pizza. You guys good with pepperoni?

HUNTER: Yep.

CONOR: Why are you texting? I'm literally sitting two feet away and Morgan is in the kitchen.

I grin at my phone before nudging the fridge door shut with my shoulder. I tuck a bag of chips under one arm and head back into the living room, taking the armchair since Phillips and Hart are hogging the couch.

Aidan is on his laptop. Conor is scrolling through movie options on the television.

It's the last weekend before finals start. Which means it's one of the final weekends of college—ever. Eve went to a concert with Harlow and Aidan said Rylan is hanging out with her roommates.

We haven't hung out, just the three of us, in a while. It's sentimental, knowing we'll never live together again. Hart won't know where he's headed until the draft next month, but I've officially committed to moving to Philadelphia. And Aidan…

Aidan sets his laptop on the coffee table next to Conor's feet. "Check this out."

Evergreen Beer Company is all I can read from this angle. I stand and move behind the couch so I can see more of the screen.

Conor leans closer. "What are you doing? Ordering beer? There's a six-pack in the fridge, Phillips."

"I'm not ordering anything," Aidan answers. "This is the website for my new brewery."

"Your new *what*?" Hart sounds stunned.

I'm only marginally less surprised.

Since our conversation on the way home from Gaffney's, Aidan hasn't mentioned what he plans to do post-graduation. I had no idea he was still considering opening a brewery, let alone acting on it.

"My new brewery. I also got a job at a marketing firm in Seattle. I start in June. So if this whole thing falls apart, I have a backup plan."

"Wow," Conor says.

I echo the sentiment, adding a "Congrats."

Aidan shows us the whole website. It's a simple layout, but it looks very official. Then, he pulls up the listing for the old warehouse he bought in Seattle, telling us about the plans for the renovations. Once they're completed, he plans to launch the website and announce the business. We're the first people he's telling, I realize.

The pizza arrives midway, so we chomp on slices as Aidan talks us through building permits and water lines.

I'm impressed. Impressed that he's doing it, and impressed

he's done it without saying a word. Aidan usually discusses everything aloud.

Then again, he kept things with Rylan a secret for a while, so maybe it just depends on how important it is to him.

"Have you heard from Sean?" Conor asks once we're caught up on Aidan's plans.

I shake my head. I told him and Aidan about my brother—the good, the bad, and the overdose—the morning after the team dinner.

And I've gotten updates from my mom—Sean was discharged from the hospital and is recovering at a rehab center—but my brother hasn't called.

Not only has he not called me, he hasn't answered *my* calls. I know he has his phone because my mom talks to him at least once a day.

But he won't talk to me.

And I don't know why, aside from the way our last conversation ended. I told him not to call me high. I didn't ask him to stop answering my calls sober.

I've realized, since I started calling, that I *stopped* at some point. That every recent time I talked to my brother was when he called me. High, but still.

I'm very tempted to drive home and confront him about it. But graduation is in two weeks. I don't have time for a thirty-four-hour road trip, and I'll be home for most of the summer before heading to Penn.

I'm planning to visit Eve at some point. She found an apartment in Greenwich Village, close to a coffee shop where she got a barista job, and is moving at the beginning of June. But otherwise, I'll be in Wyoming, and Sean won't be able to avoid me.

"Give it some time," Conor advises.

"That's what I've been doing. He could at least answer my calls."

Aidan stands and heads into the kitchen. A couple of minutes later, he returns with a stack of glasses and the expensive whiskey we broke open after winning the state championship. He pours an inch into each one.

"Seems like we should be drinking beer, to celebrate your brewery," Hart comments.

"We're not just celebrating my brewery," Phillips replies. "And this is the good shit. Show some respect." He nudges one glass toward me and one toward Conor.

"Cheers to…" Aidan raises his glass and looks to me. He knows I always *cheers* to something.

"Cheers to…us," I say. My throat is suspiciously thick, so I clear it quickly. "I'll miss you guys."

"Cheers to us," Conor echoes. "I'll miss you guys too."

"For fuck's sake." Aidan sets down his shot before we can actually knock glasses, and then walks out of the living room.

I hear his heavy steps on the stairs a few seconds later.

Conor glances at me. "That was weird."

"Very weird," I agree.

"Uh, bottoms up?"

"Bottoms up."

We clink glasses and then swallow.

"Should we check on him?" I ask.

Before Conor can reply, I hear footsteps on the stairs again.

Aidan reappears, holding two white envelopes. He scowls when he spots the two empty glasses. "What the fuck?"

"We didn't know where you went!" Conor says.

Aidan downs his shot, then refills all the glasses. "You guys know about the shit with Jameson," he starts. "How my brother is an asshole and a pain in the ass. If we weren't blood-related, I'd never talk to the guy again."

Conor nods. "And you and Morgan know the deal with Landon. He's still trying to convince Harlow to break up with me. If it wouldn't hurt her, I'd go back to pretending he doesn't exist."

I realize what they're doing, all of a sudden, and this time the lump in my throat won't clear.

"You guys have been there for me, through it all," Hart continues. "And it means…" He clears his throat. "Well, thanks."

"You're welcome, Hart," Aidan says. "Someone had to carry the team while you were slacking."

Conor rolls his eyes.

"Yeah, fine. I'll be serious. I came here at a real low point. Probably would have gotten myself kicked off the team freshman year if not for you two. And I know I was late sometimes—"

"All the time," I interject.

"And caused some problems—"

"With who?" Conor asks innocently.

Aidan slouches back on the sofa. "This is why I'm never serious, you dicks."

I reach for my glass and lift it in the air. "Cheers to choosing brothers."

Because that's what we did. We're a lot more than teammates. And we chose to be there for each other, especially when the people who were supposed to be there weren't.

"Cheers to choosing brothers," we all repeat, and then down the shots.

"Happy early graduation." Aidan holds envelopes out to me and Conor.

I take it, surprised. I figured they were related to his brewery.

"You didn't have to get us anything," I say, experiencing a pang of guilt.

I didn't get *him* anything.

I still have time, I guess, but knowing Aidan, this is extravagant, and I don't have that kind of money lying around.

"It's for me too," he replies.

I glance at Conor, and we open the envelopes together.

It takes me a couple of minutes to scan enough text to understand the gist of it.

Aidan arranged an African safari for us next summer. Two weeks, with airfare and accommodations included. I can't even imagine how much this cost. Several grand, at least.

"I picked July to make sure you were free," he tells Hart.

From the look on Conor's face, that means more than the gift itself. It's a testament to Aidan's confidence that Conor will get drafted.

Aidan glances at me. "You too, nerd."

"This trip looks amazing," I say. "But it's *way* too much, Phillips."

Conor nods in agreement.

Aidan pours more whiskey. "No, it's not. I don't know when I'll see you guys after May. I wanted to make sure we had a reunion planned. And I didn't spend my *entire* trust fund on the bar. I have the money, and I want to wear camo and see some lions with my best friends. Promise you'll show up?"

There's a tentativeness to that last question.

Suddenly I'm eighteen again, standing on a porch at a party I'm not sure I want to be at and agreeing to get lunch with a stranger.

A stranger who would become one of the most important people in my life. When I told Coach that Aidan would die for Rylan, I meant it. I knew it, because he would die for me too. Loyalty is a rare thing to come by. It can't be bought or stolen or *explained*, really. It's there or it's not.

Family can be forged. And those bonds—chosen bonds—can be a lot stronger than blood.

"I'll be there," I promise.

"I will too," Conor adds.

And for the first time, graduation feels a lot less like an ending and more like a new beginning.

CHAPTER FORTY-TWO

EVE

"Eve!" My mom stands and waves as soon as I enter the restaurant.

I smile at the hostess waiting at the stand. "I'm meeting my mom."

She smiles back. "I figured. Are you graduating tomorrow?"

"I am."

"Congratulations."

"Thanks," I say, and then head for our table.

I haven't seen my mom since the end of winter break, back in January. She smells like her lavender laundry detergent and rose perfume. I inhale the floral scents deeply as we hug.

She touches one of my curls after we let go. "Your hair looks nice."

"Thanks. I've been wearing it down more."

My mom nods. "Less breakage."

"Yep." I nod too. "That's why."

She tilts her head, studying me a little more closely. "You look happy, Eve."

"I am," I tell her.

My mom smiles as we sit down.

"The flight was okay?" I ask.

"There was an hour delay, but otherwise it was fine. I had plenty of time to check in at the hotel before meeting you here."

I nod. "Good."

A waitress appears to take our drink orders and list off the specials.

Once she leaves, I spread my napkin in my lap. "How's the salon?"

"Good. Busy. Everyone wants a spring makeover. My May candle arrived. Lilac."

I got my mom a candle subscription last Christmas. Each month is a different scent, and she always tells me what it is.

"How's Jenny?"

"She has kindergarten graduation in a few weeks, which is hard to believe. I told her your ceremony would be a *little* more elaborate." My mom smiles. "If flight prices weren't so crazy, I'd have brought her. John would have loved to be here too." She pulls out her phone and shows me a photo of my half sister clutching her dad's leg. "I took this of them after Jenny's dance recital last night."

I smile at it. "Wow. She's getting so big."

"She sure is." My mom sips her water. "Do you have any photos of your apartment?"

I still, taken aback by the question. I texted her after I signed a lease for an apartment in Greenwich Village last week. But we haven't really discussed it, maybe because there's no longer anything to say. I made my decision.

"Just a few that were part of the listing," I answer.

I unlock my phone and pull up the real estate site, chewing on my lower lip as I slide it across the table for her to look at.

I lucked out, I think. The location is perfect, right by the High

Line. And Marissa, my new roommate, seems super sweet. We talked on the phone for an hour before I committed to the apartment. Her current roommate is leaving the city to go to law school in Boston, so she has an open room. Most of the apartment is furnished, so I won't have to buy much once I move. Marissa let me know a nearby coffee shop she loves was hiring, so I called and got a barista job lined up. Hopefully it will only be temporary, until I can find something art-related, but it will be enough to pay the bills and leave me with time to paint in the evenings. The manager of the coffee shop even said she'd be open to letting me display some of my paintings for sale.

"It looks really nice, Eve," my mom tells me.

"Thanks, Mom."

She passes my phone back to me. "John has a cousin who lives in Stamford he's talked about visiting before. Maybe we can make a trip this fall."

"I would love that."

I knew my mom wouldn't *keep* me from moving to New York. That it was a decision I would get to make on my own.

But I underestimated how it would feel to have her support. It's like a weight is lifting off my shoulders. Like I could fail, and I wouldn't have to hide it from her for fear of an *I told you so*.

"What do you recommend here?" My mom opens her menu. "Everything sounds so good."

"I got the tortellini last time. The pizzas are pretty popular too."

"Hmmm." She keeps scanning the menu. "Maybe I'll get a pizza."

The waitress returns a few minutes later and we place our orders.

"So, remind me what the schedule is for tomorrow," my mom says. "I should be at the stadium at nine?"

"The ceremony doesn't start until ten thirty, but we can't reserve seats. I'd try to get there at nine just in case, yeah, but if you're running late, it should be fine."

"Nine it is. And we're getting lunch with Hunter and his parents afterward?"

"As long as that's okay?"

Hunter's mom suggested it. I've never met his parents, but based on the way Hunter talks about them, I'm sure they're lovely.

"Of course," my mom says. "I'd like to meet them. And Hunter, of course." She plucks a piece of bread out of the basket. "Is there anything I should know about the ceremony?"

"What do you mean?"

"Well, I've never gone to a college graduation before, so…"

"I haven't either, Mom. I'm pretty sure you just have to sit and try to stay awake during all the different speakers."

"Okay. I'll stop for coffee on the way."

I laugh. "Sounds good."

My phone lights up with a text from Harlow asking if I have extra boxes in my room. I reply *yes*, and then notice the time.

It's exactly eight p.m.

I stand, accidentally knocking my napkin off the table. I pick it up before grabbing my phone off the table. "I'll be right back, Mom. I just need to make a quick phone call."

I catch a glimpse of her puzzled expression before I walk outside.

I've been putting this off, telling myself it didn't matter. But I want to enjoy tomorrow, not sit and listen to inspirational speeches and regret not telling my dad why him showing up would've mattered.

If he had a good reason for not coming, it would be one thing. If his kid was sick or there was an emergency at work or some other urgent situation had come up, I would have understood.

But he *chose* not to come.

And you can't *make* someone care, the same way you can't stop caring yourself.

My father answers on the third ring. "Eve. This is a surprise."

"Because it's not a Tuesday?"

He hesitates before replying. "Because you stopped answering my calls."

"Yeah, I did. Any idea why?"

A longer pause, as the hostility in my voice registers. It's not a tone I've used with my dad before. I'm always agreeable and accommodating, trying to be the smallest burden possible.

"Life doesn't work out the way we always want it to, Eve. I have responsibilities. A job and—"

I scoff. "Mom has a job, and she showed up. She's *always* shown up."

"Your mother has a much more flexible work schedule than I do."

My father hasn't grown up. He may have gotten older. He may have had more kids. But, at his core, he's still the same self-centered seventeen-year-old who left my mom on her own.

And I'm finished accepting his excuses.

"They set the graduation date two years ago. And plenty of parents who aren't self-employed are here."

My dad sighs. "Eve, I know—"

"No, you *don't* know. You don't know anything about me, because when we talk it's about sports and then I ask about your other kids. And you know what? That's fine. That's all you could offer." I suck in a deep breath, forcing my burning eyes to remain wide open and straight ahead. "I called to tell you I'm mad. I was mad when you told me you weren't coming tomorrow, and I was too…whatever to tell you. I was mad when you never showed up for birthday parties or my eighth-grade graduation or any of my art shows, and I always pretended I didn't care. I've always been mad, and you were never there for me to be mad at. So I'm calling to tell you to stop calling. I'm done with the charade of pretending I have a dad. You never wanted me. Congratulations, Dean. You have one less responsibility, and only two kids."

For the first time ever, I hang up on my father.

And then I stand on the sidewalk, breathing heavily, simultaneously proud and sad. I needed to say all of that. But now that I have, I can't take any of it back. And if my dad listens, and never calls me again, that could have been the last time I heard my father's voice. That doesn't feel like a success.

I pull in a deep inhale, let it out, and then head back inside.

"Everything okay?" my mom asks as I sit down.

"Yeah," I reply. "I just… I needed to take care of something."

Maybe one day, I'll tell her what I just told my dad. But I don't want to bring him up now. This weekend isn't just a celebration of me. It's a testament to all the opportunities my mom gave me, all the obstacles she overcame. Not only did my father choose not to come, he chose not to contribute. Pretending he doesn't exist, same as he did to us, feels appropriate.

My pasta and my mom's pizza arrive a few minutes later. I can't recall the last time my mom and I ate dinner alone, just the two of us. It had to be well before I left for college. Before she met John or had Jenny.

As we eat, she tells me funny stories about clients at the salon. I try to talk her into listening to *C is for Crime*. The final episode is releasing on Friday, so she won't have to wait for the big reveal the way Hunter and I have all week.

After my mom pays the bill, she pulls a pink envelope out of her purse and sets it on the table. "I wasn't sure when to give this to you. It's from your dad."

I still. "What?"

"He came to the salon last week." My mom purses her lips. "It wasn't the most…pleasant of conversations, but it was a necessary one. Long overdue, probably. I know—I know I've always discouraged you from having a relationship with your dad. Most of it was to protect you from disappointment. But part of it was to punish him, and that…" She sighs. "I'm sorry about that."

I stare at the envelope like it's a live bomb that might explode.

"I think he wanted to be here, Eve. But…I don't think he knows how to be. And that's up to you, whether or not you want to teach him. How many chances you're willing to offer. Only you can decide that, and I'll support whatever you decide. I promise."

Curiosity flares as I reach for the envelope hesitantly.

My dad has never sent me a card before. I don't even know what his handwriting looks like.

The first page I pull out of the envelope is a folded drawing. Two tiny people and one person four times their height. The two shorter stick figures are labeled *Noah* and *Lily*. The tall one is *Eve*.

I set down the drawing and pull the card out.

When I open it, a check slides into my lap. A check for a lot of money, with my dad's name in the top left corner. The note on the inside of the card covers both sides, written in a slanted scrawl.

Eve,

On Saturday, you'll be a college graduate. You're

22, about to head out into the world, and I won't be there to see it.

I'm sorry. I know those are just words, and I know they change nothing.

I'm sorry I missed so much. I'm sorry that I was so selfish. I'm sorry it's taken me this long to say I'm sorry.

When we first started our calls, I thought it was better to pretend that they'd always taken place. I thought it was better to talk about my other children, so it seemed like I had some idea how to be a father.

You've stopped answering, and I don't blame you. I was surprised you ever did. You've given me many more chances than I ever deserved.

Lily wanted me to send you this drawing. She wants to be an artist like her big sister.

Happy Graduation.

Love,
Dad

I stare at the card. My eyes burn, but no tears form. Almost like I want to cry, but I'm not sure if I should.

I just decided what my dad's role would be in my life—nonexistent—and then he had to go and do this.

When I glance up, my mom's staring at me sympathetically. The conflict must be clear on my face.

"He was really hot in high school, honey."

A surprised laugh bursts out. My mom has never talked much about her relationship with my dad. All I know is it was brief and ended badly.

"And I wouldn't change a thing, Evelyn." She reaches out and squeezes the hand that's not holding my dad's card. "He might have been a terrible father, but he's not a terrible person. I got that much right, at least."

I squeeze back. "You got a lot right, Mom."

CHAPTER FORTY-THREE

HUNTER

y mom looks…nervous when she opens the door to the hotel room. But her smile is warm as she pulls me in for a hug, holding on for longer than usual. I know it's not just because I haven't seen her since January. It's because life feels extra fragile lately.

"It's so good to see you, Hunter."

"You too," I say, releasing her and walking deeper into the room. "How was the drive—"

I stop talking as soon as I see Sean sitting on the edge of the bed.

"Don't worry," he drawls. "I have my own room."

My brother looks awful.

He stopped by for Christmas dinner in December, since it was during one of his sober phases. That was the last time I saw him in person, and it seems like a lot longer than six months ago. Sean's about twenty pounds skinnier than he was then. His head is shaved, emphasizing the gauntness of his face and the dark circles under his eyes. He looks a lot older than twenty-four.

"Sean decided he was up for the drive," my mom says. Her voice is full of false cheer that sounds spread thin.

She knows Sean and I haven't talked since his overdose. Knows he's been avoiding me.

My brother stands, cracking his knuckles.

I'm taller than him by a couple of inches. I remember the day I hit his height being one of the greatest days of my life. Finally looking the guy I'd looked up to all my life in the eyes.

"Yeah," Sean says. "Sitting in the car for seventeen hours *really* takes it out of you."

"Sean," Mom chastises softly.

"Guess you still have your sense of sarcasm," I say.

"Yeah. Guess so."

We stare at each other, two brothers acting like strangers. Love and anger are battling inside of me. That frantic hour when I was terrified I'd never see my brother again is fresh in my memory, reminding me how short and tenuous life is.

But I'm also so *mad* at him. For putting me—and our parents—through that after everything else he's already put us through. And for not answering a single fucking call since it happened.

Sean rubs at his jaw. The last time I saw him, he had an unkempt beard. He's completely clean-shaven now. "Wanna go for a drive?"

"A drive?"

"Uh-huh. Seventeen hours wasn't long enough."

I snort. "I just got here."

Sean clears his throat. "Please, Hunter."

He clearly wants to talk to me alone, but I'm not sure that's a great idea. I'm less liable to say something I'll regret around our parents. And, past his bluster, I'm not oblivious to the fact that Sean just had a near-death experience. It's in both of our interests if I keep my mouth mostly shut.

I glance at my mom. She nods encouragingly.

I was expecting to have a seventeen-hour drive to decide what to say to my brother. I wasn't expecting him to be here. I'm *shocked*, actually, that he came to my graduation. I assumed he was still at the rehab center, because my mom never said otherwise.

Whatever. We'll have to do this at some point, I guess.

"Yeah. Fine." I pull my car keys back out of my pocket. "We'll be back soon, I guess."

"Have fun and be safe!" she calls.

Same thing she's always said to us.

Sean's silent as we step into the elevator and head back down to the Westin's lobby.

I am too. He's made it clear he didn't want to hear what I had to say, so I'm waiting for him to talk first.

By the time we're in my SUV, he still hasn't said a word.

I drum my fingers on the steering wheel. "So…where to?"

"What about the rink?"

"They melted the ice."

Sean shrugs a shoulder. "I didn't bring my skates."

"Fine." I pull out of the parking lot, turning up the music so we don't have to sit in stifling silence. It's the Arctic Monkeys. Eve turned me on to them.

"No. 1 Party Anthem" ends, and "Why'd You Only Call Me When You're High?" starts next.

I deliberate skipping to the next song, but then I decide to leave it on.

Sean doesn't say a word. Either he's oblivious to the lyrics' uncanny relevance, or he's choosing not to comment.

Which makes me think my brother has changed even more than I realized. Because the Sean I used to know was smart—

smarter than me. Nothing got past him. And he loved a good joke or prank.

The rink's parking lot is completely empty. Which I expected. All the underclassmen have left campus for the summer, most of the graduating seniors are spending time with their families, and the rink hasn't been used for more than a month. Officially, it closed back in March when our season ended.

Sean pops his door open and climbs out like he's fully expecting to head inside.

I have a key, but he doesn't know that.

I trail after him, studying my brother like he's a code I'm trying to decipher.

Sean crouches down in front of the door handles, slipping something out of his pocket.

"What are you doing?" I ask, reaching him.

"I wanna see the rink, not the building."

"So you're *breaking in*? Isn't your rap sheet long enough, Sean?"

"We must all look pretty tiny from your high horse, huh?"

"I have a fucking key," I snap. "Stand up before someone calls campus police."

Sean stands. "You have a key, huh? Was that part of the championship package?"

"So you *do* know we won one. I wasn't sure, since you never bothered to show up or to congratulate me."

That shuts him up.

Something that looks very similar to regret flashes across Sean's face. But it's gone a few seconds later when the hinges creak open.

My brother walks very slowly into the lobby I've entered a thousand times.

Watching him, I'm reminded that Sean never went to college.

That his hockey career ended when he was in high school because of an injury that sent him spiraling into addiction.

Anger hurts more when it's attached to sadness. It lingers and it stings and it festers.

"This is the main entrance," I say gruffly. "Concession stand and ticket booth are over there. Locker rooms and offices are through that way."

Sean's stopped by the trophy display. The national championship is front and center, a framed photograph of the team right above it. I'm in the middle, between Conor and Aidan.

"These are your best friends, right? Phillips and Hart?"

"Yeah." I've mentioned them before, but I'm surprised he remembers their names. Most of what I say to Sean seems to go in one ear and right out the other. "Rink's through here."

I shove through the doors that separate the lobby from the ice, and Sean follows me.

It's not an impressive sight. The wooden bleachers are ancient and empty. The rubber mats are scuffed and frayed in spots, and the ice is missing, just a dull slab of concrete inside the boards.

But it's been my second home for the past four years. The site of some of my happiest memories.

And something in Sean's expression makes me think that he understands that. That he sees more than the mediocrity most do.

We take a seat in the bleachers, which creak under our combined weight, and Sean glances up at the bright banner. It'll fade eventually, but right now it's the brightest, newest thing in here.

"Nice rink," he comments.

I say nothing. With Sean, it's always difficult to tell if he's being serious. That could be genuine, or it could be a jab.

"Mom said you finally got a girlfriend?"

"Finally?" I scoff. "I dated Jemma in high school."

"Yeah, but that was *high school*. It never seemed that serious."

"Well, I was…distracted."

By you.

I think it; I don't say it. But there's a wry twist to Sean's mouth that makes me think my brother read my mind.

"And now?" he asks.

"Now, I'm focused. It's serious. She's…special. She's really special."

"That's great, Hunter. I'm happy for you."

"You'll meet her tomorrow, if you—"

"Make it to the ceremony?" Sean smirks. "Don't worry. I don't have a dealer in this town. I'll be there."

"That's not fucking funny," I tell him.

Sean sobers. "I know. But as dumb as it sounds, it helps to remind myself that I have a problem. It's when I convinced myself I was cured that things got bad."

I go silent, because Sean's never mentioned his reasoning before. There were just phases when he was better, and phases when he was bad. "That doesn't sound dumb," I say quietly.

He smiles and glances up at the new banner hanging from the rafters again. "Mom said you're going to UPenn in the fall?"

"Yeah."

"For political science?" There's some amusement in his voice. "You gonna be a politician?"

"No. I'm planning to work for an organization that addresses the harms of drug use and implement policy solutions. There aren't many organizations out there, so a master's will mean a better shot at getting hired somewhere."

"Fuck," Sean says softly. He tips his head back, looking up at the bright banner again. "You won a fucking national championship, man. I couldn't believe it when Mom told me. Still can't, sometimes."

"Me neither."

"I can't believe I missed it."

"Me neither."

He exhales. "I'm sorry, Hunter. I should have been there."

I rest my elbows on my knees. "We don't have to get into it."

"Yeah, we do. I'm trying to tell you I know I fucked up. And then I fucked up again. And again. And again. Times that by a hundred. The more I did, the easier it got. But I want you to know that *I* know I fucked up, for whatever that's worth."

"You didn't answer any of my calls. You almost fucking *died*, and you stopped talking to me."

"I was embarrassed, Hunter. You don't know what it's like, to have people you love bail you out over and over again. To be so grateful and also to hate them for it. There were times I woke up and wish I *had* died, so you and Mom and Dad wouldn't have to deal with me anymore."

An awful thought occurs to me. "Did you overdose on purpose?"

Sean blows out a long sigh. "No. It was a bad batch that I mixed with booze and some other shit."

"Jesus, Sean."

"It's addictive. Not just the drugs, but doing something you know is bad for you. Dancing with the devil, you know. Or you don't. You never had that impulse. It's why you're graduating with honors and heading to an Ivy, and I'm living with Mom and Dad."

"You're just letting your demons win," I say.

"Maybe. It'll be a lot harder to get back to that place after waking up to white walls and Mom crying, I can tell you that much."

I flinch, the picture he's painting too close to the image in my head when I was speeding down the freeway.

"You didn't call that night."

"I was home. I didn't think I needed help. And—" He clears his throat. "You asked me not to."

I close my eyes. Fuck. That's exactly what I was worried about.

"I never should have been calling you, Hunter. I knew that, even high. It started because I was jealous. You were the golden boy, while I was the screwup, and I wanted to drag you down with me. And then, after you came here, it became the only way I could talk to you. I wasn't going to call to tell my little brother about the job I lost or the junkie I'd fucked for free drugs, so I called you when I was high. Nice song choice, by the way."

A reluctant smile curves up the corner of my mouth. "Thanks."

"I'm not going to promise anything, because I'm so sick of breaking them. But I'm trying to get better. I *want* to get better. And don't let me pull you into my shit. You should take whatever job you want, not—"

"It *is* the job I want," I interrupt. "Yeah, I started looking into it because of you, but there are hundreds of thousands of other people dealing with the same thing. They get in a cycle, and then they can't get out. And they get punished for it."

Sean doesn't respond right away. And when he does, his voice is a little hoarse. "I'm really proud of you, Hunter. Really, really proud."

"Thanks." My reply is a little husky too.

He claps me on the back, and then we sit in silence for a bit, staring at the spot where the ice should be. I wonder when Sean skated last. My guess is it's been a while, maybe even since high school.

"I think Mom made dinner reservations," I finally say.

And is probably sitting anxiously in the hotel room, worrying about us.

Sean shakes his head as he stands. "Don't want to be late? You're really gunning for favorite son, huh?"

"Well, you could make it a *little* more of a competition," I retort.

He grins, shoving me right as I stand. I have to turn the two steps down into one leap.

I flip him off, and he laughs. The laughter echoes, and it sounds like my childhood. Something I haven't heard in a while.

And, as we head back toward the lobby, the guy walking beside me feels a lot less like a stranger.

CHAPTER FORTY-FOUR

EVE

I'm a college graduate.

The tassel flip and the empty case I was handed to display the diploma that'll get mailed to me didn't really make it feel real. But it's starting to sink in, after a full day of photos and tears and celebration.

A happy squeal draws my attention to the left. Conor is splashing Harlow in the shallows. Rylan and Aidan are standing on the dock with Sean, looking at the boats and talking.

"What are you doing all the way down here?" Hunter's walking across the sand toward me, hands tucked in the pockets of his suit pants.

The wind picks up, flopping a piece of blond hair onto his forehead. He'll need another haircut soon.

"I wanted to stick my feet in the water," I reply.

I was also hoping he'd follow me down here and away from everyone else, since I haven't given him his graduation gift yet.

"Sean seems to be having fun," I comment.

Hunter glances toward his brother, who's still standing with Rylan and Aidan. "Yeah. He always does."

"You're waiting for him to relapse."

He exhales. "I probably always will be. But I don't think it'll happen tonight, so that's something."

Hunter leans down and picks up one of the flat rocks lining the shore. He sends it flying toward the water with a powerful flick of his wrist. It skips four times before disappearing below the dark surface of the Sound.

"Impressive," I comment.

"I'll show you. C'mere."

I take a few steps toward him, closing the distance. Hunter wraps an arm around my waist, spins me, and tugs me to him, pressing a kiss to the crease of my shoulder.

I shiver, relaxing back against his chest. Not just from the cold, although the dress I wore for graduation isn't retaining much heat in the cooling air.

"You okay?" he murmurs. "You've been quiet tonight."

"Yeah, I'm good. Just…thinking."

"Thinking about what?"

"Well, I called my dad last night and basically told him he no longer had a daughter."

"What did he say?"

"Nothing. I hung up on him. And right after, my mom handed me an envelope from him. With a nice note and a crayon drawing from my little sister and a check that means I might not need to eat ramen for every meal once I'm in New York. He dropped it off at her salon. Pretty sure it's the first time they've talked face-to-face in ten years."

"Wow." His arms fold across my chest.

I lift my hands, running them back and forth along his forearms. "Yeah. It was a lot easier to hate him when he was entirely hateable."

"You don't hate him, Eve. That's why it's hard."

I blow out a long breath, admiring the glassy surface of the Sound. Overhead, there's nearly a full moon. Everything—the water, the few boats bobbing, the rocky sand—is bathed by a silvery, ethereal glow.

Something warm and rough brushes the back of my palm. A stone.

"Here. Hold it between your thumb and middle finger," Hunter instructs. "And hook your index finger around the side. Make sure your thumb is on top. Keep your wrist parallel to the water, and then—"

I hurl the stone as far as I can. It skips and sinks in the same motion, disappearing a split second after it hits the water.

"I think you got the hang of it," Hunter says.

I laugh once, then turn so I'm facing him. "You know I'm not athletic."

He grins. "Your bowling is better."

"*Barely.*" We went with Conor, Harlow, Rylan, and Aidan last week.

"We'll practice when you visit me in Philly."

"Okay," I agree, playing with a button on his shirt. "I can't believe we *graduated*. It doesn't feel real yet."

His hand skims up my bare arm, leaving a trail of goose bumps behind. These ones have nothing to do with the temperature. "Four years went by fast."

"We're spending the first and the last night of college together," I say, a little awestruck.

Hunter twirls one of my curls around his finger. "Good start. Better ending."

I smile, but it fades fast. "I wish I could go back to the beginning."

"I don't," he says.

"You...don't?"

"Nah." He tugs gently on the piece of hair he's holding. "All the best stuff is still ahead, Eve."

"But we're going to be living ninety-seven miles apart."

Yeah, I mapped it. An hour and forty-five minutes by car. Two hours by train. Nine hours by bike—not that I'll be testing that time estimation.

It doesn't feel like I had enough time in the same place as him. Not enough of *this* time, together.

"It won't be forever. We are."

I stare at him, stunned.

Hunter raises his eyebrows. "I was kind of hoping for an agreement."

There's no way he could have known what Ben said to me. The exact words that officially ended my last relationship—*I'm not sure we're forever*—are still burned into my brain. But they fade a little more as Hunter's sink in.

"We *are* forever," I agree, rising on my toes so I can reach his mouth.

Hunter groans into my mouth as I nibble on his lower lip, his hands coasting down my back and settling on my ass. "*Why* are we at a beach with our friends again?"

I giggle. "Because they're our friends and it's our last night all together."

"I'm not feeling very social," he murmurs, and then kisses me.

I kiss him back for a minute, then slip out of his hold and jog over to the spot where I left my bag.

"What are you doing?" Hunter asks, sounding startled.

I don't usually take off while we're kissing.

"You'll see," I reply, searching through my bag.

I locate the box, stand, and walk back over to him.

Hunter raises an eyebrow when he spots it. "*Another* diploma?" he teases.

The shape *is* pretty similar.

"Not for two years," I tell him, holding the box out. "Open it," I urge.

Hunter unwraps the box carefully, folding the wrapping paper and slipping it into his pocket before lifting the lid.

He doesn't react right away. He just stares.

I chew on the inside of my cheek, waiting for a reaction.

Nothing.

"You…like it?" I finally ask, peering over the side to make sure nothing's wrong with the painting.

It looks the same as when I packaged it.

Thank God, because it took me forever. I sketched it ten times to get the positioning right before adding color to the canvas. In it, Hunter, Aidan, and Conor are standing on the blue line of Holt's hockey rink, wearing their jerseys, facing the goal. I looked up Aidan's and Conor's numbers and photos of the jerseys, so I know they're accurate. In the top left corner, you can see the championship banner that's now hanging from the rafters of the rink.

When Thea saw it, she told me I should show it to someone in the athletics department. That surely they'd want to use it as a mural or for marketing material. That it deserved to be seen by a lot of people.

But I painted it for him.

"Eve." Hunter's voice sounds choked. "I can't believe—it's perfect. I seriously…I can't believe you did this. Thank you. It's the most thoughtful gift anyone has ever given me."

"You're welcome," I say, relieved.

Hunter closes the box very slowly and sets it on the sand.

Then he wraps his arms around me, tugging me back into him. "You know how I know we're forever?"

"How?" I whisper.

"Because I don't think it's possible to love someone more than I love you."

Salty streaks roll down my cheeks. Hunter wipes them away with his thumbs. "Don't cry."

"They're happy tears. Because I love you too and I've been wanting to say it for a while and it—it feels really good to say it to you."

Hunter grins. It's the widest smile I've ever seen him wear. "You love me?"

I nod. "*So* much."

"Hey, Morgan! You guys in for burritos?" Aidan shouts.

Hunter sighs. "Phillips always knows how to make a moment more romantic."

I laugh. "Is he talking about that Mexican place you guys always go to?"

"Probably. I'm surprised they're still open. They must be doing special hours for graduation." He tucks a piece of hair behind my ear. "You wanna go?"

"Yeah. As long as we can go to Holey Moley for donuts later. They're open until three a.m. on Saturdays."

"We can do whatever you want," Hunter says, picking up the box with his painting inside like it's made of glass.

I grab my bag and sling it over my shoulder.

And we walk, hand in hand, back to where our friends and his brother are waiting by the cars.

And I decide that Hunter was right.

All the best stuff is still ahead.

CHAPTER FORTY-FIVE

EVE

FOUR YEARS LATER

My lip gloss falls out of my bag and onto the seat, promptly followed by a pack of gum. I curse under my breath as I continue rifling through the tote's contents, desperately trying to find my headphones. I'm *positive* I put them in here, and the three-hour flight to Atlanta is going to feel a lot longer if I can't listen to the latest *C is for Crime* episode I downloaded.

"Excuse me, miss?"

"One second," I say, digging deeper. That *almost* felt like the rubber coating of a wire. I can't use the ones without a wire without losing one.

The plane's loudspeaker crackles to life, preparing for some announcement, and my fingers finally close around an ear bud.

I pull the headphones out of my bag triumphantly, then glance up. There's a line of several scowling passengers standing in the aisle that I trace to my row. Specifically, to the tall figure waiting for me to move so he can take the seat I'm blocking.

"Oh, sorry—oh my God."

I forget about my headphones—and my bag, which topples to the floor—as I leap up and throw my arms around Hunter.

He grunts when our bodies collide, apparently not expecting such an enthusiastic greeting. His mistake.

"What are you doing here?" I exclaim, pulling back just far enough to see his face.

"I decided to fly to Atlanta via New York. Well, via Salt Lake City and New York. I couldn't get a direct flight to JFK."

"Excuse me, could you have this conversation somewhere else? You're blocking the aisle," the grumpy woman behind Hunter says.

"Sorry," he tells her politely, then hefts his suitcase into the overhead compartment like it weighs nothing and slides past me into the open seat.

The woman who was behind him continues down the aisle with her huge bag. How she got that past the gate agent is a mystery. I'm positive it extends beyond the allotted inches.

I focus on Hunter. "I can't believe you're here."

He leans down, picking up the lip gloss and gum that ended up on the floor and stowing them back in my bag. Then he reaches for my hand, threading our fingers together. "It's not every weekend our best friends marry each other. I figured that merited a special trip."

"You didn't need to add that much time to your flight."

"I know I didn't." He kisses the back of my hand. "Did you think of anything you forgot yet?"

"No, but I'm positive there's something."

He smiles.

"Have you talked to Conor recently?" I ask.

"Not this week. His mom flew in early to help Harlow with the last-minute preparations, and he was hoping to show her around Tampa Bay before they headed up to Atlanta. I think he wanted to make Anna feel extra special before Hugh and Allison arrived."

"That was thoughtful of him."

"Speaking of thoughtful…" He leans closer and kisses me.

I'm laughing, but it disappears as soon as his tongue touches mine. I moan into his mouth, louder than is really appropriate for a public place.

Hunter smirks when he leans back, twirling a strand of my hair around his finger. I cut it to just past my shoulders a few weeks ago, wanting to try a different style after having long hair for so long. It also means I wear it down more often, which Hunter seems to appreciate.

"How was it?" I ask quietly.

He sighs. "Sad. But mostly okay."

Hunter's grandfather passed away last week. It was sudden, a heart attack, and I wasn't able to go because my boss was out of town and I couldn't get anyone to cover the gallery for me. So Hunter went back to Casper alone for the funeral that was held yesterday. Up until five minutes ago, I thought that meant I was meeting him in Atlanta for Harlow and Conor's wedding this weekend.

"You saw Sean?" I ask.

"Yeah, he was there. He's still working at the auto shop, and seems to be enjoying it. Still showing up at NA. And he said he's dating someone, but I didn't get any details. Also mentioned coming to visit us in New York soon, but he's said that before and it's never happened, so…" He shrugs.

Hunter's good at managing expectations when it comes to his brother. Maybe too good. It's been four years since Sean's overdose, and as far as we know, he's stayed sober since. But Hunter still flinches every time Sean calls.

Some things just take time, I guess.

"My dad called last night. Lily won her art contest."

"Good for her."

"He asked about the holidays again. Wants us to come visit, maybe stay with them."

"Are you ready for that?" Hunter asks.

I gnaw on my lower lip. "I don't know. I told him I'd talk to you about it."

It took me six months to call my dad after graduation. It was right after I got a receptionist job at the gallery where I now work as a buyer. The gallery where some of my paintings hang on the walls.

Our first conversation was awkward. So was our second. Lots of them have contained awkward moments, actually. But I kept calling. And he did too. We abandoned our former strict schedule, and that lack of structure helped some.

We'll never have a normal father-daughter relationship, but we have *a* relationship. Maybe it'll continue to improve, or maybe it'll always be a little stilted. Either way, I won't have to wonder *what if.*

"I'm up for it if you are," Hunter tells me. "We went to my folks' last year."

I shudder at the memory. I loved visiting his family. I *hated* skiing. Hunter talked me into it.

He grew up skiing, and is naturally athletic. I'd never skied before, and am naturally clumsy. Honestly, I'm shocked I didn't break any bones.

"No skiing next time," he promises, knowing exactly why I'm grimacing right now. "We can go sledding instead."

"How about you do the winter sports, and I'll stay inside?"

"I'm adding it to your list."

I glare at him. "Don't you dare."

My fuck-it list has become a running joke between us.

Anytime there's something I don't want to do but Hunter does, he suggests I add it. I've caved on a few things, like skiing, but after that catastrophe I swore I was going to hold my ground on any future additions.

Problem is, I still get giddy around Hunter Morgan.

And since I admitted that to him, he uses it to his advantage.

The intercom comes to life again, this time with an announcement for the flight crew to prepare the cabin for takeoff.

I snap on my seat belt and tighten it around my waist.

Hunter's still holding my hand, rubbing lazy circles around my knuckles.

I missed him. We moved in together two years ago, when he graduated from Penn and moved to New York, and since then there haven't been many nights we've spent apart. I slept terribly the past few nights simply because his side of the bed was empty.

"Rowan had the baby," I say as we wait for our plane to leave the gate. "A boy. Ben posted a photo."

We had lunch with Ben and his wife six months ago. They came to the city for a weekend getaway, and I suggested meeting up after Hunter said he was up for it.

I hadn't seen Ben since graduation. He's running his family's seafood store on his own now, and Rowan works as a librarian in Port Haven. During dinner, Ben told me he's working on a documentary about the town's history and Rowan is helping him with the research. They're perfect for each other.

"When did we get so old people our age are having kids?" Hunter wonders.

"Ten years ago, technically. That's how old my mom was when she had me. On purpose? Now, I guess."

He squeezes my hand. "Do you ever think about it?"

My heart rate quickens. "Having kids?"

"Yeah."

"I'm not ready right now. But yes, I think about it. Maybe in a year or two?"

After you finally propose.

"After I finally propose?"

For a second, I think I spoke aloud.

Hunter smirks. "You can give me shit for it. Conor sure has. But he always has to be first with everything, so I'm not sure why he's surprised he beat me to the punch."

"I'm not going to give you shit. There's no clock. But I like the idea of being married first, yeah."

Not that you need to be married to have a baby together. But my own childhood was so *un*traditional, I like the idea of doing things in the typical order. Of having my last name be the same as my kid's.

Hunter squeezes my hand again. "Me too."

CHAPTER FORTY-SIX

HUNTER

"What *is* that?" Aidan asks, leaning so close to the glass I think his nose is touching it. Sure enough, there's a small streak when he steps back.

"A whale shark, I think."

"Fuck. Now *I'm* scared of sharks. Why did Hart's wedding have to ruin surfing for me?"

"This isn't his wedding. It's the rehearsal dinner."

"Same difference, Morgan." Aidan sips his drink.

Conor and Harlow are having their rehearsal dinner at the Georgia Aquarium. It's the entire reason they're getting married in Atlanta, actually. Because Harlow loves the ocean and Conor loves Harlow.

It's a cool venue, I have to admit. We're inside a glass dome, a giant tank, filled with fish and stingrays and coral and seahorses and one gigantic shark surrounding us. Her name is Nina, according to the sign.

"Hey, you guys made it."

I turn toward Conor's voice. "Made it? I took three separate flights to be here, Hart. Like I'd miss your fucking wedding."

"I'm sorry about your grandfather, man," Hart says, punching me gently in the shoulder when he reaches us. "Eve told Harlow why you were out of town."

Since he got drafted and became the star of the National Hockey League, I don't get to talk to my best friend as much as I'd like to. Half the time, we communicate through our girlfriends. Well, his fiancée and my girlfriend. Soon to be his wife and my fiancée.

"Thanks," I say. "It was quick, at least. He didn't suffer."

"Was Sean there?"

"Uh-huh."

"Still sober?" Aidan asks.

"Yeah."

It's been four years now. A hell of a lot longer than Sean ever stayed sober before. But I'm still scared to trust it.

Addiction doesn't have a cure.

I do hope it means Sean has found some better ways to cope. We went skating together while I was home for Gramps's funeral. The local rink where we both learned to play hockey stays open year-round. I suggested to Sean he join a local league, like I did in New York, and he said he'd think about it.

"Oh. Hey, I almost forgot." I dig my phone out of my pocket. "This guy in the airport was wearing your jersey, so I snapped a photo. I told him I know you, and he told me to fuck off. New Yorkers, you know."

Aidan starts laughing. "You took a photo of a guy who told you to fuck off just because he was wearing Hart's jersey?"

"Well, yeah," I say defensively. "It probably would have gone better if I'd been wearing mine."

Conor sent me one to wear to his first game. I still have it. And I bought five more, so Eve had one to wear, and some extras because I was proud as hell of my best friend.

"Where's Rylan?" Conor asks Aidan. "She here?"

"No, I left her in Seattle to run the brewery," Phillips says sarcastically. "She's over by that orange fish with her parents."

Conor invited Coach Keller and his wife to his wedding.

We all glance that way. Rylan waves at me and Conor, then blows a kiss to Aidan.

He pretends to catch it.

"You guys all travel together?" I ask.

"Yes," Aidan grumbles. "And Coach picked the five a.m. flight, so I haven't slept since yesterday, practically."

"That's nothing," Conor says. "I haven't gotten a good night's sleep in two months. My mom or Allison is calling all the time about wedding shit, and they forget about the time difference a lot."

"Well, it'll all be over after tomorrow, right?"

Conor lets out a relieved sigh. "Right." He glances between me and Aidan. "So which of you two is going to take the plunge next?"

"Well..." Phillips says, rubbing his jaw.

We both stare at him, but that's all he says.

"You proposed to Rylan?" I finally ask.

"Yep. Except...she said no."

"Wait, what?" Conor asks.

I frown, just as confused as Hart.

Rylan's a year younger than us, so maybe she doesn't feel ready? But she and Aidan have been together almost as long as Conor and Harlow have. And they're nearly *married* now, not just engaged.

Aidan nods. "Yeah. She started crying, saying I was over-reacting."

Conor and I exchange a puzzled look.

Not only does Rylan's reaction to the proposal make no sense, but the two of them are either excellent actors or actually on excellent terms right now. Which also makes no sense.

"Overreacting to *what*?" I ask.

"Oh. Yeah. She's pregnant. That's why I proposed."

Conor makes a choked sound that's either a laugh or a shocked cough.

"Holy shit," I say. "Does Coach know?"

Aidan scowls. "That's your reaction to finding out I'm having a kid?" He glances at Hart. "Guess it's down to you for godfather."

"*Does* Coach know you *knocked up* his *daughter*, though?" Conor questions.

"I hate both of you," Aidan says, then downs the remnants of his whiskey. He groans. "Damn, that's good. I gave up drinking alcohol, in solidarity. Tonight's a special occasion."

"Well, wow," I state. I've been here the whole time, but I still feel like I'm behind in this conversation, somehow. "Congratulations, Aidan. Seriously. Way to, uh, bury the lede with the whole bad proposal thing."

"Thanks, man." He taps the side of the glass with one finger. "But to be clear, my proposal was not bad. Just…bad timing. I did overreact, a little."

If I know Aidan—and I do—I guarantee it was more than a *little*. He likely went out and bought the biggest ring he could find and then rented out the Space Needle or something.

He and Rylan live in Seattle. Aidan's expanded Evergreen Beer Company to two locations, and Rylan works as a financial analyst for a huge company. I'm not clear exactly what she does, except that it has to do with numbers and she's super successful at it.

"Congrats?" Conor says, sounding unsure if that's the right response.

Only Aidan would tell us he was about to be a dad like this.

"Thanks, Hart. It's all good. I like a challenge. I had to work to get Rye to date me, so this is just like one extra step." He glances at me. "What about you, Morgan?"

I look around for Eve, finding her whispering with Harlow in the corner.

Furtively, I pull the ring out of my pocket. I bought it six months ago, and I've carried it around with me ever since. No place seems safe enough to store it, and I don't want Eve to find it accidentally. Not that me proposing will be a huge surprise—we've been together for over four years. But I want to witness the moment she sees the ring I picked out for the first time, not for her to find it while she's putting folded socks in the drawer.

I crack open the tiny black box so my best friends can see it.

"Damn," Aidan comments. "I didn't know policy organizations paid that well. It's almost as big as Harlow's rock."

Conor does an admirable job of keeping his laugh contained, but a little amusement slips out.

"Thanks for your concern about my salary, Phillips." I roll my eyes as I slip the ring box back into my pocket.

Aidan slaps my back. "Just kidding. You did great, Morgan. When are you proposing?"

"Next week. Eve thinks we're headed back to New York from here, but I'm taking her to Paris. She's always wanted to go. We're doing a trip to Versailles one day, and I'm planning to ask her there."

Conor whistles. "Damn. Nice one."

"Conor!"

He glances toward Harlow, who's waving him over. "See you guys later?"

"Yeah, we'll be here," Aidan replies. Once Conor disappears, he glances toward Rylan. "I should go check in with Rye, actually. See if she wants another ginger ale."

Eve is standing alone now, watching Conor and Harlow greet more of their guests. "We're at table five," I remind Aidan, then head for her.

She sees me coming and smiles. "Saw you talking to Conor."

"Saw you talking to Harlow."

"So convenient, that our best friends are together."

"It was very considerate of them," I agree.

Harlow and Conor started dating first. But Eve and I met first, so…

"I know a secret," I whisper to her.

"Does it have to do with why Rylan is drinking ginger ale?"

"Fuck," I say. "Do you think anyone else noticed?"

Like Coach? I don't envy Aidan for having to have that conversation.

"Nope. I was watching, because she texted me and Harlow a couple of days ago to tell us she was pregnant."

I stare at her. "Seriously? Aidan *just* told us."

Eve pats my chest. "Girls communicate better, babe."

Well, damn. At least I still know one secret she doesn't. Unless Aidan tells Rylan or Conor tells Harlow and they tell Eve. That possibility is just occurring to me.

I said the proposal was a surprise, right?

Crap. I'll have to clarify later. Conor mentioned the three of us going out tonight, since he didn't have a proper bachelor party, so I'll swear them to secrecy then.

"They're starting to bring out the food," Eve says. "We should go sit down."

I follow her over to table five, one of the coveted few closest to Conor and Harlow's spot, since we're all in the bridal party. We're the first to take our seats.

Eve glances up at the glass ceiling overhead, separating us from thousands of gallons of water and a lot of fish. "This place is pretty cool, huh?"

"Unless it cracks."

"*Hunter.*"

"I'm sure it won't."

Eve smiles and leans closer. I stare at her, and she stares back.

"I missed you," she whispers. "Three nights was too long."

I drape an arm over the back of her chair, playing with the ends of her hair. "I'm here now."

She tilts her head, holding eye contact. "And from now on?"

"Yeah. From now on." I lean closer, sealing the promise with a kiss.

The best is still ahead.

THE END

ALSO BY C.W. FARNSWORTH

Standalones

Four Months, Three Words

Come Break My Heart Again

Winning Mr. Wrong

Back Where We Began

Like I Never Said

Fly Bye

Serve

Heartbreak for Two

Pretty Ugly Promises

Six Summers to Fall

King of Country

Left Field Love

Rival Love

Kiss Now, Lie Later

For Now, Not Forever

The Kensingtons

Fake Empire

Real Regrets

False God

Anti-Hero

Truth & Lies

Friday Night Lies

Tuesday Night Truths

Kluvberg

First Flight, Final Fall

All The Wrong Plays

Holt Hockey

Famous Last Words

Against All Odds

From Now On

ACKNOWLEDGMENTS

This was the first book I've written knowing that it was going to be the end of a series. Saying goodbye to the Holt Hockey world was more than a little sentimental, but I love Hunter and Eve's story and I truly couldn't think of a better way to close this chapter. Working on this trilogy has been my happy place for the past eighteen months, and I hope you had as much fun reading these books as I had writing them!

Sophie, you are a ray of sunshine. Your support and encouragement has been invaluable for so many of my releases, and I'm incredibly grateful for all your feedback on this book.

Megan, this story was infinitely improved by your attention to detail and suggestions. Thank you for being so thorough and thoughtful! I appreciate your time and insight so much.

Britt, working on this series with you has been one of the highlights of my career. You approached the editing process with such infectious joy and enthusiasm, and your excitement means more than I can say. Thank you for sharing your wit and wisdom with this project, in addition to your eagle eye for errors!

Judy, thank you for being so lovely to work with. I hope this was the first of many manuscripts!

Alison, thank you for another amazing proofread. I always love working with you!

Mary Scarlett, I am forever in awe of your talent. The covers for this series were everything I could have hoped for and more. I feel so lucky to have gotten to work with you.

My family, for being unfailingly understanding and supportive. This was the last time I'll set a deadline just before the holidays, I promise!

My agent, Lauren, thank you for all your hard work!

Katie and the team at Lyric Audiobooks, thank you for being so incredible to work with. Christian Fox and Rose Dioro, thank you for bringing Hunter and Eve to life!

Valentine and the entire team at Valentine PR, thank you for helping Hunter and Eve reach as many readers as possible!

And finally, thank YOU for reading. The love readers have shown this series is incredible and thrilling and I am so grateful.

ABOUT THE AUTHOR

C.W. Farnsworth is the author of numerous adult and young adult romance novels featuring sports, strong female leads, and happy endings.

Charlotte lives in Rhode Island and when she isn't writing spends her free time reading, at the beach, or snuggling with her Australian Shepherd.

Find her on Facebook (@cwfarnsworth), TikTok (@authorcwfarnsworth), Instagram (@authorcwfarnsworth) and check out her website www.authorcwfarnsworth.com for news about upcoming releases!